One look

"Look, Alex. It's pretty simple. I don't want to do this; you certainly don't want to. So . . ."

I hadn't realized he was slowly bending his knees until his chin entered my line of vision, followed by the rest of his face. He wasn't grinning now. He looked very serious. "Ella. I really do want to do this. Help you, if you'll let me." He sighed again. I was completely fixated on his eyes. They're a pretty amazing combination of green and bronze. "I don't know what's going on, but it's weird, and it shouldn't be. I'm a decent guy."

"Of course you are." I sighed. And caved. Apparently, my Phillite defenses were worthless around this particular specimen, no matter that he couldn't seem to make up his mind whether I was worth noticing or not.

Truth: Yes, I am that naive.

Other Books You May Enjoy

THE FINE ART *of* TRUTH OR DARE

melissa jensen

speak

An Imprint of Penguin Group (USA) Inc.

For my guys.

Chris, Aidan, Duggan.

And my dad, who used to take me

to the de Young Museum on Sunday afternoons,

and who first took me to the Louvre.

SPEAK
Published by the Penguin Group
Penguin Group (USA) Inc., 345 Hudson Street, New York, New York 10014, U.S.A.
Penguin Group (Canada), 90 Eglinton Avenue East, Suite 700,
Toronto, Ontario, Canada M4P 2Y3 (a division of Pearson Penguin Canada Inc.)
Penguin Books Ltd, 80 Strand, London WC2R 0RL, England
Penguin Ireland, 25 St Stephen's Green, Dublin 2, Ireland (a division of Penguin Books Ltd)
Penguin Group (Australia), 250 Camberwell Road, Camberwell, Victoria 3124, Australia
(a division of Pearson Australia Group Pty Ltd)
Penguin Books India Pvt Ltd, 11 Community Centre,
Panchsheel Park, New Delhi - 110 017, India
Penguin Group (NZ), 67 Apollo Drive, Rosedale, Auckland 0632, New Zealand
(a division of Pearson New Zealand Ltd.)
Penguin Books (South Africa) (Pty) Ltd, 24 Sturdee Avenue,
Rosebank, Johannesburg 2196, South Africa

Registered Offices: Penguin Books Ltd, 80 Strand, London WC2R 0RL, England

First published in the United States of America by Speak, an imprint of Penguin Group (USA) Inc., 2012

3 5 7 9 10 8 6 4 2

LIBRARY OF CONGRESS CATALOGING-IN-PUBLICATION DATA IS AVAILABLE

Speak ISBN 978-0-14-242090-4

Printed in the United States of America

*THAT I AM VALUABLE, I KNOW.

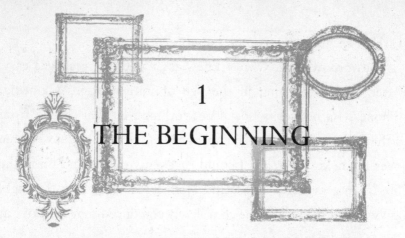

1
THE BEGINNING

Truth (according to Edward Willing): People who rely on first sight are either lazy or deluded.

Truth (according to Ella Marino): I fell in love with Edward Willing the first time I saw him.

It was Day Three, Freshman Year, and I was a little bit lost in the school library, looking for a bathroom that wasn't full of blindingly shiny sophomores checking their lip gloss.

Day Three. Already pretty clear on the fact that I would be using secondary bathrooms for at least the next three years, until being a senior could pass for confidence. For the moment, I knew no one, and was too shy to talk to anyone. So that first sight of Edward: pale hair that looked like he'd just run his hands through it, paint-smeared white shirt, a half smile that was half wicked, and I was hooked.

Since, "Hi, I'm Ella. You look like someone I'd like to spend the rest of my life with," would have been totally insane, I opted for sitting quietly and staring. Until the bell rang and I had to rush to French class, completely forgetting to pee.

Edward Willing. Once I knew his name, the rest was easy. After all, we're living in the age of information. Wikipedia, iPhones, 4G networks, social networking that you can do from a thousand miles away. The upshot being that at any given time over the next two years, I could sit twenty feet from him in the library, not saying a word, and learn a lot about him. Enough, anyway, for me to become completely convinced that the Love at First Sight hadn't been a fluke.

It's pretty simple. Edward matched four and a half of my *If My Prince Does, In Fact, Come Someday, It Would Be Great If He Could Meet These Five Criteria.*

1. *Interested in art.* For me, it's charcoal. For Edward, oil paint and bronze. That's almost enough right there. Nice lips + artist = Ella's prince.

2. *Not afraid of love.* He wrote, "Love is one of two things worth dying for. I have yet to decide on the second."

3. *Or of telling the truth.* "How can I believe what other people say if I lie to them?"

4. *Hot.* Why not? I can dream.

5. *Daring.* Mountain climbing, cliff diving, defying the parents. Him, not me. I'm terrified of an embarrassing number of things, including heights, convertibles, moths, and those comedians everyone loves who stand onstage and yell insults at the audience.

5, subsection a. *Daring enough to take a chance on me.*

Of course, in the end, that No. 5a is the biggie. And the problem. No matter how much I worshipped him, no matter how good a pair we might have been, it was never, ever going to happen. To be fair to Edward, it's not like he was given an opportunity to get to know me. I'm not stupid. I know there are a few basic truths when it comes to boys and me.

Truth: You have to talk to a boy—really talk, if you want him to see past the fact that you're not beautiful.

Truth: I'm not beautiful. Or much of a conversationalist.

Truth: I'm not entirely sure that the stuff behind the not-beautiful is going to be all that alluring, either.

And one written-in-stone, heartbreaking truth about this guy.

Truth: Edward Willing died in 1916.

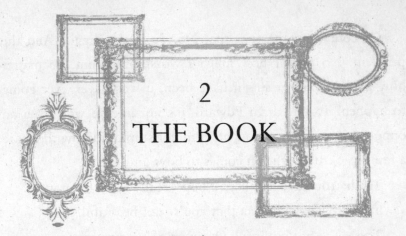

2
THE BOOK

You might think lunchtime at Willing would be different from other high schools. That everyone would be welcome at any table, united by the knowledge that we, at Willing, are the Elite, the Chosen, stellar across the board.

Um. No. Of course not. High school is high school, regardless of how much it costs or how many kids springboard into the Ivies. And nowhere is social status more evident than in the dining room (freshmen and sophomores at noon; upperclassmen at one). Because, of course, Willing doesn't have a cafeteria, or even a lunch hall. It has a dining room, complete with oak tables and paneled walls that are covered with plaques going all the way back to 1869, the year Edith Willing Castor (Edward's aunt) founded the school to "prepare Philadelphia's finest young ladies for Marriage, for Leadership, and for Service to the World." Really. Until the sixties, the school's boastful slogan was "She's a Willing Girl."

Almost 150 years, three first ladies, and one attorney general—not to mention the arrival of boys—later, female members of the student body are still called Willing Girls. You'd think someone in the seventies would have objected to that and changed it. But Willing has survived the seventies of two different centuries. They'll probably still be calling us Willing Girls in 2075. It's a school that believes in Tradition, sometimes regardless of how stupid that Tradition is.

I eat lunch under the plaque that tells me for three years running, 1948–1950, Gertrude Wharton was Willing Oral Girl of the Year. And the one memorializing 1919, when eight girls were given the award for Willing Service to Soldiers of the Great War. Really.

Apparently, there is a plaque on the window wall for Willing Contribution to Nature. Honestly, I don't know if that's organic contribution or monetary, all those rich Philadelphia families spreading their money like fertilizer over verdant fields. Frankie says the first name on the plaque is Edna Moore Willing. I'm not sure if I believe him.

There is one not too far away for Willing Contribution to the Arts. The entire plaque is definitely Willing-, Moore-, and Biddle-heavy; Frankie says it could use a good Marino to shake things up.

For the most part, I don't know what's on the plaques between the windows. I've never wandered between those tables, let alone had a meal there.

This is how it works.

Tables 1 through 4, near the big windows that overlook the lawn:
The Phillites.

The term was coined by a local journalist and Willing alum a few years ago in a magazine article titled "Supreme Court: Philadelphia's Young Royalty." Really. Phillites (Phil-Elites) are expensive, smooth, and shiny, and they stick together. Like caviar. They're the product of impeccable genes, cutting-edge orthodontia, and weekly sushi. Most of the Phillites are sporty; some are brainy. Two or three are on scholarship. They are all a little blinding.

Tables 5 through 8, one row from the windows, middle of the room:
The Bees.
Less wealthy and less beautiful than the Phillites, still cherished by the school for their sheer usefulness. The yearbook and school paper editors, the leads in the spring Shakespeare play, the student tour guides and class fund-raising chairs. Once a Bee Boy, always a Bee Boy, but the girls occasionally move up by dating well. Miss Edith would probably approve.

Tables 9 through 11, west corner: *The Stars*.
Extra smart, extra talented, completely unconcerned with fashion, popular culture, or social mobility. Mathletes, chamber music society, debate team. Will absorb people from the bottom tier, providing the commitment to the activity is sincere and complete. Love mathletics or leave. There is no halfway.

Tables 12 and 13, flanking the kitchen doors: *The Invisibles*.
Willing can't have outcasts. That would look really bad in a school

that prides itself on social and academic excellence. Anyone who needs to be alone—or has a visible drug problem or pierce-toos—quietly disappears between semesters. The ones who go to rehab sometimes come back. The others don't. Leaving the bottom tier to the kids who write obsessive *Lord of the Rings* fan fiction, who don't have enough money to make up for chronically bad skin, who just don't shine or fit in anywhere else.

⌁

So, as usual, Sadie, Frankie, and I were at Table 12, under Gertrude. Having arrived last, I was in the death seat, the one that gets pounded every time a member of the kitchen staff comes through the swinging doors. I scooted my chair forward for the third time since sitting down, ending up with the table edge wedged firmly under my ribs. It's hard enough to breathe in that seat, let alone eat.

"So what are you going to do with it?" Sadie whispered.

The European history book lay on the table in front of me, Winston Churchill scowling up at the ceiling. He was not pretty. Alex Bainbridge is. It was his book, with his name written in sharp, bold script inside the front cover. Unlike at Sacred Heart, where every year you hoped to be handed books without desiccated pizza cheese between the pages, Willing students always buy their own books. Then they write in them.

I can't do that. The Sacred Heart nuns still scare me, two miles and two years away. The name inscribed in gold ink inside my history book is Erin Costantini. I've never met Erin Costantini. She graduated from Willing before I arrived, charitably leaving her used books, some of which I got as part of my scholarship, and a plaque near Table 5. She won the Willing Sportsmanship Award two years in a row.

Alex's book was new, of course, and filled with markings that have nothing to do with European history. *"D'oh!"* occupied a speech bubble next to Napoleon. Stalin wondered if we *Got Ex-Lax?* There was a phone number scrawled across Marie Antoinette's chest. No name with it.

I wondered if Amanda Alstead knew about that phone number. Amanda, queen of the Phillites to Alex's king. I wondered if it was Amanda Alstead's number.

"Ella?" Sadie nudged me. There was a huge button on the elbow of her gray sweater. It didn't fasten anything. Her mom is into deconstructed Japanese couture. On her, it says *"Vogue."* On Sadie, raw seams and upside-down pockets say "Schizophrenia."

"The book?"

"She'll give it to him." Frankie poked at his burger and winced. It was the same color as Sadie's sweater. "Simple."

Only it wasn't, and Sadie knew that.

"Maybe you should just leave it in front of his locker. Or drop it off in the office," she suggested. "They'll get it to him."

She'd finished her bagged lunch (celery and an off-season plum from Australia) ten minutes ago and was now chewing on the ends of her hair, making one thick strand sleek and dark. When she let go, it bounced back into her mass of slightly fuzzy brown curls. Her mother takes her to Alphonse (his extreme talent with hair-care products renders a second name unnecessary) for thermal conditioning treatments once every four weeks. Sadie comes out looking like she's been greased. Frankie and I say nothing, and a few days later, she's back to normal.

Sadie's one of the rich kids. Which means she should be able to walk up to Alex Bainbridge, hand him his book, and make a quip about being an American in Paris. She's been, multiple times. She has also known Alex pretty much all her life.

She thinks she might have hit him with a pretzel wand once when they were in the Society Hill Tiny Tots program. She's not sure; they both left SHTT to start kindergarten at Madison, so the pretzel incident would have been at least twelve years ago. She doesn't think they've spoken to each other since.

It works that way sometimes.

"Oh, for God's sake." Frankie rolled his eyes under his green porkpie hat. The color perfectly matched the VINCE stitched onto the pocket of his brown bowling shirt. Frankie is all about vintage chic. "Give me the book. I'll throw it at him."

Frankie's daring. He's also conversant in postmodern art and tells me he loves me on a regular basis. He does lie like a rug, but only to people he doesn't care about, like the gym teacher. "Badminton?" he gasped once, early in our friendship, when I assumed I'd found a gym partner (him) who would actually talk to me. "And risk this nose?"

It's a good nose. In a really, really good face. Frankie's mom is Korean; his dad is a former model from Bryn Mawr. Frankie's theory is that his dad is gay, too. "Four years with an ordinary Asian girl who, no offense to her, looks like a pretty Asian boy?

Then, poof (pardon the pun), off to raise goats in California? Please."

He reached for the book. I held on. I might even have hugged it a little.

Frankie groaned. "No. No no no no no. Not you, too! Is there *one* girl in this school who doesn't have a thing for Alex Bainbridge?"

He looked to Sadie, who shrugged and offered, "He is gorgeous."

"He's a Neanderthal."

Frankie was a slightly earlier entrant into the Phillite solar system than I was. He did seventh and eighth grades at Madison, entering just at the point when boys started flexing their muscles and noticing whose shoes came from Kmart.

He'd explained it to me freshman year when the miraculous score of a pair of clearance D&G chinos (it helps to have a twenty-nine-inch waist) loosened his tongue about his pre-Fab days. "Gaysian? Poor? Five foot nothing? I might as well have had 'dunk me' tattooed on my forehead."

They dunked him.

"Now be fair." Sadie is all about being fair and open-minded. She insists it's because she's a Libra. I credit ten years of being the bat her parents use to whack at each other. "Alex never actually put you into a toilet. It was his friends."

"Oh, excellent defense, counselor. Case dismissed."

"Pissy does not become you," she informed him.

"Neither does piss," he shot back.

I completely understand how that sort of thing would be hard to get past, even after a couple of years. You don't forget the mean stuff, even when the mean stuff ends. Or at least gets less obvious. It might have been Frankie's growing seven inches in two years that ended the dunkings. Or the Phillite boys growing up a few years. More likely it was the whispers that Frankie's twin brother, Daniel, had joined an Asian gang. Whatever—he hasn't forgotten.

"Ah, the Bainbridge Fan Brigade. I thought better of you, Fiorella." Frankie doesn't keep his opinions about anything to himself. I usually admire that a little desperately. This time it stung. "I really did."

Why? I'm only human. And invisible. In part (not that I kid myself that it's the major part) because I am still not much over five foot nothing. Alex Bainbridge is a foot taller than I am, with bronze hair that turns up at the front and a mouth that turns up at the corners, even when he's not smiling.

"It's better than her obsession with a dead man," Sadie said gently.

"Not much," was Frankie's grumbled reply.

He's probably right. I can sit blissfully under Edward's portrait in the library, scouring the Web for auctions containing his paintings, reading and rereading his letters and the handful of biographies about him, and no one notices. This year, it's even legit: research for my honors art history project. Besides, Edward was real. Everything he wrote and said was real, true. Unlike Fitzwilliam Darcy, who, drool-worthy as he might be, was really just Jane Austen in breeches. And look how many women dream about marrying him. I know for a fact that two of the girls at Table 13 are regular contributors to an online Darcy fanzine. They read aloud from it during lunch. It's not bad.

As for the possibility of Alex . . . well, he's *alive*. I could reach out and touch him almost any day September through May. I could actually invite him to a movie or pizza, or Marino's, where my nonna would make the calamari and my brother would have to serve it to us at a table in front. But I wouldn't. More the point, I *couldn't*. Because of his seat near the windows. Because of Amanda Alstead and lacrosse and the fact that he probably doesn't eat squid. I know the closest I'll get to Edward Willing is his portrait and an honors thesis. Of course I know that. As for playing footsie under a red-checked tablecloth with Alex . . .

Truth: For me, it's easier to accept the impossible than the pitifully improbable.

I should probably have left the book where I found it, half hidden under the statue of Samuel Windsor Willing, Edith's grandfather (the Revolutionary War uniform is misleading; a little math tells us that he was only nine in 1776, but the Willings were never short on ego). I was coming out of the east corridor girls' room, which makes me wonder if school bathrooms are going to have ongoing significance in my life. I wish it didn't seem so likely. I certainly don't spend much time in them. Even at Willing, they smell like dirty water and that industrial pink soap that doesn't come out of the dispensers, no matter how many times you pump. Besides, I'm not a mirror girl. I have Frankie and

Sadie to tell me if I have lettuce in my teeth. I don't have shiny lip gloss to check. I don't do anything that necessitates Visine. Still, sometimes I'll come out of a stall or look up from washing my hands and catch sight of myself: a small, startled person behind a curtain of dark hair who looks away quickly, as if embarrassed by being caught staring.

This time, I could have used the bathroom closer to math class. I mean, I didn't have to pee all that badly. But Amanda and her cadre can usually be found in the bathroom closer to math class before math class. Since the only word she has spoken to me since freshman year was *"Ewwwww!,"* it makes sense to avoid her.

Beyond that, it's a Girls' Declamation (formerly known as "Oral") Week at Willing, which means we have to memorize scarily long poems and recite them in front of our class. Declamation has this bizarre and overblown importance at Willing. Like all our future success depends on being able to remember that love is like a red, red rose. The week's subject was Robert Frost. Meaning the school has been overrun for the last few days with nervous girls reciting "The Road Not Taken." It's the poem of choice for the Phillites and Bee Girls. They've been coaching each other all week, filling the halls and bathrooms with bouncy rhythms and rhymes that I don't think Frost intended, even though he wrote them.

During Dec Weeks, we at Willing live a life that's something like a cross between a Broadway musical and Christian hip-hop. Everyone walks around mouthing unfamiliar, old-fashioned words. The halls become littered with increasingly dog-eared printouts of poems. We skip a little as we walk, like ponies in iambic quadrameter: bah-*dum*, bah-*dum*, bah-*dum*, bah-*dum*. Endless blonde ponytails swishing down the halls.

"Two roads diverged in a wood and I—

I took the one less traveled by . . ."

Bah-*dum*, bah-*dum*, bah-*dum*, bah-*dum* . . .

So I used a quiet bathroom. Coming out, eyes on the scuffed toes of my Chucks, I saw the book. It was tented near Cornelius's feet, a few papers loose under the bent pages. I leaned over and picked it up. And that, as Robert Frost would say, made all the difference.

From Table 12, I had a fairly good view of Table 2. Alex always sits there (Table 1 is for Phillite *seniors* only) usually in the same seat, back to the room, facing the window. It's a cool guy's seat. It says,

- I know you won't throw things at the back of my head because you wouldn't dare.
- Ditto making faces or rude hand gestures.
- I'm not worried about missing anything that might go on in the rest of the room.
- I don't care if you notice what I'm wearing, or that my hair is perfect today.
- Nothing inside is more interesting that what's outside, away from school.

Except, of course, Amanda Alstead, but she always sits half next to Alex and half on him, so he could see her just fine.

Today, she was sitting sideways in her chair, as usual. She could see part of the room (the Table 1 part, actually); most of the room could see her outfit (all shades of white, very cute, I wouldn't dare), her cameo profile, and the fact that she had her legs slung over Alex's lap. What I could see of him was the perfect triangle of his back in a green Lacoste and the pale edge at his hairline, the divider between the last of his summer tan and his October haircut.

"*Hey, Alex.*" I composed the words in my head. "*I have your book . . .*"

D'oh. I would be standing there, holding his book.

"*Alex. Thought you might want to have this back.*"

Nope. Sounded like I'd taken it, which would be bizarre, or that he'd given it to me, which would be ludicrous.

"*Hey. This was on the floor in the upstairs hall, and I figured you probably didn't know where it was.*"

Truth is always good.

He would look blank for a sec (he probably had no idea he'd dropped it; European history was first period), then smile gratefully, hazel eyes crinkling at the corners, that mouth turning up in that unbelievably cute way.

"*Wow. Thanks, Ella! I didn't even know I'd dropped it.*"

See?

And I would hand it over—if our fingers brushed, no complaints—and say, "*I saw the stuff inside. It's really . . .*"

"El. *Ella.*" Sadie bumped me with her button again. "Coming?"

"Hmm?"

"Where were you? Oh, yeah . . ." She followed my slightly unfocused gaze and nodded. On her other side, Frankie snorted.

She elbowed him. No button on the other sleeve. "Wanna practice before class? I mean, I know you don't have to; it's imprinted on your brain. But there's that line at the end I just can't get right. El?"

As I watched, Amanda swung her legs off of Alex and stood up. My legs felt a little rubbery as I did the same. "See you in class," I said quickly, leaving Sadie to remember that, in "Mending Wall," the line is: *We keep the wall between us as we go.* It's my favorite Frost poem. No pony rhythm, no rhyme. About walls.

I wove my way between the tables, pulling my hair forward over my shoulders as I went. Alex was still sitting when I reached him.

"Hey. This was on the floor in the upstairs hall . . ."

I stood behind his chair. Completely frozen.

I might have stood there for a very long time if he hadn't pushed himself away from the table to get up. The chair thumped me in the stomach first, then in the knees. I think I made a noise. I dropped his book.

"Oh. Oh, crap. I'm really sorry!" Alex jerked the chair out of the way and bent down a little. He had to, to see my face. "You okay?"

I did manage to nod.

"Seriously. I must have really pounded you there. You sure you're all right?"

"Yes, fine," I whispered.

Across the table, Chase Vere laughed. "Dude, she was, like, standing right behind you."

Alex ignored him. He stared at me for a long second, then bent down to pick up my book. Only, of course . . .

"This is my book."

I nodded again. "Um, yeah. I found it. Upstairs—"

"Oh, right. I was running to trig. It must've fallen out of my bag. Thanks." He was already turning away, already forgetting the moment. "It's Freddy, right?"

It kinda felt like the chair, again, in my stomach. Usually the name doesn't bother me. When I'm prepared for it, anyway. But this time, I wasn't. I let more of my hair fall forward. "Um, no," I said softly. "Ella. It's Ella."

He faced me again, looked confused for a second. Then he shrugged. "Huh. Okay. Ella. Well, thanks."

I heard the muffled giggle. Or maybe it wasn't muffled, just quick and quiet. I didn't want to turn around. I would much rather have crawled under the table, only I'm not quite that pitiful.

I turned.

Amanda hadn't really left. She'd gone to get a bottle of water. Another Willing perk: all the Poland Spring we can drink, and handy recycling bins to keep it Green. She was standing three feet away, flanked by her inner posse, Hannah and Anna. The Hannandas, we call them. Not that they look alike. Amanda is what guys picture when they hear the words *Swedish Massage*. Anna is dark, like me. Hannah has the gold-brown hair and awshucks look of a Kansas farm girl. But they are alike. Perfect features, the right shoes, luminescent lip gloss, and the instincts of barracudas.

Amanda bared her teeth. It wasn't really a smile. "Let's go," she said to Alex.

He went.

I could have counted. *On three. One . . . two . . .* The whisper came, followed by the whinny. I'm not noble enough to call it a laugh. Not from the Hannandas. Skirts and ponytails twitching behind them as they went. Bah-*dum*, bah-*dum*, bah-*dum*, bah-*dum*.

"*. . . Freddy . . . Don't you remember . . . tries to hide it . . .*"

I followed, at a distance, as we all left the room. We keep the walls between us as we go.

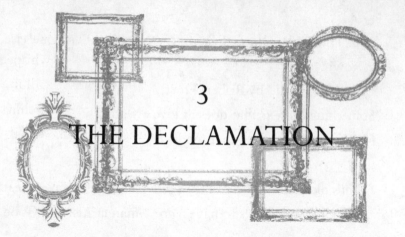

3
THE DECLAMATION

"... I shall be telling this with a sigh
Somewhere ages and ages hence:
Two roads diverged in a wood and I—
I took the one less traveled by,
And that has made all the difference."

"Thank you, Hannah. That was very nice. Now ... ah ... Fiorella Marino. All the way up front, please, Fiorella. Okay. Whenever you're ready ... ?"

"Ella."

"Sorry? I didn't catch that."

"It's just Ella, Mr. Stone."

"Oh, is that something new and hip that you're trying out?"

"Not really."

"I'm sorry, I didn't hear that, either. Quiet, people, please. Miss Marino is speaking."

"It's always been Ella, Mr. Stone. Since before I came here."

"Oh. Ha. Well. Okay, then. Carry on. Ella. Everyone else, *quiet*. Now!"

"'Mending Wall,' by Robert Frost.

'Something there is that doesn't love a wall,

That sends . . . um . . . that sends . . .

. . .'"

"That's okay. Ella. You can try again next week. Have a seat. Now. let's see. Who wants to have a go? Amanda Alstead. Good, great. Carry on, Amanda . . ."

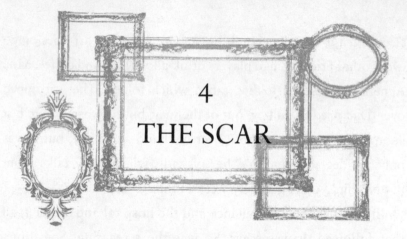

4
THE SCAR

To his credit, Alex obviously didn't remember why people call me Freddy.

It's after Freddy Krueger.

I'm not scary. I'm nothing like a nightmare movie monster. Objectively, I know I'm not even ugly. It's the scar.

Most of the time, you can't see it. If I wear sleeves, even short ones, and my neckline isn't too low, all you can see is the section on my neck. Turtlenecks hide it almost completely, but Philadelphia is too warm for turtlenecks half the year. So I wear my hair down all the time, and try to keep it in front of my shoulders.

It's what's known as a hypertrophic, hyperpigmented scar. Meaning it's raised and it's darker than my natural skin. In my case, it's red and looks a little like a web, over all of my right shoulder, about four inches down my right breast, and about five inches up my neck. It was a hot-water burn. I was seven. Ironically, maybe, it didn't happen in the kitchen at Marino's, or in our—the Marinos'—kitchen, where there's often a big pot of soup or pasta water boiling on the stove. Nope. This was the doing of an electric tea urn in the church basement. Sacred Heart does bingo every other Friday. Bingo players drink a lot of tea and coffee. Mrs. Agnelli bumped the folding table, which folded. The urn tipped over. Dad tried to pull me out of the way, but he wasn't quite fast enough. He got burned, too, over his hand and wrist, but it was only first degree. "Nuthin'," he says sadly whenever he talks about it. "Nuthin' I don't get every week at the stove."

It was bad—the ambulance and the hospital and all the stuff that followed. It was scary. So was the screaming. Sometimes Mom at Dad (Why hadn't he moved faster, for Chrissakes?), sometimes Dad at the insurance company (What did they mean it doesn't merit extensive cosmetic treatment—isn't *covered*, for Chrissakes?), sometimes me (It hurt.).

In the end, it stopped hurting, although it's still sensitive to the touch. Nonna stopped praying about it, and Mom and Dad stopped yelling about it. There was no extensive cosmetic treatment. Extensive means expensive, and it's ten thousand dollars no one has. I think Dad had a meeting with some of the more important Sacred Heart people. He never talked about it after. All these years later, I can imagine why he went and what was said. *"We understand that your daughter's injury would be upsetting to you, Ronnie."* They would have called him Ronnie, not Mr. Marino. *"But as neither the urn nor the table belonged to the church . . . Lawsuit? Well, you are aware we have seventeen attorneys on retainer . . ."*

Father Sanchez and Mrs. Agnelli came a lot, always with cookies. Mrs. Agnelli offered to sell her 1986 Cadillac and give us the money. Father Sanchez is still trying to find someone to do laser treatment for free. I think that's why Dad still goes to Mass. But only on the holidays. I don't go very often, either, but that has more to do with things the Church doesn't want me to do than with the scalding. Nonna still goes every day. And my sister, Sienna, is having her wedding there in December.

Life goes on. Even for a timid kid who got more timid after she got burned. In another story, the plucky heroine would have filled her wardrobe with halter tops and organized loose change collections for the Children's Hospital burn ward. But this was me. I put T-shirts on over my swimsuit when we went to the Shore. I stopped wearing sundresses. I tried to be charitable about the Freddy Krueger stuff. After all, the scar was pretty horrendous and huge then. I've grown; it hasn't. I thought Freddy would be left behind when I got my Willing scholarship and got out of Sacred Heart.

Of course it wasn't.

I have my theories about how the name followed me. The nicest one is that Philly, for all its big-bad-city rep, is really not all that large. For those of us who live pretty much in the middle of it, it's a village.

Since freshman year, when everyone at Willing had to try it out, I don't hear it as much. I don't expect it. And I really, really don't like surprises. Which made going home at the end of the unexpectedly catastrophic day okay. There are exactly no surprises to be found there.

I stopped at the restaurant first. Marino's takes up the first two floors of the building; there are three apartments above that. My dad and uncle Ricky grew up in one. When they got married, they each moved into one of the other two. My grandmother stayed, even after Poppa died and the crazy old lady next door died, and Mom made sure to get the listing so she and Dad could buy the house. Nonna finally moved in with us four years ago. My brother, Leo, moved into her place. Ricky and his wife moved down the block, and my sister took their apartment. Uncle Ricky stays in the closet-size attic studio when Tina kicks him out of their house.

My family doesn't believe in long-distance anything. Or quiet, either.

The noise hit me before I even had the back door into the kitchen all the way open.

"So I'm sitting there at my own table, trying to have a quiet bowl of cornflakes," Uncle Ricky was yelling to no one in particular over the chugging of the industrial dishwasher, "and she's tearing into me about my friggin' socks . . ."

". . . six cases of the plum tomatoes, and two pounds of dried oregano . . ." my dad shouted into the phone. He and Ricky look a lot alike—short, solid, with serious Roman noses—but Ricky still has all his hair. Stress, Dad says. ". . . okay, okay, throw one of those in, too, but make sure it's good . . ."

Leo shoved through the serving doors, glowering in a way his last girlfriend told him makes him look like Johnny Depp. "Mr. Donato wants more *pepperoncini* in his antipasto." Leo hates waiting tables, especially when Sienna is hosting. He is planning on running Marino's when Dad retires. She has been planning her wedding for a year and isn't above showing bouquets and garter samples to the customers to get their opinion. "And there's some pickled asshole from Society Hill saying the mozzarell's off."

"*Taci, Leonardo!* Watch your mouth!" Nonna swatted at him with a wooden spoon. She was standing on a milk crate in front of the big stove, like she does whenever she makes sauce. Leo grinned and dodged just enough so the spoon grazed him instead of smacking into his bicep. If she'd missed completely, Nonna would have climbed off the crate to try again, and lively as she is, she really shouldn't be hopping on and off boxes. "Take Salvatore his *pepperoncini* and the other gentleman an *insalata mista* on the house." She swatted again at his departing butt and got back to stirring.

Technically, Dad owns Marino's. Nonna knows that; she sold it to him. She just likes to ignore that fact. I don't think he minds. He's happiest when the customer is happy. Ricky has no interest whatsoever in running a fifteen-table family restaurant in South Philly. He's always had big plans, most recently involving *Top Chef*—for which he auditions every season—and a move to New York. Nonna likes to stand in the kitchen and tell everyone what to do. The system works.

"Eh, Rinaldo, you need to put more anchovy in that puttanesca! *Ancora!*" Nonna clanged her ladle against one of the big stainless colanders hanging over the workstation for emphasis, sending it into a wobbly arc.

"Sure, Ma." Phone wedged between ear and shoulder, Dad dropped a fistful of fresh fettuccine into a waiting pot, stopped the colander midswing, and plated a slab of codfish. Fred Astaire in a red-stained apron. "Leo!" While Nonna wasn't looking, he slid the anchovy container a few inches closer to the stove. Consider them added. "*Leo!*"

"... so I tell her, when I get to New York, Padma Lakshmi's not gonna be hassling me about my friggin' Fruit of the Looms ..."

"A little service here!" Dad yelled. "No, not you, hon. My son who puts the word *wait* in *waiter*. Now, you promise me those eggs are gonna be fresh? Keeps me up at night, thinking about E. coli ..."

I thought about slipping silently back out. But that would have defeated the purpose, which was to be seen. Otherwise, someone would come over to the house looking for me, and probably want to chat. I needed to make an appearance, so I could go home to unwillingly and helplessly relive the dismal day over and over in peace. I braced myself and stepped onto the honeycomb floor mat.

They saw me.

"Hey, Ell-*a*!" Uncle Ricky lunged with a spoon. I tasted garlic and strawberry. "Mmm," I managed.

"It's my new sauce. The producers will love it."

Maybe. I grabbed a slice of bread from a basket.

"That's no good!" Dad scolded. "No, not you, hon. My shrimp of a daughter. Thinks she can make a meal out of bread. Harvard girls eat dinner!" I saw him reach for a pan. Knowing he would be stuffing me soon with something expensive and unappealing, and probably fishy, I headed him off by filling a mug from the *zuppa di giorno* pot. Then I did the rounds, kissing him, Uncle Ricky, and Nonna, who pinched my cheek, hard, like always, and started my escape. Through the porthole windows between the kitchen and dining room, I could see Sienna bouncing toward us. I wanted to get out before—

"Get the lead out, youse!" She banged through the doors like a force of nature, masses of curly hair and eyelashes and J.Lo booty squeezed into a tight black skirt. She's the hostess on Tuesdays and Sundays, and on nights like these, when Uncle Ricky and Aunt Tina are fighting and Tina refuses to come to work. "We're all turning gray out here!" Someone in the dining room must have said something funny, because there was a ripple of laughter.

"You're a pup, Mr. Donato," Sienna called back over her shoulder, then slipped in for a lipstick-and-VPL check. She gave me a quick once-over and rolled her eyes. "Would it kill you to put on a little mascara? You could be such a hottie if you just tried . . . Okay, okay," she muttered when Dad, Ricky, and Nonna gave her looks I pretended not to see. "I'm just saying."

They all have their own ways of trying to fix me. Dad's usually involves food. Mom's is a continuing stream of rhinestone-embellished tops that would cure my Willing invisibility in decisive and unfortunate ways. Sienna goes for vague threats of makeovers.

"Hey, don't you go sneaking off on me," she commanded as I edged toward the back door. "I got pictures of shoes to go with the bridesmaids' dresses. You just gotta tell me which you like best."

Fortunately, when there are options, Sienna circles her preference in pink Sharpie. It makes my participation much simpler.

Leo came back in with the plate of "off" mozzarella salad.

"Look at that. Ass—" Nonna hissed. "Jerk eats most of it, then sends it back. I *hate* these guys. Yo, Insania, there are people waiting to be seated."

"So they'll wait." Sienna carried a bowl of minestrone to the office in back. I could see our mother, magenta suit jacket and matching pumps off, frowning at a stack of papers on the desk in front of her. Generally, she's at work from eight to late, showing houses to people who, for the most part, don't buy them. Lately, she's around more, studying the books and trying to convince Dad that shrimp and steak for a hundred and fifty wedding guests is not excessive. I watched as Sienna traded the soup for a shiny catalogue. Whatever she said, probably something about shoes, got her a big smile. They're most alike, Mom and Sienna, but we're not exactly a wildly exotic family.

I'm like the period at the finish of a sentence, the end of the line. We all have the Marino dark hair and eyes, even Mom, who was born a Palladinetti and has aspirations of being a redhead. We're all short, although Leo swears he's five ten, and kind of curvy. Even Leo and Dad. We burp when we eat celery, have decent singing voices, and have never had our names on a single plaque. There are a thousand families just like us within twenty blocks.

"Ella," Mom called from the office, "did you wear those ratty jeans to school again? No wonder you haven't got . . . Oh, fine, Sienna. I get it already. Ella? Come in. You gotta look at these shoes. Absolutely to die!"

I didn't think I could face pictures of purple diamante pumps just then. Mug in hand, I crept out.

"Stay, stay!" Dad called. "Salmon. It's brain food!"

"Anchovy!" Nonna banged again. I closed the door behind me.

I stepped from the restaurant's four-car lot into our backyard, skirting the rock bed and empty koi pond Mom insisted on when Zen was all the rage. Personally, I miss the scrubby lawn and cracked cement patio. It was good for sprinkler jumping in the summer. From the front, the house is pretty much like every other one on the block: narrow, three stories, brick at the bottom and white vinyl siding at the top. Dad nixed Mom's idea of replacing the porch supports with plaster Greek pillars. But on theme, she stuck a trio of fat, faux-stone planters complete with cavorting nymphs on the front porch. She never remembers to water the stuff she plants, so there's usually an assortment of browning weeds in front of the thriving rosemary that Nonna snuck in. Inside, it's beige and cabbage roses, the toile throw pillows that were all the rage three years ago, and the occasional bright blue Madonna statue that, yeah, Nonna snuck in.

My room was pink, typical ruffly princess pink, until I started at Willing and had my first art class with Ms. Evers. She took one look at the watercolor I did of the rose she'd given us and laughed. In a really good way. Then she gave me a pad of the whitest, thickest paper I'd ever seen, a box of charcoal pencils, and sent me off to roam the halls.

"Think bold," she said.

Now my room is black and white. *"Sfortuna!"* Nonna mutters whenever she looks through the door. "No good fortune in this room."

But she likes my drawings, which replaced the pink floral wallpaper, and she's partial to black, herself. She hasn't worn anything else since arriving from Calabria fifty years ago ("Oh, this city. So dirty!").

Nonna is obsessed with dirt, *American Idol*, and bad luck. Since my birthday is March 17, she's convinced I was born with bad luck hanging over my crib. According to her, the fact that I am barely five one is due completely to Evil Number 17. Mom says the fact that I was due to be born on the twentieth—of *April*—has a lot more to do with my shrimpyness. Dad says that considering the fact that I only weighed three pounds then and weigh a hundred and three now, I should consider myself a champion grower. Mom also likes to point out that Nonna doesn't top five feet even in her black church shoes.

According to Mom, I was a perfectly beautiful little shrimp. According to everyone, Nonna went ballistic whenever someone *called* me a beautiful baby. *"Malocchio, malocchio!"* she spat at doctors, nurses, and visiting friends, hurrying to counteract their well-meant compliment (and, apparently, evil-eye curse), by waving the protective *corno*—pinkie and pointer up, other fingers folded—over my tiny head. "Like a wrinkled Ozzie Osbourne in a dress," Mom mutters.

Mom and Nonna don't agree on much. Well, they are both completely convinced that they come first with Dad. And they love me with the same combo of high hopes and fierce, if misguided, helpfulness, leaning on me like mismatched bookends. Mom shoves from her side: "Such a diamond in the rough! Everyone can see that. Gorgeous bones. Bright as anything, absolutely endless potential, just needs some work . . ."

She speaks in Realtor-ese. I don't think she can help it.

Nonna shoves from her side: "*Bellissima! Bella bella Fiorella.* No, no, no purple! Always green, like the spring . . ."

She spends a lot of time telling me how *bella* I am. Apparently, it's okay now that the damage has been done. She puts all of her ninety-odd pounds behind the word, so it always sounds kinda like she's spitting, cursing the curse of the curse. That's Nonna.

I think maybe she believes that if she says it often enough and with enough force, it'll come true. Or I'll buy it, like the emperor's clothes.

Nonna is okay with faking things. Her favorite handbag is one she bought off the street from a guy who was also selling incense and diet pills. It's stiff and black, big enough to swallow small people, and she pretends not to notice that the metal plate on the front says FRADA. According to Nonna, if she believes and God doesn't mind, it's all good. She has pictures of Jesus, the Pope, and Robert De Niro over her bed.

I have my sketches, mostly of architecture—like cornices and pediments and bow windows, although I've been going through an ornamental door knocker phase lately, so the top layer has a lot of eyes and gaping mouths—covering two walls. Above my desk, I have one bit of Edward. There are plenty of prints of his work, but he did only two self-portraits (one is in the library at Willing), and only one has been reproduced, on a museum poster advertising an exhibition. It's my very favorite piece, a portrait bust in bronze.

Here's the thing. Edward's self-portrait in the school was like a first date. Through it, he said everything about himself that he would have wanted me to think: that he was handsome, sexy, confident. All true, but that's only the obvious stuff. Not the whole picture. By the time I found the bronze, I'd already read the bios and the collection of his letters that Edith's granddaughter published after his death. It was later in our relationship. I *knew* him.

The bronze is a completely different Edward, the warts-and-all Edward. He's older, by about ten years. It's the same broad forehead and thick hair waving back from it. The same slightly hooded eyes; in the painting, they make me wonder if Edward didn't go through life looking a little sleepy, and if that didn't make a lot of women feel wide-awake. But there are shallow lines next to the bronze eyes, and deeper ones bracketing the mouth, which is thinner than the painted one, and really sad.

Which makes sense when you see that the center of the piece, the most important part, is the jagged, gaping hole in the middle of his chest where his heart would be. It's called *Ravaged Man*, dated 1899, which is the year his wife died. Diana. He never got over her. I like the bronze. It's truthful. In it, he's truthful.

"Does all life suck?" I asked him as I slumped into my desk chair. I noticed the white paint I'd used was starting to chip. The pink was creeping back. "Or just ours?"

"Life sucks," he agreed. He sounds a little British, even though he . . . well, wasn't. "Although I think that if I could live for seventeen years after having my heart wrenched from my body, you can survive another nineteen months until graduation."

"You'd think, wouldn't you? I'm not so sure."

"Not a good showing with the Frost, certainly."

"Don't even go there," I warned him. "I can't even think about that yet."

"Fine. How is the weather?"

"I mean, I *knew* I would see him in class." I let my head drop onto the desk with a well-deserved thunk. *D'oh*. "I see him in *every* English class. But today, after . . ."

"After the unfortunate Freddy moment?"

"Don't go there. I really don't want to talk about that."

"Fine." Edward shrugged. He does have shoulders. "Have you read any good books—?"

"He's so cute. And, you know, I kinda get the feeling he's *nice*, even if he is dating Cruella De Vil . . . And the *drawings* . . . Sorry," I offered. "I probably shouldn't be talking about another guy."

"I completely understand." Edward is very understanding. "Besides, I am ravaged. I have no heart to give you. And the Bainbridge fellow is rather talented. The mermaid was really quite impressive."

"Yeah, it was." There had been two loose pages tucked into Alex's book. They'd been covered with incredible, unreal figures: slinky animals dressed up like forties movie stars, ghostlike people who looked like they were from Japanese woodblock prints, and an unfinished mermaid, with incredible wild hair and dozens of teardrop-shaped scales, half of them filled with smaller pictures: fish, cameras, airplanes. "I wanted to tell him how great his stuff is, but I completely froze."

"No great surprise, that."

"Thanks. Why do I bother talking to you?"

"Because you can, I suppose" was his reply. "I don't frighten you."

"You should. You have a huge hole in your chest."

"That's what you like about me, darling."

"Maybe," I conceded. Edward hadn't needed words to tell the world how he felt about Diana. "So what do I do about Alex?"

"Talk to him."

"Yes, again, thank you. How do I start?"

" 'Hello'?"

"Masterful. And then?"

Edward sighed. "For heaven's sake, Ella, you're a smart girl. Think of something. What was it Evers said? 'Be bold'? Be bold. Tell Alex his drawings remind you of Suzuki Harunobu, Hieronymus Bosch, and Hilary Knight all in one."

"Oh, *that* would make me sound cool and normal." My fingers traced the edge of the scar where it peaked under my ear. "It's hopeless. I'm hopeless."

"Absolutely. Give up now."

"You're not helping," I said. "Why can't you be doting and supportive and say all the *right* things?"

Edward shrugged again. "You prefer the truth. Besides, I'm a metal head. What do you expect?"

Fair enough, although you'd think imaginary conversations with an object of desire would be a lot nicer.

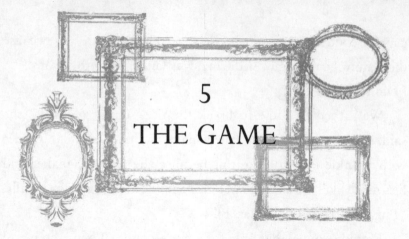

5
THE GAME

"Okay. Sing first, or Truth or Dare? Sing, right?" Frankie had scanned the crowd at Chloe's. Apparently, he'd seen something he liked, because he knows his singing—his enthusiastic, reliably flat singing—will bring him to the attention of everyone in the room. He freely acknowledges that Sinatra he is not. "We believe in the importance of dancing well," he informed me once, speaking for millions of gay men who might or might not agree. "Singing well is not mandatory. It's all about presence."

I almost never sing in public, for all the expected reasons (cowardice, cowardice, cowardice, and cowardice) and because, between Sadie's good singing and Frankie's everything but, I would just disappear again. When I'm between Sadie and Frankie is when I'm most visible. Why would I mess with that? For me, Chloe's is all about the hummus and hanging with my friends. For Frankie, it's so much more.

"Truth or Dare," I said around my first mouthful of spanakopita.

"Puhleeze," he muttered. I didn't know if it was because I

usually choose ToD and almost never choose Dare, or because the skinny, goateed guy at the mic was launching into "Oops! . . . I Did It Again."

We turned to Sadie to break the tie. "Truth or Dare," she said, surprising me a little. She usually and understandably sides with Frankie on stuff like this because she's a peacemaker and he's more likely to sulk than I am. Then she added, apologetically, "I'm starving. If I don't eat, I'll cry."

Frankie pouted, but only for a few seconds. When it comes to Sadie and food, he's a prince. Especially when her diet is not going well, which is almost always. "Greek salad," he said, sliding the platter in front of her, "takes almost as many calories to digest as it has in it. Really."

I nodded my agreement. Sadie smiled (she's no dummy, but she has a great ability to believe in fairies and magic when it's important) and scooped a pile of salad onto her plate.

Chloe's: Greek restaurant, karaoke bar, and shoe-repair shop, is our favorite hangout for three very good reasons.

1. The food is cheap and decent.

2. The karaoke options are many.

3. No one else from Willing ever goes there.

We'd managed to snag our favorite table—one away from the stage, such as it is. It's really just a big sheet of plywood raised up on bunch of cinder blocks, large enough to hold a mic and a singer (or poet, stand-up comedian, or emcee, depending on the night) comfortably. It's not uncommon for a Motown song to inspire backup singers, but it's also not uncommon for them to fall off the back, especially if the song is "Stop! In the Name of Love" and the Supreme-alikes are enthusiastic.

"God, shoot him," Frankie muttered, stabbing a pita triangle in the direction of the stage. "Shoot me."

Sadie, clearly feeling much more cheerful with some sustenance in her, popped him with a gun forefinger. "Truth or Dare."

"Truth. I'm eating."

"Okay." She sucked thoughtfully on an olive, then, "If you could commit one serious crime—and I mean a lots-of-years-in-jail kind of crime—and get away with it, what would it be?"

"Ooh." Frankie narrowed his eyes in gleeful contemplation. "I like that one. A raid on the men's department at Barneys, maybe? A slow, painful death for certain elected officials? A forged check from a member of the Walmart family? Hard choice. Ah. I have it. I would steal the Hope Diamond."

"It's cursed," I told him. "Everyone who has owned it has died a terrible death."

"Don't care. I want it."

"Why?" Sadie was genuinely curious. "You couldn't exactly wear it around."

"Absolutely true. Maybe I'd keep it in a shoe box. Or send it to Haiti. No one would ever know where it went, or what brilliant criminal mastermind was able to take it. I would be the eternal Who."

I have to give Frankie credit; his answers are never boring.

ToD, as we play it, has two rules: no lying, ever, and no dares that would cause the sort of humiliation that follows you into adulthood. Since it's just the three of us, we're pretty good at respecting those boundaries. After two years, we've gotten pretty creative. You'd think we would know every last thing there is to know about one another, rendering the game something less than entertaining. We know *most* everything about one another. We also each know something about the others that keeps ToD fresh.

Like:

Frankie exaggerates. Everything. So ToD is a good way for Sadie and me to find out whether he actually did meet Marc Jacobs as he hinted after a trip to New York (no, but he did see him coming out of Bergdorf's), or locked lips with the cute sales boy at Sailor Jerry (yes, but cute sales boy has a boyfriend). It's also the only way we ever find out *anything* about his life at home. He never volunteers. He will, however, answer what we ask, even if he looks like the words are burning his tongue while he does it—as long as it's not about his brother's shadier side. And Sadie is desperately curious about Daniel.

Of course, Frankie almost always chooses Dare. And the one time Sadie tried to do an end run around that one by (gently) daring him to tell us the worst thing Daniel had ever done in his presence, he growled, "Not cool. Not cool at all," and got up and walked out of Chloe's. He was there waiting for us at school the next morning, and nothing was ever said, but we haven't dared him to tell or asked about his twin since.

When daring Frankie, it helps to know that, deep down, he is just as shy and insecure as anyone. Yes, his fave pastime is dancing in front of the mirrors at Neiman Marcus in Helmut

Lang clothing he can't afford. True, he sings frequently and enthusiastically at Chloe's. Absolutely, he walked up to the drop-dead gorgeous guy in the vintage Bowie shirt at Head House Books last week and asked his favorite ice cream flavor. Turned out the guy was straight ("No, just closeted" was Frankie's take), but nothing ventured, nothing gained. And it had, after all, been a dare. He probably wouldn't have done it otherwise. The price of rejection is, quietly, too high.

As for Sadie, in ToD it helps to know that she loves to be asked about her plans for the future. She's not naturally garrulous, and no one outside our little cadre ever asks her anything about herself. She used to go to a therapist (one of *Philadelphia* mag's Top Docs, of course), but her mother put a stop to that when Sadie wouldn't tell her what happened in the sessions. Mrs. Winslow is pretty narcissistic. Sadie probably doesn't need therapy half as much as her mother—or most of the people we know. She's pretty centered. But she still likes to be asked. We never dare her to talk to strange boys. The only thing that scares her more than that is the concept of being naked in front of anyone.

And me? When it comes to dares, on the rare occasion when I take them, anything is possible. I trust my friends not to humiliate me; they take great pleasure in making me do things that involve climbing. "Life is short," Frankie likes to announce with great solemnity as I examine walls, trees, and statues of dead patriots for footholds, "and so are you!"

The truths are often of the wolf-in-sheep's-clothing variety: serious stuff in fluffy wrapping. Like, "A genie grants you three wishes, but they all have to involve sex…" or, "If you had to confess one of your biggest fears to Amanda Alstead, what would it be?" ToD and Edward are my therapy. Which means the undertruths Frankie and Sadie ask can be a little brutal. But interesting.

Sometimes ToD is fun; sometimes it's legitimized prying. Sometimes it's our way of checking in. "How *you* doin'?" isn't in any of our characters. Well, okay, maybe Sadie's a little, but she's too sensitive to pry, and when someone tells Sadie to bug off, even if they don't really mean it, off she bugs.

"Why do you think we ended up here, together?" Frankie asked once at lunch when the three of us were crammed into a two-chair space at Table 12. Even Invisibles have a stratum, and to sit at 13 would be an admission of . . . well, something. When I started to point to my scar, he slapped my hand. "No. No no no. It's because we have private inner lives. They"—he gestured to the Phillites—"don't."

I'm not sure that's entirely true. I mean, everyone must have some sort of inner life. The alternative is a little too zombie-creepy. But I know what he means. Social networking sites, texting in class, and vaguely incestuous dating practices all make secrets a lot less secret, and a lot less interesting. With the Phillites, it's all out there for everyone to see.

Frankie waited until the next singer started her rendition of "You Oughta Know" before turning to me. "Truth or Dare?" He always asks, just to remind all of us—lovingly, of course— just what a complete coward I am.

"Truth."

He sighed, but clearly had one on tap. "Five things you find adoration-worthy about Alex Bainbridge, and if you mention his eyes, I will spit hummus on you."

"I hardly adore—"

"Five. No eyes. Now."

"Fine." I thought for a sec. "One: He seems like actually a halfway-decent guy."

Frankie snorted. "Halfway-decent? Such praise."

"Oh, stop. Really nice, then. He seems really nice." Despite the Cruella De Vil girlfriend. "Two: He looks like a god when he plays lacrosse. Ah! Don't you dare roll your eyes at me. We, as female animals, are genetically programmed to go for the potent combo of grace and power. Right?" I looked to Sadie for backup. She nodded with enough enthusiasm to make her hair bounce in a wild pouf.

I turned back to Frankie, who, I could tell, was going to launch into snarky mode. "Before you go all fake-wounded on me, Mr. Hobbes, I will remind you that you have admitted to having crushes on David Beckham, Roger Federer, and Gene Kelly—who is every bit as dead as Edward Willing."

"Whatever. Third?"

"Third. You saw the drawings. Need I elaborate?"

"No," Frankie conceded sulkily. "I'll give you that one."

"Thank you ever so. Now, fourth . . ."

Fourth . . . It wasn't so much that I was stumped, as that I was reluctant. I just didn't want to share the fact that watching Alex in action, or even just watching him lounge in one of the school desks that are not quite big enough for tall boys, makes me feel just a bit breathless—and a bit angry (mostly at myself) that there isn't likely an Alex Bainbridge in my foreseeable future.

I hadn't wanted to look at him during the declamation disaster. Partly because looking at him, then at Amanda, who stared back with a combination of amusement and utter contempt, as I was getting started had been part of the problem. *Freddy . . . Freddy . . . Freddy.* But I had looked at him, helpless, after, and had seen him punch a snickering Chase hard on the arm.

Alex Bainbridge just might be a little bit wonderful.

"Can't do it?" Frankie poked me out of my thoughts. "I rest my case. This is not an adoration-worthy specimen."

I could have conceded. It certainly would have been the easiest thing to do. I'm ordinarily a big fan of the path of least resistance. Not this time. "I'm merely sorting through the options." I poked him back. "Just what is your problem with him? Even you've admitted he never did anything nasty to you. So what is it, really?"

Frankie gave me his lizard look, flat mouth and lowered eyelids. "I am the one doing the asking, madam. The next time I choose Truth and you're asking, feel free to waste your question on such inanities. Finish the list. If you can."

"Fine. Fine. His breathtaking smile. And his money. If I had that money, I could do anything . . . everything I want."

I'd just make a whopping kink in the rules, if not a fracture. I'd kinda lied. Not that having the kind of money the Bainbridges have would smoothly open the world to me, but that I cared. I could see Sadie and Frankie staring into me, trying to decide whether to call me on it. They let it go. Sadie is rich and, not her fault, doesn't really understand. Frankie, coming from a family with even less money than mine, does.

"Truth or Dare," Frankie offered Sadie. I decided not to mention it was my turn to ask.

"Dare." Sadie's not afraid of dares when she's had real food.

"Sing. Something old. Decent. And I mean *decent*."

She nodded, flipping through the grease-spattered playlist. "I'm thinking about 'Every Rose Has Its Thorn.'"

"Oh, God," Frankie groaned. "Too maudlin. I don't think I can handle maudlin tonight. Besides, it's a terrible song."

"You just don't like anything recorded after 1970," Sadie said tartly.

"Wrong. Very wrong. I do not like terrible things recorded after 1970. If you have to stick to"—he made a quick gagging motion—"power ballads, splash out. Aretha: 'I Never Loved a Man the Way I Love You.' Otis Redding: 'Try a Little Tenderness' . . ."

"Those are from the sixties."

"I'm sure Christina Aguilera has mangled them in concert."

"How about 'I Want to Know What Love Is'?"

"I'll vomit, Sadie. I really will. All that wailing. Nope."

"But you're not the one singing it," Sadie pointed out reasonably.

Frankie blinked at her. "Your point?"

"Fine. 'You Don't Have to Say You Love Me'?"

"Excellent choice."

Sadie's mother had dressed her again. This time, it was a shapeless black sack of a dress with an artfully shredded hem.

"She looks like a crazy cat lady," Frankie said sadly as Sadie climbed the single step to the plywood stage.

She did.

She got a smattering of applause. Other regulars. Everyone else just went on with their hummus and playlists. The table behind us was in the middle of a raucous game of quarters. "Powel freshmen," Frankie had dismissed them after getting a glimpse of their fake IDs and oversize sweatshirts. All straight, none cute enough for him. Just loud and growing louder with each successive pitcher.

The music started. The collegiates howled at what must have been a masterful shot. We ignored them. They were big and drunk, and we're small (me), confrontation-averse (me, too), and rational (Frankie). We knew what was coming.

"When I said I needed you," Sadie began. The quiet came on so suddenly, it was a noise in itself. By the time she got to the end of *"You said you would always stay,"* the only sound was the faint whirring of a quarter spinning to rest on the table behind us.

Here's the thing. When Frankie suggests Aretha or Dusty Springfield or even Adele to Sadie, he means it. Because when Sadie sings, everyone listens. Her voice is deep and velvety, and makes me think of smoky bars in 1940s Casablanca, where everyone wore white and drank contraband champagne. Of course, I don't have the slightest idea what a 1940s bar in Casablanca was really like, which says a lot of what there is to be said about Sadie's singing. It takes you.

She looks pretty, too. She does this thing where she tilts her head and half closes her eyes and holds the mic really close to her mouth. When she sings, guys watch and occasionally get a slightly glazed look. I've seen a few come halfway out of their chairs as she sings her last note. Then she slumps back to the table, they slide back into their seats, and the moment's totally gone. Sadie hasn't had a date since . . . well, birth, unfortunately.

I don't get it. She's fab. She's certainly not unattractive. She has perfect skin, the best eyebrows I have ever seen, and no matter how much she and her mother insist to the contrary, an entirely decent body. Round, absolutely, but only in the right places. But she wears her shredded sacks, and when she's not singing, I guess that's what guys see. The one time I hinted that a belt would be a nice addition, all she did was give my turtleneck a long look. I didn't think it was entirely the same thing, but point taken.

"You don't have to say you love me . . ."

Sadie could kill people in the bland musicals that Willing puts on every spring, knock everyone right out of their seats and through the back wall of the auditorium and onto the manicured lawn. But she won't. No one at Willing has a clue. She pours her heart out in three-minute power-ballad measures on the Chloe's stage and leaves it there.

"You know," I suggested quietly to Frankie during a long pause in the lyrics, "maybe this isn't the song you think it is. I mean, she's telling some guy that he doesn't have to love her as long as he comes home. Is that a message we want to send?"

Frankie speared a bite of feta. "Who's 'we'? And who are you, the Censorship Fairy? It's a killer song. Just listen."

I did. Everyone did. Some of the guys in the room looked like they'd been drugged. Of course, a few of them probably had been; it's South Street, after all, but a bunch were just vibin' Sadie's voice.

"Jeez, Marino, don't you want to feel that?" Frankie rapped his fork against his plate. "To love so much that you don't *care* if he loves you back? To be so into someone that pride goes out the 'effing window?" When I got very interested in my olive pits, he sighed. "It doesn't count, your sad, sad thing for Edward Willing."

"He won't leave," I offered, trying for levity.

"He won't come, either."

"Nice."

"Virginity is not a commodity in our world, my vestal friend."

Maybe not, and no one had expressed all that much interest in mine recently. There was Dieter, a German exchange student freshman year, who smelled a little like paste and spent nine weeks in perpetual surprise that I wouldn't let him feel me up before dumping me for a yearbook girl who would. And there was Bryan, who I met during my week at the Shore last summer. He had carroty hair and wore high-necked, long-sleeved sunblock shirts because he was prone to crisping. I let him get a half of a good feel under mine. He e-mailed once, from his home in North Jersey, ten words with six of them misspelled. I didn't reply. I'll take dead over dumb.

Much to my don't-wanna-have-this-conversation relief, Sadie slipped back into her seat. "Sublime," Frankie told her, and she glowed a little, because while he might exaggerate, he never lies to us. Then, "My turn."

He glided into place, did an expert hair toss that brought all attention to his model-perfect face, and acknowledged a wolf whistle from behind us with a flick of his fingers. I glanced over my shoulder at the table full of pretty boys. None were familiar, but I pegged one as Frankie's type to a tee: Norse godling, all icy blond and blue.

"This is for you, Marino," Frankie said, and my attention snapped back to the stage.

Yes, he did. The first notes of "Like a Virgin" came on, and seconds later, Frankie was channeling Madonna for all he was worth. He was saved from cliché-dom by the sheer fact that he can't sing for his life. No one minded, and after the first curious glances, no one was looking at red-faced me. Because, of course Frankie wasn't singing to me. Every word, every wink, every shimmy and hip thrust was for Gunnar-Björn behind us. By the second verse, most of the audience was singing and thumping along.

He finished to full-blown appreciative howling from the crowd. He waved it off as he strolled back to us, eyes sliding once, and again, toward the pretty boys. Once seated, he folded his hands neatly on the table and looked at us expectantly.

There was no question what he wanted. He was silently and eloquently daring us to dare him.

We're good friends. "Truth or Dare?" Sadie asked.

He pretended to think about it. "Ah . . . dare."

Sadie pretended to think about it. "I dare you to go ask for his phone number," she said with perfectly earnest enthusiasm. She pointed discreetly. "The cute blond one."

"Ragnar-Knut-Thor," I elaborated.

Frankie blinked at me in surprise. "You know him?"

"Of course not."

"Very funny." He leaned into me, until his lips were inches from mine. He blew. "Okay?"

"A little garlicky."

"Hummus," he muttered. "Doctor?"

Sadie was already on it. From her huge, fringed bag (Balenciaga runway, one of her mother's rejects), she pulled a tin of Altoids. She also can be counted on for Kleenex, Band-Aids, bottled water, and dried seaweed snacks. Frankie popped his pill, bared his teeth so we could do a spinach check, and was on his way. He moves like a cat. Within thirty seconds, he was seated next to his object of desire.

"I watch," Sadie said in wonder. "I watch and I take notes, and I still can't master it."

"Me, either," I admitted cheerfully.

"There has to be more to it than the fact he's beautiful. There *has* to be. Otherwise, I might as well give up now."

I squeezed her hand. "Of course there's more. Frankie's . . . he's . . . Well, he's . . ."

"*Frankie,*" we said at the same time. We laughed, jinx-dibsed each other, and dug into the remains of the baba ghanoush.

Frankie is beautiful. He's also sharp as broken glass, fierce and charismatic, and out of the confines of Willing, he glows.

Especially when he meets a new Mr. Maybe. Frankie loves to date. "Would you buy a pair of shoes without trying them on and walking around for a while?" he demands. He likes shoes, too. But the truth about Frankie is that he's really looking to be half of one good pair.

Aren't we all?

"It'll happen," Sadie announced, mind reader and eternal optimist that she is.

The words were barely out of her mouth, my pithy retort just forming, when Frankie slid back into his seat, a good ten minutes too soon. He looked crushed.

"Oh, sweetie." Sadie scooted over and put an arm around him. "Clearly, he's a taco short of a combo platter."

"Elvis has left the building" was my contribution.

"A few fries short of a Happy Meal." Sadie is very fond of food analogies. Who can blame her?

Frankie focused. A little. "What?" he asked vaguely.

"To say no to you." Sadie smoothed a shiny comma of hair from his forehead. "He's obviously insane."

"He didn't say no to me. We barely got past introductions before I had to leave."

"Why?" Sadie and I demanded in unison. "He looks like a Norse godling!" I added.

"I know. I know. Ragnor-Knut-Thor! . . . Only, his name is Biff," he moaned. "I can't go out with someone named *Biff*!"

I patted his back. Onstage, one of the college boys was just launching into "U Can't Touch This."

6
THE DOOR

Once upon a time, before Willing was a school, it was a house. Not the Willings' house; they always lived in Society Hill, until the various and sundry branches moved out to the Main Line and vast acreage. The house-that-became-a-school was built by a South Philly man named Vittore Palladinetti, who made a fortune building railroads. Literally building them. He started as a laborer and ended up owning a big chunk of the Reading Railroad (Monopoly, anyone?). He bought the equivalent of an entire city block and built his four-story, sixty-two-room mansion, complete with an acre of Italian gardens, an aviary for his daughter, and a hundred-seat theater for his opera-loving wife.

Just over a year after moving in, Vittore caught the flu—most likely from one of his daughter's beloved birds—and died. His wife and daughter moved, married, changed last names, and so, while I might have been a student at the Palladinetti School, which would have been coolly ironic as my mom is descended from Vittore's far-less-successful younger brother, Beppo, it wasn't to be. Edith Willing swept in, disinfected, and this Wednesday morning in October, I was sitting on the floor outside what had once been Daughter Palladinetti's bedroom and was now the Regina Pugh Willing Romance Language Room, sketching the door. It's copied from a bronze abbey door in Rome, filled with angels and demons that look like they are having a hell of a party.

Downstairs, the period bell rang. It's actually an antique gong that lives in the back hall. The school secretary has to leave her office once an hour to whack it with a really big, padded stick. She puts on construction earmuffs to do it. It's loud. A couple of times a year, humor-impaired students make it disappear until it becomes clear that no one really cares. They always bring it back. Until then, Mrs. Maus cheerfully uses an electronic signal horn. I think she likes watching people in the vicinity jump.

I didn't bother moving when the gong went. I had double AP studio—meaning I get to draw, for credit, for two periods in a row. Ms. Evers pretty much lets me do my own thing on the days when she doesn't think I'll benefit from whatever the rest of the class is doing. Every so often, she tries to get me to draw people. "We know you can do doors, Ella. Why not try faces? Fascinating stuff behind them, too. I bet anyone you ask will be happy to sit for you . . ."

I think she's matchmaking, or at least trying to help me expand my social horizons. She's a former debutante from North Carolina who looks like Jessica Simpson. I would hate her, except she's an incredible painter and really decent human being. So I nod and smile and go off to find an interesting window to draw.

I figured angels have faces, even if these were almost too small to draw, so I was half honoring her suggestion. I was just starting on a wing when the door banged open, spewing a mixed crowd of juniors and seniors into the hall. Some were still speaking French. More were instantly on their iPhones, communicating with BFFs downstairs or down the hall. We're not supposed to have electronic stuff out during the school day. Yeah, right. I would say with confidence that 250 of Willing's 311 students can text without looking.

I made myself as small as possible, tucking my legs in and pressing back against the wall. I still got bumped and stepped on a few times by oblivious texters. One stopped for a second. "Oh, hey, sorry. Didn't see you," she offered. The rest just kept going.

My lowly French 2A class meets in the basement. I tried to take Italian, unsuccessfully, as a freshman. "This seems rather . . . er . . . well, not quite . . . right," Mr. Donaldson, my freshman adviser had said carefully when he saw my course request list. "The goal is to learn a new language. Is it not?"

Well, maybe, but they weren't stopping all the Phillites who'd been summering in Provence since infancy from taking French. And my Italian is pretty nonexistent. According to my dad, that's the way it is with the grandchildren of Italian immigrants. He and his siblings all understand Italian from hearing it being spoken around them, but none of them speak it. Sienna speaks Gucci; Leo has a pretty decent arsenal of Sicilian insults. I arrived at Willing knowing a lot of food names and a couple of curse words. But Mr. Donaldson nixed the Italian request. I guess he just assumed I was already fluent. I assume because my name is Marino. They called Frankie into the office once freshman year to ask him to inform a table-linen deliveryman that there were holes in several of the tablecloths.

"He was Vietnamese," Frankie grumbled on returning. "I don't even speak enough Korean to have a conversation about table linens. I told them to call me if they ever needed someone to translate Sanskrit. That oughtta make their heads spin a little."

Of course Frankie doesn't speak Sanskrit, either. He takes Spanish. His last name is Hobbes. Must be the eyes they were going on.

The last of the French 5 class filtered down the hall. "Hey, I got one for you," a skinny Bee Boy in a kilt and Timberlands announced. "How did the slumlord end his suicide note?"

"How?" someone dutifully asked.

"J'ai le cafard!"

There were as many groans as laughs. A girl already in her soccer kit bumped the jokester with her shoulder. He bounced off the wainscoting.

As they turned the corner at the end of the hall, I half levered myself off the floor. I needed to close the door so I could start sketching again. Suddenly, Alex Bainbridge was there, framed by cavorting angels. I froze.

He didn't even look at where I was crouching. *"Merci,* Madame Grey," he called over his shoulder. *"Salut."*

"Ahem. Monsieur Bainbridge. *Salut . . . ?"*

Alex rolled his eyes, knowing Mrs. Grey couldn't see him as the doors, weighted for fire code, started to swing shut behind him. *"Pardonnez-moi, madame. Au revoir."*

"*Très bien. Au revoir.* Dude."

Alex grinned and slung his backpack over his shoulder. It gaped open. *No wonder he loses books.* He turned toward me then, and I suddenly felt like a spotlight had flashed on. I swallowed. And waved a little. He blinked.

"Jeez . . . uh . . ." I could see the wheels turning. It had, after all, been almost a week. "Ella. I didn't see you. I mean, I did, I guess, but I thought you were . . ." He gestured vaguely down the hall. There are busts and standing statues all over the place at Willing.

The Willings, of course, were patrons of the arts. Some of the sculptures are really beautiful: gods and goddesses and the occasional family member. Others are pretty creepy. There's a bumpy Vulcan in the dim hallway outside the biology lab that makes people move a little faster. I wondered for a sec what sort of statue Alex thought I was.

"You going in?" he asked just before the silence got deafening. He reached back for one of the doorknobs. Willing boys are supposed to be that polite. Most of them aren't.

"Oh, no," I managed finally. "I'm . . . um . . . sitting . . ." I pointed to the floor under my butt, like a complete idiot, and slowly sat back down. "Well, drawing. The door." I dipped my right shoulder quickly and lowered my chin, my long-perfected move to make sure my hair is covering me and my eyes are down. Alex was wearing retro-looking suede Adidas. One of them was coming untied.

"Drawing the door. Right. Do you draw a lot of doors?"

Truth: Yeah.

"Um . . . well, yeah. Doors, windows. Railings." I heard myself, but too late, of course. Ella Marino. Freak. She draws windows.

I looked up, and waited for him to walk off. Or roll his eyes, or whatever. He narrowed them. Then turned around to look at the door. He touched a dancing demon. "Wow. Cool. I can't believe I never noticed that before. Is it the same on the inside?"

I shrugged. "I don't know. I'm in Basement French. Shoulda known better. Italian girl."

"Yeah? *Sonno davvero allergico ai palle!*" He turned back and smiled at me, clearly delighted with himself. There are so many parts of Alex Bainbridge to stare at. But that mouth, the way it actually curves up at the corners . . .

It almost killed me to tell him, "Sorry. I have no idea what you just said."

"Yeah? Crap. It's all I remember from our trip to Tuscany a few years ago. My mother made me say it, like, a thousand times until I had it down. It means, 'I'm majorly allergic to nuts.'"

"Oh. Are you?"

"I am. Not go-into-anaphylactic-shock-and-die allergic, but I get pretty sick. So is it my accent? I mean, that you couldn't understand."

"Actually, it was everything other than *sonno*," I admitted. "And *allergico*, but that one just because it sounds like it does English."

"Wait. I thought you said you were Italian."

And here we go. "One grandmother came over. Everyone else

is old-school South Philly. We speak menu Italian." Which gave me a pretty good idea that whatever Alex was telling people he was allergic to, it wasn't what he thought it was.

I don't know what I expected, but it wasn't another killer smile. "I hear that. My mother's from Ukraine. I can name thirteen types of vodka, but not much else."

"No words for homicidal almonds?" *Who is this girl?* I almost asked aloud. Chatting with Alex Bainbridge like it was no big deal. I had a feeling I wouldn't recognize her in a mirror.

"Not a one. The only time I was there, we ate meat and potatoes. All the time. But, man, the food in Italy . . . Amazing, isn't it?"

"Never been."

"But . . ." He seemed to think better of whatever he was going to say. "You will."

"I will." And I did yet another thing so completely unlike me that it made me a little dizzy. I shared something only maybe three people know about me. "It's the very top of my Things to Do Before I Die list: Go to Florence. For the art."

"Cool. And what else?"

"In Florence? Well, I guess I would like to see—"

"No. On your list. What else is on it?"

It's a long and occasionally lofty list, but of course all that sprang to mind was the unmentionable: boring *Cut my hair short once* and humiliating *Lose my virginity.*

"Oh . . . uh . . . Paris," I managed, which is somewhere in the top twenty. "I'd like to go to Paris."

"For the art." His mouth curved.

Well, no. For the lights and cafés and boys with floppy dark hair and sultry accents, but I wasn't going to say that out loud. So I just nodded. Then, because it seemed like something I could do right then, I asked, "What does '*J'ai le cafard*' mean?"

Alex stared down at me. "Really?"

"Basement French," I reminded him. I didn't mention that I was, at best, scraping by at Basement French, and only that because Sadie, of French 3 excellence, insisted on checking my homework. "So?"

"It means you have *la tristesse*." When he didn't get so much as a glimmer from me, he repeated, "Really?" Only it wasn't mean, just kinda teasing. "Melancholy. The blues."

"Ah." I wondered if Bee Boys were generally humor-impaired, or just ones in kilts and lug soles. "Okay."

"Of course it literally means you have a cockroach."

"Ah," I said again. "Okay."

Alex braced one arm above my head and leaned forward, tenting me between his legs and the wall. There was a small, L-shaped tear in the left knee of his jeans. Through it, I could just see a patch of shadowed skin. He smelled like fabric softener and fresh grass.

"Do you?" he asked.

"Do I . . . ?"

"*Avoir le cafard.*"

I laughed. I couldn't help it. "*Non.*"

"That's good," he said. "That's *good.*"

If all rational thought had not fled my brain, I would have figured out that he was having a look at my drawing. I would probably have covered it. As it was, I simply swallowed as he leaned down farther and pointed to one of the demons I had sketched.

"Especially that one. He looks like he's going to jump that angel." We both jumped as his backpack swung forward off his shoulder. He caught it just before it thumped me in the forehead. I saw the corner of a book wobble precariously in the open flap. "I should go," he said, shoving away from the wall, away from me.

"I saw yours." It was out before I could think about it.

"My what?" He sounded slightly alarmed, and I imagined what he was thinking. That I'd been peeping in the locker room or something.

"Your drawings. The ones in your history book."

"*What?*"

"They're good," I said. "No, amazing. Like Suzuki Harunobu. Or Utagawa Kuniyoshi, maybe. The mermaid, especially, with all the detail. But modern. With all the little pictures. I really, really liked the rocket . . ."

All of a sudden he was looking at me like I was *un cafard*. I shut up, fast, but too late.

"Those are private."

"Right." It started, that quiet rushing sound in my ears. The one that would turn into a roar, the Niagara Falls of humiliation. *Something there is that doesn't love . . . doesn't love . . .* "I didn't—"

"What the hell? You went through my stuff?"

It didn't matter that I hadn't, that the papers had fallen out of the book and that it would have been almost impossible not to see them. I can't handle it when people go angry-flat like that, closing up like oysters or freezer doors. It makes me want to curl up and disappear.

"I'm sorry," I whispered. "I didn't mean—"

"Right. Whatever. I have to go."

I'm sorry, I'm sorry, I'm sorry, I'm . . .

It was the worst moment imaginable. Until it got even worse.

"Hey, Romeo. I've been calling you for, like, five minutes. Did you lose your phone again?"

Amanda Alstead was catwalking down the hall, hips and hair swinging. A half step behind her were, as always, Anna and Hannah. They all glided to a swishy stop next to Alex. I could tell the instant Amanda saw me. Her smile wavered for a nanosecond, then went sharp.

"Oh. You. Did you fall down?" she asked, so sweet.

"I'm sitting."

Someone, either Anna or Hannah, like it mattered, stifled a giggle.

"Sitting. Okaaay." Hannah, angelic in a fuzzy white sweater, looked down her button nose at me. "Things a little . . . challenging for you these days?"

Alex's feet were still so close that I could have bumped his toes with mine. He didn't say anything. When I darted a glance up, I saw that he wasn't even looking at me. He was staring at the wall. He looked bored.

Amanda tossed her hair back, displaying a column of perfect pale skin. "You know, if you need to talk about . . . problems, I've worked on the school crisis line since freshman year."

I could almost see the graphic bubble over her evil goddess head: *Knowledge is power, and I know everything.* I couldn't think of a single person I would be less likely to confide in. With the Hannandas of the world, it was no wonder I talked to Edward.

"It's all completely confidential." Another hair toss, more perfect skin.

If I decide to use what I hear, the bubble read, *believe me, I will, and I'll still come out smelling like a rose.*

"I'm fine," I managed, the two words coming painfully through my tight throat.

"Because mistakes like drugs and alcohol," she went on, as if I hadn't spoken, ". . . whatever . . . can have even more damaging consequences than just loss of memory and motor functions. I mean, you can seriously screw up your whole life with a few bad choices."

Like talking to my boyfriend.

I got it already.

"I'm fine," I repeated.

"Whatever. I'm just trying to help." She exchanged looks with her attendant duo. *What did I expect, trying to be nice to a loser?* "Come on. I hate this hallway. It's like something out of a bad horror movie."

They went, Alex and the Hannandas.

Anna hadn't said a single word. That wasn't surprising. Anna hadn't talked to me in more than two years, since our first day at Willing. That wouldn't be surprising to anyone at the school, either, unless they learned that Annamaria Flavia Lombardi and I had known each other since infancy and had, through our Sacred Heart middle-school years, even been pretty good friends, part of a group of a half-dozen girls who moved as a happy, woolly pack. Even when her dad's building business started mushrooming and her mom arrived one day to pick her up from school in a huge, sparkling Escalade, we stayed friends. We took the Willing entrance tests together, joked about burning our Sacred Heart uniforms in the courtyard trash can.

Then, the July before freshman year, Annamaria disappeared. It turned out she was in Loveladies, at the Jersey Shore, in her new five-bedroom beach-block house, two streets down from the Alsteads' eight-bedroom beachfront house. In September, it was Anna Lombardi who arrived at Willing, tan and skinny, paying the full tuition, and dealing in gossip.

I suspect it was Anna who brought "Freddy" to Willing. Of course, I can't prove it, and I'll never ask, but it's the only explanation that makes sense. In a school where almost everyone has lots of money, gossip is killer currency. Anna shucked South Philly and her past as easily as her Sacred Heart plaid skirt. And burned it all, like bridges, without a single backward glance.

She didn't look back—none of them did—as they walked away, Amanda twining herself around Alex and her flunkies following behind. Why would they look? There was nothing to see.

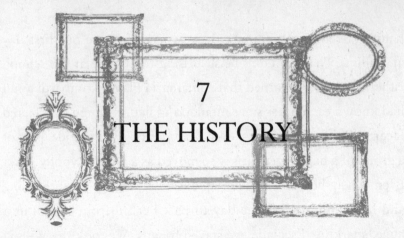

7
THE HISTORY

From *Incomplete: The Life and Art of Edward Willing*, by Ash
Anderson. University of Pennsylvania Press, 1983:

September 7
Hotel Ritz
Paris

Dearest Spring[12],

    What biblical plagues shall I bring upon myself should
I begin a letter cursing my parents? Shall we have
cockroaches in our basement? Hurricanes lifting the tiles
from our roof in August? Water that runs rusty-red
from our pipes? But wait, we have those things already!
You should well know, having picked beetle legs from your
brushes. Aunt Edie, of course, beetles her brow and says
nothing.[13] O Philadelphia, what domestic adversities lie
beneath your stately edifices.

So, to hell with them, my love.

I am entirely serious. Why should you care that my parents think you beneath me?(14) We know better, you and I. We know that you are to me as champagne to beer—superior in every way. Yes, I know your soft heart would like all to be flowers and frolicking kittens, but my nature is such that I will think of the wasps and fleas. How perfect a pair we are, beloved Train,(15) completely unlike in such complementary ways.

So my father loathes your lack of fortune? How fortunate that generations of unhappy intermarriage have given my family more money than can possibly be good for it. There is irony, too, in my mother scorning your lack of domestic skills when she has not so much as arranged a flower in twenty years. There is a housekeeper, a maid, a poor relation or two to do everything for her, including, I would imagine, pore through a Roget's to find adequate words to express her disapproval. There are not words enough in heaven and earth to express my devotion.

Shall I try a few, darling Post?(16) Immeasurable, mythic, dizzying? Boundless, fierce, orange? Passionate? Occasionally quite painful?

I wake every morning, wishing you were beside me. I then pass the better part of the morning wishing you wished you were beside me when I awake. Yes, yes, I know, and I would beg your pardon if I felt any less impatient. December is far too far away.

My love, My Love, is eternally yours.
Edward

(From the private Willing Archive, courtesy of the Sheridan-Brown
Museum of Modern Art, Philadelphia. Reprinted with permission.)

Notes

Chapter 11 (cont.)

(12) In his early letters to Diana, Edward addresses her by a variety
of names, including "Spring," "Penelope," and "Cab." There is no
documented explanation or key, and most suggestions, including
that in which the names were derived from newspaper stories of
the day (Hearst, 1946), have been debunked. In her letters, both
before and during their marriage, Diana most often addresses
Edward as "Darling Clod."

(13) (14) Diana Drummond was descended from a respectable
Scottish family. By the mid-nineteenth century, however, the
family fortunes had been so depleted that her father, James,
a third son, chose to emigrate. He landed in Philadelphia in
1864 and, in partnership with fellow Scot Gordon Gibson,
became a grocer. By 1912, Drummond and Gibson's, under
the management of the founders' sons, was the third largest
grocery business on the East Coast (now, as D&G's, it has over
twelve hundred stores, in eight countries), but in 1887 was
still a small, if successful, local business. Diana Drummond,
then eighteen, took a post as art teacher in the school founded
by Edward's aunt Edith Willing Castor. It is assumed that she

and Edward met that year during one of his visits home to Philadelphia from abroad. By January 1889, their engagement was official, much to the unconcealed distress of his parents. In a letter to her sister, Maude Pugh Willing referred to Diana's father as "that fishmonger."

(15) See (12).

(16) See (12).

⟨⟨⟨✦⟩⟩⟩

From the article "Diamonds on the Muse," in *Jouel Magazine*, Issue 137, September 1999:

. . . In the spring and summer of 1889, Willing was in France. While the majority of the eleven weeks was spent in Aix-en-Provence, studying with Cézanne, he did stay for a period at the Hotel Ritz in Paris. It was during that time that he purchased a twenty-carat diamond-and-platinum bracelet from Cartier.

While Willing records show that Edward purchased many fine pieces for his wife during the course of their marriage, mostly from such purveyors as Tiffany in New York and J. E. Caldwell in Philadelphia, the bracelet was clearly a favorite piece. It figures prominently in six portraits of Diana Willing (including, perhaps most notably, the scandalous Troie) *painted by her husband, as well as numerous photographs.*

On the death of his wife in 1899, Edward gave the bracelet to her niece Julia Drummond Jones, who subsequently moved to California. In 1954, it was acquired in a private sale by baseball legend Joe DiMaggio as a gift for his wife, actress Marilyn Monroe. It appears in many photographs of the couple during their brief

marriage, and occasionally on Marilyn thereafter, and remained in
her possession until her death in 1962. As part of her estate, it was
bequeathed to her friend Lee Strasberg, and is part of the collection
to be sold at auction at Christie's, New York, next month. Bidding
is expected to begin at $70,000.

"Marilyn would be horrified," a close friend of the actress who
wishes to remain unnamed insisted over the phone from her home
in Beverly Hills. "She never intended for her things to be sold,
especially not to benefit Lee's wife! Marilyn specifically asked that
her belongings be distributed among her friends. She promised me
a Cartier ring, from the diamond bee collection . . ."

"Is everything really about money?" I asked Edward later that night
as I tried, yet again, to think of something to write about Paris for
my homework assignment that wouldn't (a) show just how mediocre
my French was and (b) make it glaringly obvious, yet again, that I
was one of oh, maybe, four students at Willing who'd never been.

He gave a short laugh. "I rather think so. And passion,
occasionally. All great acts in history, and all dastardly ones, seem
to have been motivated by one or the other."

"Oh, come on. *All?*"

"You're a student of history, Miss Marino." He jerked his
chin at the untidy pile of papers I'd shoved to the side of my desk
in favor of Paris. "What does it say?"

"I am a student of *art* history," I corrected him. "And this is
my honors project, which, I feel compelled to remind you, is all
about you."

"Your choice," he shot back. "With all that glorious oeuvre that is *le maître* Cézanne . . . *C'est dommage*." He pretends to think I could have made better use of my time and options. But there's nothing modest about Edward. I'm convinced he is tickled black and white that I'm writing about him, even if his expression in the postcard doesn't show it. "Try anyway. Aunt Edie always found history of unnecessarily great importance, especially if there was a Willing involved in it somehow. I'm sure they feed it to you with a trowel at that school."

"Fine. How about 1066. The Battle of Hastings."

"Too easy, Ella. France wanted England, and all the wealth it would bring."

"The Emancipation Proclamation?"

"Noble as Lincoln was, it all came down to the fact that the South couldn't survive without slave labor. The Proclamation only freed the slaves in the South, after all."

I thought for a second. "The moon landing. Gotcha."

"What? You believe there is ever exploration for the sake of anything other than money?"

"We're not exactly raking in the lunar bucks these days," I said dryly.

"Ah, but NASA and the White House had no way of knowing that forty years ago. I expect they had visions of holiday resorts with private suites owned by Aristotle Onassis and Bill Gates."

"Bill Gates was, like, my age then. He was an unknown quantity."

"Your point?" Edward yawned.

"What do you know about 1969, anyway? It was after your time."

"I know everything." He gave me that sleepy-eyed smile of his. "Love or money, I'm afraid."

"Great," I sighed, unable *not* to think about Alex and trips to Europe and the Hannandas with their Prada bags. "The two things that show absolutely no hint of ever coming my way. Shoot me now."

"I can't, darling girl. No arms. Besides, even if I had the ability, I would never do such a thing. It would be dastardly. And . . ."

"And?"

"Ah, Ella. Fond of you as I am, there is no passion in my feelings."

"Love or money," I droned.

"Love or money," Edward agreed.

8
THE MENU

"My sister taught me the best trick. When the salesclerk isn't looking, you make Sharpie marks on the front of all the others so no one else will buy them. I mean, how embarrassing would it be to have someone else show up at the dance wearing the same dress! This way, I know I'll be the only one."

"God, I wouldn't have the guts. What if you got caught!"

The Sharpie-wielding Phillite shrugged. "I would put them all on my dad's card. But then I wouldn't be able to buy the Manolos . . ."

She and her impressed friends headed down the hall. Frankie banged his locker closed with unnecessary force. "Mind-boggling," he muttered. "All that money, and they can't buy a clue."

Around us, there was a nearly tangible hum of excitement. The theme for the Fall Ball had been announced at assembly. Straight from the minds of the intrepid Bees who make up the dance committee, this year on Halloween, we would all officially be in "Davy Jones's Locker."

For the next two weeks, there would be no rest for the weary. Many a Bee Girl and Boy, not to mention a few Stars and even a handful of Phillites, would be working like ants to get the school ready. As far as Sadie, Frankie, and I were concerned, the best part of it all was that, for the week leading up to the dance, there would be no gym class. Apparently, it would take the Decorating Committee that long to turn the gym into an underwater paradise.

"Correct me if I'm wrong," Frankie told us, working on the principle that he is never wrong, "but isn't Davy Jones's Locker the *antithesis* of an underwater paradise: all drowned sailors and sea demons?"

It actually wasn't a bad theme for a Halloween dance. It was infinitely better than last year's "Sleepy Hollow," also chosen by the Johnny Depp fan brigade, which turned out to be a tactical disaster, with too many headless freshmen banging into one another. This brought to mind ghost pirates, skeletons, monkfish. But so far, the chatter was all about smuggling rum into the school (senior Phillite boys) or mermaid costumes (no fewer than thirty girls across the social spectrum). Which meant, of course, that these girls would appear in the minuscule shimmery dresses that seemed to be in every shop window lately—or, more likely, tiny, embellished bikini tops with minuscule shimmery skirts. I wondered what lucky boutique would be most Sharpied, Willing's apparent alternative to toilet, papering trees on Halloween.

"Oh, God," Sadie groaned. "Swimsuits!"

This would be the third year that she would try halfheartedly to keep her mother unaware that there even was a Fall Ball, let alone the theme. But there was no question that Mrs. Winslow would get the info somehow, probably within six hours of the announcement. It didn't matter that she was presently in the Caribbean. She was connected. By morning, she would be on the phone to someone in New York or Paris or Milan, finding the perfect costume for her daughter.

The last one was a historically accurate replica of an eighteenth-century dress, appropriate to rural New York State gentility, no less. It had possessed a wig, corset, and padded butt. Sadie, itchy and unable to breathe, let alone eat or drink or shake her extended booty, had spent the four hours of the dance sitting in a dark corner. I, dressed in a high-necked, tattered, and "blood"-splattered white dress and veil (Bride of the Headless Horseman), sat with her. Frankie'd had a date, a beautiful blond boy he'd met at PrideFest, who came dressed as Cupid, in little more than white boxers. ("What?" Frankie had defended him. "They put cherubs on everything in 1790!")

"She'll find me a tail made of real fish scales," Sadie predicted now, only half kidding, "with its own free-floating pond. Or an authentic Japanese pearl diver outfit from Okinawa. For once, one time, couldn't the theme just be 'Halloween'? I could do witchy. Witchy is easy."

"Witchy is not sufficiently sexy," I said, watching as Amanda held two shell-shaped paper cutouts in front of her breasts, making every guy within twenty feet start panting, and laying her claim early on mermaid-dom. "Be a siren."

Frankie pushed his tweed cap back on his head and actually gave a whistle. "Marino, you are brilliant. That is *exactly* what Sadie should be. A siren."

"What do sirens look like?" she demanded, more than a tad suspicious.

"Mermaids," Frankie and I said together. "No, no. No scowling!" he scolded her. "It's what they *do* that's important. Phone, please." He held out his hand. Sadie gave a furtive glance around the hall. The three faculty members on dismissal duty were all busy stalking Bees for contraband electronics. We, as usual, were invisible. "Oh, please. It's three thirty-three. Phone!" Sadie passed over her iPhone. Seconds later, Frankie waved it in our faces with a flourish. "Voilà. Sirens."

He'd Wiki'd. Some were beautiful women with Amanda Alstead boobs and mermaid tails. Some were beautiful women with feathered wings and no tails at all. Some, apparently, were manatees.

"Great. I'll be a manatee. I can wear my own clothes." Sadie was wearing the gray sweater again. I'm not sure she was entirely kidding about the costume. "At least I'll be able to breathe."

"Shut up." Frankie waved her into silence and read out loud, "'A siren's sole purpose was to enchant. On hearing a siren's song, men would unquestioningly fling themselves into the sea, caring for nothing but the sound of the last notes as they drowned.' You, madam, should be a siren."

"No tail," Sadie said firmly. "No singing."

"What lame sort of siren is that?" Frankie demanded.

She gave him a humorless smile. "Asked and answered, counselor."

Frankie rolled his eyes. "Mind-boggling. *Et tu*, Marino? Shall you also go the low and cowardly route? Or will you, for a second, consider showing off that hot little bod? Work that tail."

"Ick." The idea of baring any part of me was almost comical. I thought of a high-necked, tattered, blood-spattered dress and veil. "Bride of Davy Jones?"

"Why do I bother?"

Frankie was thwarted in his impulse to flounce off by a trio of effortlessly cool senior girls walking by. Like everyone else, they were talking about the dance. "As long as we keep the music out of Adam's hands . . . Hey, maybe we can get Genghis Khan's Marmot to play!"

"Or the Razor Apples. How sick would that be!"

"Edith would roll!"

I knew the middle girl, tall and pretty with metallic gold streaks in her hair, and band buttons all over her Union Jack messenger bag. I didn't recognize any of the band names. She, however, recognized me.

She paused. "Hey, Ella."

"Hi, Cat."

"How's life with Edward?"

"Complicated," I answered. "JMW?"

"Sketchy. Thanks for asking." She grinned and waved as they moved on.

Cat Vernon and I have AP art history together. She's doing her honors project on J. M. W. Turner portraits. "He didn't do nearly enough of them," she told me cheerfully when I once suggested that she might be confusing one painter named Turner with another. Cat's the sort of person who is nice, even to people who say incredibly stupid things to her. She's also the kind of person who wouldn't find it necessary to mention that her boyfriend's family owns several Turner paintings, including two portraits. I knew only because I heard her explaining to Ms. Evers where the images came from.

I don't think she has conversations with Turner. She doesn't seem the type. And she has the English boyfriend.

". . . I'm thinking maybe we should go as the Monkees," she was announcing to her friends. "You know, Davy Jones, Mickey Dolenz . . . 'Oh, what can it mean, to a daydream believer and a homecoming queen . . .'" she sang as they rounded the corner. She can't sing. Which clearly doesn't faze her in the least.

I envy Cat. I want to be Cat. Last year, she and her friends wore silk pajamas to the Sleepy Hollow dance. They looked a little sleepy and totally glamorous, like thirties movie stars.

I wouldn't have admitted it to either of my friends, but I'd sort of enjoyed the two Fall Balls I'd been to. It was a little like watching the Oscars pregame show: Hollywood royalty walking the red carpet in over-the-top gowns and tuxes. Only I was watching a strangely hypnotizing combination of kiddie dress-up and opening night at the Met.

Now the hall was filled with a combo TGIF/party-hearty

cheer. As we made our way toward the front doors, I listened to sound bites of people's weekend plans.

". . . party at Harrison's . . . parents are in Munich . . ."

". . . watch Teigh Bowen on YouTube. Omigod, so cute!"

"The Razor Apples are playing at the Rotunda!"

"I gotta pick up some condoms."

". . . Rag & Bone trunk sale . . ."

Sadie, Frankie, and I would do what we did nearly every weekend: Java Company for coffee and bagels. Maybe Chloe's. Head House Books. Deconstructing Frankie's last date with him, when he had one. Sunday at the art museum if I could drag one or both of them with me. Otherwise, we'd just sklathe in front of one of the Winslows' numerous plasma screens.

"Have you even heard of the Razor Apples?" I asked.

Neither had. "Rag & Bone, however . . ." Frankie sighed. "Ah, what fabulous damage I could do with Rich and Clueless Daddy's platinum card."

I tend not to think about it too much, the music we've never heard of, clothes we can't afford. Frankie likes the odd sarcastic aside, but I know it goes deeper than that. I know his dream castle includes a walk-in closet with floor-to-ceiling sweater shelves. Sadie keeps her mouth shut. She isn't overly concerned with either, but knows better than to say anything. There's little in life quite so obnoxious as hearing "God, I couldn't care less what I put on!" from a girl wearing four-hundred-dollar shoes and a Cartier watch.

"Anyone want to go to South Street?" she asked as we hit

the pavement. "I would kill for a slice at Lorenzo's."

Sadie's mother was in St. Bart's for another ten days. Sadie was staying with her dad, who, between work and an endless string of much younger girlfriends, rarely got home before eleven. His usual method of feeding his daughter during these visits is to leave twenty-dollar bills and take-out menus scattered over the otherwise unused kitchen counter. Her mother, after every trip, goes on a weeklong rant about how each time Sadie stays with her dad, she gains five pounds. This time, Mr. Winslow had persuaded whatever stick insect he was dating at the moment to stock the freezer.

"It was only one pound last time," Sadie grumbled. "And I lost it in three days. I've been subsisting on Lean Cuisine grilled chicken for two weeks now. I need pizza."

I would have gone, but I was broke. And as happy as Sadie always is to pay, I really really hate letting her do it.

Frankie answered before I could. "Can't. It's a family-dinner night. Mom's making *chap chae*, and she will go ballistic if I'm not there."

Frankie's mom is big on family dinners, even if she can only get both her sons in one place once or twice a week. It's not that Frankie and Daniel don't like each other; they do. It's just that their lives are so completely different. Frankie has Willing and me and Sadie and his string of pretty boys. Daniel goes to a public high school, hangs out in parts of the city I've never even been to, and has . . . well, I'm never sure what he has beyond tattoos and some dodgy friends.

Sadie looked hopeful, but we all knew no invitation was forthcoming. Frankie's mom is a seriously private person; they're a private family. I've been to their apartment only once. It's really small, scarily clean, and the room that Frankie and Daniel share smelled like a taxi. "Disgusting, I know," Frankie muttered, wrinkling his nose. I wouldn't have said anything. "Dan smokes; Mom yells. Then she sprays." We left soon after and went to Chloe's.

Family dinners for us happen exactly twice a year: Thanksgiving and Christmas. Every other day, Marino's is open, and most of the family is there, together, serving dinner to other people's families. Our two holiday family get-togethers inevitably involve many assorted Marinos and Palladinettis eating way too much, and at least three good screaming matches, which aren't necessarily angry. With Thanksgiving approaching, I quietly hoped this would finally be the year I wouldn't find myself at the children's table.

Sadie spent last Christmas at an Ayurvedic spa with her mother, who gave her a gym membership and a diamond Om pendant.

"We had lentils for two" was all Sadie needed to say beyond that.

I took pity on her now. "Come with me. I'm sure Dad will make you a pizza."

Not that I was in any great hurry to go home. Wedding plans had gone into overdrive in the past week, along with the drama. I'd taken to waving through the back door of the restaurant before fleeing home to PB&J and silence.

We stayed at school long enough for me to conjugate, excruciatingly slowly, many irregular French verbs and a few regular ones (*Elle a le cafard . . .*), for Sadie to do her math homework, and for Frankie and me to copy most of it. By the time Saddie and I got to my street, the air was cold and pizza was very appealing.

For a change, everything at Marino's seemed remarkably peaceful. As always, the kitchen greeted Sadie with delight. "Serafina!" Dad shouted, his pet name for her that makes her giggle. He was chopping a huge pile of garlic with a careless speed that always makes my fingers tense up. I could see a row of dough balls resting on the counter behind him, one already flattened into a disk.

"You're in luck," I told her. Then, to my father, "Sadie needs pizza. They're starving her at her place."

"Criminal." He scowled and chopped harder. "Gotta feed the young brain. So, what appeals, ladies? Sausage and mushroom? Meatballs? Peppers? The works?"

I'm a garlic-and-spinach girl, myself, with the occasional and unbroadcasted craving for anchovies. Sadie had gone a little moon-eyed at the mention of meatballs, however, so I shrugged. "Whatever you want," I told her.

She wandered over to the toppings station and checked it out as if it were a spread of diamonds at Tiffany. "Meatballs," she said happily. "And onions and olives and extra cheese."

"Done." Within a minute, Dad had a pizza in the oven.

"Hey, was that for my table?" Leo came out of the back,

carrying a dusty bottle of white wine, which he gave a quick swipe with a towel. "They wanted pepperoni."

Dad was beaming. "You got someone to buy the Grizzo. Good boy!" He took the bottle from Leo and gave it a much more thorough cleaning. "This pizza's for the girls. They're starving. Your table won't know the difference between five minutes and ten."

Leo shrugged. It was still early enough that everyone was calm and cheerful, and Sienna wasn't in the kitchen. "Hey, Sadie."

Sadie hurriedly swallowed the little mozzarella ball Dad had slipped her. "Hi, Leo." She coughed and blushed. It's a cute-boy thing.

"Say-dee." Uncle Ricky lunged, waving a loaded and dripping fork in front of her. "My new ravioli. Taste!" She did, and chewed, slowly and thoughtfully.

"Mmm," she said eventually. "It's really a unique combination. Um. Beef and rosemary and . . . blue cheese?" she guessed. Ricky beamed. "And something else . . . I just can't . . ."

"Pumpkin!" he crowed. "In a fig-and-wild-mushroom sauce. It's autumn ravioli. Move over Rocco DiSpirito!"

Sadie loves coming to the restaurant. From her point of view, I can understand why. Everyone is tickled to see her, and no one acts like her putting food in her mouth is anything other than a really really good thing.

She discreetly picked a woody bit of rosemary from her tongue. Dad clucked his. "Pumpkin ravioli," he sighed. "Who's gonna order that here?" Still, it was up on the specials board. It's a deal they have, Dad and Ricky. Weird is okay, as long as it tastes good. If no one orders it, or anyone complains, it's gone for good. Or until *Top Chef* calls. So far, the system has worked. Smoked salmon pizza with cream cheese and capers became a menu staple and neighborhood fave. Manicotti stuffed with clams, asparagus, and roasted pears is never to be seen again. "Watch the rosemary twigs in the mix!" Dad called to Ricky, who scowled and waved him off, then promptly started sifting through the herbs for the next batch.

"Bella Sarah." It was Nonna's turn. She pinched Sadie's cheek, not too hard, then gave her a head-to-toe once-over. She sighed. "Your mama is a beautiful woman," she said sadly, "but she has no idea how to help her beautiful daughter. Real food and none of this silly . . ." She flapped her hands, unable to even find a word for the disaster of a brown canvas jacket Sadie was wearing. It looked like a cross between a straitjacket and an army tent.

"Sì, signora." Sadie has spent enough time with my grandmother to know the quickest and most useful response.

"And you"—Nonna turned her sharp eyes on me—"in those jeans. They look like they belong on Leonardo."

"It's the style, Nonna. They're called 'boyfriend' jeans."

"Boyfriend. *Magari!* We should be so lucky." She pinched my cheek, hard, her way of softening her words. "Too much salt!" she scolded Ricky, and went back to eviscerating chickens at her station.

Sadie and I stayed out of the way for the next five minutes, sneaking mozzarella and watching the action, such as it was. Sienna came in once for an antipasto plate and a glowering lipstick check. She clearly had a bee up her butt, but she wasn't talking, and I wasn't about to shatter the relative quiet by asking. She flounced out; Leo came back in, delighted to report that his table was chugging down the last bottle of the Grizzo, one of Ricky's less-successful wine purchases, with gusto.

"Farewell, horse piss!" he sang. Dad lifted a handful of shrimp shells in salute.

"Hey!" Ricky objected, but it was a halfhearted protest at best.

Dad pulled our pizza out of the oven, crisp and bubbling. Sadie looked ready to swoon. Even my mouth was watering. Waiting only long enough for him to slice and slide it onto a serving plate, we slipped into the office to eat in peace. Mom was hosting an open house in an old school building that had been converted into condos. "They just don't build them like this anymore!" I'd heard her begin her spiel to a potential buyer over the phone. "A classic in stone and steel, updated but not renovated into unrecognizability, for the modern city dweller."

Meaning it was a big, ugly, old fortress that, no matter how much pale wood and copper was put in, would be freezing in winter, stifling in summer, and that even the grimmest of bureaucrats hadn't wanted to keep. The units wouldn't sell for six months, when the ticked-off developer would slash the price and sack the realty company.

We'd made it through half of the pizza when Sadie's phone squeaked, telling her she had a text message. She sighed and deliberately looked away from her bag. A text comes to an ordinary sixteen-year-old—lipsticks fly as she scrambles to get the phone out of her bag. But neither Frankie nor I has unlimited texting on our phones ("It was either live without bells and whistles or get a job," he explained. "No-brainer. No bells."), so when that sound sounds, Sadie knows it's one of her parents.

She set down her half-eaten slice—half sad, half guilty— wiped her hands, and dug out her phone. "Oh, fabulous," she sighed again. "I'm being summoned. Dad's having dinner with Russell Tarrant at Le Bec Fin later and wants me there."

Again—ordinary teen, the city's most famous restaurant, and two-time Oscar-winning actor? Back handsprings. Or at least a giddy rush to try on six different outfits and the latest vibrating mascara. Sadie looked like she'd just discovered the gym showers didn't have curtains.

"Sades, how does your dad know Russell Tarrant?" I asked. Her dad knows lots of name-in-the-news people, but they're usually not international celebrities who've recently been knighted by the Queen.

"Oh, they were roommates at Cambridge the year Dad spent in England." She was eyeing the remains of the pizza with longing. I thought of dinner with a movie star with just a tiny bit of longing.

We both jumped a little as "I can't friggin' *believe* this!" thundered through the closed door. Sienna's voice has been known to cut through solid steel.

I'd been ignoring the slightly raised voices coming from the kitchen. It's not uncommon for a shouting match to break out on any night. It is almost guaranteed on nights when Tina is hosting and Sienna has to wait tables.

Tina was hosting. She's a thirty-five-year-old version of Sienna, only bottle blonde. Same blind-you lipstick, same taste in clothes, same complete disregard for anyone else's opinion on anything.

They hate each other.

"You hate me!" Sienna wailed.

It wasn't Tina's voice that snapped back, but Dad's. "Oh, no. I am not playing that game with you. Do you have any idea what a hundred pounds of filet is gonna cost me? And now you want *lobster*?"

"But it's my *wedding*! Daddy—"

"Don't you Daddy me, princess! I'm already five grand in the hole for the damned hotel, not to mention two for the dress, and every time I turn around, you and your mother have added a new guest, bridesmaid, or crustacean!"

First of all, Dad was yelling. Almost. Second, he was swearing. Even *damn* is fighting talk for him. I set down my pizza and debated the best route for a stealthy escape.

I'd seen the dress. Pretty, in a Disney-princess, twenty-yards-of-tulle, boobs-shaped-into-missiles sort of way. Sienna looked deliriously happy in it. She looked beautiful. The less said about the bridesmaids' dresses, I'd decided, on seeing the purple sateen, the better.

"No lobster!" he yelled.

There was a dramatic howl, followed by the bang of the back door. When I peeked out, it was like a photo. Everything was frozen. Dad was standing over the massive pasta pot, red-faced and scowling, wooden spoon brandished like a sword. Leo and Ricky had retreated to the doorway of the freezer. Nonna had her eyes turned heavenward, and Tina was halfway through the dining room door, smirking a little.

No one looked in the least concerned or embarrassed by the fact that Sienna's outburst could probably have been heard all the way out on the sidewalk. Our dramas all tend to play themselves out in the kitchen, occasionally to the amusement of the customers, most of whom have heard it all before. There's no such thing as privacy when you're a Marino. Not all that much in our little corner of Philadelphia, but none whatsoever in our family. When I got my first period, when I got into Willing, when Dieter dumped me for Feel-Me-Up Girl, that's where the news broke, because that's where everyone was.

Everything was still for an instant, then Dad sighed and lowered the spoon. Tina went back to the dining room, letting the doors swing to with a muffled thump behind her. Ricky went back to his herbs, and life went on.

"Ella, grab a shirt and apron," Dad commanded, "and take your sister's last table. They're still waiting to order, and Leo can't handle any more."

"Dad, no—"

"Ella, please."

It wasn't really a request. When Marino's needs us, we chip in. I just hate when chipping involves waiting tables. I have to write down orders so I won't forget them, am scarily clumsy with hot plates, and, humiliatingly, have to get someone else to bring the wine or beer when customers order it, because I'm not eighteen, and it's illegal for underage me to serve alcohol.

"Can I help?" Sadie asked quietly. She meant it.

"God, no." I handed her her bag and gave her a light shove toward the back door. "Save yourself. Go have escargots with Russell Tarrant."

"No, really—"

"Go. We'll talk tomorrow."

She went. I dragged myself across the office and pulled one of Leo's spare white button-downs from his cubby. He's not a big guy, but it was still large enough that I ended up leaving the buttons undone, then wrapping it around me and tying it in back. Efficient, but problematic. Even if I could button it up all the way, the collar wouldn't hide all of the scar. Worse than that, waiting tables necessitated a ponytail. No arguments. I'd tried before.

"I get it, I get it!" Dad had finally shouted me down. "But the health department doesn't know from vanity!"

I tied my hair, gypsy-style, on my right shoulder, and hoped the customers wouldn't be gawkers. They're usually not. In fact, ten minutes after ordering, I bet most diners couldn't pick their waiter out of a lineup. We're invisible. I'm used to it.

"Table three," Leo said cheerfully as we passed in the kitchen doorway. "Better you than me. They stink of Mercedes leather."

It's hardly unusual for Marino's to get people from Society Hill or Rittenhouse Square. A lot have even become regulars. We've been in 'Best of Philly' twice in the last three years ("Best Eggplant Parm" two years ago, "Best Place to Eat While Channeling Tony Soprano" last year). You'd think Leo's animosity for waiting on rich Philadelphians would have been tempered somewhat by years of good tips. But the fact is that the only ones who tip lavishly are the ones trying to prove how egalitarian and generous they are: "Below South Street, Above South Street," they seem to be saying; "What's the diff?" Plenty diff, actually, and they're inevitably the ones who make you jump through hoops, just to show how valuable their business is: no butter, fresher butter, vegetarian Bolognese, "Oh, you don't have Château du Cochon '63 . . . ?"

Of course, Sout' Philly Made Good is just as bad with the hoops, but loads better with the tips. The last time he came in with his brothers, Anna Lombardi's dad left Sienna $50 on a $120 bill. But he also had Nonna make his linguine fresh, almost right at the table, to make sure she didn't try to give him pasta from the afternoon batch.

The two people I could see clearly as I approached the table didn't look like they came to South Philly very often, certainly not for food. She looked like she didn't eat. She also looked vaguely familiar. Her husband had blindingly white teeth; she had brilliantly white-blonde hair. They had matching wristwatches that I was sure cost more than both our cars. Diner Number Three was obscured by the tall menu. All I could see was a pair of large hands. I set a basket of fresh bread within reach.

"Hi, welcome to Marino's," I said in my best Isn't This Lovely? voice. "Can I get you something to drink?"

Diner Number Three emerged from behind the menu. *"Ella?"*

9
THE APOLOGY

I was wearing no makeup and my brother's shirt.

"Alex. Hi." It only came out slightly squeaky.

The woman's beautiful face broke into a smile, and suddenly, I knew exactly who she was: Karina Romanova, co-anchor of the Channel 4 Evening News. Seen smiling out of thousands of televisions and bus kiosk ads. Wife of Paul Bainbridge: current U.S. representative and senatorial hopeful. Mother of Alex.

"You know each other!" she said brightly, just enough Ukraine in her off-screen voice to make her sound sexy and a little exotic. "And we thought we were just choosing from 'Best of Philly.'"

"I . . . ah . . . I didn't know." Alex's eyes flicked from his own hands to my mostly hidden scar. I did my shoulder dip, so very automatic, wondering whether he could see my skin, and whether his parents could see my discomfort. After all, my last contact with Alex had been . . . strained.

I wondered what adjectives were sliding through his mind while his parents looked at him expectantly. *This is Ella. She's, um . . . well, weird, a social misfit, intrusive at best, and potentially stalker-psychotic.*

But Willing boys are supposed to be ever so polite. And Alex, after all, was the poster child for the school.

"Mom, Dad, this is Ella . . ." He glanced at the menu, and I saw the little figurative lightbulb blink on. "Marino. She goes to Willing, too."

His father, who, I noticed now, had Alex's eyes and jaw, thrust out a big hand. "Paul," he said, waiting patiently for me to shift my order pad and pen so I could shake. "It is a very great pleasure to meet a Marino."

As if he knows anything about us. As if we are important. For a second, I felt important, and understood exactly why he is going to win that Senate seat in two years. "Thank you. Nice to meet you, too."

"Karina." She wanted to shake, too. She had a decent grip, but her bones felt pin thin against mine. "So, how do you like Willing?" *Villink*. It sounded better that way. I am a *Villink* Girl.

"Love it," I answered by habit. "I mean, it's Willing."

"Mmm." I wasn't sure she believed me, but then, I was pretty sure she didn't really care one way or the other.

"Good. Good." Paul beamed at me. "Great school. Just great. Although, around exam times, you'd think we were sending our son to reform school from the way he moans and groans."

I managed the expected chuckle and darted a glance at Alex. He didn't look particularly embarrassed by his dad's practiced joviality. I guess when said dad is jovial on a national scale, you wouldn't be. Alex still hadn't looked directly into my face.

"Do you live near here?" Karina asked.

"Next door."

"Ah, so Willing is a neighborhood school. How convenient."

Well, yes. Except not too many kids from the neighborhood get to take advantage of that convenience. Maybe they didn't know that, the senior Bainbridges. Maybe they genuinely thought that there was space and money and interest enough to bring lots of South Philly kids into the rarefied world of Willing. Either that, or they assumed we were all just one big happy Family (Soprano, Corleone, Scarfo . . .) down here, with lots of ill-gained money floating around. Or maybe they were just shinily polite.

I noticed that neither asked if Alex and I were friends. Most parents would. But not a reporter and a politician. They know every dangerous, loaded question in the book. Beyond that, I can't imagine it being more obvious that, no, Alex and I weren't friends.

I smiled. Politely. "So. Any drinks to get you started?"

Karina asked for sparkling water; Paul wanted a German beer to go with his Italian food. I wondered if I could get Leo to serve it without smirking. I turned to Alex. "A Coke. Please," he added, looking past the tip of my nose.

"I think we should probably order." Karina took a discreet peek at her watch. I readied my pad. "How is the special ravioli?"

"Delicious," I lied automatically. Well, not lied, precisely. Sadie had seemed to like it.

"Mmm. Well. I think I'll have an *insalata mista*. Dressing on the side, please." She did have the grace to look both regretful and slightly apologetic.

I turned to Alex's dad. "*I* will have the special ravioli," he announced, handing over his menu with a flourish, "with the soup of the day."

The soup of the day was curried carrot. Not exactly a Tony Soprano standby.

So here's something everyone should know about diners and Italian family restaurants. Order the obvious. On the rare occasion when Sadie, Frankie, and I forgo Chloe's for the South Street Diner, Sadie inevitably orders something that just shouldn't be on a diner menu. Osso bucco, sole almondine, sweetbreads. She's always disappointed. Me? Grilled cheese and tomato sandwich on wheat, side of fries, every time.

"How do you know what you'll like, if you won't even try?" Sadie scolds.

"Yes, Frances. Have some bread and jam" is Frankie's helpful refrain.

Truth: I have seen sweetbreads in their natural state. Gimme bread and cheese any day.

Diner or Italian joint: Regulars have their faves; smart diners go for classic. People pleasers order the specials.

I turned to Alex.

"Minestrone. Please. And spaghetti carbonara."

Smart boy. Smart boy who still hadn't looked me full in the face. Growing up in South Philly, it's no big deal, giving and taking orders from people you know. There could be any one of the Giordano kids behind the counter at the bakery; Mom's best friend from forever cuts our hair. The Ryans down the street handle all our insurance, and I buy way too much unnecessary stuff to camouflage the tampons when Sam Nguyen is manning the register at his parents' pharmacy.

I know there's a division north of South Street. Your friends are never, ever your servers. But then, Alex wasn't really my friend.

"On its way," I said cheerfully. And went into the back, back to my family.

We keep the walls between us.

I gave the food order to Dad. I'd debated not saying anything, but couldn't. "Persons of interest," I told him.

It's code. Police-speak for suspects; Marino for regulars, suspected restaurant critics, and anyone who might be in a position to help or hurt the restaurant's reputation. Everyone gets good food at Marino's; persons of interest get the best.

It galled me a little, giving Alex's family the designation. But I'm a pragmatist. A good word from Paul and Karina could bring in extra business. And the more extra business we get, the less money I'll have to beg, borrow, or steal for college.

"Who?" Dad asked as he scanned the order.

"Karina Romanova from Channel 4 and Congressman Bainbridge. With their son."

He let out a low whistle. "Well, lah-dee-dah. Good for us." Then, "You forget something here, hon? There's only two entrées."

"She's skinny," I explained, then, before Dad could give a

familiar opinion on women who eat naked salads for dinner, I told Uncle Ricky, "The congressman ordered the ravioli."

"Hot damn!" He grinned, actually rubbed his hands together, and swung into action. Flour flew.

"Heaven help us," Dad muttered under his breath. "Now, you take an antipasto plate out to them, on the house—"

"Dad, no!"

"What? We can't let Whatshernameanova sit there with just a pile of lettuce. Trust me, she'll pick at a pepper, nibble some prosciut, and all will be well in the world."

Not exactly. Karina wouldn't touch the platter, with its meat and cheese and oiled peppers; I knew that. And there it would be, sitting on the table in front of Philadelphia's Most Beautiful Family, like a gift from peasant to king. It's always a pig in fairy tales, hauled in from the grateful subject's backyard and trotted up the hill to become royal prosciutto.

"Dad . . ."

I closed my mouth. I couldn't say it. My dad's no peasant, and he's no brown-noser. He's a decent guy who thinks an empty stomach leads to an empty head. I watched as he deftly arranged the peppers, the anchovies, the mozzarella, creating a pretty mosaic on the plate.

As he added salami, I grabbed a chilled beer and a glass and waved them at Leo, who was on his way back to the dining room. "Can't," he snapped. "Overloaded as is." True enough. He had full plates halfway up both arms, and two more orders coming up. "Christ. Sienna and her f—"

"*Leo!*"

"*Scusi,* Nonna." But he still managed to get a good, quiet curse or two out as he backed his way gingerly through the swinging door.

"Here. I got it." Tina took the beer and glass from me. "Ya know them?"

I nodded.

"She looks like butter wouldn't melt. But her kid . . ." She pursed brilliantly pink lips. "All that and a bag of baked tofu chips?"

I had to smile a little at the image. "No. He's not . . . He doesn't act like . . ." I wasn't entirely sure why I was defending him. He hadn't exactly been the Prince Charming of Dinner Orders. Come to think of it, I couldn't completely vouch for Alex Bainbridge being Prince Charming of Anything. Except my own little *Villink* fantasy. "Maybe."

"Cute, though."

"Yeah."

"Yeah?" I have no idea what is was Tina saw in my face. Something. "Aw, sweetie." She sighed. "Want me to shake up Daddy's beer a little?"

"No," I answered, "but thanks for the offer."

I got a drinks tray and added Karina's Pellegrino. The Coke dispenser spat pale brown liquid at me. Then it hissed. "And typical. Syrup's low. Will you tell them the Coke's on its way?"

"Sure thing." Tina deftly lifted the tray onto her fingertips. She was a cocktail waitress at Delilah's before she got married.

As a matter of fact, she met Ricky there. She won't talk about the job much at all, but she tells anyone who will listen that Ricky looked so uncomfortable when he came in with a bachelor party that she knew he had to be okay. I don't know whether the club had hired her for her agility, or whether she'd learned it there, but she could probably dodge a barrage of bullets while holding two loaded trays over her head. I drop dish towels. Which is why I'm rarely given anything weighty, hot, or valuable to carry.

Ordinarily, Dad would have reloaded the soda machine. I have to stand on a box, and the syrup is heavy. But he was in the walk-in, getting the special For Royalty Only pancetta from whatever crevice he hides it in. As I wrestled with the machine, trying to get the bag-in-a-box syrup locked into place, the door thumped again.

"Um . . . Excuse me?"

I very nearly slopped a gallon of Coke syrup over the floor. I did fall off my box, but at least I landed on my feet. Alex was standing in the doorway, half in and half out of the kitchen. He didn't see me. I crept back up onto my perch.

"Can I help you?" Ricky was closest. He had so much flour on him that his hair was gray.

"I . . . ah, wanted to talk to Ella."

"You go on back out. I'll send—"

Tina, who apparently hadn't gone anywhere just yet, promptly smacked Ricky on the back of the head with her free hand.

"*What?*" He didn't have a clue.

Tina did. She could probably hear my heart thundering from

across the kitchen. "There she is," she told Alex, pointing. Then she looked at me and jerked her chin toward the back door. "Go. I'll take the table." She scooped up the antipasto and bumped her butt through the door, doing a quick, arms-raised, hips-pivoting cha-cha with Leo to avert a collision.

Tina can be a B–, and she's high maintenance in every possible way. She's also prone to asking questions like whether vegetarians can eat animal crackers. She actually once asked Frankie what Asians throw at weddings, since Americans throw rice. He said shredded math tests. I think she believed him. But she's surprisingly smart when it comes to people's complicated love lives (in the last six months, she's correctly predicted two marriages and three divorces among Marino's regulars), and is usually pretty nice to me.

I took the hint. I snapped the valve onto the syrup, pushed the button, and a minute later, had two glasses of Coke in hand. "Come on," I told Alex, crossing the kitchen and pushing the screen door open. "It's cooler out here."

He followed me out onto the stoop. Someone had swept; the little parking lot was free of leaves and the usual soggy take-out menus from the Thai restaurant up the street. There was a Porsche SUV squeezed in next to the Luccheses' Buick. I assumed it belonged to Alex's parents.

I sat all the way over to the right, so he had no choice but to sit to my left. He did. He was wearing the same green Lacoste from the disastrous declamation day. I could see a trail of bread crumbs running down the front. Nonna takes her *pane* seriously.

She bakes it on a stone in the pizza oven and mists it while it's cooking, as if it were some sort of bizarre tropical fern. The result is pretty amazing. The crust shatters like glass, but the center is so soft you almost don't have to chew.

Alex folded himself up and rested his crossed arms on his knees. The stoop isn't very high. With his legs bent, his knees were almost even with his shoulders. He looked like a really beautiful human umbrella.

"You're not going to get in trouble for this, are you?" he asked.

"No." I handed him his Coke and prayed silently that it wouldn't be flat. "I'm good for a few minutes."

I had no idea what else to say. So I drank. A little sweet, but plenty fizzy. Like I thought I should probably be. Peppy. Perky. Civically minded and fond of pastels.

"I really didn't know this was your family's place," he said after a minute. "It was *Philly* mag. The 'rents were looking for authentic Italian. They're big on authenticity."

"'The best place to eat while channeling Tony Soprano'?"

He winced. "You make it sound so . . . cheesy."

"Yeah, well, what can we do? People like . . ." I stopped myself. *People like you think we're all tied to the Mob.* ". . . the idea of old South Philly. The checkered tablecloths and rubber grapes. Men in hats. We have pictures like that from when my grandparents opened the restaurant."

"Ever had a hit here?"

See?

I sighed quietly. "Not in my lifetime." Then, since I was feeling none too eloquent, and "What do you want, Alex?" was a little too Frankie and not at all Ella, I asked, "Shouldn't your mom be in the studio or something?"

"They're sending her down to D.C. to interview the Russian president, so she's not on tonight. If she's home and Dad's home and they don't have an event, we go out to dinner."

"Happen often?"

"Often enough. Once a month or so. They like to play happy families."

Oh, I was dying to ask, *Aren't you a happy family?* I know, of course I know that money isn't enough, but it has to help. I can't remotely imagine how it's possible to be unhappy on trips to Florence.

"Is it just you?" I did ask. "No sibs?"

"Just me. Public figures have to have at least one. It makes them look trustworthy." He took a quick look at my face and laughed. "I'm kidding. Trust me, you can't believe most of what I say."

I had absolutely no idea what to say to that.

Truth: I want people to tell the truth.

Truth: Yes, I am that naive.

"Siblings are . . . complicated," I said. "You met my sister."

"Not really. I *heard* your sister. I mean, I didn't mean to listen, but it was kinda hard not to . . ."

And there it was, suddenly, the elephant in the room. We both went completely quiet. Alex looked at his wrist, like he was checking the time. Only he wasn't wearing a watch. Finally, he sighed.

"Look. I'm . . . uh . . . When you told me you'd looked at my stuff. I didn't . . . I shouldn't have . . ."

What is it about those two words—*I'm sorry*—that makes otherwise articulate guys into babbling idiots? I mean, *I love you,* I get. That's a tough one, putting yourself so completely, nakedly out there. I haven't ever said that to a guy. A guy other than Frankie or my dad, anyway. But *I'm sorry*? I say it twenty times a day. To Nonna, when I just can't face a three-course breakfast at seven in the morning, to the half-dozen people I bump into on my frantic rush up those eight blocks to school. To Sadie, for having to copy her algebra homework for, like, the thousandth time, because I didn't get to mine.

I'm still waiting for Leo to apologize for totaling my bike three years ago. I forgave him eventually. Riding a bike in the middle of the city is a little like playing Russian roulette with a bus. Still, it would have been nice to have gotten an *I'm sorry* instead of a litany of excuses. I figure I'll be waiting forever.

That said, I was ready to let Alex off the hook in, oh, about a second.

"Yeah," I said. Then, "I'm sorry I looked. Or saw, I guess. I didn't go digging through your book. The pages fell out."

"Yeah. I kinda figured that might have been what happened." He scuffed one heel against the cement. "The book fell out of my bag again. . . and, well . . ."

And, well, there he was, forgiven.

"Zippers," I said. "One of mankind's better inventions. Your bag has one; I've seen it."

"You see much, Grasshopper."

I blinked at him.

"C'mon. *Kung Fu?*" He let go of his knees and sliced both hands through the air in a choppy spiral. "Shaolin monk fighting against injustice while searching for his long-lost brother in the Old West?"

I shook my head. "Nope. Sorry."

"Sad. I bet you wouldn't recognize 'Live long and prosper,' either."

"Nope."

"How did I know? My dad got me into seventies TV. It's awfully brilliant. Or brilliantly awful, maybe." He had relaxed and was looking monumentally pleased with seventies television or himself or something.

You're awfully beautiful, Alex Bainbridge.

I managed to keep that one to myself, but . . . "You're really good." That one got away from me. "Your drawing, I mean."

He shrugged. "Not really. Besides, what difference does it make? It's not like I'm going to do anything with it. What's the point . . . ?" He winced. "Jeez, I'm sorry. You're probably heading for MoMA via the Sorbonne and Bennington."

"NYU if I'm really really lucky." I smiled, letting him off the hook. I still couldn't quite wrap my head around the fact that I was bantering with Alex Bainbridge. "After that, not a clue. You?"

"Yale, then Powel Law." No *With luck* or *I hope* or even *If all goes as decreed.*

"Wow. It must be nice to be so certain in your path." I didn't mean to sound snide. I really didn't. "No starving artistry in your future, that's for sure."

Occasional stupid Mafia comments aside, Alex is no dummy. "It must be nice to be so certain in your convictions. No moral low road for you, that's for sure."

I felt myself blushing, felt that Blood Surge of Humiliation beginning. But then I realized how silly the whole thing was. I sighed. "I guess I take art very seriously."

He didn't say anything for a long moment. Then he nodded. "That's okay," he said. "I . . . can't."

There was a soft cough behind us. I turned to see Tina framed in the upper half of the door. "Your food's out," she told Alex.

"Oh. Yeah. Right. I guess I should go in."

"Yeah." I couldn't think of any possible universe where wrapping myself around his knees to keep him in place would be construed as anything other than psychotic.

"Okay." He unfolded himself from the stoop, six feet of splendid, and actually held out his hand.

For a second I thought he wanted to shake. I levered myself halfway up before realizing he was offering to help me up. What a gent. What a spaz. Me, that is. I crouched there, helpless, sat back down a little, then realized how incredibly stupid *that* must look, started up again. By the time I finally took his hand, I was almost upright, and if I hadn't let go almost immediately,

I would have looked even more ridiculous than I felt.

"So, I'll see you Monday, maybe," he announced. "On the floor somewhere."

"Not unlikely," I managed. "I can often be found on floors." Whatever that meant. I winced inwardly. Then compounded the idiocy. "I watched a *Brady Bunch* marathon once when I had strep throat."

He laughed. "Nice try, Grasshopper, but no dice." He held the screen door open for me and followed me into the kitchen. "Thanks," he said to a hovering Tina. He nodded to my father and Ricky, and stepped through the swinging door into the dining room.

I stood in the middle of the floor, not sure what to do.

Tina gave my wrist a squeeze as she walked past. "I gotta go back out. I'll see if they need anything."

"Thanks."

Tina took over for me for a while, and nobody commented. The Bainbridges got their check early. No coffee, no dessert. We watched through the back door as Karina slid her slim legs into the Porsche. "I bet that one's never seen anything like the inside of one of your *nonna*'s cannoli," Dad said a little sadly.

"Betcha cannoli's never seen the inside of that one," Tina said with a snort.

She told me later that Paul Bainbridge had left a thirty-dollar tip on an eighty-dollar meal. She gave me five of it.

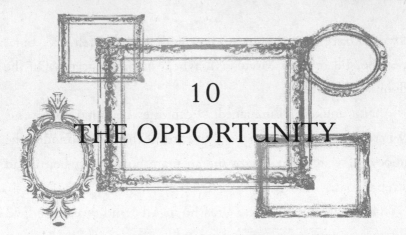

10
THE OPPORTUNITY

I don't mind Mondays, more than is absolutely necessary, anyway. After history, which I occasionally enjoy, and French, which I *très* don't, I have double art. The art studio hasn't been changed in, like, a hundred years. The floors are battered and creaky and covered with so many layers of dried paint that it looks like Jackson Pollock Was Here, minus the cigarette butts.

Apparently, past generations of Willing Art Girls had tossed their cigarettes onto the tiled window well outside rather than onto the floor. "They were more ladylike," Cat Vernon told me once, pointing out the window beside her easel. The butts are gone, but there are burn marks, scattered like leopard spots, over the terra-cotta surface.

Cat was nowhere to be seen. In fact, the art studio was deserted except for me and one Juicy-clad senior whose space was forever filled with colored-pencil drawings of frothy gowns. She was on her way to Paris, I'd heard her tell Ms. Evers, as soon as the ink on her diploma was dry. Apparently, there's a spot waiting for her at Dior.

She ignored me, as always. Ordinarily, I didn't mind, but I was quietly dying to ask her if my lipstick was too pink. She would know.

I had my door sketch in front of me. One little devil was making me crazy. He kept coming out cute, rather than menacing. The corners of his mouth kept turning up in an unmistakably adorable way. I thought about erasing again, but couldn't really be bothered to draw in yet another sneer that wasn't. Truth be told, I was just killing time until the end of the period, when I could go lurk in the entrance hall.

The studio door banged open. Dior Girl didn't even flinch. She was listening to loud Europop through earbuds that looked like pearls. Ms. Evers came striding across the floor, three-inch boot heels clacking on the wood. She looked like Miss North Carolina. She always looks like Miss North Carolina, but this time it was Miss North Carolina after learning that Miss Alaska had a smack habit and would not be making it to Las Vegas this year.

"I," she announced with a thousand-watt smile, "am occasionally startled by my own cleverness." I suspect lots and lots of people are startled by her cleverness. "C'mon, Ella. I'm waiting." She tapped her foot and looked at me expectantly.

"How clever are you?" I asked obediently. I waited for the *bah dum ching*.

I half expected her to tell me that she'd finally arranged with the Powers That Be to turn the dusty trophy room into an art gallery. She's been trying since she arrived at Willing. No one thinks it will ever happen. Dusty past glory trumps condom-wrapper collages every time.

Instead, I heard, "I am so clever that I got you a backstage pass into the Willing Archive."

I got a chill. No one got into the Willing Archive except the occasional septuagenarian scholar from the Louvre or PhD candidate from Yale. The archive belongs to the Sheridan-Brown Museum of Modern Art. It is completely, fiercely unavailable to the general public. I didn't know anyone who'd ever been there. I envisioned a steel-walled vault somewhere thirty feet below the museum, where molelike archivists had to submit to retina or armpit scans to open the doors.

Apparently, Edward's will was a little vague in places. I would assume he hadn't expected to die at fifty-three. However it happened, the contents of his personal library were at the S-B. His books were there, the books he'd bought and held and maybe read as he sat beside Diana in the evening. His papers were there, too. Some letters to Diana. Some from Cézanne in French, and a series from Edith Wharton that were supposed to be so steamy that a never-ending lawsuit kept them under permanent lock and key.

"So?" Ms. Evers was still tapping away.

"But they *never* let students in." Not since three Willing girls and one errant joint had set off the sprinkler system directly above the set of first-edition Trollopes they were perusing. That was thirty years ago. "How—"

"I lied." Only, it was *"Ah lahd,"* accompanied by a smile that hinted that Misses California, Texas, and Rhode Island were going down, too. "I told them you are doing some preliminary recon for a student-run cooperative retrospective between UArts, the Willing School, and, I hinted, the Maude Pugh Willing Foundation. Who, as it happens, are loaded."

It actually almost made sense. Revenue trumps dusty past glory every time.

Still, this was me. "But I don't know anything about any of that!" I admitted miserably.

"So fake it."

I gaped at her.

"Ella, you know Edward Willing better than his mother did. Spout some details about his inspiration and vision, and no one will be the wiser. It's all about money in the museum world anyway." She flapped her hands at me. "Go forth and Google. Memorize a few trustee names. Work on an expression of complete ignorance to be used when questioned on anything involving dollars. For heaven's sake, wing it. Maxine Rothaus is expecting you at the archive Wednesday at four."

"This Wednesday. No—"

"Absolutely. You may begin thanking me profusely now."

"Thank you." I was going to the Willing Archive. "Thank you!" I was going to walk right into the hallowed halls in my battered Chucks and jeans, to sit among first-edition Trollopes—assuming they'd restored them. Walk right up to whatever heavily armed security troll was at the door and demand admittance.

They wouldn't let me over the threshold. "I'm not sure I can. I mean, I'm sixteen. I'm nobody—"

"Ella." Ms. Evers looked at me sternly. "If you don't learn to carpe the diem, you will be, while most certainly not Nobody, something less than a Somebody. Now scoot. I have to talk to Lucinda here about gouache."

I scooted. I had to go find Frankie, who, at least, would tell me what to wear. My wardrobe would render any suggestions moot, but the suggesting would make him happy.

I found him in his usual Monday prelunch spot in the curve of the main stairs. He was in full autumn splendor: camel cardigan, striped polo, gray flannel pants cuffed over vintage loafers. I'd managed to dodge him so far that day. I hadn't wanted to explain the lipstick. Or the mascara. Or the skinny jeans I'd snagged from Sienna's laundry and washed under cover of darkness and paired with a black turtleneck that a jaunt through the dryer had made, to be honest, a size too small. But this news about the Willing Archive trumped all of that.

He gave me a careful once-over. "Well."

I sat down next to him, aiming for casual. I should have aimed my butt. I sat on his geometry book. "Well what?"

"Don't even. The day you become a good liar is the day I leave you for one of the Hannandas."

"I have an appointment at the Willing Archive."

I will say this for Frankie: He pays attention. "The utterly-off-limits, place-to-bury-your-face-in-Edward's-old-knickers archive?"

"Nice. But yes, that one. Ms. Evers got me in."

"About time someone did." He bumped a shoulder against mine. "I really do hate to burst your bubble, Fiorella, but Edward is a century past appreciating the sight of you in tight jeans. So tell me whassup."

I squirmed a little.

"What sort of idiot do you think I am?" He sighed. "You look good, but I am concerned about the inspiration."

"It's not a big deal. It's some makeup."

"When I want a boy to look at me, it's a day that ends in *y*. You, it's something else. It's a big deal."

He dug in his bag for a real handkerchief. Usually, he finds them at his vintage stores, yellowing at the creases in their unopened boxes. Sadie and I bought him a brand-new set at Brooks Brothers for his birthday last year. They were fifteen dollars each. I bought two; Sadie the other ten. Frankie had had to use one (reverently) to wipe his eyes. This specimen was old and soft, monogrammed with a *J* in the corner. "Makes it interesting," he told me once, after finding a box monogrammed with *M* for fifty cents at a sidewalk sale. "Was it Max or Michael? Maybe Marco . . ."

"Here," he said now. "You have lipstick halfway down to your chin."

Humiliated, I scrubbed at my face.

Frankie held out his hand, palm up. "Okay, let's have it." I pulled the tube out of my pocket. "Not really my thing, madam, but since I've seen what happens when you don't use a mirror . . ." I'm sure it helped that he was holding my face, but he read it like a pro. "You had a mirror."

"I did. I'm hopeless."

"Maybe. Open." He squinted as he filled in my upper lip. "I don't like this."

"The color? I knew it was too pink—"

"Quiet. You'll smear it. The color is fine. Better for Sienna, I'm sure . . ." He surveyed his handiwork. "I don't like that you're doing this for *him*."

"Don't start. I told you how nice he was."

"In excruciating detail."

Given, the post-Bainbridge family dinner e-mail to Frankie and Sadie had been long. But *excruciating* stung, especially from the boy who'd used every possible synonym for *hot* in describing his Friday-night bookstore acquisition. No name, just detailed hotness and the play-by-play of their flirtation over the fantasy section.

I reminded myself that Frankie had suffered some serious indignities at the hands of the Phillite boys. And I got that it kinda didn't matter that Alex hadn't been one of the frontmen. He'd been there. And he hadn't made it stop.

"He came to find me," I offered, a small indication, maybe, that this was a Phillite boy who'd grown into doing the right thing.

"I'll give him that. He could have just sucked down his spaghetti and gone." Frankie stuck the cap back on the lipstick. "You look very pretty in . . ." He flipped the tube over and read. "You've gotta be kidding. *Poysonberry?* Who comes up with this stuff? Anyway. I'm sure Alex Bainbridge will agree."

"Thank you."

"Anytime. Just keep this in mind, if you would, please. *I* know that you look very pretty every day, with or without the ridiculously named wax products."

"Saint Francis," I teased, feeling just delightfully poysonous enough in the glow of his approval. "Too good for this world."

"That's just what Connor said." Frankie's most recent boy. They met in a bookstore.

"Bookstore Connor of the fantasy realm?"

Behind us, the gong went. Frankie started to scoop his stuff together. "Careful. His fantasies do not involve one-dimensional Phillites or dead men."

I tapped him on the tip of his perfect nose. He hates that. "How do you know? He might have a thing for dead, one-dimensional Phillites."

"Speaking of . . ."

The first of the junior-senior lunchers flowed into the hall. Mostly Stars at first; they had food to scarf, meetings to attend. Without realizing I was doing it, I leaned forward, waiting.

I saw Chase Vere first. Partly because he was wearing a vibrantly orange sweatshirt with the Princeton insignia splashed across the front. No secret where his aspirations lie. Partly, too, because, regardless of what Chase was looking for, his eyes found me. Force of habit had me looking away, but not before I saw him wink. By the time I glanced back, he was jostling another lacrosse player and not looking at me at all. Not that it mattered in any case. Alex was a couple of feet behind him, heading straight in my direction.

I got up. It would be too easy to get completely lost in the flow, especially for someone like me. I knew when he saw me; I could see the moment of recognition on his face. I smiled, raised my hand, started to wave.

Another member of their insular little team shoved him from behind. Alex turned and said something that made all of them laugh. They reminded me of the noisy, surging amoeba tag games the inept gym teachers made us play in sixth grade—where everyone caught had to join hands and move as a unit, hungrily swallowing the slow of foot (or eager to join the crush) as it went. I was chronically among the slow, but entire games would go by when I could stay on the edges of the gym and not be consumed. There were always classmates who were just as terrified of coming into close contact with my puckered skin as I was of being swallowed, and they would steer the teeming, laughing mass in other directions.

I got a pretty good view of Alex's profile as he walked by, surrounded by his friends. I was close enough to see that he'd shaved recently and maybe hurriedly. There was a nick at the corner of his jaw, healing, but fresh enough to look a little sore.

I might have stood there for a long time, hand halfway up like a religious statue, if Frankie hadn't gently pulled it down and held on.

He stood behind me, vibrating with anger. "That is *not* an honorable man, Fiorella."

Without thinking, I lifted my free hand toward my neck. But I was wearing a turtleneck and my hair was down. There was nothing to see, and all my fingertips found was the rigid peak under my jaw.

"Don't do that," Frankie hissed. "Don't you dare. It's not the scar and it's abso-freakin-lutely not you."

I dropped my hand. "Yeah, right." I sagged against him a little. For being skinny as he is, Frankie's really solid. "It's never me."

I felt his sigh against my shoulder blades. "'*We are young; heartache to heartache we stand.*'"

"Let me guess," I said. "Old Korean proverb."

"As if. Pat Benatar. 'Love Is a Battlefield.'"

I laughed. I had a feeling I might cry later, but not there and then. "Thanks."

"Don't mention it." Frankie wrapped his free arm around me so my chin rested on his forearm. "Enough, right? That was enough of Alex Bainbridge—for all of us. Promise?"

"Yeah. Promise."

11
THE ARCHIVE

There was no retina scan or security troll. Just a small, round woman behind a desk at the museum's back entrance who tiredly checked my name off a handwritten list and waved me down a long hall. "Elevator to the third floor, Room 312."

So no trip to the bowels of the building, either.

Frankie had planned my imaginary ensemble for me with care. Sadly, I didn't have an asymmetrical knit dress or distressed boots. So instead, I was wearing a skirt. Gray wool, boring and itchy, even through the tights I'd dug out from among the wear-only-when-everything-else-is-dirty underwear in the back of my drawer. My plain heels clacked loudly on the pale wood of the third floor, making me cringe as I walked. I passed a series of doors, indistinguishable except for their gold-painted numbers: 302, 308. 312. *The Willing Archive*. I took a deep breath and knocked.

I waited, heart pounding. And waited.

I knocked again.

Across the hall, a door flew open. "Oh, for heaven's sake! *I* am here." She was definitely there, a six-foot Amazon in a black wool dress with a dramatically uneven hem. "Are you the Willing scout?" In the second it took me to try to decide exactly how to answer that, she expended her patience. "God, students and their brilliant ideas. I hate budgets."

She disappeared into the office. I stood right where I was, probably looking as completely clueless as I felt.

"Okay, then." She was back, stalking toward me on endless legs and tall boots. Up close, I could see she was probably my mom's age, only she didn't henna out the gray in her hair, and she had lines around her mouth and between her eyebrows that looked deep enough to stand a toothpick in. She looked like she might have been beautiful once, before she got angry. "I'm Dr. Rothaus. This, unfortunately, is my domain."

She twisted a key in the lock of Room 312 and opened the door with a flourish.

It looked like a storage room at Willing. Light filtered through a single small, high window. On one wall, a floor-to-ceiling bookshelf sagged a little under the weight of hundreds of books. A pair of old-fashioned file-and-document storage drawers sat in the middle of the floor. In one corner, a leather sofa vied for space with an overstuffed ottoman and a black lacquered table.

It got stranger. What looked very much like a fireplace poker leaned against a mahogany desk with a broken corner. A heavy-looking bronze clock took up a quarter of the surface. It was made up of a trio of fat, smug-looking nymphs and was ticking away with a slightly annoying *click-hiss-click*. I wondered if Dr. Rothaus came in every day to wind it up. I wondered if she touched anything else. Everything was covered in a fine film of dust.

"I . . . I . . ." I was pretty speechless.

"Expected something else, mayhaps?" Dr. Rothaus said scornfully. Then, "God, *students*. This isn't Rembrandt here."

I took in the black fireplace screen and andirons, the fat footstool with carved cat feet, the dusty rug beneath. It was a little *Addams Family*, actually. I wasn't sure exactly what I had expected. Light, maybe. At least more of it. Tidy shelves and cardboard file boxes. Books arranged in colorful rows. Framed pictures lining the walls: antique explorer's maps from Italy, Cézanne watercolors Edward had brought back from France, his own paintings of Diana. The only thing on the wall, besides the shelves, was a big red fire extinguisher.

Dr. Rothaus must have read the direction of my gaze—or thoughts. Wouldn't have surprised me. "The bequest was for the contents of Edward Willing's library," she said tersely, "and did not include the paintings. Those went . . . elsewhere." Her already disapproving expression became even more pinched with the word. Like *elsewhere* was Hell, or Overseas, or MoMA.

"I can't even begin to imagine what you thought you might find here. But that's your problem, not mine. You have access to those drawers." She pointed to one set. "Do not remove anything that is in a protective cover from the protective cover. I suppose you may look at the books, but be sure to put them back where you find them. It's now four ten. I leave at six thirty. You will have finished by six. Where are your gloves?"

Head spinning a little, I looked down at my hands. They seemed smaller than usual, and even in the dim light I could see that I hadn't managed to scrub all the charcoal from the side of my index finger. "It's not cold out—"

"*Archival* gloves. For handling the objects. Don't tell me . . ." She blew out an exasperated breath. "I'll find you some. It's your responsibility to replace them."

"Right," I managed. "Thank you." I wandered into the room and started to put my bag down on the desk. A quiet hiss from Dr. Rothaus had me hurriedly stowing it on the floor.

"*You* may sit there." She gestured to a much smaller desk with an attached chair, one that looked like it belonged to some Dickensian charitable school.

"Was that Edward's?" I asked, trying to imagine him there. Even in posed, formal photographs, he always looked relaxed, loose.

"That is from a fire sale at St. Ignatius. I bought it. People need to sit somewhere in here."

Not on the sofa, clearly, or the large leather desk chair. There was something a little malevolent about the old school desk. I figured I would be working on the floor.

"I will be back with your gloves. Don't touch anything until you have them on."

I gazed around, a little hopelessly. Where to start? The files? The topmost row of books . . . ?

Dr. Rothaus was back way too quickly. I thought of witches. She thrust a pair of white cotton gloves at me, then demanded, "Just what is it you're looking for?"

Everything I'd crammed about artist retrospectives zipped through my mind: *enduring themes, aesthetic revival, licensing revenue.* I'd written a line; Frankie had honed it. I was going to say, if asked that question, "I'm looking for the crux, the quintessence of American Post-Impressionist art as seen through the eyes of one of its preeminent painters."

Instead, I said, "I'm looking for the true Edward Willing."

She stood for a minute, arms crossed, scowling at me. Then she shrugged. "Fine."

She wedged the door open as she left. I noticed that she left her office door open, too. So she could keep an eye on me, no doubt, in case I decided to grab the andirons and make a run for it.

I stood for a minute, taking it all in. Not what I'd expected at all. And Edward hadn't been any help: "Heavens, how should I know what's there? Whatever was left after my collective vulture of a family descended, I assume . . ."

The first thing I did was to sit down on the sofa. The old leather creaked loudly enough to make me flinch. But it was worth risking the return of Dr. Rothaus to sit where Edward had sat. Only, it didn't feel very significant. Just cold and little slippery.

I ran my fingers over the nail-studded arm. There is a famous painting of Diana stretched out on a sofa, but that one was blue damask silk. I could think of one other sofa painting, *Mrs. John Girard Hamilton*, a pretty but not-particularly-happy-looking young society wife in a pink velvet dress. Edward liked the outdoors. Even his portraits were usually set outside. The truth was that I just couldn't picture him in this room.

I slipped on the archival gloves. They were soft and smelled like newspaper. Then I got up and headed for the file cabinets. They seemed the most likely place to find something I could use in my paper. They seemed the only likely place I was going to find anything useful. Kneeling in front of the bigger of the cabinets, I slid the top drawer out slowly. Inside I could see files, separated by thin wooden dividers, labeled by year. I ran my finger over the top: 1885, 1886, 1887.

The last file in the drawer was 1890. It was the year Edward painted *Across the Delaware* (acquired in 1961 by Jacqueline Kennedy and now hanging in the White House foyer), the year he married Diana (April), and the year he nearly made her a widow on their extended honeymoon (May) when he overestimated the water temperature at the cliffs in Brontallo, Switzerland, and had to be pulled, nearly unconscious and hypothermic, from the water by a pair of passing Norwegian tourists in a rowboat.

I slipped a page from among the collection. It was written on yellowed onionskin paper, a series of faded lines. Heart thumping, I brought it close to my face and began to read.

Dear Mr. Willing,

Thank you for you letter of 3 December. I am very pleased to inform you that we have managed to locate seven of the ten items you requested. Available as follows:

6 bottles 1877 Mouton Rothschild

12 bottles 1893 Margaux

7 bottles 1895 Yquem . . .

It went on. It was a lot of wine. Which meant pretty much nothing to me. I put it at the front of the file and chose another paper.

Dear Mr. Willing, Enclosed please find an invoice for the month of November . . .

Twelve yards of Indian muslin . . .

Dear Mr. Willing, I write most humbly to describe to you the charitable efforts we envision for the following year . . .

. . . I am at your disposal, sir, any day this month. And while I am thinking on the matter, I would certainly not say no should you generously offer to sponsor me membership to your club . . .

From what I could see, most of the file was shopping lists, tradesman's bills, notes from charities and schools and local arrivistes, all wanting something from Edward—usually money or time. None were particularly interesting, although I got a kick out of a note from the Philadelphia Zoo suggesting that since the tiger was not entirely reliable around humans, perhaps Mr. Willing would consider a leopard for his painting instead. It had been a pet until the demise (natural) of its owner and would, if not firmly admonished, climb into a person's lap, purring, and drool copiously.

I pulled a sheet of scrap paper (the Stars spent a lot of time sending all-school e-mails about recycling) out of my bag and made a note on the blank side: "Leopard in *The Lady in DeNile?*" It wasn't my favorite, *Cleopatra Awaiting the Return of Anthony.* It was a little OTT, loaded with gold and snake imagery and, of course, the leopard. Diana hadn't liked the painting, either, apparently; she was the one who'd given it the *Lady in DeNile* nickname. I wondered if the leopard had drooled on her.

None of the papers were personal, but they were Edward's and some were special, if you knew about his life. There was a bill from the Hotel Ritz in Paris in April 1890, and one from Cartier two months later for a pair of Tahitian pearl drop earrings. Diana was wearing them in my favorite photograph of the two of them: happy and visibly tanned, even in black and white, holding lobsters on a beach in Maine. "I insisted we let them go," Diana wrote in a letter to her niece. "Edward had a snit. He wanted a lobster dinner, but I could not countenance eating a fellow model."

I added "lobsters, earrings, *Beach at Trouville,* 1898?" to my sheet.

There was a receipt for silk stockings from London (June) and another for "cycling trousers" in New York (July). I vowed to tell Frankie that Edward had paid seventy-five dollars for three custom linen suits and six dollars for a pair of straw boater hats. It was just the sort of thing he would appreciate.

One sheet with a sketch on it made me catch my breath before I realized it wasn't Edward's work. It was a tailor's design, a picture of a big coat that looked like an upright bear. I hoped Edward hadn't bought one. I put the paper at the back of the file.

I was disappointed, but not terribly surprised, to find more of the same in my quick scan of the drawer below. Another time, I might read carefully, but even if I did, I had a feeling I would be more charmed than informed. I looked at the ugly clock. It was a quarter to six.

"Okay, Edward, where are you?" I asked quietly. I didn't particularly want Dr. Rothaus to hear me chatting with empty air. I'd always made a point of talking to Edward only when I could look him in the face. Otherwise, it seemed a little too nutso, even to me.

I got up and headed for the bookshelf. "You wanna know something," was Dad's refrain while we were growing up, "get a book." Of course, he predates Google, but it stuck with me.

I pulled down a blue, leather-bound book the size of a tombstone. Remembering Dr. Rothaus's command, I noted its exact location. Not that I was likely to forget where it went anyway, but there didn't seem to be much of an order to things. I was holding *Geography of Southeastern Pennsylvania: A Government Survey*, which had been stacked on top of *Teutonic Mythology*, on top of *Experimental Researches Concerning the Philosophy of Permanent Colours*.

I opened *Geography*. It was full of big maps of small sections of the state. I put it back and scanned the nearby shelves. "We will be discussing your taste in reading materials later, Mr. Willing," I muttered.

It was a pretty dull collection. *The A.B.C. Guide to the Making of Autotype Prints in Permanent Pigments. Art Work of*

Utah. Mosses and Liverworts: An Introduction to Their Study, with Hints as to Their Collection and Preservation. I couldn't even work up a tingle in holding *An Account of the Manners and Customs of Italy; with Observations on the Mistakes of Some Travellers, with Regard to That Country.* I figured people had been making goombah jokes even in 1768.

Edward had held these books, I reminded myself. He'd opened them, learned from them. Maybe fallen asleep while reading them. I took down *The Hand: Its Mechanism and Vital Endowments,* cupping it between mine, but it was cold and had sharp corners.

Then I found a little pocket of poetry and fiction. *Jane Eyre. Treasure Island. The House of Mirth* by Edith Wharton. I haven't read that one, but I've read *Summer,* about sex and longing and growing up. It was published in 1917, the year after Edward died. In the one letter from Edith to him that has made it into print, she talks about it. At least she's probably talking about that book. I tried to remember the letter. *"I am consumed by this fierce compulsion to tell a true fiction,"* she'd written. Or was it *"an honest fiction"*?

I flipped carefully through *The House of Mirth.* There weren't any letters tucked inside, but on page 89, I found a note in the margin. *"How true,"* it read. I couldn't be sure, but I thought it probably referred to the line *"The real alchemy consists in being able to turn gold back again into something else."*

My search changed. Now I gently fanned hundreds of pages and I found notes. Most were single words: *"Check," "Rubbish,"*

"Hah!," but sometimes there was more. I discovered *"Read to Diana, pref. in bed"* inked next to an Ezra Pound poem called "Fish and Shadow." There was a mention of a woman and bed, but the important part apparently was in French: *"Qu'ieu sui avinen, Ieu lo sai."* I didn't understand a word of the French. Or the poem, for that matter. The notation was pretty obvious.

I could feel myself blushing a little as I put the book back, but not before I'd copied the line on my note sheet. Then I went back and stood in the middle of the room. There was something there for me. There had to be.

"Let me guess—" I spun to find Dr. Rothaus standing in the doorway. "You're having a large disappointment," she drawled, "with a side of rare pissed-offedness."

I thought about lying outright. But as it was medium disappointment with a side of self-pity, I just shrugged. "It's not what I expected, but that doesn't mean I'm not finding interesting things."

She leaned one sharp shoulder against the doorframe. "How well do you think you know Willing?"

I figured *"I chat with him in my bedroom on a regular basis"* wasn't the right answer. "Fairly well. He's my favorite artist."

"Mmm. Cute, wasn't he?"

"Gorgeous!" I took the line, hook and sinker.

Dr. Rothaus rolled her eyes. "God, devotees." She sighed. "Let me give you some advice for your future, Willing Girl. If you idolize someone, stay away from where they live. You're never going to see what you want to see. Whatever good they produce is usually somewhere else, and there's always a poo stain on the toilet. Now go home. It's closing time."

I scooped up my bag. She stepped back to let me out of the room. I got a few feet down the hall, then stopped. "Thank you," I said.

"For what?" she asked sharply. "The advice?"

"For letting me in," I told her. "Being here was . . . an honor."

She snorted, and pulled the door shut with a snap.

⁂

"She had a point, you know," Edward commented a few hours later. "Unnecessarily crude, perhaps, but apt. Our public personas frequently do not match our private ones. You, of all people, should know that."

"This isn't about me," I said grumpily. "This is about needing to find more information about the private you. Something I don't already know."

"I have terribly ugly feet."

"Not what I had in mind. And probably untrue anyway."

Edward glanced down at the empty space below his rib cage. "Probably. So, what did you have in mind?"

"A letter, maybe. From Diana. Something that connected your love to your work."

"I rather thought I did that through my paintings."

"You did. I mean, that's what attracted me to you in the first place. Well, no, that was your smile, probably, but the paintings helped. It's just that I need to know more about your muse."

"Ah, darling Ella, the artist's muse is Ego. Nothing more."

"You don't mean that. You married Diana because she made

123

you feel like no one else in the universe ever did or could."

He nodded. "She was extraordinary."

"But not everyone saw that. Your family went nuts. Half of your friends stopped inviting you over, at least for a while."

"Their loss. She was a woman who comes along once in a lifetime."

"And . . ." I was on a roll. "Your sales increased dramatically after your marriage."

"Ah, now that wouldn't stand up in a thesis, and you know it. My sales increased after my 1902 show at the academy, and more after I died. It wasn't the love story, perhaps, so much as the end of it."

Of course I suspected as much, but hated saying it out loud.

He didn't. "You've read my letters, Bella Ella. According to you, the museum shop is now selling the sixth edition of the appallingly illustrated version my niece put together. It's a simple truth: people like you better if you've suffered a little. Vincent van Gogh wouldn't have half so many calendars and coffee mugs had he been quieter about his demons."

I'm inclined to agree, although I think van Gogh was a pretty amazing painter. I never mention that to Edward, especially since van Gogh's *Portrait of Doctor Gachet* sold for eighty-two million dollars, and the Sheridan-Brown got Edward's *Portrait of Doctor Tapper* for forty-two thousand.

"You'd think that philosophy might have put the kibosh on some of the Freddy Krueger stuff," I mused, tilting my jaw until I felt the pull of the scar.

"And well it might, if you ever let on that it hurt."

I'm inclined to agree with that, too, but there's a limit. "So I should start going strapless."

"Don't be snotty. You don't have to show your pain literally. You insist you are an artist, Ella. Be an artist. Use your joys— and your traumas. Tell me, how much did Vincent's *Self-Portrait with Bandaged Ear* sell for?" When I kept my mouth shut, he shrugged. "Fine. I am simply suggesting that you could be just a tad less self-protective. Show some scar."

"You sound like Frankie."

"Of course I do. So . . . ?"

"A hypertrophic, hyperpigmented scar is just ugly. An irrevocably broken heart is beautiful and poetic."

"The breaking is not nice," Edward said, a little sharply. "I don't recommend it."

"Yeah. Sorry."

He grunted. "What is it you *want,* Ella?"

"What you had," I answered softly, "with Diana. That once-in-a-lifetime connection that makes everything good."

"Fine. But you do realize that in order to be loved like that, you have to let the lucky gentleman see you. I mean truly *see* you, scars and all."

"Yes, Edward, I am fully aware of that."

"But you don't want anyone to really look at you."

He had me there. "Well, no."

"Good luck with that, then," he said, then yawned and closed his eyes, telling me the conversation was over.

12
THE REVIEW

From *The Collected Correspondence of Edward Willing*, edited, enhanced, and with illustrations by Lucretia Willing Adamson. Henry Altemus Company, Philadelphia, 1923:

Absence Makes the Heart Grow Fonder

October 23
The Plaza Hotel

My Darling,

Well, it is settled. The Metropolitan Museum shall buy Cleopatra. You may send your profuse thanks to Mr. F. W. Rhinelander for his invaluable assistance in removing it from your sphere to his.

I lunched with him today and was introduced to his granddaughter, Edith Wharton, who is visiting. She is not especially pretty, but is quite clever and excessively well read. She prefers the design of gardens, I believe, to that of art, and dabbles in both poetry and prose. She is not entirely well; she and her husband will be returning to Europe soon, she hopes, so she may take some cures in France. She recommended several spas there from which you might benefit.

Shall we go to Paris next spring? You will certainly be well by then. I agree that Dr. Tapper is far more intelligent and sensible than many of his profession. If he tells you that you are not to be slogging through the Wissahickon in this weather, you must desist with your daily slog. Your lungs are fragile, my love. I would not have you expiring for a sight of interesting lichen. Love is one of two things worth dying for. I have yet to decide on the second. It is most certainly not colorful fungus.

I shall be home as soon as this business is settled, certainly no more than a week. My mother complains that you will not have her to dinner. Good for you. Take pity on Hamilton's new wife and have her to tea. Fire the cook, please. I cannot face another dish of sweetbreads.

With all my love always,
Edward

꧁꧂

From *Incomplete: The Life and Art of Edward Willing*, by Ash Anderson. University of Pennsylvania Press, 1983:

The academy exhibition of April 1902 marked a notable departure from Willing's past style. Rather than the small brushstrokes and sunlit colors so characteristic of his earlier works, this collection was bolder and darker. Missing, too, were his familiar depictions of single persons. A local critic wrote:

While one might expect either the complete absence or overwhelming presence of the late Mrs. Willing in this collection, one would, perhaps, be justified in feeling startled by the complete lack of any people whatsoever. It is as if Willing has excised all human contact from his sphere, finding his muse instead in the flat gray of the Schuylkill River or the lumpen boulders of the Wissahickon Valley. While there is no question that Willing's work has been, through the years, alternately tolerable and uninspired, his pitiable loss of just over two years ago might inspire a bit of sympathetic latitude. However, for my part, I left the exhibition feeling very low-spirited and slightly damp. (9)

For the next three years, Willing traveled extensively (see Chapter 20), and completed the eight uniquely abstract landscapes that came to be known as the Elysium series. (10) The only known portrait from that time was one commissioned by a Willing family friend, art collector, and philanthropist John Girard Hamilton, before Diana's death. As it was to be of Hamilton's wife, the sittings were understandably postponed, and the picture was not completed until mid-1905. For the remainder of his life, Willing would paint very few portraits, although he did resume the use of models for figure studies sometime in 1906 . . .

Notes

Chapter 19 (cont.)

(9) Stuyvesant Gumm, *The Philadelphia Inquirer*, April 17, 1902. Gumm was never kind in his reviews of Willing, and in fact once publicly called him a "s**t-shoveler."

(10) A somewhat ironic term, as the titles: *Limbo, Lust, Gluttony, Avarice, Wrath, Heresy, Violence,* and *Fraud* are reminiscent of Dante's Circles of Hell. While there is no direct evidence of its presence there, *Betrayal* is assumed to have been lost in the Jordan Cooper Gallery fire of December 1905.

13
THE MAGIC

"Okay, people. I'm throwing all caution to the wind. Ha. Taking a leap of faith. And assuming you finished reading *Gulliver's Travels*. I thought I'd shake things up a little, upset the status quo, so to speak, and try something new. Let's really splash out here and have you be . . . Reviewers. Like in the *New York Times Book Review*. Lay it on me. Tell me what you think . . . Anyone? . . . Anyone? Yes, great, Alexander. Your review."

"It was somewhat lacking in magic, Mr. Stone."

"*Excuse* me?"

"Well, this class is called the Magical World. So, if I were to compose a review, I think I would have to begin with, 'For a book intended to represent a magical realm, it was somewhat lacking in magic.'"

"Mr. Bainbridge, I would expect such glibness from some of your . . . *peeps*, is it? But you are usually a gentleman of sensibility."

"Thanks, Mr. Stone. But I'm being totally serious. *Gulliver's Travels* is at best an adventure story. Maybe not exactly the wildest and hairiest . . . but, anyway. It's not magical. It's just satire, pretty much aimed at government. It tells us the stupid, ineffective way things truly are. Okay, so some of the folks in charge are actually talking horses, but that's not magic. That's just Washington."

"Quiet, people. Yes, yes, very clever. Your point, Alexander?"

"My point is this. In magical things, it's all about the way things *could* be. Right? If we just look at them a little differently. And about that feeling that the whole world has been, I don't know . . . repainted. Or totally turned upside down."

"I'm still not getting you. So . . ."

"So, maybe, Mr. Stone, and I say this with all due respect, we should be reading *The Lord of the Rings*. Or *American Gods*. Harry Potter. Something where the magic is . . . well, there."

"Ah. Of course. Harry Potter. Believe me, I know how you all feel about anything older than you are, but established and classic does not necessarily imply difficult and without value."

"Believe me, Mr. Stone, I hear you. But wouldn't it stand to reason that if you follow the same logic, new and different doesn't automatically imply inferior and worthless?"

"Rejoice, Mr. Bainbridge. We will be reading *Le Morte d'Arthur* later in the term. And our next subject is Shakespeare's *The Tempest*. Oh, people. Come *on*. It's about beaches and monsters. Great stuff. Just great . . ."

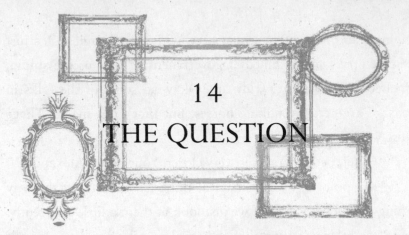

14
THE QUESTION

Chloe's was crowded, even for a Saturday. Sadie and I had to settle for a table near the back. We knew Frankie would complain, but there wasn't much we could do about it.

"Fried cheese," Sadie said, not even bothering with the menu. "Moussaka, tiramisu, and something with lots and lots of olives."

"That bad, huh?"

"Today," she informed me, "I have eaten a cup of miso soup and three sheets of toasted seaweed." Her mother was back. "She weighed me."

"Oh, Sades."

"She actually made me stand on the scale in her bathroom. After she'd been on it."

Mrs. Winslow has one of those scales you see in doctors' offices, with the slidy metal bars. It gets you right to the ounce. And doesn't go back to zero unless you make it.

"Oh, Sadie," I said again.

"Guess."

"No, I wouldn't—"

"Not me, you doof. *Her.*"

I didn't want to do that, either. "Um. One twenty-five . . . ?"
Sadie snorted. "As if."

It's rare to see her upset like this. When Sadie goes all hard-edged and humorless, it's serious. I never know quite what to say to make anything better, let alone everything. That's her domain.

Thank God Frankie arrived just then, paper bag from the repair counter in hand. He dropped into his chair with a sniff. "You couldn't have gotten a table all the way out in the alley?" He hadn't seen Sadie's face. Momentary blissful ignorance. He pulled a pair of vintage wingtips out of the bag and examined one heel closely. "He's good," he announced after a minute. "Schizophrenic, but good, our friend Stavros."

Stavros was, at the moment, somewhere in the recesses of the building, cooking. When at Chloe's, I tend to avoid thinking about the fact that the hands making my souvlaki and *tsatsiki* have spent at least part of the day holding the bottoms of other people's shoes. When neither of us said anything, Frankie looked up. And sighed. "Right." In the smoothest of moves, he stowed the shoes under the table and folded his hands on top. "Who?"

I tilted my head toward Sadie.

"Guess how much my mother weighs," she challenged him.

He didn't miss a beat. "Your mother is a cow. A skinny cow, to be sure, but a cow nonetheless."

That earned him the ghost of a smile. "One-seventeen," Sadie said sadly. "Soaking wet. I could still see her footprints from when she got out of the shower."

Frankie looked to me. "Weight check," I mouthed.

"Ah. Well, shall we send her an anonymous note that Marino here weighs fifteen pounds less than that?"

"Ella is five-one. My mother is five-seven."

She had us there.

"She told me I look like a potato."

"That," Frankie snapped, "might just be unforgivable."

"It's true."

"It's not!" We didn't jinx-dibs each other; it wasn't the moment. Beyond the fact that, in her shapeless canvas jacket, Sadie actually did look a little like a potato, we were both hating her mother pretty fiercely just then. Frankie leaned forward and pancaked her hands between his. "Truth or Dare?"

"Frankie—"

"Truth or Dare?" he repeated, a command we knew Sadie would no way disobey.

"Truth."

"Okay. Who died and made your mother arbiter of anything that has to do with anything?"

"What?" She blinked at him. "What kind of truth is that?"

"An important one." He tugged until they were nearly nose to nose. "Seriously. Much as it pains me to say it, your mother has pretty crap taste in . . ." He let go of Sadie's hands to tick the items off his fingers, right in front of her face. "Gifts, men, clothing, men, music, men, food, and constructive criticism. All the things that matter. Fiorella?"

"You're perfect," I told Sadie, and meant it.

She snorted again. Frankie snorted back. "Fine," he said. "You might never take our word for it. But let's get one thing clear, shall we? Your mother's current stud has badly capped teeth, a weave, and a spray-on tan."

"He does not!"

"He does. Which tells us everything we need to know about her taste and your eyesight. Hence . . . Fiorella?"

"You're perfect," I said.

Sadie shook her head, but she was smiling. "You're nuts."

"Whatever." Frankie flagged down the original Chloe, Stavros's daughter. She favors black lipstick and spikes, hates waiting tables, and is getting her PhD in infectious diseases. I try not to think about that when she is handing me food. "Order for the table, Miss Winslow."

"Moussaka," Sadie said almost immediately. Then, a little sadly, "No. Wait. Chicken kebabs. Falafel. And a Greek salad." She paused, opened and shut her mouth, then added, "Extra feta."

"You go, girl." Chloe signaled her approval with a raised fist, and stomped off toward the kitchen.

Sadie sighed and propped her chin on her hand. Her hair slid forward over her face. Mrs. Winslow's return had precipitated a trip to Alphonse. "So why is it all about food?" she demanded. To me, "Your family is constantly trying to feed you. Mine starves me. Your mother," to Frankie, "gives every family dinner the importance of Thanksgiving. All about food, food, food."

"But it's not," I disagreed, trying not to regret the loss of the moussaka. "Food is just a convenient tool."

"Convenient tool." Frankie was eyeing me with barely veiled amusement. "Do tell."

"Look. The thing about food is that we can't live without it. Right? I mean, barring a life on an IV drip, we have to *eat*."

"I wish I didn't," Sadie sighed. "Every day, I wish I could just say no. Admit I am powerless, abstain, and be thin one day at a time."

I reached over to squeeze her hand. "Oh, Sades. I think you say no way more often than you should anyway. Because your parents tell you to. Because magazines tell you to. Because it's all about love or money."

"Okay, Fiorella. Have you been drinking?" Frankie demanded.

"Love or money," I insisted. "Everything is about love or money. Magazines? All about spending money. Shampoo. Cars. Size-two dresses. And Sadie said it: my family, yours . . . I mean, Marino's isn't really about food; it's about money. Right? And Frankie's mom is all about making her kids stay still so she can love them."

"I'm intrigued." Frankie folded his arms *à la* Tim Gunn. "I can't wait till you explain how Sadie's Joan Crawford of a mother fits into that tidy little equation."

"If food is love, I'm screwed," Sadie agreed.

"Too rich or too thin." I sighed. "Someone famous said that. You can never be too rich or too thin."

"The Duchess of Windsor." Frankie tilted his head thoughtfully. "You might be onto something. The English king gave up the throne to be with her. Skinny bitch. A lot like your mother there, Sadie."

"So you're saying my mother thinks no one will love me if I'm not skinny?"

"Nope." He put his hand over mine over hers. "Not really. She can't imagine how anyone would love *her* if she weren't."

Sadie gave us both affectionate if exasperated glances. "You're insane. Love or money. Nothing's that simple."

Sure it is.

"So, Fiorella the Wise. Home Truth time." This is Frankie's variation on Truth or Dare where he gets to ask and answer. Sadie and I have never been quite as enamored of Home Truths as he is. "Ready?"

"Okay," I said reluctantly. Better to just get it over with.

"So, if it's all love or money, which is Alex Bainbridge?"

I blinked at him. "What?"

"He's a turd, Ella. He looked right through you like you were a ghost, but you still have a thing for him."

"I do n—"

"Don't even. You've gone through the whole week watching for him. So what is it? I would really like to know. Love or money?"

"I have not been watching for him!" I snapped. Oh, but I had, in every hallway, at lunch, when I took my seat at the edge of English class. "And if I have, it's just so I can look away first."

Frankie rolled his eyes. "Shall I get you a pail of water?"

"Why?"

"Your pants are on fire."

I actually looked down at my lap. "Oh, very funny." I shot Sadie a look when she giggled.

"Listen, Liar Liar, you promised. Enough with Alex Bainbridge."

Home truths are not meant to be comfortable, I know. Frankie knows it, too, and for a teeny tiny second, I hated him just a teeny tiny bit for knowing just where to stick the pin.

I glared at him. "How did this go from being about Sadie to an assault on my honesty? Huh?"

He shrugged. "I love you, Fiorella. We ain't got no money, honey, but we got love."

I've never been able to hate Frankie for more than a second at a time.

"Christ. Who died?"

We all jumped a little. Daniel Hobbes was there beside the table, looming over us, and no one had seen him arrive. Sadie promptly went wide-eyed and still. Frankie grinned. "What are you doing here?"

With that same feline grace that awes me in Frankie, Daniel snagged a chair and slid into it, all without looking like he'd moved a muscle. "Ax got busted, and without our guitarist, there is no session. I was on my way home and figured you'd be here. Seemed as good a place to eat as any, although the company might leave something to be desired. You are one sorry-ass-looking trio."

"Who asked you?" Frankie shot back. "You can take your uninvited and sorrier-ass face and stuff it elsewhere."

It can be dizzying, this insult-as-affection that Frankie and Daniel fling at each other. In the eight or so times I've been in

Daniel's presence, I've heard him say maybe two nice things to his brother. But it never occurred to me for a second that they weren't a fierce, unbreakable, and completely united unit.

People just assume they are identical twins. "It's the eyes," Frankie says snarkily. Okay, so beyond the fact that he's convinced the non-Asian world thinks one epicanthic fold is just like the next, the differences are more subtle than not. Or would be, if it weren't for ink and accessories. They have the same killer cheekbones and thick, slippery black hair that requires impressive amounts of gel to look Hollywood, the same sculpted mouth. Daniel is taller, but Frankie likes gel, so he adds a good two inches in hair. Frankie looks like he might break your heart a little. Daniel looks like he might rip it from your chest, still beating, and bite it.

"So who do you have to do around here to get a beer?'" The words were still hanging over his head like a cartoon bubble when Chloe appeared. Our food was nowhere to be seen. She actually batted her spider-leg eyelashes at him. "Whatever's local and on tap," he ordered.

I saw her hesitate, take a step back and then forward again. It was a dance I'd seen waitresses do with Daniel before. To card or not to card; was it worth risking his disapproval? Or, in this case, Stavros's liquor license?

I watched the silent battle in awe. Daniel waited patiently, giving Chloe a half smile that was less a friendly expression than a display of his incisors, which are slightly longer than the teeth on either side. It makes him look even more feline than he already does.

"Oh, go ahead. Card him," Frankie said wearily. "He doesn't mind."

"No, no. That's okay. I'll be right back . . ." And she was gone.

Daniel bared more tooth. "Nice, bro."

"What? You're disgustingly proud of that ID."

Daniel laughed. "I am," he agreed. "I totally am."

He shoved up his sleeves, displaying several thin leather bracelets and the red-and-black tip of a dragon tail just above his right elbow. I've never actually seen the head. It's on Daniel's back, Frankie told us once, between his shoulder blades. "So, my children, what is up?"

"We're trying to figure out how to get a soul-sucking, male lower life-form out of Ella's head," Frankie explained.

"Kill him," Daniel said casually. "Unless there's a symbiotic thing going on and Ella would have to die, too. That would be a shame."

Here's the thing about Daniel. He has always scared me a little. I don't bother going through the scar-hiding motions; I'm convinced he can see right through clothing. Not that he leers. He's not a leerer. He has two facial expressions: cold and amused. He also has a second tattoo, on the inside of his left wrist, that looks exactly like how I would expect a gang mark to look. Frankie has never said a word about that tat. Or much about his brother's friends. Who have names like Ax and spend time in police custody.

Here's another thing about Daniel. He completely fascinates Sadie. She was leaning forward, mouth open a little, watching every move he made.

Chloe was back with his beer in a blink. He accepted it with a slow, wider smile that had her looking a little dazed as she wove away between the tables. He took a long swallow and shook his head. "Man. This place."

Onstage, a skinny girl in what looked like a real mink jacket was crooning her way through "Hey There Delilah."

"Nice gate, Ella."

I looked back at Daniel. He waved toward my lap.

"Oh." I draw on my jeans when I don't have paper. My bus had gotten stuck behind a trash truck, right in front of a seriously old churchyard. "Thanks." I wasn't sure how I felt about Daniel staring at my thigh, even if he had recognized the sketch for what it was.

"Here." Suddenly, he had a booted foot on the rung of my chair, legs spread, one pressed against mine. "Draw something."

"Oh, please," Frankie muttered from his other side.

I shook my head. "I don't have a pen."

Sadie promptly disappeared beneath the table. I could hear the clank of Marc Jacobs chain handles and had a feeling in a second she would be asking, "Blue ink or black?"

"Don't you dare, Sadie," Frankie said cheerfully. "Ella does not want to be inscribing my brother's crotch."

True, I didn't. Except I'd had the clearest vision of how a little Italian portal devil would look on the faded denim . . .

"Fair enough," Daniel said, sliding his foot off my chair. But he actually looked disappointed. For a second, anyway. "I assume there's food coming?"

"There is," Frankie answered. "I'm sure it will come a hell of a lot faster if you do your vampire boy thing on Chloe again."

"Tsk, tsk. Jealousy, Miss Thing."

They bared their teeth at each other. It was scarily pretty.

"What did you order?" Daniel asked. Frankie told him. "That is not a Chloe's meal. That is penance." He scanned the room for Chloe. She was already on her way over. "Spanakopita," he called to her. "Fried zucchini. And a loaf of thou." She giggled and headed for the kitchen, ignoring a dozen waving hands and several annoyed "heys."

Frankie rolled his eyes. Daniel laughed and drained half his beer. Across the table, Sadie was hunched into her jacket, looking deflated.

Mink girl finished to polite applause. A pale, wispily goateed regular took her place and launched into "Buffalo Soldier."

Daniel stood up and loomed over Sadie. "Sing?"

"Sorry?"

"Do. You. Want. To. Sing. With. Me?"

For a count of five, nothing happened. Then, a thousand sad wallflowers at a thousand loud dances were redeemed in that moment. Sadie positively lit up. "Yes," she said, sitting up straight. "I do."

"Okay." He started for the stage. "Lose the jacket."

She paused halfway out of her seat. "What?"

"The jacket," he said over his shoulder. "It's freaking ugly."

I watched as Sadie froze.

"C'mon, Sadie. I'm aging here."

Sadie slid the jacket off her shoulders. It caught at her elbows for a second, then she let it drop to the chair. Underneath, she was wearing jeans and a red cashmere sweater. She looked terrified, mortified, and really good.

"Excellent," Daniel said. "Let's go."

Sadie folded herself up a little, but she went. Frankie snagged Daniel's beer and took a sip. He wrinkled his nose and slid the mug back where it had been. None of us are drinkers, really, but Sadie occasionally sneaks a bottle of champagne from her mother's many cases. Frankie never turns down the expensive stuff. He sips it with reverent joy, then inevitably has a Fred Astaire or Frank Sinatra moment. My fave is "The Way You Look Tonight." Sadie likes "Someone to Watch Over Me."

"He got her out of her jacket. In less than ten seconds." Frankie shook his head. "God help her if he tries to get her out of something else."

"Oh, no. He wouldn't . . . You wouldn't let him . . ."

"For the record, I was kidding. But try to give them both just a little credit, if you would, please."

As he and Sadie waited for their turn, a good twenty female gazes latched onto Daniel. I suspected the hungry-looking guys were staring at him, too, no matter how good I thought she looked.

"But it begs the question . . ." Frankie went on, reaching over to tap my wrist, "Truth: What is it about boys who are bad for you? Huh? And I don't mean just you. I mean every otherwise intelligent girl who has lusted after a guy who bites or shreds, or even just never calls when he says he will. It's mind-boggling."

"Right. Saint Francis," I shot back at this, one superior snipe too many, "who has such an excellent record with—"

"Ah! Careful," Frankie warned me, eyes narrowed, giving me the Hand. "You might want to think before you finish that sentence. I might not have found Mr. Right, but I never, ever go for Mr. What-Are-You-Thinking."

"Ow. Hot, hot, hot!" A steaming plate replaced Frankie's tight face in my line of vision. Chloe slapped the fried squash onto the table, following it with the spanakopita. Then she grimly examined her pinkened and empty hands. "Anything else?"

"The chicken kebabs?" Frankie said. "Salad. Falafel."

"Oh. Yeah." Chloe stared at Daniel's empty chair. She sighed. "Right." She gave Frankie an absentminded pat on the shoulder and wandered off.

"Well?" he demanded.

I picked up a wilted paper napkin and waved it in surrender. "I'm hungry."

He gave me a long look, then reached for a piece of zucchini. "Ow. Hot." I know Frankie; I knew it was a temporary reprieve. There was a squawk from the microphone. "If they sing 'Endless Love' or 'No Air,' I'm disowning them both."

They didn't. They sang "I Got You, Babe" and it was amazing. Daniel kept his eyes on Sadie pretty much the whole time, like he was singing just to her. And, unlike Frankie, Daniel can *sing*. For the first few lines, Sadie kept her face down, hidden by her unnaturally sleek and heavy hair. Then her fab Sadie heart kicked in, and she faced him, chin up, and matched him note for note.

The applause was thunderous. And it was a good few minutes before anyone else dared to take the stage.

The clapping followed them back to our table in the boonies. Instead of walking in front of her this time, Daniel let Sadie go first. One of his arms circled but didn't quite touch her back, like he was protecting her from her greedy fans. He still managed to look cool and a little amused, his usual. By the time Sadie reached the table, she'd folded back up a little. But she was smiling, and she left her jacket off and she hung on to some of the glow, even when a model-faced stick insect wiggled up to the table and cooed at Daniel until he went with her. They sang "No Air."

Frankie stayed off the stage for once, even when Daniel abandoned it for food. "I know when to sit it out," Frankie said, waving a chicken-laden fork first in his brother's direction and then toward the room. "Tonight I will let 'em watch and yearn."

I kept my head down and my mouth full. I didn't want Frankie's sharp eyes or tongue focused on me any more than necessary. It was a lot easier with Daniel taking up half of the food and most of the air.

"What about it, Ella?" he asked when everything was gone except the parsley garnish. "When do we get the pleasure of your vocal stylings?"

"I don't sing."

"You mean you won't sing," Sadie corrected. I tried to be

charitable about her treason; she goes pretty brainless around Daniel. "Ella sings really well."

"I'm sure she does." Daniel tipped his beer glass in my direction. "In fact, I bet she could totally murder 'Don't Stop Believin'." A song that is actually one of my guilty pleasures. I think he probably knew that. I think he probably had himself a lovely chuckle over it. Then he whispered, "*Coward.*"

In another story, the plucky little heroine would have slapped both hands onto the table, making it wobble a little on its predictably uneven fourth leg. She would then have taken both hands, ripped the long scarf from around her neck and, chin high and scar spotlit, stalked to the dais, leaped up, and slayed the audience with her kick-ass version of "Respect." Or maybe "Single Ladies," for the sheer Yay factor.

In this version, I gave Daniel what I hoped was a slayer look and busied myself refolding my napkin.

He was, not surprisingly, unfazed. "Can I ask you a question?"

I sighed. "Will my answer to that one make any difference?"

"None whatsoever."

"Fine," I grumbled. "Ask." I didn't have to answer. He wasn't my Hobbes.

"Why are there interstate highways in Hawaii?"

I gaped at him. "That's your question?"

"Nope." He leaned back in his chair, propping one foot on the other knee. "That's *a* question. My question is this: What's the one thing you should ask yourself before getting involved with someone?"

"Seriously?"

"Do I look serious?"

Maybe not serious, but vaguely deadly. Still, it was an interesting question, especially coming from Daniel Hobbes. I thought for a second. "'Will he make me happy?'"

"You think?" Daniel asked, then unfolded himself and got to his feet. "I'm outta here. Who's coming?"

We drove home in his battered Jeep. It smelled like smoke and cinnamon, even with the plate-size rust hole in the back that let in steady gusts of cold air. Daniel and Frankie were going to hear Be Cruel, the ska Elvis cover band that Frankie loves and Daniel tolerates. I hoped they would be able to talk Sadie into going with them. I just wasn't up for it. I'd had enough mediocre covers for one night, and more than enough of Daniel and his brain-numbing pheromones.

He drove with one hand at the bottom of the steering wheel and sifted through a pile of hand-labeled CDs with the other. Next to me in back, Frankie had his panama hat pulled low over his forehead, deliberately not looking. In front, Sadie was having a grand old time. Daniel found something he liked and shoved it into the player, which promptly spat it back out. "Put your hand here," he told her, guiding her. "Hold it in until it sticks." She did, it did, and a wailing guitar started competing with the wind and engine.

"Genghis Khan's Marmot," Daniel yelled over the noise. "They're playing the Farm next Saturday. You should come. It would, and I say this with all due respect, be good for you."

None of us mentioned that the following weekend, we would

be floundering in Davy Jones's Locker. We all knew better. And anyway, Daniel probably knew all about it.

My clock read 1:10 when I flicked on the light in my room. I was quiet when I came home late, but not too quiet. I knew my dad would be half awake, listening for me. He was always exhausted after a Saturday night at the restaurant, but he wouldn't really sleep until he was sure I was home.

My clothes smelled like roasted chicken and shoe polish. I dumped them into my hamper, pulled on a *Top Chef* T-shirt—gift from Uncle Ricky—to sleep in, and dug my reliable costume out of the back of my closet. It would do. The painted blood looked fresh enough for the Bride of Davy Jones. Truth be told, it looked a lot better to me than when it had arrived, pristine, two years earlier. "Shred it. Paint it. Wear it to his funeral!" my cousin Alyssa had snapped as she dumped the dress, shiny and perfectly preserved in its carrier bag, onto the floor next to my bed. "Just don't you let a guy promise you a damn thing when you're wearing it. Swear?"

I swore. Then I shredded, painted, and wore it to the Fall Ball.

I'd decided not to go to this one at first. I thought I couldn't take it, the undulating mermaids and their drunken pirate partners. I thought I wouldn't be able to sit with Sadie and Frankie and watch Alex dancing with Amanda, her shells flattened against his chest, his hands on her sequined tail.

I'd changed my mind somewhere in the middle of Chloe's. Sad I could allow, even scared. I just wasn't willing to succumb to *coward*.

The shredded wedding dress was heavy in my hands. I thought I might add a paper anchor and chain this year, maybe a few wilted starfish. Black pearls would have been a nice touch, but the only pearls in the house were on Mom's wedding choker. There had been more pearls, fake ones, in the vertical lace spray that had topped her veil. More still sewn onto her fingerless lace gloves. Not her fault, I thought every time I passed their wedding photo in the living room. It was the eighties.

"Oh, that dress!"

My grandmother stood in my doorway, optic in a furry leopard-print robe. It was hardly her style, but one glance into the window of Victoria's Secret and she'd fallen in love. It was, she believed, exactly the robe Robert De Niro had worn in the boxing ring in *Raging Bull*.

"Hi, Nonna. Did I wake you up?"

"Oh, no. I watch Steven Tyler on the *Saturday Night Live*." She stalked into my room, giving the dress the evil eye. "Bad luck, that."

"Only for Alyssa."

"Hmph. You have another party?"

"The Fall Ball," I told her. "Our Halloween dance."

"Ah. You have a boy to go with?"

"Absolutely. Frankie."

She sighed, and perched on the edge of my bed. Her feet dangled a good six inches off the floor. "I like your Frankie, but he's not going to make pretty *bambini* with you."

"Nonna!"

"Well, is he? No." She leaned forward. "Now, that boy with the nice voice and bony mother. He might do."

I sighed. "He might do a lot of things, Nonna." *I'm not one of them*. "Dancing with me is not one of them."

"He liked my *pane*."

"Yup. He did."

"And you. He likes you."

"Nope. That he does not."

"Hmph. You with all the answers about boys."

That made me smile. "Apparently, I don't even know the right questions."

"Who does? Even kings don't know the right questions. Eh, did you know there is a love story between a king and a queen in your history? Here." She patted the bed. "Get in, *cucciola*. I will tell you."

15
THE FOLKTALE

"This, *bellissima*," Nonna began, "is true love story . . ."

"The Costas, we were born to the sea and proud, very proud. Son after father after son build their boats and follow the fish. My *bisnonno*, father of my *nonno*, is proudest of all. He is the only son of a widowed mother—king of the sea. But he is . . . ppffftt . . ." Nonna blew out a breath and fluttered her fingers maybe an inch or two above her own head. "*Basso. Piccolo.* When he was young, his uncles and cousins at first fear to take him on board. They think the smallest of waves or biggest of *tono* . . . *tono* . . . What is it?"

"Tuna," I said.

"*Sì.* Silly word. A *tuna* would flip him from the boat. But no one looks down on him. Ah, you laugh, you. Go on, laugh. They are not much bigger than he. So he is little, but he is proud, because his boat sails highest on the waves and soon brings in the most fish. Like gold, it makes him rich. And when a man becomes rich, he must think of marriage, or the village mamas will think of it for him. *Capisci?*"

I smiled. "Yeah, I get it. 'It is a truth universally acknowledged that a single man in possession of a good fortune must be in want of a wife.' "

"Ah, *sì!*" Nonna nodded, delighted. "Austen. So smart."

"You know *Pride and Prejudice?*" I asked. She flicked my ear. "Ow!"

"You think you have the only brain in this family? *Eh?* Ah, Darcy. My *bisnonno* is such a man . . . Fine, you laugh again. Not so handsome, I think, but just as proud. He struts though the square with his new shoes. He buys a carriage. But he gives to the poor, too, to the Church. He is kind to his sisters; he is a friend to many. He is *raffinato*, a gentleman And the girl he chooses? Hmm? Hmm?"

"I don't know, Nonna. Elizabeth Benedetto?"

"Hah!" Nonna slapped her hand hard against her knee. It bounced soundlessly off the leopard plush. "*Elisabetta.* Elisabetta, daughter of a man who works on another's boat. Elisabetta who has many sisters and who is intended for the Church if she does not marry. I don't remember her family name, if I ever knew. Maybe Benedetto. Why not? It does not matter. What matters is that no one understands why Michelangelo Costa chooses this girl. No one can . . . oh, the word . . . to say a picture of: *descrivere.*"

"Describe?"

"*Sì.* Describe. No one can describe her. Small, they think. Brown, maybe. Maybe not so pretty, not so ugly. Just a girl. She sits by the seawall mending nets her family does not own. She is odd, too, her neighbors think. They think it is she who leaves little bit of shell and rock when she is done with the nets, little *mosaico* on the wall. So why? the *piu bella* girls ask, the ones with long, long necks, and long black hair, and noses that turn up at the end. Why this odd, nobody girl in her ugly dresses, with her dirty feet?

"Michelangelo sends his cousins to her with gifts. A cameo, silk handkerchiefs, a fine pair of gloves. Again, the laugh. Then, you would not have laughed at a gift of gloves, *piccola*. Oh, you girls now. You want what? E-mails and ePods?"

"That's iPods, Nonna."

"Whatever. See, that word I know. Now, Elisabetta sends back the little gifts. So my *bisnonno* sends bigger: pearls, meters of silk cloth, a horse. These, too, she will not take. And the people begin to look, and ask: Who is she, this nobody girl, to refuse him? No money, no beauty, no family name. You are a fool, they tell her. Accept. Accept!

"And my proud *bisnonno* does not understand. He can have any girl in the town. So again, he gathers the gifts, he carries them himself, leads the horse. But Elisabetta is not to be found. She is not at her papa's house or in the square or at the seawall. Michelangelo fears she has gone to the convent. But no. As he stands at the seawall, a seabird, a gull, lands on his shoulder and says—"

"Nonna—"

"Shh! The bird tells him to follow the *delfino* . . . *delfin*? Dolphin! So he looks, and there, a dolphin with its head above the water says, 'Follow!' So he follows, the sack with gifts for

Elisabetta on his back, like a peddler, the horse trailing behind. The dolphin leads him around the bay to a beach, and there is Elisabetta, old dress covered in sand, feet bare, just drawing circles in the sand. She starts to run, but Michelangelo calls to her. 'Why,' he asks her. 'Why do you hide? Why will you not take my gifts?' And she says . . . ?"

I'd been fighting a losing battle with yawning for a while. I was failing fast. "I have no idea. 'I'm in love with someone else'?"

Nonna snorted hard enough to shake the mattress. "With who? There is no one else like Michelangelo. He is king of the sea! In love with someone else. Pah."

"Okay. Fine. Tell me what she said."

Nonna leaned toward me, eyes bright. "She says, 'You do not see me.' And my *bisnonno*, he says, 'Of course I see you! Every day I see you by the seawall. I see you in my mind, too, in pearls and furs and silk. So, here, here I offer you these things.' And she says . . . ?"

" 'Thank you?' "

"Per carita!"

" 'No, thank you?' "

"Ah, Fiorella. I think you are not the child of my child! *Rifletti*. Use that good brain."

"Nonna . . ."

"She says, '*You do not see me!*' And she sends him away."

I wasn't sure I was getting the point. Here's an ordinary girl in ratty clothes who's going to end up a nun if she doesn't get married. Along comes a decent guy with money, promising to take her away from it all . . . Wasn't that where it usually faded to Happily Ever After?

"So." Nonna tucked each of her hands into the opposite sleeve, a wizened Confucius in a leopard bathrobe. "Michelangelo, he goes. For days and days he stays away from Elisabetta. The other girls, the prettier girls, have hope again. And then, there he goes once more, carrying only his *nonno*'s ugly old glass—his telescope—and a bag of figs. These he lays at her feet.

"'I see you,' he tells her. 'Every day for months, I watch. I see you. Where you sit, the sea is calm and dolphins swim near you. I see your mended net looks like a lady's lace. I see you dance in the rain before you run home. I see the jewel mosaic you leave to be scattered and remade again and again, *piu bella* than gold and pearls. You are *piu bella* than any other, queen of the sea.

"'You do not need silk or pearls. I see that. But they are yours if you wish. I am yours if you wish. If you like what you see.' He gives her the glass. She takes it. Then she asks, 'What about the figs?' My *bisnonno*, he laughs. 'It might take time, your looking to see if you like me. I bring lunch.'" Nonna slapped her knee again, clearly delighted with little Michelangelo's humor. "There is the love story. You like it?"

I swallowed another yawn. "*Sì*, Nonna. It's a good story." I couldn't resist, "But . . . a talking seagull? A dolphin guide? That kinda stretches the truth, dontcha think?"

Nonna shrugged. "All truth, not all truth, does it matter? My *nonno* Guillermo came to Michelangelo and Elisabetta, then my papa Euplio to him, then me, your papa, you." She lowered her feet to the floor. Then pinched my cheek. Hard. *"Buona notte, bellissima."*

"Okay, Nonna." I yawned and pulled the white eyelet quilt up. I'd inked abstract swirl-and-dot patterns all over it when I redecorated my room. They're a little optic when I'm that tired. *"Buona notte."*

As I was dozing off, I heard her rummaging in the linen cupboard next to my door. Reorganizing again, I thought. She does that when Mom can't see her. They fold things completely different ways.

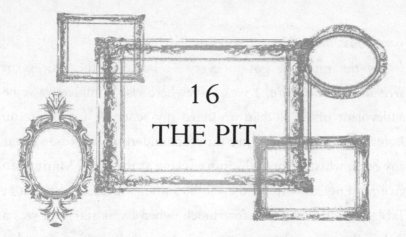

16
THE PIT

There aren't many classrooms in the school basement. Most of the space is for storage and utilities. As far as student use goes, the darkroom is down there, along with yearbook and the school paper. Places that either don't require much light or are used by students so happy to be there that they don't care. The only illumination comes from the fluorescents overhead and what filters in from the hallway through the glass upper half of the doors. It usually takes me about ten minutes in French to lose my focus completely.

This time, it took less. We were learning the past imperfect tense, which, as well as being completely incomprehensible in practice, in theory describes a state where every action was either left incomplete, unfulfilled, or repeated over and over.

It was me, Sadie, and Frankie, European version.

"*Ah, si j'étais riche!*" Miss Winslow (distant cousin to Sadie, direct descendant of Abigail and John Adams, reminiscent of a buff-colored French bulldog) recited. "If I were rich!"

"*Nous croyions aux contes de fées.*" We believed in fairy tales.

"*Vous cherchiez . . .*" You are searching.

By the time she got to everyone being in the process of *arrivaient* somewhere, I was somewhere else completely. Some malevolent office elf had arranged my schedule for the term. Actually, it was probably just the office underling, who didn't hear any bells, whistles, or cash-drawer clang at the name Marino. To give me English with all the Phillites after I'd just had lunch at Table 12—and French before lunch, when I was starving, was a little evil, as far as I was concerned. At *we believed in fairy tales,* I'd started thinking about Nonna and Michelangelo, which had quickly devolved into thinking about his bag of figs.

"*Mademoiselle Marino?*"

It didn't fully register that the words meant me until the freshman Bee Boy behind me snorted and kicked the back of my chair.

"Ella!"

"*Oui, mademoiselle?*"

"*Dormez vous?*"

"Ah . . . *oui?*"

There was a flutter of laughter in the room. Mademoiselle Winslow crossed her arms over her chest. She had a sailboat on the front of her sweater. Scrunched up, it looked like a nunchuck. "*D'accord. D'accord. Avez-vous de bons rêves?*"

It took me a sec. Then I felt the blood rising in my face. "No. *Non.* I mean. I wasn't dreaming . . . revving."

A few people weren't even bothering to muffle their laughter now. Mademoiselle Winslow's mouth thinned, making her look more bullfrog than dog. "*Vous me parlerez après la classe,*" she snapped. "*Compris?*"

I got it. Just. I would be staying after class.

It took her a while to get to me. I waited miserably in my seat while a stream of mostly freshmen, all of whom were more proficient than I at the language, said their *au revoirs* and accepted their *bien faits*. I don't think I've ever gotten a "well done" from a French teacher. Art, absolutely. Math and science, sometimes. English, sure—before Mr. Stone.

"So, Ella." Mademoiselle Winslow sat down heavily in the desk next to me. "So, so." The story is that she lived in Paris for a year between Vassar and coming to work at Willing. Apparently, she picked up the French habit of repeating words there, and has clung to it fiercely ever since. "What are we going to do with you?"

I felt myself flushing again. "I'm really sorry, mademoiselle. I have stuff on my mind, and I wasn't paying attention. It won't happen again."

She almost looked sympathetic when she replied, "It happens all the time, Ella."

That wasn't fair, but I was getting a faint sense that maybe if I kept my mouth shut, I would just get a scolding before she let me go.

"Is this stuff something you would share with me?" she asked.

Not likely. I shook my head.

"Okay. Okay." She tapped a blunt fingertip on her desk. Elegant Frenchwomen, she'd informed the enraptured freshmen girls who thought having us translate a French *Vogue* in our 2A class was brilliant, don't wear nail polish. "Have you thought about talking to a peer counselor?"

Like Amanda Alstead, of the Chanel rouge-noir nail polish and black heart? I actually shuddered. And was about to come clean and admit I was just hungry and tired, when she added, "Look, Ella, I can't force you to talk to anyone, but I can put my foot down about this class. You're teetering on the wrong edge of a C-minus, and while that might be acceptable to you, it isn't for me. So we're going to strike a deal. We're already nearly in November. I'll hold off giving you a midterm grade; you'll do the work. *D'accord?*"

I was ready to sign over Frankie and my firstborn to get out of this particular hole. It would kill my dad—and possibly my scholarship—if I got a D in anything. *"D'accord."*

"Excellent. I have a few upperclassmen who tutor some of my French 1A students. I think even an hour a week would make a difference, providing you put in the effort."

"Fine." I could do it. I could stomach an hour a week with some earnest Star who would quiz me on conjugations and probably try to recruit me for the French Club. They do a cabaret each year, which consists of lots of striped shirts, one mime, and a few Liza Minnelli-alikes crooning into a mic. I sighed. "I'll put in the effort. I promise." Mademoiselle Winslow looked satisfied. "Can I go to lunch now? *S'il vous plaît?*" I drew the line at saying it twice.

"Meet with the tutor first. There's one here now, waiting to use the room." She waved toward the door.

As soon as I turned, my stomach dropped. Even through the mottled glass, there was no mistaking the figure there, even from behind. Of course. It would have to be . . .

"Oh, no. No," I whispered. Then, before I could stop myself, "Can't you find someone else?"

Mademoiselle Winslow blinked at me in surprise. "Why?"

Oh, I wasn't about to answer that one. "There has to be something else I can do. I'll read Dumas. I'll listen to Celine Dion. I'll join a Johnny Depp Fan Club. He lives in France—"

"Ella. You are just being silly." The patient bonhomie (Frankie likes to use that word about Dean Martin; it had nothing to do with any hidden French aptitude on my part) was gone, replaced by a sort of sugary snobbishness with a dash of impatience. "He's just a boy who happens to speak French well. You mustn't let where you come from make you feel"—I don't think she meant to look at my neck—"at a disadvantage."

I actually felt the ache of tears at the back of my throat and swallowed angrily. Trust this product of thin blood and fat bank accounts to completely misunderstand. She hadn't had an instant's concern that I might have even the smallest of valid reasons for not wanting to learn French from Alex Bainbridge. It all came down to money.

Then she made it worse. "You have an advantage," she said brightly. "It's so much easier to develop true facility in one Romance language if you know another. *Capisce?*"

She smiled at me brightly. Just call me Scar Fascia, I thought.

"So." She tapped her unpainted fingers against the knees

of her cords. "So, Ella. Keeping in mind that it might be the difference between failure and your future, what will it be?"

My stomach growled. "Figs and tuna fish, apparently," I answered.

Mademoiselle Winslow's eyes bugged out more than normal. Before I could explain that it had just slipped out, that I wasn't being a smartass—not that it would have mattered, probably— she shouted, "Alex! *Entrez!*"

He shoved his way through the door, looking far too cute and cheerful to be in a basement. ". . . *tu me fais chier, il me fait chier . . .*" he was saying slowly to the small and slightly awestruck-looking freshman boy behind him.

"Alex!" Mademoiselle Winslow managed to sound disapproving and totally charmed at the same time. "Really!"

He grinned at her and shrugged. Then he saw me. And kept grinning. "Hey."

I lifted one hand halfway off the desk in greeting.

"Sebastian, you can wait with Ella in the hall while I talk to Alex for a minute." Mademoiselle Winslow shooed the boy out. I got up to follow. "Don't even think of disappearing," she ordered me grimly. "And close the door behind you."

I slung my bag onto my shoulder and followed Sebastian. He was even shorter than me, and he leaned back against the wall in a gravity-defying way that made him look even smaller. "Is Alex helping you, too?" he asked after a couple of silent minutes.

"No." It wasn't a lie if I meant it. "Is he a good tutor?" I couldn't help asking.

The kid's face lit up. "Awesome! He's teaching me all the cool words. I will kick butt. No. *Je démonterai*," he corrected, then giggled.

"In French 1A?" I asked. I didn't mean to be critical; it just sounded like an empty victory.

"Chamonix" was his reply. "We're going for winter break, and my parents want me to be conversational."

Fortunately, the door opened again, and both Mademoiselle Winslow and Alex came out. She patted me on the shoulder and stumped off down the hall in her nautical-blue clogs. Alex levered Sebastian off the wall by the front of his shirt. "Go in. I'll be there in a sec." When Sebastian, clearly delighted to be treated like one of the guys, didn't move, Alex bared his teeth. *"Dépêche-toi!"*

Sebastian dépêched. Alex turned back, all Cheshire cat smile.

"No," I said.

"No what?"

"No, you are not going to teach me all the cool words so I can go to Chamonix and be conversational."

"Good." He leaned in so I could see the faint dusting of freckles on his nose and smell spearmint gum. "Chamonix is so 1990s. Everyone who is anyone goes to Courchevel these days."

I turned on my heel and started to walk off.

"Jeez. Ella." He loped after me. "What is your problem? Conversational, my ass. Talking to you is like dancing around a fire in paper shoes."

I stopped. "What is that supposed to mean?"

"It's an expression my Ukrainian babushka likes. I'll explain it at our first tutoring session."

I scowled at his shirt. This one had what looked like a guy riding a dolphin instead of the ubiquitous alligator or polo player. "There isn't going to be a tutoring session."

"Winslow seems to think otherwise."

"Wouldn't be the first thing she's wrong about," I muttered.

He gave an impressive sigh. The dolphin lurched, but the little guy on it held tight. "You don't want to fail *French*, do you? That would a serious admission of weakness from an Italian girl."

I almost smiled. Instead, I announced, "Fuhgeddaboudit. I'll buy a 'Teach Your Poodle French in Ten Easy Lessons' online. Problem solved, and Winslow will never be the wiser."

"Yeah. Good luck with that. So how's this Friday? I don't have practice." When I shook my head, he demanded, "What is it? I'm a good tutor. Ask Sebastian. I was just teaching him how to tell the obnoxious French dudes on the slopes that they suck."

That did make me smile just a little. "Look, Alex. It's pretty simple. I don't want to do this; you certainly don't want to. So . . ."

I hadn't realized he was slowly bending his knees until his chin entered my line of vision, followed by the rest of his face. He wasn't grinning now. He looked very serious. "Ella. I really do want to do this. Help you, if you'll let me." He sighed again, but I couldn't see the fate of his dolphin logo person. I was completely fixated on his eyes. They're a pretty amazing combination of green and bronze. "I don't know what's going on, but it's weird, and it shouldn't be. I'm a decent guy."

"Of course you are." I sighed. And caved. Apparently, my Phillite defenses were worthless around this particular specimen, no matter that he couldn't seem to make up his mind whether I was worth noticing or not.

Truth: Yes, I am that naive.

"Good. So. Friday after school. We can meet down here."

I could just see Amanda's face when she caught us on our way into the dark depths of the school. "No."

"Fine. Your house."

"God, no!"

"Do you make everything this complicated?" he asked. "No. Don't answer that. Would you come to my house?"

That sounded doable. If we were at his place, I could leave whenever I wanted. "Okay."

As I watched, he did a slo-mo, surprisingly graceful flop onto the floor. "Finally!"

I stepped over him and headed for the stairs.

<hr />

"There's a rumor Barsky's Chemistry Club is cultivating some fierce bacteria in the lab," Frankie informed me a few minutes later, after I'd related Mademoiselle Winslow's ultimatum, and my soon-to-be tutoring sessions with Alex. "I bet we could break in and get you a good dose of something. Put the kibosh on the tutoring. Could be a little pinkeye, could be leprosy . . ." He took a cheerful bite of his taco, which flaked everywhere.

"Frankie!" Sadie scolded. "That's awful." She'd already finished her apple and Belgian endive. To me, "If it's this or fail French, well, you don't know; Alex might be just what you need."

"Oh, yeah, he's a prince," Frankie muttered. "Abso-friggin-lutely guaranteed to man up and do the right thing."

With that, he reached over and stole my french fries. He'd already eaten the baggie of almonds Sadie had decided had too much fat. Apparently, she and I were both obsessing with our appearance. She was having a hate-hate day with her upper arms. I was wondering if I was about to be at the tutorial mercy of the guy who'd looked right through me, or the guy who looked at me like I'd never been scarred at all.

⌒⌒⌒

"Honestly, the pair of you" was Edward's response. I brushed cracker crumbs off my homework folder; I'd needed a snack after giving up most of my lunch. "Silly infants. Don't you know the way people see you has absolutely nothing to do with the way you actually look? Beauty is all sleight of hand. Just ask Holbein. Or Bobbi Brown."

"I thought Beauty was Truth," I said wearily. I had a headache, and three pages of French to translate.

"*That* is Keats. I am not overly fond of Keats. Had he not died so poetically early, people might have realized he was not quite what they thought he was."

"The same could be said of you," I shot back. I was a little annoyed by the "silly infants" comment.

"Oh, so clever. What's the worst-case scenario, should you give the Bainbridge boy a try?"

"Well, gosh. Lemme see." I ticked off a few possibilities on my fingers. "Humiliation, humiliation, mortification, and humiliation."

Edward sniffed. *"Qui craint de souffrir, il souffre déjà de ce qu'il craint."*

"And what does that mean?" I recognized it from the second page of my homework.

"Well, gosh, darling Ella. You'll just have to ask your new tutor, won't you?" he said silkily. Right before he went back to emulating a lump of metal.

17
THE LIST

I bought some cotton archival gloves the next day at Blick. They didn't really fit; the only available size was Large. I felt like the Scarecrow in the Oz books, clumsy and dressed in someone else's rejects. I'd drawn the line at another skirt. I was back in jeans. Dr. Rothaus ignored them but gave the gloves an almost-approving nod when she let me into the archive. "I didn't think you would come back."

I paused, the second glove halfway on. "Why?"

"Most people don't. They spend a few hours being overwhelmed by this"—she flapped a hand at the sagging shelves and motley collection of furniture—"and decide they're not going to find anything valuable."

I flinched. I'd pretty much decided as much, too. She gave me a thin smile. "You, too?"

"I'm here." A few hours among Edward's possessions was a good thing in itself. Beyond that, the idea of having to call and explain to Maxine Rothaus that I wasn't coming was infinitely more terrifying than a little disappointment brought on by boring books. She was wearing a textured gray sweater that looked like chain mail, and a necklace made up of opaque glass beads that were strongly reminiscent of human teeth. "I came back."

"You did." She leaned against the desk, mail-clad arms crossed over her chest. "Why?"

"Why? To be honest . . . ?"

"Absolutely. Be honest."

"I'm a little obsessed with Edward Willing and a little desperate to find material for my honors project."

"Well. I believe both."

Truth: Despite the impressive number of lies I tell in my day-to-day life, I'm not particularly good at it.

Dealing with my French teacher is one thing; she wears pants with little whales on them. But I was convinced Dr. Rothaus could smell a lie from ten words away. I found myself feeling sorry for any children she might have. I imagined them as shadowy figures with excellent posture and skill at declamation.

She stared down her long nose at me. "I called the Willing Foundation."

"Oh." My stomach sank.

"Funny. They had no idea who you were."

"No," I said sadly. "They wouldn't. I'm sorry."

I waggled one loose fingertip nervously and waited. I figured I deserved whatever was coming. Of course, it would have been sufficiently humiliating for the desk guard to have refused me entrance. Sufficiently humiliating for me, anyway. I wasn't sure about Dr. Rothaus. I looked at the necklace again and decided a little torture might be right up her alley.

She just stared at me through hooded eyes.

"Okay. I should probably leave now," I said, starting to strip off the gloves. I wasn't about to walk away with my droopy scarecrow hands.

"Probably," was her bland reply, "although that would completely eliminate any possibility of finding something useful here."

I stopped, fingers tangled. "You're not throwing me out?"

"I am not. Not yet, anyway. And for the record, I didn't betray your little charade to the Willing People."

"Why?" I couldn't help but ask.

"I don't like them," she said crisply. "They think their money makes them important. And a chimpanzee knows more about art. Besides, you completely reorganized 1899."

I winced. "Sorry."

"Are you? Why? Every paper was put back right side up, right side out, and staggered, so they weren't all crammed in. They were also in chronological order. Either you're compulsively neat"—she gave my inky jeans and faded turtleneck a quick, brow-raised glance—"or you're reverent."

Somehow, reverence didn't seem like much of a crime.

"Plus," Dr. Rothaus added, "you left your notes." She reached behind her and lifted a sheet of blue paper from the desk. When she held it up, I could see the badly drawn undersea locker of the Fall Ball flyer on the side facing me. She reached into her pants pocket and pulled out a pair of gunmetal-framed reading glasses. She flicked them open, switchblade-style, with a snap of her wrist, and shoved them onto her nose. "'Lobsters,'" she read. "'Earrings. *Beach at Trouville?*'" Then, "Roses and Wharton *Summer?*'" She studied me for a long moment. "You actually seem to know your Willing."

Of all the things I hide, that's not one of them. "I do."

Now her brows went up. "That sounded like pride. Favorite painting . . . ?"

"Painting? *Odalisque*," I said.

"Really. His non-nude nude. Interesting."

It was, to me. Edward's most famous painting of Diana is *Troie*, where he painted her as Helen of Troy: naked except for the diamond bracelet and the occasional tendril of auburn hair. It had caused quite a stir at its exhibition. Apparently, Millicent Carnegie Biddle fainted on seeing it. It wasn't quite what she was used to viewing when she sat across from Mrs. Edward Willing every few weeks, sipping tea from Wedgwood china cups.

Odalisque was more daring in its way, and infinitely more interesting to me. Most of the Post-Impressionist painters did an odalisque, or harem girl, reclining on a sofa or carpet, promising with their eyes that whatever it was that they did to men, they did it well. An odalisque was almost compulsory material. But unlike any of them, Edward had painted his subject— Diana—covered from neck to ankle in shimmery gauze. Covered, but still the ultimate object of desire.

"Why that one?" Dr. Rothaus asked.

"I don't know—"

"Oh, please. Don't go all stupid teenager on me now. You know exactly why you like the painting. Humor me and articulate it."

I felt myself beginning the ubiquitous shoulder dip. "Okay. Everyone is covering up something. I guess I think there's an interesting question there."

"'What are they hiding?'"

I shook my head. "'Does it make a difference?'"

"Ah." One sharp corner of her mouth lifted. I would hesitate to call it a smile. "That is interesting. But your favorite Willing piece isn't a painting."

"How—"

"You hesitated when I asked. Let me guess . . . *Ravaged Man?*"

"How—"

"You're a young woman. And"—Dr. Rothaus levered herself off the desk—"you went through the 1899 file. I know the archive."

"But I thought you didn't like being in charge of it." Her vague approval was making me bold.

"Who says I do?" She flipped a rucked-up corner of the rug into place with the pointed toe of one shoe. "I am the world expert on the influence of Cézanne on early twentieth-century American painters. Edward Willing was just one of many. I wanted this job; he came with it. Of course, the librarians get the interesting papers. Along with all my curatorial duties, I get the kitsch."

I had to ask. "Are his letters to Diana downstairs?"

She sighed. "What is it about girls and letters? My husband left me messages in soap on the bathroom mirror. Utterly impermanent. Really wonderful—" She broke off and scowled. I would have thought she looked a little embarrassed, but I didn't think embarrassment was in her repertoire. "Anyway. Most of the correspondence between the Willings is in private collections. He had their letters with him in Paris when he died. In a noble but ultimately misguided act, his attorney sent them to his niece. Who put them all in a ghastly book that she illustrated. Her son sold them to finance the publication of six even more ghastly books of poetry. I trust there is a circle of hell for terrible poets who desecrate art."

"I've seen the poetry books in the library," I told her. "The ones with Edward's paintings on the covers. I couldn't bring myself to read them."

"Smart girl. I suppose worse things have been done, but not many. Of course, there was that god-awful children's television show that made one of his landscapes move. They put kangaroos in it. *Kangaroos*. In eastern Pennsylvania."

"I've seen that, too," I admitted. I'd hated it. "Hated it. Not quite as much as the still life where Tastykakes replaced one orange with a cupcake, or the portrait of Diana dressed in a Playtex sports bra, but close."

"Oh, God. I try to forget about the bra." Dr. Rothaus shuddered. "Well, I suppose they do far worse to the really famous painters. Poor van Gogh. All those hearing-aid ads."

"Yeah." We shared a moment of quiet respect for van Gogh's ear. Then, having waited as long as I could, I prompted, "Any suggestions . . . ?"

She shrugged. "Willing didn't keep much after 1899. What we have is fragments, mostly, things that scavenging relatives missed because they were on the flip side of bills or business correspondence. But . . ." She stalked over to one of the cabinets. The bottom file drawer grated and clanged as she pulled it out. "I found this one in the 1902 file, stuck to a receipt for snowshoes. He'd written a critic's home address on the other side. There's a rumor said critic once found a pile of manure on his front step, but I've never seen it verified. Anyway." She handed me a single sheet of yellowed paper encased in a clear archival sleeve. "This ought to speak to you . . . Not like that! Hold the edges!"

I flushed and held the edges. The writing was familiar: bold and spiky, the ink faded a little to indigo. *Stuyvesant Gumm*, it read. *1966 Spruce Street.* All around the writing were small, raised lines. The *t* of "Street" ran into a tear where a pen had come through the other side of the paper. I turned it over. Edward had scrawled:

1. She snored like a bear.
2. She left her shoes in the middle of the floor and right in front of the door.
3. She thought it amusing to put asparagus and beans in the menu when entertaining my parents.
4. She insisted that kale was good for my digestion.

5. She insisted more firmly that solitary walks in the rain were good for my temper.
6. She hid the chocolate.
7. She had feet like a goose.
8. She filled my coat pockets with ~~█████~~

The list stopped there, the final word ending in a slash and a smear.

"Wow," I said.

Dr. Rothaus was clearly less moved. She was picking invisible lint off her sweater. "I've never been able to decide whether it's incredibly romantic or just plain pitiful."

For me, it was no contest. All I could think was that Edward was so devastated that he was past being comforted by remembering the good stuff, the things about Diana that he'd loved. That, maybe, the only way he could get through this particular day was to make himself focus on the things he hadn't.

I said as much. Dr. Rothaus snorted. "How did I know you would go all rhapsodic over that list? God, youth. Are you in love or just an annoying romantic in general?"

"Neither," I said. "I just think this is amazing."

Holding Edward's heartbroken list, I felt weepy. Fine, the time of the month didn't help, but I was feeling pretty sorry for myself. Nonna would say it was a curse; I figured I must have been a three-timing lap dancer named Ginger in a past life to deserve where I was in this one. Adoring a guy without a heartbeat, all in knots over a live one who had absolutely no interest in making my heart beat a little faster.

"Why is it amazing?" Dr. Rothaus's sharp voice yanked me out of my pity party. "To borrow a page from your book, does it make a difference in who Edward Willing was as an artist? Or could it possibly just be sentimental drivel?"

I thought maybe she would have been an okay teacher. If she hadn't been guaranteed to scare the opinions right out of just about anyone at Willing who might possess one. Or maybe I was just pitifully grateful to be able to have a real conversation with anyone about Edward.

"I think he painted the way he did," I answered, "because he had something perfect with Diana."

I braced myself for her next scathing insight and nearly fell over when she reached out to pat my hand. Her wedding ring was a heavy, hammered gold band that could probably pound nails.

"Nothing but the occasional espresso is perfect," she said, not unkindly. "Let me share some wisdom, Willing Girl. Relationships are like Whack-a-Mole. You squash one annoying deformity and another one pops up in no time."

Not your classic sentiment, there. Or a particularly heartening one. It seemed well meant, though, so I figured it might be a good time to inform her, "Um, my name . . . is Ella. Marino."

"Oh, I know who you are, Miss Marino," she shot back. "Shall I mention again that the Willing Foundation doesn't?"

"No, Dr. Rothaus," I said meekly. "No need."

"Excellent." Dr. Rothaus headed for the door. "You may call

me Maxine. Good luck finding something I haven't. And don't cry on the materials."

⌘

Three hours later, I slung my book bag onto my desk chair at home. "Don't say anything," I told Edward. "Today I waded through another file of deadly minutiae. I do not want to know that you probably smelled like red wine and blue cheese. Ah!" I held up a hand. "Not a word."

I was tired, hungry, and beginning to understand why every curator I had ever met was grumpy. I took off my jacket and headed for the closet.

It was hanging front and center, a long flow of pale blue cotton sateen. I recognized my parents' pre-toile-redecoration bedsheets even as I took in the fact that this was no longer bedding. It was very clearly a dress. I reached out to touch the intricately draped and pleated top.

"Pretty, eh?"

I jumped a foot. "Nonna!"

She was standing in my doorway, beaming like a demented gnome. "For your underwater dance."

"It looks like . . . a toga."

"Toga," she sniffed as she stalked across the room to lift the dress from its hanger, "is for boys at silly parties. This is for a goddess." She held it up to me. "You will be Salacia, Roman goddess of water."

It still looked like a toga, and not a very big one, although it did almost reach the floor. My legs would be covered, which was all well and good, except that, other than going a little too long without defuzzing, I didn't have much of a problem with my legs. I did know this wasn't going to work. I just had no idea at the moment how I was going to make it not happen.

"This is awfully . . . pagan of you, Nonna."

She rolled her eyes. "*Ai*, sixteen, with the smart mouth and such certainty. You think I just read the Bible? A goddess, she has more fun than a saint."

"Nonna!"

"Ah!" She poked me in the center of the chest with her middle finger. "Fun, *sì*, but a bad end if she thinks to hold the heart of a boy who wants only to play. Salacia, she let Neptune chase her and chase her and prove his heart was true."

I didn't argue. My grasp of Greco-Roman mythology is shaky at best, and derived mostly from the Percy Jackson books. I had my doubts about Neptune's heart, but figured it would only be smart-assy to mention that to my grandmother.

I ran a hand over the perfect pleating. "It's amazing, Nonna. I just don't think—"

"Don't think. Try. For me. If you don't like it, you don't wear it to the dance."

Again, I held my tongue. What was the point in trying to explain that liking something and wearing it in public had pretty much nothing to do with each other?

"Okay. I'll try."

She was already on her way out the door. "I will come back."

As I shucked my jeans and sweater, I did some quick thinking.

I figured I could make her happy and still be comfy in my shredded wedding dress. I would store that in my locker; I could leave the house as Neptune's bride and arrive in the gym as Bride of Davy. Sadie would help. Frankie probably wouldn't, I thought as I reached around to unhook my bra. He would be on Nonna's side all the way.

I opened my closet door and lifted my bathrobe from the hook over the mirror so I could see. I don't usually do that when I'm undressed. But I was distracted.

There's a moment everyone knows, when you look down at your fresh white shirt and realize you've spilled Coke or egg yolk or spaghetti sauce down the front. There's that flash of denial, followed by the realization that the shirt is probably ruined; it'll certainly never be the same. Then, for some people, it's "Well, that's life. Move on."

I still haven't reached that point with the scar.

Straight on, it can look kind of like a closed handprint, like something hellish stood behind me, grabbed my shoulder with a massive fist, and squeezed. I don't face it straight on very often, especially not naked from the waist up. Once in a blue moon, I'll stand in profile, left side to the mirror. If I push my hair behind my shoulder and get the angle just right, all I can see is what could have been: smooth skin, longish neck, breasts I would actually have been proud of.

Like I said, I don't bother often. I don't let anyone else look, either, if I can possibly help it. Because almost as much as the scar itself, I hate the lies:

"Oh, it looks so much better than it used to!"

"Honey, it's not nearly as bad as you think it is."

"Believe me, no one is looking."

And the very worst one:

"The scar doesn't have anything at all to do with who you are!"

Yeah, right. Try going through the whole day with egg on your chest and see who you are at the end of it. See if you don't want to squeeze the shirt into a tight little ball and throw it away, even though there's a big bottle of bleach above the washer.

I turned my back on the mirror and slid Nonna's dress over my head. I owed her that much, especially considering the effort she'd made. She had stitched a sort of half sleeve on the right side, flowing but designed to cover the top of my arm. The fabric was gathered high on my shoulder in a tall, intricate knot that stopped just below my ear, then draped down across my chest, leaving my entire left arm bare. She'd attached one of the gold drapery cords from the pre-toile-redecoration days onto the back. When I tied it, pulling some of the material up and through, the skirt fell to the floor in a graceful column.

"Oh. Oh, Fiorella. *Molto carina.*" Nonna was back. She stood in the doorway, both hands over her heart. "You are beautiful."

I turned reluctantly to face my reflection again.

What little makeup I'd put on in the morning was long gone, I probably should have washed my hair that morning, and my stripy toe socks were peeking out from under the blue hem. But I looked okay. Maybe even just a little bit better than that. The dress certainly hid the scar. I still couldn't wear it to the dance, but . . .

"*Grazie*, Nonna. It's beautiful."

She shuffled into the room, grabbed my hand, and pressed it open until it was flat, palm up. "Your *nonno* give this to me the month before he passed. Now I give it to you."

It was warm from her grip. I felt it and knew what it was even before I looked. "Nonna, I can't. It's your Tiffany necklace—"

"It is yours now, my sea girl."

She folded my fingers closed, pinched my cheek, hard, and walked back out of the room, closing the door behind her. I unfolded my hand and the chain slithered between my fingers. The silver starfish pendant glowed softly. It looked completely different against the warm beige of my skin than it always had against Nonna's stark black dresses. It had seemed too whimsical on the occasions when she'd worn it, a quirky and impractical gift from a husband who hadn't lived to see her wear it. I never thought about the fact that, as Estella Marino, she was literally Star of the Sea. My grandfather had.

"I don't suppose I have much of a choice now," I said aloud.

"The admirable thing, darling Ella," came Edward's reply, "is that you ever thought you did."

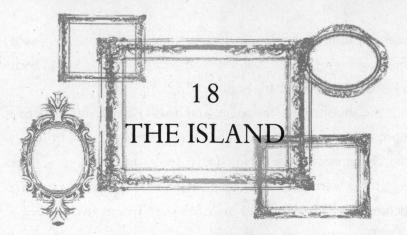

18
THE ISLAND

"So, how important is the setting of *The Tempest*? Anyone? Yes, Chase."

"Well, it's an island. You know. Like *Lost*, with a whole bunch of people who were there first and then the group who got shipwrecked. Fighting."

"Right, and . . . ?"

"And . . . what?"

"Okay. Maybe I should be more specific. Let's talk about why the setting is important to the Miranda-Ferdinand love story. Anyone? How about you, Ella?"

"Honestly? It's everything. I mean, she's been on the island almost all her life. It's her world. She doesn't know anything else. Then suddenly, she's surrounded by all these new people who are like aliens—"

"Shh. Quiet. Let's let Ella run with this. Go on, Ella."

"So, fine, she sees Ferdinand, and it's love at first sight. But what if they'd been from the same world, or what if she'd known more men from his? They pretty much *have* to fall in love, don't they? Otherwise, the whole story falls apart. But what if they'd had more information about each other? Or what if they'd been in Naples when her father was the duke . . . ?"

"A fair question. You've been to Naples. Imagine it five hundred years ago. Would it have made a difference?"

"I've never been to Naples, Mr. Stone. But yeah, anywhere would have been totally different. It's not about Italy. It's about isolation and freedom and wanting more than you have."

"True. True. But . . . I was so sure. Didn't you talk about Vesuvius when we read *The Last Days of Pompeii*?"

"I think you might be confusing me with someone else."

"No, no. I'm quite sure it was you. Wasn't it?"

"No. It wasn't."

"Oh, now, Ella. I distinctly remember something about the cleansing aspects of fire . . . Oh."

"Wrong aspects, Mr. Stone."

"Right, right. Of course. My mistake. Okay. No harm done. So, about islands . . ."

19
THE BATHROOM

"Mr. Stone is a jackass."

That was Alex's greeting when he found me in the hall Friday afternoon.

"Probably," I agreed, levering myself out of the corner where I'd been waiting, on nervous Hannanda alert, for him to show up. "But I don't think he can help it."

"Generous of you." Alex swung his backpack from his left shoulder to his right, then, like it was the most natural thing in the world, pulled mine out of my hand. I was too surprised to stop him. *"Allons-y."*

We turned a few heads as we went. I would have happily met him a block away from school, but he'd preempted my cowardice, sliding a note into my locker that morning. *Front hall, 3:15.* I ignored the stares as Alex held the big front door open for me, my heavily inked bag dangling from his wrist. I figured any speculation would last only as long as it would take for us to hit the street in front of the school. By then, at least one "Wait. Wait. Alex Bainbridge left with Freddy Krueger?" would have been met with "Yeah. He's tutoring her in French. Winslow's making him."

Because he would have told Amanda, and Amanda would have told anyone who cared. That's the thing about Willing: There's always someone happy to let you know exactly what your place is.

I started to turn toward the closest bus stop. Alex turned the other way. *"Suivez-moi,"* he commanded. So I followed. *"Bon. Je pensais que nous irions—"*

"Alex."

He stopped. "Ella."

"Don't do that, the immersion thing."

"Mais, c'est très important."

"Alex."

"Ella."

"Please. I know you do this with other linguistic losers, but it makes me feel like I should have a great big *L* lipsticked onto my forehead in some swirly French calligraphy."

"Do you often contemplate decorating yourself in such a manner?"

I took a quick look down. I was wearing Sienna's turtleneck again, but my own jeans. There was a large blue sea horse from the art museum fountain running from my knee to the crease of my thigh. "Yeah," I admitted. "I do."

"Quelle horreur!" he declared, eyes round in mock distress.

"Casse-toi."

He let out a bark of laughter that sounded just like a seal. *"Très bien,* Mademoiselle Marino. Got any more?"

"A couple. Frankie gave me a copy of *How to Offend the French* when I managed to get a B in 1B last year."

"Well, I never trade insults on a first date. Not that kinda guy. But after two or three . . ."

I liked that he'd said "date," instead of "tutoring session." Even if it wasn't and he totally didn't mean it. I couldn't help it.

He jingled his keys in his hand as he walked. "Y'know, I've looked for you around the floors. You haven't been drawing our door."

Of course, there wasn't an *our* anything. Unless, of course, he meant *our* as in "we the people of means who visit France regularly enough to be in French 5." "I figured I should give up," I said shortly.

"Why?"

Because you looked right through me. Because I might be pitiful, but I'm not stupid. Because I promised the one boy who never disappoints me. "There was no way it was going to turn out the way I wanted it to."

"Too bad."

"Yeah."

We'd reached a parking lot. Alex stopped.

"You *drive* to school?" I demanded.

He gestured me ahead of him through the break in the chain fence. "We don't all live five blocks away," he shot back.

"It's eight, actually."

"Fine, eight. And sometimes I walk."

I pictured the stretch between Willing and Society Hill, where

I knew he lived somewhere near Sadie. It was quite a distance, and not a particularly scenic one, especially at seven thirty in the morning. "Yeah? When was the last time?"

He didn't answer immediately, leading the way now between the parked cars. He passed a big Jeep that still had its dealer plates, a low-slung two-door Lexus, and a slick black BMW that all looked like just the sort of cars he would own. "April of last year," he admitted finally. "But it pissed rain on me the whole time, so that's gotta count for something." He stopped by the dented passenger door of an old green Mustang. "Your carriage, my lady."

"Really? *This* is your car?"

The door made a very scary sound when he opened it. "It's clean," he snapped, and I realized he'd totally missed my point.

"It's amazing."

And it was. I know a whole lot of nothing about cars, but I do know that the saddest day of my father's life was the day he sold his 1972 Mustang to his nephew Paulie. He'd bought it from his own uncle, the original owner, and spent ten years of Saturday mornings vacuuming the floor and polishing the whitewalls.

There were pictures of him, full head of hair and huge smile, leaning on the racing-striped hood or beaming out from the driver's-side window. There was a photo of the back, "Just married" written in soap on the rear window, cans of ribbons trailing behind as it carried my parents to their honeymoon in Atlantic City. There are two or three of a fat, scowling baby Sienna strapped into the back. After that, all car pix are of the chain of Toyotas that came along in the wake of the Mustang.

Alex's was even older than Dad's had been, and in visibly rougher shape. But like he said, it was clean, and it was very, very cool.

I told him so. He beamed. Then ordered, "Seat belt!" as he stowed our bags in the backseat. I was trying. I'd already scanned the duct-tape-patched roof in vain. The clip was where I expected it to be, next to my left hip on the bench seat. Not so the other half. "Oh, yeah. I forgot to mention it's a lap belt."

He reached over me, his arm brushing against my chest, his hair just grazing my cheekbone as he pulled the belt from the crevice between the seat and the door. I caught my breath. And jumped a little when he shoved the pieces together with a loud click.

"Old parts," he apologized.

Quivery parts, I thought as my insides settled. Kinda.

"I found it online," he told me, patting the steering wheel with affection. It was hard plastic, with bumps for gripping. "It's a '68 GT Coupe, only two owners before me. I'm going to restore it over the summer."

"By yourself?"

"I wish. No, there's a guy in West Philly who specializes in vintage Fords. But I want to do some of it by myself. Whatever he'll teach me."

I thought about telling him about my dad and his '72. I didn't.

"Look." He tapped the odometer. "Only eighty-five thousand miles. And," he added with obvious pride, "it's an AM radio. *Just*

AM." He pushed one of the chipped buttons. We got an earful of static before he spun the dial. A fuzzy "Ain't Nothing Like the Real Thing" came through the speakers. It's one of Frankie's faves.

I sat back, wondering what Frankie would have to say about the car. He'd been uncustomarily reserved, if stinky, when I'd mentioned that the tutoring sessions would, in fact, happen, and at Alex's house, no less. "As long as the entire lacrosse team doesn't think they can get a date with you after . . ." was pretty much all he said on the matter. Sadie's input, after a long and heavy pause: "I think their house is an I. M. Pei." I'd promised to e-mail her if anything interesting happened. I'd told Frankie, "I'll make sure you're cc'd by the team."

There was a little pair of crossed lacrosse sticks dangling from Alex's rearview mirror. I tapped them, and they spun in a wobbly circle. "How's the season going?" I asked. It seemed a safe conversation: his sport.

"Okay. We're three and two so far. But Chase might be out for a few weeks. He has tendinosis."

"That's too bad," I muttered. As far as I was concerned, Chase Vere's continued absence from anywhere could only be a good thing.

Alex shot me a quick look, but didn't respond.

He drove the way he seemed to do everything: smoothly, confidently, with very little visible effort. We cruised up Broad Street, the rough asphalt vibrating up through my seat, the white stone walls of City Hall looming ahead. There's something pretty awesome about coming into Center City from South Philly, something impressive and encouraging and even beautiful.

There's a statue of William Penn, the state's founder, on top of City Hall. For a hundred years, nothing in the city could be built that was taller than Billy's hat. Then, one at a time, bigger buildings went up. Blue glass, black steel, arches and spires. But somehow, Billy is still visible from a dozen different angles, from all the way down in my neighborhood.

I waited as Alex turned right off of Broad Street. Every time Leo and his friends drive near the City Hall circle, they yell, "Boner!" It has to do with one of Billy's hands and how it looks when you see the statue from certain vantage points. Even Frankie has been known to salute the hand. I was thrilled when Alex didn't say anything.

We were heading east now. The big commercial buildings turned to smaller ones, then to houses only, and then to big houses. Alex steered the car down one narrow street, and then another, this one lined with tall brick walls and big wooden garage doors. He fiddled with the plastic box attached to his visor, and one of the doors slowly rolled open to reveal the Porsche I'd seen at the restaurant and enough empty space for the Mustang to pull in beside it.

"Dad's in D.C. all week," he said as we climbed out, "so I get to use the garage. Parking's a bitch around here."

I didn't know whether to roll my eyes or sympathize.

"Is your mom home?" I really didn't know how I felt about seeing Karina Romanova in her own home. Well, no.

Truth: I was worried how she would feel about seeing me in it.

"Will she mind my being here?"

"Why would she?" Alex gave me an odd look as he pushed open a small door onto a wide brick patio. "But no, she's at the studio until midnight. It's just you, me, and the lacrosse team."

I could see myself with amazing clarity in the huge glass wall that was the entire back of the house. I was small, dark, and frozen. "You're kidding, right?"

Next to mine, Alex's reflection looked twice as big and just as still. "*You're* kidding. Right?"

I nodded. Clearly not emphatically enough.

"Christ, Ella. Who do you think I am?"

I sighed. Honestly, I didn't know. "I think you're probably a terrific guy, Alex. But let's be truthful here. We don't really know each other."

"Oh, come on. We've gone to school together for two and a half years. I've been to Marino's . . ." He stopped. Sighed. "Okay. Fine. So let's change it. Now." And he unlocked the door to his house.

It was huge, even for the neighborhood. It was surprisingly modern, especially for the neighborhood, all cathedral ceilings and huge expanses of stone floor. Everything was steel and granite and glass. I recognized a Calder mobile, a dozen axe-blade-like black metal plates connected by silver wire, over the glossy white dining table. The chairs were Eames black plastic. When I looked past the dining room into the palatial living area, I saw a leather-and-steel sofa that probably had a twin in MoMA. It was a modern rich girl's dream, this place.

I didn't like it.

"Nice house," I said politely.

"Thanks," Alex said flatly, and led the way into the black-and-chrome kitchen. "Personally, I think it's like living on the set of *Alien*."

"Oh, no. It's not . . ." As I watched, he pressed a button on the front of the blindingly shiny fridge. A panel slid up, displaying four spigots. Alex lifted one eyebrow. "Oh."

"Yeah. You never know what's lurking. So, can I interest you in flat water, fizzy water, iced green tea, or Diet Coke? Or . . ." He opened the door with a flourish, showing a space that looked nearly as big as the walk-in at the restaurant. It was startlingly empty, except for . . . "Regular Coke, milk, soy milk, grape juice, lemon soda—Italian, I will add—and three types of champagne, which, much as I would like to offer them, are not for first dates, either."

I was more in my comfort zone here than he might have imagined. It looked very much like Sadie's mother's fridge, right down to the single nonfat yogurt, bottle of green olives, and unopened, foil-wrapped box of Belgian chocolate truffles that someone completely unclear on guest-of-the-pin-thin etiquette had brought as a gift.

I pointed to the lemon soda. "Smart girl," Alex said. He handed me the bottle, then reached into a nearby cabinet for two glasses. My heart stuttered twice, first when I nearly dropped one, it was so heavy, then again when I realized that a glass weighing that much cost more than my monthly allowance.

By the time I had everything gripped tightly, Alex had unearthed a bag of gourmet soy crisps from the very back of the tallest cupboard. "My mother resisting temptation," he said dryly. "Sorry. I ate all the Doritos."

"Not a prob." In my house, I have to stand on the top pad of the stepladder to get at the Doritos, Milanos, and peanut butter. *My* mother resisting temptation.

"Onward and upward." Backpacks and soy chips in hand, Alex headed toward the front of the house. It was eerily quiet, none of the usual street sounds you get living in the city. I could hear each little squeak of my Chucks on the marble floor. It was just a few degrees too cool, too. Like a museum.

I would have liked to have wandered a little, like in a museum. There were sculptures scattered through the downstairs, including a life-size reclining blob that I was dizzily certain had to be a Moore nude. There were paintings, too, that I'm sure were original and probably priceless, and probably by very famous contemporary artists. Not my forte.

We went up a huge flight of stairs, and another. And another. Alex opened a door to bright light, welcome warmth, and a very faint smell of socks. It was clearly his room.

Here, everything was colorful and a little untidy: the big, low bed, made but obviously hurriedly, a single sports shoe in the middle of the floor, unidentified papers and a few graphic novels scattered over the counter/desk that ran the entire length of one wall. There was a huge, built-in TV, and a small Bose cube holding an even smaller iPod. It was a rich boy's room. I liked it.

Alex shrugged out of his jacket and slung it onto the bed. When he reached for mine, I tried to remember if I'd taken the tampon out of the pocket. I could just imagine it winging across the room. But Alex hung the jacket carefully over the back of his desk chair.

"Okay. First things first. Three things you don't want me to know about you."

"What?" I gaped at him.

"You're the one who says we don't know each other. So let's cut to the chase."

Oh, but this was too easy:

1. I am wearing my oldest, ugliest underwear.
2. I think your girlfriend is evil and should be destroyed.
3. I am a lying, larcenous creature who talks to dead people and thinks she should be your girlfriend once the aforementioned one is out of the picture.

I figured that was just about everything. "I don't think so—"

"Doesn't have to be embarrassing or major," Alex interrupted me, "but it has to be something that costs a little to share." When I opened my mouth to object again, he pointed a long finger at the center of my chest. "You opened the box, Pandora. So sit."

There was a funny-shaped velour chair near my knees. I sat. The chair promptly molded itself to my butt. I assumed that meant it was expensive, and not dangerous. Alex flopped onto the bed, settling on his side with his elbow bent and his head propped on his hand.

"Can't you go first?" I asked.

"You opened the box . . ."

"Okay, okay. I'm thinking."

He gave me about thirty seconds. Then, "Time."

I took a breath. "I'm on full scholarship to Willing." One thing Truth or Dare has taught me is that you can't be too proud and still expect to get anything valuable out of the process.

"Next."

"I'm terrified of a lot of things, including lightning, driving a stick shift, and swimming in the ocean."

His expression didn't change at all. He just took in my answers. "Last one."

"I am not telling you about my underwear," I muttered.

He laughed. "I am sorry to hear that. Not even the color?"

I wanted to scowl. I couldn't. "No. But I will tell you that I like anchovies on my pizza."

"That's supposed to be consolation for withholding lingerie info?"

"Not my concern. But you tell me—is it something you would broadcast around the lunchroom?"

"Probably not," he agreed.

"Didn't think so." I settled back more deeply into my chair. It didn't escape my notice that, yet again, I was feeling very relaxed around this boy. Yet again, it didn't make me especially happy. "Your turn."

I thought about my promise to Frankie. I quietly hoped Alex would tell me something to make me like him even a little less.

He was ready. "I cried so much during my first time at camp that my parents had to come get me four days early."

I never went away to camp. It always seemed a little bit idyllic to me. "How old were you?"

"Six. Why?"

"*Why?*" I imagined a very small Alex in a Spider-Man shirt, cuddling the threadbare bunny now sitting on the shelf over his computer. I sighed. "Oh, no reason. Next."

"I hated *Titanic, The Notebook*, and *Twilight*."

"What did you think of *Ten Things I Hate About You?*"

"Hey," he snapped. "I didn't ask questions during your turn."

"No, you didn't," I agreed pleasantly. "Answer, please."

"Fine. I liked *Ten Things*. Satisfied?"

No, actually. "Alex," I said sadly, "either you are mind-bogglingly clueless about what I wouldn't want to know, or your next revelation is going to be that you have an unpleasant reaction to kryptonite."

He was looking at me like I'd spoken Swahili. "What are you talking about?"

Just call me Lois. I shook my head. "Never mind. Carry on."

"I have been known to dance in front of the mirror"—he cringed a little—"to 'Thriller.'"

And there it was. Alex now knew that I was a penniless coward with a penchant for stinky fish. I knew he was officially adorable.

He pushed himself up off his elbow and swung his legs around until he was sitting on the edge of the bed. "And on that humiliating note, I will now make you translate bathroom words into French." He picked up a sheaf of papers from the floor. "I have these worksheets. They're great for the irregular verbs . . ."

"Not today."

He shot me a look and kept shuffling papers.

"Okay," I said. *"D'accord. Pas de papiers aujourd'hui. S'il vous plaît, Alex. Je . . . je fais les choses la dernière fois."*

"Prochaine."

"What?"

"La prochaine fois," he corrected. "Next time. *Dernière fois* is 'last time.' I'm not even going to start on your verb usage."

"Right. *La dernière . . .* sorry . . . *prochaine fois.* How do you say 'I'm *begging* you'?"

"Je t'en supplie," he answered. Then, "You are aware that in order to speak better french, you actually have to speak French."

"Oui, monsieur. But the Eiffel Tower will still be standing next week, and french fries will still be American."

"Belgian." Alex sighed. "French fries started in Belgium. Look, I'm not going to force you to work. It's your choice and not my job."

"Next week," I promised. "I promise."

"Right." He rubbed the back of his head, pushing his hair into a funny little ducktail. "Okay, fine. How 'bout a movie?"

Worked for me. "Sure."

He got up, crossed the room, and slid open a drawer under the TV. Inside were maybe a hundred DVDs. I was impressed. Until he grunted, "Nope," and opened the drawer next to it, displaying another hundred. By then I was just resigned, and wriggled deeper into my seat to wait.

He found what he was looking for. I got a brief glimpse of the cardboard cover as he loaded the disk. It was unmistakable. "*Jurassic Park*? We're going to watch *Jurassic Park*?"

"Yup . . . in French."

A while later, while the awful lawyer ran from the T-rex into the Porta-Potty, his dubbed "*Aidez-moi! Aidez-moi!*" trailing behind him, Alex polished off the last tofu crisp and sighed happily. "I love this movie!"

I had to admit it, I did, too.

By the time it was over, I'd learned all the right words for all the dinosaurs (pretty much the same as they were in English), and multiple variations of "Help, for the love of God!," which might come in handy should I ever take up any of the activities that scared me most. It was also past five o'clock. Time to go. I extricated myself from the chair, leaving a distinctly Ella-shaped imprint, and retrieved my jacket.

I scanned the several closed doors on the room's periphery. "Um . . . bathroom?"

Alex pointed toward the stairs. "Next floor down, first guest room on the right." He gave me a brilliant smile. "My bathroom is strictly No Girls Allowed."

I wondered if he was lying, if Amanda got to use it.

I went downstairs into a magazine-perfect bathroom. I peed. I washed my hands and smelled the Diptyque fig candle. Twice. Sadie had bought me one once, lavender scented, after she'd caught me going back into her bathroom three times to smell hers. I was on my way out the door when I saw the sketch.

It was maybe eight inches square, in a carved gold frame. I'd seen ones like it before, in books and museums, quick studies for pleasure, or for bigger paintings. The Philadelphia Museum of Art has about a dozen on display. This one was a female nude, seen from behind, seated at what might have been a dressing table. She was brushing her long hair. It was clearly Edward's work, a model other than Diana. Diana was long and angular. This woman looked smaller; only her toes touched the floor under her padded stool. She was softer, too, rounder.

There was something written in pencil in the bottom corner, smudged and faded. I leaned in until my nose was almost pressed against the glass. *Narnia*, it looked like.

I must have stared for a lot longer than it seemed.

A tap on the door had me jumping. "Ella?" A second later. "Um . . . Ella? You okay in there?"

Alex looked red-faced and startled when I jerked the door open. Even more so when I grabbed his wrist with both of my hands and pulled him into the bathroom. Another time, I might have been equally red-faced. I would definitely have been uncomfortable, even if it wasn't in a bad way. But at the moment, I was too busy in a different part of my head.

I let go of him and pointed to the sketch. "That's a Willing."

"Is it?" He didn't look particularly impressed. More relieved that I hadn't fallen and hit my head or had some similar mishap.

"Edward Willing. You *have* to know who Edward Willing is."

He peered past me. "Philadelphia painter. Early twentieth century, right? I was in your art history class last year, you know."

I didn't. Not really. "You were?"

"I sat in back. You sat in front. Never saw your face during class, but I remember you arguing with Evers about Dalí. I remember. You don't like Dalí."

"Not much."

"You like this guy?"

"Yeah." I took a breath. "Yeah. I do. And you have one of his sketches. In your *guest bathroom*."

He caught on. At least as much as I could have expected him to. "Ella, my parents buy what their decorator tells them to buy, and they display it where she tells them to display it." He looked again. "This one might actually have come from my grandmother's house. Most of the older stuff did."

"Are there more of Edw—of Willing's pieces?" I was feeling giddy now.

Alex looked apologetic. "No. I'm pretty sure there aren't. But there's a Picasso in the living room. And a really, really small Matisse in the den." He held both hands out, like he was offering me . . . everything, maybe. "Look, I'll move this one now. I'll put it somewhere more visible . . ."

He actually reached for the frame. I stopped him. "No. You can't. But thanks."

"Sure."

It hit me, then, while he stared down at me with a slight frown. I was standing almost chest to chest with Alex Bainbridge in a very small space. I backed up a step and bumped into the toilet. "I should go," I said, a little shakily. "I should get home."

"Right." Always polite, he let me walk out first. "Next week . . . Next week, we can have our tutoring session in here. We'll discuss art. Or bathroom fixtures. You can sit up there"— he pointed to the counter— "next to the Willing."

Now, out of the bathroom, and a few feet away from him, I could laugh—"Okay. Before you start to think that I am obsessive and insane, there has to be something, the sight of *something,* that would make you go all goofy."

He didn't miss a beat. "Mademoiselle Winslow in a tutu. No . . ." He looked a little goofy when he said, "*Spider-Man versus Doctor Octopus.* July 1963."

"That's a comic book, right?"

He sighed. "Oh, Ella." Then, "Come on. I'll drive you home."

"You don't have to—"

"Yeah, I do."

The sun was setting as he pulled up in front of my house. There weren't any lights on there, but I could see into the restaurant. It was already busy; Sienna and Leo were both waiting tables.

I got out of the car and closed the door. Then I leaned back through the window. "Thanks for the ride. It was really nice of you."

"No worries. Since I'm down here, maybe I'll swing by Geno's for a cheesesteak." He shook his head. "You saw what was in my fridge."

"I did. Alex . . ."

I could ask. It would be so easy. A pizza, some of Nonna's fettuccine . . .

"I had a good time," I told him. *Coward*, I scolded myself. "I didn't expect to."

"Yeah, well, you can't beat a good raptor attack. Next time, before we get started, I'll show you my French comic book collection . . ." He wiggled his brows at me in perv fashion. "*Then* we'll work."

"Okay," I agreed. "Sounds good." I started up the sidewalk. Instead of going home, I'd decided to go over to Marino's. Offer to peel garlic or something. Dad would appreciate it.

"Hey, Ella."

I turned. "Yeah?"

"I'll see you tomorrow."

I must have looked blank.

"At the dance," he added.

"Oh. Yeah. See you tomorrow." I turned back toward the restaurant.

"Hey, Ella."

"Yeah?"

"*J'ai passé un très bon moment, aussi.*" When I just stared at him again, he snorted. "Work it out."

I did, but not before he'd driven away. He'd had a really good time, too.

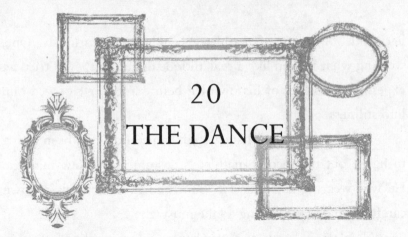

20
THE DANCE

The floor was full of crepe streamer seaweed and decomposing pirates. Or at least so it seemed. Half of the male population of Willing was out strutting its stuff in frilly shirts, head scarves, and gruesome makeup. Although, to be fair, some of the contorted faces had more to do with exertion than costume-store goop. Some boys need to concentrate really hard if they want to get their limbs to work with the music. It looked like "Thriller" meets *Titanic*.

Of course, the other half was blinding. As predicted, sequins reigned. Also as predicted, the costume of choice was some sort of skirt (the smaller the better) paired with a bikini top (ditto). As I watched from my seat at the edge of the gym, a mousy physics teacher dressed in a rotund foam sea-horse suit had a brief, finger-waggling argument with a mermaid over the size of her shells. I couldn't hear what they were saying, but the hand gestures said plenty. The teacher won; Shell Girl stalked off in a huff. She stopped halfway off the floor to do an angry, hokey-pokey leg shake to disentangle a length of paper seaweed from around her ankle. A group of mathletes watched her curiously. One, wearing what looked like a real antique diving suit, even tried an experimental shake of his own leg before another elbowed him into stillness.

"Teddy Roosevelt?" I suggested. Sadie and I had been trying to figure out the second mathlete's costume for a few minutes. He was wearing a 1930s-style suit, had his hair slicked down carefully, and was sporting a fake mustache.

"No glasses. And I can't even begin to imagine the connection between Davy Jones's Locker and Teddy Roosevelt." Sadie pulled a long gold hair from her pumpkin-orange punch and sighed.

Maybe her mother hadn't topped her Sleepy Hollow triumph, but it wasn't from lack of determination. What Mrs. Winslow hadn't achieved in creativity (she'd gone the mermaid route), she'd made up in the details. The tailed skirt was intricately beaded and embroidered in a dozen shades of blue and green. It was pretty amazing. The problem was the bodice: not a bikini, but not much better as far as Sadie was concerned. It was green, plunging, and edged with itchy-looking scallops. She was managing to stay covered by the wig, but that was an issue in itself. It was massive, made up of hundreds of trailing corkscrew curls in a metallic blonde. To top it all off, the costume included a glittering, three-point crown, and a six-foot trident, complete with jewels and trailing silk seaweed.

"Sadie," I'd asked quietly when she'd appeared at my house, shivering and tangled in her wig, "why don't you . . ." *Just tell her where she can shove her trident?* But that would just have been mean. Sadie gives in and wears the costumes because it's infinitely easier than fighting. ". . . come next door and we'll see if Sienna has a shawl you can borrow?"

Sienna has been a bridesmaid eleven times. She has a faux pashmina for every occasion. We left for the dance with Sadie wrapped in sparkly silver, Nonna waving from the front porch. Nonna likes Halloween, but draws the line at a costume, although she's been known to scare small children as she looms over them in her stark black, screeching at them to have some M&M's.

Within the hour, Sadie and I were settled at the edges of Willing's underwater paradise-slash-hell, watching the show and having a not-bad time. I was doing fine in my water goddess costume and Sadie was dealing. Unlike previous years, she looked more resigned than uncomfortable. To me, trident aside, she looked pretty great.

On seeing my costume, she had actually clapped her hands and shrieked. "Oh, Ella, you're gorgeous!"

When we'd met up with him in the school rose garden, Frankie had let out a low whistle. "Way to go, Marino."

I'd waved them both off, muttering, "It's just a dress." A dress made just for me by a loving, if deluded, fairy grandmother, and hair and makeup thanks to a painful hour at the hands of a determined sister.

"Sit still and stop with the whining already!" Sienna snarled as she twisted my hair into long, loose spirals and transferred the contents of a dozen bottles and tubes onto my face. "See?" she'd demanded at the end, dragging me in front of her big mirror. *"See?"*

It was just me. Only, even I had to admit, not quite. I looked softer, shinier, just a little bit luminous. Now, in the light of hundreds of fake ship's lanterns, I could still see the shimmer of whatever fragrant lotion Sienna had rubbed into my arms.

Twenty feet away, Frankie was writhing gracefully to the music, his bell-bottoms swinging with him. His date, dressed in a matching vintage sailor suit, wasn't quite as graceful, but he was just as pretty. "Naval surplus," Frankie had explained the uniforms on arrival. "We're 'Don't Ask' . . ."

"'Don't Tell.'" Connor finished. He seemed okay. He didn't say much: "Don't Tell" personified. But he clearly liked to dance, seemed to like Frankie, and had complimented Sadie on her shoes, which were fish-scale-sequined Jimmy Choo (Frankie ID'd them in a heartbeat) flats, and very cool.

"Maybe a young Jacques Cousteau . . . ?" Sadie was still working on the boy in the suit. "But that would just be silly. I mean, a suit . . . ? Oh. No."

Apparently our scrutiny hadn't gone unnoticed. Teddy-Jacques-Whoever was bearing down on us, smiling broadly under the mustache that, I noticed, was coming loose at one corner.

"Good evening, ladies!"

He was a senior, I thought. We didn't have any classes together; he was AP everything, but I thought I remembered seeing him during Performance Night in the spring, part of a co-ed a cappella group. They'd done a Black Eyed Peas song—

pretty well, too. He was cute, too, in a pale, lanky way.

"Walter Elias Disney," he said with a bow. "At your disposal."

"Walt Disney?" Sadie was obviously too intrigued to be shy. "Um . . . ?"

He grinned and waved his arm at the spectacle behind him with a flourish. "The myriad talents of Johnny Depp aside, it is debatable whether any of this would have come about without me. It seemed only appropriate that I should make an appearance."

I nodded. "I'll buy that."

He bowed again, but his eyes stayed on Sadie. "Would you care to dance?"

"Oh. I . . . Oh." Several emotions flooded her face in an instant: terror, pleasure, uncertainty, and why-the-hell-not. She darted a glance at me. I gave a quick, emphatic nod. I would be fine. She absolutely should dance. "Sure," she said.

And off they went.

I watched for a few minutes. Sadie did well, despite the heavy skirt. She watches *Dancing with the Stars* religiously. Walt wasn't bad, either, not too much flailing. He said something that made her laugh. She looked terrific. Nearby, Frankie and Connor were doing a decent version of the sixties "Swim." I scanned the sea of undulating limbs and happy faces for, well, anything interesting.

It didn't take long. The Phillites were in the middle of the dance floor, a happy group of shiny hair, flashing teeth, and skin on display. The girls were all in embellished bikini tops and shimmery skirts. The guys wore loose white shirts open to a point that would have been laughable any other time, but seemed roguishly appropriate now. I saw Anna and Hannah, in crimson and aqua, then Chase, who was wearing an eye patch and flashing a gold earring. It wasn't hard to find Alex; he was the tallest of his crowd. I got a glimpse of white shirt and square jaw, but he was facing mostly away from me. I couldn't see Amanda at all.

I got up. A couple of skinny pirates were eyeing me speculatively. A wallflower, especially without a wall, was an easy target. Trying to look like I had a destination, I skirted the floor. I thought I might do a slow circuit, then come back and dance for a few minutes with Frankie and Connor. I knew Frankie would be delighted; he likes seeing me dance in much the same way he enjoys sending me up trees.

I'd done a quarter round when I came up against a knot of Bee boys. I tried to get around them but found myself tangled in one's octopus costume. My "Um. Excuse me?" got precisely no response. It didn't take long to find out why. Amanda Alstead was in their direct line of vision.

She was doing the universal dance of confident girls: arms clasped overhead, eyes closed, hips swaying to whatever the beat of the moment was. This was midtempo, not so slow as to allow for in-your-face sexiness, but slow enough to get a good roll. Her uplifted arms had her shells doing their own dance.

It was certainly mesmerizing. I watched for a minute, wondering if I would ever have the guts to move like that in front of one person, let alone several hundred. I wondered if I even had the ability. She looked like a silk ribbon on ball bearings.

When my ego couldn't stand it any longer, I looked past her.

There, of course, was Alex. He wasn't watching Amanda. He was looking over her head, his bored gaze skimming over the room. Before I could turn away, it had found mine. He didn't smile; he certainly didn't wave. But he didn't look away. And I had absolutely no idea what to do.

"Hey, Ella!"

Someone jostled me from behind. I turned to find myself face-to-Willing-mascot. The track jersey sported a familiar stylized bee. We are the Willing Hornets, but the image didn't change when the name did (until the arrival of boys, Willing teams were, believe it or not, the Buzzies); it was engraved on too many surfaces. This one had been provided with an inked diving helmet and flippers. The rest of the ensemble included a snorkeling mask, a pair of shiny running tights, and the pièce de résistance: a sequined jock-strap. Inside it all was Cat Vernon. I laughed. I couldn't help it.

"Pretty clever, huh?" She grinned. "The contents of Davy Jones's Locker." Behind her, a couple of her friends were similarly attired. They all looked cheerful and relaxed. "What are you doing wandering? Come on. Let's dance."

She pulled the mask down over her eyes and linked her arm through mine. Then, gently but firmly pushing aside the still-gasping boys, she pulled me into the middle of the floor, into a knot of gyrating seniors. There was a girl pirate and a boy dressed as Neptune, but not a mermaid among them.

I danced. I turned my back to Amanda and did my own arms-half-up wiggle. I even shimmied for a minute with a cute senior dressed like a lobster. Cat's crowd was loud and lively, and no one looked at me like I didn't belong right where I was. By the time the third dance was over, I was giddy and a little sweaty. Everyone else in the knot jumped right into the next song; Neptune was pogoing for all he was worth. I waved good-bye to Cat and slipped from the dance floor.

As I made my way toward the side door, I saw Frankie and Connor, now doing a synchronized brim-tapping, foot-scuffing sailor dance. They had an appreciative audience. Beyond them, Sadie was still with Walt. It seemed absolutely the right time to disappear for a little while. I was feeling the urge.

I knew most of the classrooms would be locked, either from the outside by suspicious teachers or from the inside by single-minded couples. There was no way Ms. Evers would leave the art room open. Available paint was just too much of a temptation for mischief, even on a night that didn't include Halloween pranks. For that reason, when she wasn't around, the room was closed up tight, and locked. For that reason, she told a select few students where a key was hidden. I was one of the few.

Five minutes later, armed with a fresh sketch pad and a handful of charcoal pencils, I was on my way out a side door and onto the brick patio that ran the southern length of the building. It overlooked the gardens. In the moonlight, the shadowed balustrades and ornamental urns took on new and interesting shapes. I settled myself on a stone step and began to draw. As the minutes passed, strange and satisfying images took shape: the curve of a fin in empty air, posts that looked like teeth . . .

"I was wondering where the real party was."

I jumped, sending my pencil in a sharp line across the page. Alex was standing two feet away, one booted foot on my step, hands thrust into the pockets of what looked too much like Emo pants: black and tight.

"Sorry," he said. "I didn't mean to surprise you."

"You didn't surprise me," I gasped, left hand plastered to my chest. "You scared the crap out of me. Who raised you? Wolves?"

He actually grinned. "You've met my parents. What do you think?"

I wasn't going to touch that one. I just shrugged.

"Why aren't you inside?" he asked after a few seconds.

"It was too hot," I lied, closing my sketchbook as casually as I could. "Oppressive. Why aren't you?"

"It was too . . . God, I don't know. Oppressive's a good word. Some fresh air seemed like a good idea."

I looked past him, relieved not to see anyone else there. "All by yourself? That's . . . bold."

His brows went up. For a second, I thought he was going to turn around and leave. Instead, he took his hands out of his pockets and pointed at my step. "Big words for a small person. Can I sit down?"

I swallowed. "Sure."

He did, ending up with his elbows resting on his thighs and his right knee not quite touching mine.

The silence went on just long enough to make it uncomfortable. But I wasn't going to help him with his small talk. I'm not very good at it in the best of circumstances. Sitting almost thigh to thigh with a guy who turned me into a mental pretzel was nowhere near a good circumstance.

"So . . . Quite a scene in there tonight." He jerked his chin toward the open patio doors. The music was just loud enough that I could hear the lead singer mangling the words of "Beyond the Sea." The original is one of Frankie's faves. I guessed he was probably entwined with Connor at the moment, in slow-dancing ecstasy. Which was good for several reasons, including the one about how much snark he would give me if he caught me chatting away with Alex Bainbridge.

"Yup," I agreed.

"Typical Willing."

"It is."

"Well," he asked, "whaddya expect?"

It was so obviously a rhetorical question that of course I answered it. My truth impulse seemed stronger around this boy, my impulse control way under par.

"I would expect you to be dancing."

His expression was unreadable in the limited light. "Is that an invitation?"

"No. An observation."

He shrugged. "Okay. I needed a break. It was either keep an eye on Chase while he pukes up a fifth of cheap rum in the guys' bathroom or follow the girls into the ladies' room."

I almost smiled and told him about Willing's bathrooms and me. Instead, some truly horrific and irresistible impulse had me announcing, "Amanda looks really pretty tonight."

"So do you."

Bizarrely, I felt my breath catch in my chest, and for a long, awful second, I thought I might cry. I gripped the top of my pad tightly, concentrated on the spiral metal binding where it dug into my skin.

"It's a cool costume," he said. "Water nymph?"

"Sea goddess," I answered quietly. "Roman."

"Hmm." Alex was staring out toward the garden now, looking so at ease that I went from pretzel to knot. Could it really be that easy for him? To say things like he did without thinking? Without meaning anything at all? "Too many mermaids tonight. Not that I have anything against mermaids. Mermaids are hot. I mean, you saw my drawing."

I nodded.

"You know," he went on, "that day in the hall, you compared my stuff to two Japanese artists—"

I nodded again, even though he was looking out into the darkened gardens now and not at me. "Suzuki Harunobu and Utagawa Kuniyoshi. They were eighteenth- and nineteenth-century woodblock print masters—"

"Ella," he interrupted. "I know who they are."

"Oh."

"In fact, I have a couple original Kuniyoshi prints."

"Oh. Wow. *Wow.*"

He shrugged. "They're not that rare. What I'm really hoping to get is one of his *Princess Tamatori* series. Do you know it?" When I shook my head, he explained, "You know he did all these illustrations for books and folktales. Right? Some like cartoons or graphic novels. Princess Tamatori sets off to recover this massive pearl from the Dragon King underwater. She has to fight him and all these crazy creatures on her way back. So I had this idea for a graphic novel about . . ." His voice trailed off.

"A mermaid," I finished for him.

"Yeah."

Neither of us said anything for a minute. Then, "Your drawings are really, really good," I said softly. "You should do that book."

He grunted. "You ever hear of a rich graphic novelist?"

"You ever hear of a happy lawyer?" I shot back, less surprised at myself than amused by just how much of Frankie and Sadie had rubbed off on me in two years. I didn't say, "You're already rich," which would have been too much Frankie and no Sadie whatsoever.

"Who knows?" Alex sighed, and I let that rhetorical question go. From inside, I could hear the opening notes of "Come Sail Away." "Why is it," he asked after a few bars, "that they always play these schizo songs at dances? They start out slow, so you're all psyched, then get fast halfway through, so you end up feeling like a total idiot, trying to decide what to do. One person always chooses to keep doing the slow thing—"

"And the other one jumps back and starts boogying."

"Exactly! You've been there," he said, smiling. I wasn't about to mention that *there* for me had always been the wallflower seat. "My dad loves this song."

It was my turn to smile. "So does mine."

"So . . ."

"So?"

He bumped my knee with his. "Wanna dance?"

"You're kidding, right?"

Even in the limited light, he looked offended. "I am not." In a second, he'd levered himself off the step. "C'mon. We'll dance fast at the beginning and slow when the music speeds up."

"Slow . . ." I was totally distracted by the image of the two of us on the floor.

Not, apparently, for the same reasons he was. "I'll do a Quasimodo," he offered, bending and twisting *à la* the Hunchback so he was closer to my height. "C'mon, Ella. It's just a dance."

"Okay." This time, I got it right. With my butt still firmly planted on the step, I reached up and took his hand. I didn't yank mine back, either, once I was upright. In fact, I held on to him for what was probably a beat too long; he was the one to let go.

I'm not sure why I thought it might actually happen. It was probably the whole Japanese woodblock/graphic novel thing. He had me at Kuniyoshi.

We only got as far as the hallway inside the door.

"Yo, dawg!" We both turned. Chase Vere was walking toward us, weaving a little and grinning. "Where were you? I just did some serious Technicolor spewing."

"Good for you," Alex answered. He thrust a protective arm in front of me as Chase came to a lurching halt a foot away. I got a faint whiff of alcohol and something even less pleasant.

"Oh. Hey." Chase squinted at me. "Her."

"Ella," Alex said tightly. "Her name is Ella."

"Okay, sure. Ella." Chase nodded. This time, his unfocused gaze did a slow roam from my head to my toes. It came back to rest on my breasts, which, I discovered, was in no way preferable to my scar. "She looks hot."

"Jesus, Vere—"

Whatever else Alex was going to say was lost as Chase did a slightly wobbly pivot and yelled back down the hall. "I found him! With the weird girl. Only she's hot tonight."

"Vere, you jackass." Alex turned to me. "I'm really sorry. He's wasted."

"It's okay. I'll just go. Now." I'd seen them; Alex hadn't because he was facing me. The Hannandas had rounded the corner and were on their way toward us, a fierce trio wearing pretty sequins and ugly expressions.

"What is going on?" Amanda demanded, eyes blazing from Alex to me and back.

"Nothing," I answered automatically, knowing even as the words left my mouth that I probably shouldn't have said anything at all.

For all the times I'd played and replayed the lunchtime hall scene in my head, for all the times I'd imagined how it might have been if Alex hadn't ignored me, if he'd stopped and said hello, or even just acknowledged my existence, I cringed when he announced, "Ella and I were on our way back into the dance."

He didn't even have to say that we were actually planning on dancing. Amanda's eyebrows shot up; her nostrils flared. For an instant, she looked like a really angry sea horse.

"Who'd'a thought she had such a sweet little bod? Cover the bad part; I'd do her," Chase mumbled. Then, almost in the same breath, "Oh, man. I'm gonna hurl again."

"I hope it hurts," Alex muttered, even as he was moving, shoving Chase quickly and efficiently toward the garden door. "Not here, you dipshit." They disappeared into the shadows. A moment later, the unmistakable sounds of retching filtered through the music.

I started to creep away. I didn't get the chance. Amanda stalked toward me, eyes narrowed, effectively pinning me to the wall. Anna and Hannah lockstepped behind her. I thought of jackals, watching the kill. Amanda stopped a few inches from me. She was just tall enough to loom.

"Look, Freddy Krueger, if I thought there was a chance in a gazillion that Alex would even feature you in a nightmare, I might not be saying this so nicely. But I feel sorry for you, so I'm going to give you a tip." The *p* was sharp, harsh. She leaned in, close enough that I could see the pale, shimmery lipstick caked in the corners of her mouth. "This thing you have for him just makes you look like the world's most pitiful loser. Did you really think you had even the smallest chance with him? Did you?"

I didn't answer. Maybe a no would have satisfied her. Maybe not.

"You are a skank and a freak," she snapped, the hard sounds

making me flinch. "You don't belong here. Go back to your greaseball 'hood. The sight of you makes me sick!"

Any girl who has ever been face-to-face with another angry girl, especially one with infinitely more spite and social standing, knows to run. It's innate, from bunnies to baboons. Don't mess with the alpha female. She'll tear your throat out. So I ran, but not before I got a glimpse of Anna's face.

In the second before she turned away, she looked like someone had slapped her. Funny, seeing that didn't make me feel any better.

I hit the dance floor just as the song tempo changed. Around me, couples faltered, clearly caught in that slow/fast dilemma. I found Frankie and Connor easily. They were a solid white column in the middle of the floor, wrapped around each other and barely moving. I tapped Frankie on the shoulder.

"I'm going," I told him.

"What? Why?"

But I was already walking away. "Make sure Sadie gets home," I called over my shoulder.

He caught up with me quickly. "Hey. What happened?" he demanded, fingers finding mine and pulling me to a stop.

"Nothing." When he narrowed his eyes at me, I sighed. "Hannandas. Nothing major. I just want to go."

"We'll go, too," he declared. "We'll walk you home then come back for Sadie." He jerked his chin toward the sidelines. She was sitting with Walt and his friends. They were laughing. "You cannot walk home alone."

I snorted. "It's Halloween in South Philly. The streets are full of little ghouls and their parents." I remembered being maybe eight, in a nylon fairy costume, walking next to Annamaria Lombardi in her equally flammable princess dress, our mothers following ten feet behind, chatting like they'd known each other all their lives, because they had. "If I get attacked, it will be by a pack of small goblins looking for a candy fix."

For a second, I thought Frankie was going to argue. Then he shrugged. "Fine. Call me when you get home."

I went before he could change his mind. Behind me, I thought I heard someone call my name. I didn't stop. Once on the street, I gathered up my skirts and ran, barely pausing at intersections to look for cars. Even at this hour, there were trick-or-treaters still out. I dodged a few ghosts, sidestepped chattering moms, and was home in a matter of minutes. The house was dark, the porch light off. I figured Nonna had left her post to go over to the restaurant. It was a Saturday; they would need her in the kitchen.

I didn't turn on any lights in the house. My bedroom window is visible from both the kitchen and the restaurant office. I figured my parents were there, and I didn't want them to know I was home already. Their disappointment would be tangible.

I kicked off my shoes and reached for the tie at my waist. But I didn't undo the knot. Instead, I sat down at my desk, still fully dressed. My cell phone was there. I had a message.

It was Sadie, yelling against the music. "Where did you go? I looked . . . thought I saw . . ." Whatever she said next was lost." . . . want me to leave, it's fine. Jared wants . . . outside. Call me!"

I didn't. I didn't call Frankie, either. I texted him. I didn't think he would complain about the charge. *Got home OK,* I typed. *Tell Sadie. XO.*

XOOXOOXOOX, he sent back.

I turned off my phone. Above me, Edward was staring out of his card, expression unreadable in the dark.

"An excellent young man, your Frankie," he said.

"Yup. He is." Exhausted suddenly, I folded my arms on the desk and dropped my head onto them.

"Oh, Ella. I wish you'd had a better time at the ball."

"Fuhgeddaboudit," I muttered. *Greaseball. Freddy. Freak.* "It's not like she and I were ever going to be BFFs."

"I wasn't just referring to Amanda."

Of course he wasn't.

"I'll try," I moaned into the crook of my elbow. "'Oh, Lord, I'll try to carry on.'"

"That sounds rather dramatic, even for you."

"It's Styx," I told him. "After your time, before mine. I don't know all the words, but those work for the moment. And for the record, I'm being ironic, not dramatic."

"If you say so."

I ignored him. "I have had my last flutter over Alex Bainbridge. I mean it. Frankie was right. How many signs do I need that we are never, ever going to have . . . anything . . . before I get it? Obviously, it doesn't matter that we relate to the same schizo seventies songs. Or that we can discuss antique Japanese woodblock prints. Or that when he sits next to me, he kinda takes my breath away. You would think that would count for a lot, wouldn't you?"

Edward gets the concept of rhetorical questions, so I went on. "I wouldn't even want to hazard a guess about what makes Amanda's pulse go all skittery, but I would bet anything it's not Alex. And he's still with her. He doesn't belong with her, but apparently he feels he belongs *to* her. Explain that, please."

"Oh, Ella. We men are not always the best at looking beyond the . . . er . . ."

"Boobs, Edward. You can say it. Amanda Alstead is all boobs and blonde hair. Beyond that, I can't see a single thing that's special about her."

"Because there isn't a single thing. Beyond the . . . er, obvious. You, on the other hand, are a creature of infinite charms. Shall I list them alphabetically or from the top down?"

I scowled up at him. "Y'know, you are beginning to sound a little too much like Frankie and Sadie, my deluded Greek chorus."

"Yes, well, I rather thought that's what friends were for."

"You're not supposed to be my friend," I muttered. "You're supposed to be my Prince Charming."

"Ahem." Edward's sculpted lips compressed into a grim line. "Have you looked at me lately? I am *supposed* to be startling and even a bit scary."

"Nope. Neither." I rested my chin on my forearm. "To me, you are perfect. You are loyal and reliable and completely lacking in surprises."

"That is a good thing?"

"Absolutely," I said. "It's an excellent thing. I don't want any more surprises, ever."

"Hardly an admirable goal, that."

"Maybe not," I agreed, "but pleasant. Among all the other bizarreness tonight, I found something new to be afraid of. Evil girlfriends."

"Now, Ella. You can't go on being afraid forever."

"Oh, yes, I can. As far as Amanda Alstead is concerned, I can."

Edward tilted his head and studied me for a moment. He looked annoyed. "Why do you insist on having these conversations with me when you ignore everything I have to say?"

It was a pretty good question. "Fine." I sat up straight and folded my hands in my lap. Home Truth time. "Go ahead. On this night when we celebrate the mysteries of life and death . . . Say something profound, something startling."

There was a long silence. Then, "Boo," Edward said.

"Thank you, Mr. Willing."

"Don't mention it, Miss Marino. I am yours to command."

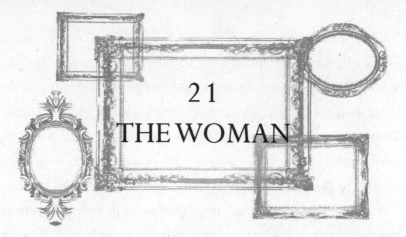

21
THE WOMAN

I decided the Monday after Halloween would be a very good day to cut classes. Not all of them. That would have provoked a call home, and I just didn't feel like explaining to my parents why I preferred not to go to Mr. Stone's English class with Chase and the Hannandas ever again. So I went to history, where I paid a little attention, French, where I paid none, and then to art.

I convinced Ms. Evers that I (a) would benefit from outside time, and (b) should be excused from all further classes because I was running out of time at the archive and I needed to be there ASAP. I have no idea if she believed me. She wrote me a note anyway.

So, long before the lunch bell rang and any possible encounter with Alex or Amanda, I was on my way to the Sheridan-Brown. I could have gone shopping; I could have gone home. I could have gone anywhere. But without Sadie or Frankie, it was all similarly uninspiring. Besides, we'd spent all of Sunday together, drinking too much coffee at Java Company and eating contraband Cinnabons in Sadie's room.

My sudden departure from the dance had taken surprisingly little explaining. A bent-truth tale of an Alex encounter in the hall, a brief recap of Scary Amanda's psycho-bitch moment, and the suggestion that Chase Vere is subhuman, and they left me alone. Probably they wouldn't have, ordinarily, but they took me at my I-don't-want-to-talk-about-it. Possibly because there were other matters to discuss. Frankie needed to analyze the end of his date. ("If he only kissed me once, does that mean he's seeing someone else?" "Is 'dinner with Grandma' code for something?" "Do you think his teeth are too shiny?") Sadie thought she might kinda, possibly, but no, really probably not have had a very nice time with Jared-the-Walt, and wouldn't mind it if he called but couldn't possibly, absolutely not, no way could she call him. All of which effectively kept the attention off me.

I was still suffering very slightly from that fourth Cinnabon as I took the elevator up to the archive floor. I could have gone home to a bottle of ginger ale and an afternoon of TV talk shows. Inevitably, at least one would have been about Girls Who Love Dead Guys or Live Guys Whose Girlfriends Would Like Them to Be Dead. There always is. But for all my faults, I'm not lazy. My term project on Edward was barely a blot on paper, and December was coming faster than it should. I wanted to have a really complete outline done before winter break. So far I had half a title: *Ravaged Man: Edward Willing (something something Diana something)*. I figured I had plenty of time to work on that part.

I heard the music when I was still only halfway down the

third-floor corridor. It was faint, but not so faint that I couldn't make out a wild drumbeat and a series of screams. Some, I thought, were guitars, the others human. I tried to walk quietly in order to hear. I didn't think I was getting the lyrics quite right.

"*Under armadillo, we are green . . . Under armadillo, we scream.*"

Words aside, it wasn't bad. I could imagine Cat Vernon and her friends dancing to it in a club. A little Red Bull, an earnest but mediocre opening band, and this could even seem pretty good. It got louder the farther down the hall I went. I kept following, not quite believing the evidence, but knowing there wasn't really an alternative.

Maxine's office door was open partway. Through it, I could hear the music (*"Kick me in a hairy pot"*) and see her sitting behind her desk. Today she was wearing a pair of thick-framed black glasses with dramatically sharp corners. I stood in the doorway, uncertain whether to knock. I waited. I was too curious about the lyrics.

"*. . . under armadillo, feed me the rubber boots. Whenever you kick me, I know we're green roots . . .*"

I gave up and knocked on the doorframe. She gave a visible start, then slapped at a button on her keyboard. The music cut off mid-armadillo. "Oh," she said on seeing me. "Ella."

"Hi," I offered, then waited, face turned slightly toward her computer.

It didn't take long. "My son's band," Maxine said stiffly. "They're called Genghis Khan's Marmot."

Oh. I'd actually heard of them, which said something. "I've heard of them," I told her. "And I'm pretty clueless when it comes to local music. The people in the know at Willing think they're great."

"Really?" For an instant, her face lit with pleasure and, I thought, pride. "They've had some interest from a couple of indie labels. Of course, it's a rough business, the recording industry."

I figured anything Maxine Rothaus called rough was, in fact, vicious and lawless and inclined to eat its own young. "They'll get a deal," I said. "It's just the sort of stuff my generation wants to listen to."

Like I knew anything about that. But it seemed just the sort of assurance her generation would swallow.

She hit another button with a flourish. "Give me your e-mail address. I'll send you their demo file."

I did. She even hummed a little as she typed. When she was done, she folded her hands on her desk and looked at me almost pleasantly over her glasses. "So, what do you hope to find today, and is there any way I can help in the next three minutes? I have a conference call with Berlin. They have an original Man Ray photograph they might consider selling us."

I thought of spiky irons and disembodied eyes. "Doesn't seem like your . . ."

"Bailiwick? Territory? Thing?"

Actually, it seemed exactly her thing. "I was going to say niche."

She shrugged. "Man Ray was from Philadelphia. Plus, I speak

more German than the Dada curator. So . . . your plans?"

I didn't really have any. I didn't think I should mention that. I figured Maxine probably had bathroom trips preplanned and efficiently choreographed. "I'll go through the files one more time in case there's something I missed. Unless there's more . . ." I said hopefully.

She smiled slightly, but shook her head. "Even if I had the time and desire to take you downstairs, nothing I could show you would be of much use. His niece put most of what we have into that ghastly book of hers, and trust me when I tell you that there's a reason the rest never was published. Deadly dull." She almost sounded apologetic when she said, "I can't let you handle the Cézanne letters. Besides, they're in French, which you've told me you don't speak. Most of the Wharton letters are in French, too, although I wouldn't show you those even if I could."

"Too racy?" I asked.

She snorted. "Too asinine. For being such a brilliant woman in all other respects, apparently, she was completely flummoxed by sex. When she wrote about it, it was either all buttoned up or completely, pardon the expression, screwy. Between you and me, the letters to Willing are just sloppy and boring. The spicy bits read like old *Cosmopolitan*s now. The rest is just simpering and scolding him for not writing in kind."

"Of course he didn't. He loved Diana."

Maxine swept a shred of paper from her desk with a quick backhand. "Oh, for heaven's sake." She huffed out a breath. "The heart of the teenager." She reached into her desk drawer and pulled out a single key attached to a ruler-size wooden strip with a jump ring. She slid it across the desk to me.

Hand-printed along the wood was "I SHALL WRING HIS NECK LIKE A GOOSE. —*Tomb Curse, Egyptian 6th Dynasty*."

"Bring that back when you're ready to leave." I thought I might have seen a ghost of a smile as she added, "Don't lose it!" Then she turned back to her computer screen, as clear a dismissal as could be.

I didn't pull her door shut all the way behind me. I stood in the hall for a minute, waiting. The music didn't come back on.

I let myself into the archive room and carefully balanced the key over the door handle. Then I weighed my options. I'd pretty much expended the file cabinets. Not that I didn't enjoy the tailors' bills, but they wouldn't tell me anything I didn't already know.

An hour later, proven absolutely right, I slid the last drawer closed, sat on the dusty floor, and had a good, sorry-for-myself "what now?" moment. My eyes fell on the bookshelves. I wasn't optimistic, but I had time on my hands and nowhere else I especially wanted to be.

I decided to be bold, splash out, cross a line. I would start from the bottom right this time. Most of the books there, I discovered quickly, were just like the ones on the upper left: old, obscure, and uninspiring. *Heat and Light: An Elementary Textbook, Theoretical and Practical.* Goethe's *Theory of Colours. Instructive Rambles Extended in London and the Adjacent Villages, Designed to Amuse the Mind and Improve the Understanding of Youth.*

Occasionally, I am convinced that the amount of my brain over which I have control could fit into a pistachio shell. Taking its cue from no message I was sending, it led my eyes right to the faded, green leather spine of *The Flora of St. Croix and the Virgin Islands* by Heinrich-Franz-frigging-Alexander. Then to *Love, from the French,* followed by *The Romances of Alexandre Dumas.*

Okay, so I was feeling grouchy and a little sad, but I figured I could at least take a gentle flip through that one. Who doesn't like a good musketeer or three? The book was sandwiched firmly between *Analytic Keys to the Genera and Species of North American Mosses,* and the *Complete English–Russian Dictionary* by A. Alexandrow, which had me actually speculating on just what terrible crimes I might have committed against love and peace in a former life to have earned myself this one.

I reached for the Dumas. As I started to pull it out, my watch caught on the frayed binding of the Alexandrow dictionary. Before I could catch it, it had tipped from the shelf, landing at my feet with a crash that sounded like it could have been made by a cannonball. My heart gave a lurch; the spine had cracked. I had broken one of Edward's books. I started to bend, then froze, certain I'd heard the clack of heels in the hallway. He would forgive me; Maxine, I was sure, wouldn't. But it was only the nymph clock, sounding abnormally loud in the still air.

The scene was eerily familiar: a heavy book tented on the floor, a few loose papers underneath. One small one had landed upside down a foot away. Its edges were deckled, raw like an old novel. I scooped up the book first, with the loose sheets under it. When I went back for the smaller paper, I realized it was a photograph. I turned it over and felt my pulse skitter.

It was Edward. Not young, but still beautiful, his hair thick and wavy, his jaw firm. He was sitting on the ground on a cloth in some sort of park or garden; I could see what looked like a row of peony bushes behind him. He was in shirtsleeves, an arm resting on his bent knee, the other leg stretched out in front of him. He was smiling. But not at the camera. I followed his gaze to the figure next to him.

It was a woman, dressed in the pleated blouse and flowing skirt of the first decade of the twentieth century. Even seated, I could tell she had a nice rounded shape, curved like a violin. Like a Man Ray photo. The woman's face was completely hidden by the wide brim and feathery spray of her hat. I could see part of a knot of pale hair. It was impossible to tell for certain in black and white, but I assumed she was blonde, rather than white-haired. Edward's blond hair had the same glowy look.

So did his face. Even in profile, I could read the expression. It was happiness, adoration. I knew him. I'd seen dozens and dozens of photographs, spanning his life. I'd seen the almost goofy joy in his engagement picture. The young, arrogant pride in the formal wedding portrait. I knew how he looked beside Diana on the gangplank of a yacht bound for the Caribbean, how he looked at her in the garden of Cézanne's Aix-en-Provence house. This photo wasn't of that garden.

This photo wasn't of Diana, either, whose hair had been the shiny dark auburn of wet autumn leaves.

I might have stood there for a very long time, picture of the other woman Edward had clearly loved gripped in my fingers. But the dictionary got heavy fast in my other hand. I knew what I should do. No question, the right thing was to tuck everything back inside the book and hand it over to Maxine with an apology and an "Isn't this *amazing*?"

I sat down on the floor again. There were three folded sheets of paper that I'd picked up with the book. I didn't open any of them at first. Instead, I carefully checked for anything else that might be tucked inside, no mean feat, considering the dictionary had several hundred onionskin pages. Finally, heart still going a little too fast, I unfolded the first sheet.

There were five words there, in familiar handwriting:

My Dear, I must express

He got a little further on the second sheet:

Dearest, How confounding I find to be at any loss for words. The importance of secrecy

The last one just said:

I dream, Dorogaya

I looked toward the door I had closed behind me, the curse-bearing key still balanced on the handle. I wondered if Maxine was in her office. I slowly got to my feet. Then I tucked the dictionary back onto the shelf, right where it had been.

I put the photograph and the aborted letters into my bag.

Heart hammering so loudly now that I thought it had to be audible, I headed out of the archive. I allowed myself a shaky sigh of relief when I saw that the pebbled glass on Maxine's door was dark, no light shining behind it. I knocked anyway. When I didn't get an answer, I pushed the key under the door. She would get it when she was done with Man Ray.

Then I walked, stiff but not too fast, down the hall, into the elevator, and past the security desk, where the guard barely even looked up.

The house was empty when I got home. I still shut my bedroom door behind me. Then I made my shaky way over to my desk. The pad I'd taken from the art room Saturday night was there. Opening it, I chose the most complete sketch: the urn base that, in the dark, had taken on the shape of a sea creature, the half-fish, half-mythological beasts that had been so popular on sixteenth-century maps of the world. Cartographers had marked the waters where they were with the words *Here Be Monsters*. I tore out the drawing and tacked it to the wall above Edward, covering his image. I couldn't face him yet.

I completely ignored the faint protest. "Now, Ella. You don't know the whole story . . . Diana was gone . . . 'The heart will go on.'"

I gagged inside my head at that one. Hate that song.

I lowered my bag, with its incriminating contents, to the floor and myself into my chair. On autopilot, I turned on my laptop, opened my mail folder. There were three new e-mails. One informed me that I had two million dollars waiting for me in a Bulgarian bank. All I had to do to claim it was e-mail my full name and address, along with my savings account and Social Security numbers, within the next twenty-four hours.

The next was from Frankie to me, Sadie, and an unfamiliar address I was afraid might be Connor's.

From: fhobbes@thewillingschool.org

To: fmarino@thewillingschool.org

swinslo@thewillingschool.org

condonelly@centennial.phila.edu

Date: November 2

Subject: Ten Reasons (Most) Boys Suck

1. They (not I) smell like Parmesan, taste like tuna, and have hair in all the wrong places.

2. The top of "Please, God, Give Me . . ." lists is Muscles. Followed by large metal objects, small electronic ones, and cast members of *Baywatch 2015*.

3. They're all convinced they have a sense of humor and good taste.

4. The ones with good taste in music have lousy taste in clothes. The ones with good taste in clothes eat Stilton. The ones who know what Korean BBQ is have never heard of Dusty Springfield.

5. They're obsessed with hair gel and hair loss.

6. If there's something they hate about themselves, they're totally phobic about it in other people.

7. They keep texts from other parties, then yell at you for snooping when you call them on it.

8. They chase you like you're tequila on wheels, then when they catch you, drop you like an empty can of Colt 45.

9. They only want what they can't have.

10. They lie.

I hadn't talked to either Frankie or Sadie in twenty-four hours. Something must have happened between leaving them in sugar shock around five and—I checked the time stamp—four a.m. Something not good. I should have gotten the e-mail first thing in the morning. But our wireless router is in Leo's apartment. He turns it off by accident at least twelve times a week. Inevitably, when I've forgotten to charge my phone battery.

I thought about calling Frankie right then, but realized he would still be in chemistry, probably causing little explosions all over the place.

The last e-mail was from Maxine Rothaus. No greeting, no message, just an MP3 file, labeled "OMCL." I double-clicked on it. A few seconds later, the familiar screaming came through my speakers. I looked where it had installed itself in iTunes.

So much for armadillos. The song title was "Our Mad Cold Love."

22
THE ADVICE

From *The Collected Correspondence of Edward Willing*, edited, enhanced, and with illustrations by Lucretia Willing Adamson. Henry Altemus Company, Philadelphia, 1923:

Advice from an Artist to a Young Man

March 31, 1916
Belvoir, Chestnut Hill

My Dear Mellon,

The very best thing about advice is that one may heed or heave it at will. Why it is your mother has chosen me to impart my dubious wisdom as to how you might better live your life remains to be seen, but I suspect it has something to do with the fact that I am, at present, in Philadelphia with an exhibit on at the Academy, while you are in Mexico cavorting like a savage," as she phrased it. Whatever the reason, I shall do my best.

First, my young friend, I shall say this: Change your socks and drawers daily. Or, if you will not, I have found a bit of ground coffee in a mesh pouch in one's pockets is a marvelous thing. Ah, but the redoubtable Mrs. Mellon does not wish me to bore you with such trifles. No, she wishes me to tell you how to be a great Man and Artist. Preferably much closer to home.

So, I shall advise, as concisely and helpfully as I might manage at this time of night. I say, go to Europe whenever possible, and never alone. I shall be leaving, myself, for Paris next week. Drink as much as you like, but refrain from smoking in the studio. It does not go well with the turpentine. Be patient and kind to your models, keep them no longer than a year, and dismiss them firmly. Buy French. Everything. Except perhaps automobiles. I am rather enamored of my Packard Twin Six.

Never grant interviews, and immediately dispose of all correspondence from anyone with whom you would not want to be seen in public (I trust you shall burn this as soon as you have read the last line!). Do not socialize with persons who wish to discuss your work. Your life is not your art, even if your art is your life, but understand that no patron, curator, or critic will ever accept that.

Understand that <u>nothing</u> is forever. Our passions, our words, our dabs on canvas, may well end their days moldering in an abandoned attic.

Wear good linen. Eat figs.

For God's sake, do not come back before summer.
Your friend,
Edward Willing

"Beauty is truth, truth beauty,"—that is all Ye know on earth, and all ye need to know. —Keats

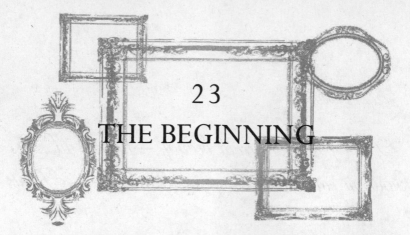

23
THE BEGINNING

Frankie turned back and forth in front of the three-way mirror. "I have absolutely no ass whatsoever."

A few feet away, a woman whose designer velour fit her like a sausage casing, gave an amused snort. "Honey," she said over a display of two-hundred-dollar T-shirts. "I have been waiting forty years to say those words."

Frankie padded toward her in his socks and Alexander McQueen pants. He thrust his hands into the pockets, pulling the fabric tighter, and presented her with his outthrust bottom. "Honestly. *This* is what you want?"

She lasted about five seconds before grinning—and sighing at the same time. "No, I guess not."

He turned around, leaned in, and informed her conspiratorially, "There is not a T-shirt on earth worth that much."

She looked down at the plain blue cotton in her hands. "You are so right." She put it back. "And with that face, sweetie, you could have the ass of a rhino and no one would notice. I'm just saying."

"What does she know?" he muttered when she'd gone. "What good has this face done me?"

Apparently, Connor hadn't been quite as available as he'd let on. Apparently, along with dancing, juggling was one of his talents.

"You couldn't have known," Sadie said gently.

"Oh, yes, I could. I mean, he's a guy, isn't he?"

There's not much you can say to a boy when he makes a statement like that. So we just scooted in until we were up against Frankie's thin shoulders, bookending him.

"I am going to end up alone," he moaned.

"Not in any conceivable universe!" One of Sadie's best qualities is the ability to say "Are you effing insane?" with such sweet conviction and nicer words.

"I am going to end up alone in a one-room apartment over a dry cleaner."

"A dry cleaner?"

"He could have said a bar," I offered.

"True," she conceded.

Frankie was on a roll. "I am going to end up alone in a one-room apartment over a dry cleaner with a cat. Who bites me."

"Oh, Frankie—"

"I am going to end up alone in a one-room apartment over a dry cleaner with a cat who bites me and pees in my closet full of moth-eaten sweaters."

"Well, maybe," Sadie said, reaching around to hug both of us. "But the sweaters will be Dolce & Gabbana." One of her other fabulous qualities is that underneath the sweet conviction, she does have a sense of humor.

Frankie did laugh. Then he gave a sigh that I could feel all the way through me. I knew Sadie could, too. "I liked him," he said, very quietly. "I really did. And I thought he felt the same way. I bent and twisted and distorted everything that happened between us to fit my pretty little picture. God, I believed my own hype. How stupid, how incredibly *stupid* was that?"

"Not stupid." Sadie squeezed. "Hopeful. And if we're not that, what's the point? El? Help me out here."

I wanted to. I really did. But all I could think of was the fact that at home, exactly where I'd put it in my bag, which was still exactly where I'd dumped it on the floor, was the evidence that Edward had let me down. I was keeping that to myself, at least for the moment. *Twisted it to fit my pretty little picture.* I didn't think I could take Frankie's complete lack of surprise that a guy (even a dead one) had let me down—or Sadie's sympathy. Not on top of my own anger.

Because, plain and simple, it wasn't okay to look at another woman like that, not when you met the love of your life and gave a big flipped finger to the people around you so you could be with her. Not okay even if she was dead, because I, Ella, really really want to believe that sometimes love does conquer all, and sometimes some things do last forever.

Truth: Yes, I really am that naive.

"You're perfect," I said to Frankie. And I meant it.

Sadie and I waited for him to shuck the trousers. Once he

was out of the dressing room, filled now with discarded designer clothing he insisted on returning neatly to its hangers, he wrapped an arm firmly around Sadie's shoulders and guided her toward the escalator.

"It is time, my darling."

"Oh, Frankie, no—"

"You chose dare," he reminded her.

"I did," she agreed sadly, stepping up. "You're right."

It hadn't been entirely fair of him, starting the game in the middle of Neiman Marcus. The King of Prussia Mall, a zillion acres of retail-and-food-in-a-box, is many people's idea of perfect therapy. Me? If given the choice, I might opt for swimming with sharks instead. But today was about Frankie.

"So," he told her, "I pick out three outfits, head to toe. You put them on."

"Fine." Sadie pulled her jacket closer around her. This one was a muddy purple, and had a third sleeve stitched to the back. "But if you pick anything like that"—she pointed to a tiny tartan dress that seemed to be missing its entire back—"I will cry."

"Have faith," he replied with a slightly twisted smile, and dragged her toward women's sportswear. "What our sport is," he said apropos of very little save the sign on the wall, "I have no idea."

Ten minutes later, Sadie was heading into the dressing room with an armful of autumn color and a look like she was on her way off a cliff. Frankie and I sank into two of the cushy husband chairs that are scattered all over the store.

"Okay," he said the minute I was settled, "Truth or Dare."

"Not fair. You already had a turn."

"Correct me if I'm wrong, but this little excursion was to make me happy."

I sighed, knowing I'd already lost. "You're right."

"Do I look happy to you?" He visibly deflated in his seat and pulled down the corners of his mouth. He looked like a very pretty scarecrow. "Well?"

"No, Mr. Hobbes, you do not look happy."

"So . . ."

I eyed the racks around us. There seemed to be an awful lot of jungle and orange. "If I say 'dare,' are you going to make me put on leopard print?"

"I might."

"If I take 'truth,' will you promise not to ask any more questions about Alex?"

"I will not."

For all of Frankie's insistence that he never wanted to hear the name Alex Bainbridge again, he'd been a little relentless in trying to get the details about the tutoring, about the encounter at the dance. It was like he was trying to catch me at something. I still hadn't mentioned the fact that exactly twenty-four hours later, I would be conjugating again. I'd given the bare minimum of info, especially after—hypocrite that he is—Frankie made such dramatic gagging motions at my description of the Mustang that a passing shopper had asked if she should call 911.

So I braced myself. "Dare."

Frankie's brows went up. "Well. All right, then." He scanned the floor. "I dare you to stand up next to that mannequin over there, and list the five best Unrequited Love songs of all time."

The mannequin, of course, was up on a plinth. I glanced around nervously, but there wasn't a saleswoman in sight. They were all in the premier designer section, following people who, unlike us, were likely either to shoplift or to buy. I climbed up. Then I thought for a minute.

"One," I said, "'Wicked Game.' Chris Isaak . . . Two: 'Someone Like You' by Adele . . . Um . . ."

How hard could it be? Three more songs about love that wasn't gonna happen. It's the backbone of country music, alternative geek, and the blues. "Ah. Three: 'You Don't Have to Say You Love Me.' Dusty Springfield."

"Excellent," Frankie approved.

I took a good look at the mannequin. She had a platinum Dutch-boy wig and was wearing a cropped orange sweater, a short, shirred cargo skirt, and very high red booties. I guessed she looked chic, but I didn't quite get the look she was going for. Urban Jungle Jane? Preppy with a naughty streak? Desperate but not serious? "Kanye West. 'Love Lockdown.'"

"This is me vomiting here, madam."

"Fine. 'You Oughta Know.' Alanis Morissette."

"Better. Slightly."

I thought of Edward and Alex. I thought of Chloe's, of all the wispy girls with prominent eyes and overbites who got up and sang what none of us ever want to say aloud: that sometimes no matter how many eyelashes or dandelion seeds you blow, no matter how much of your heart you tear out and slap on your sleeve, it just ain't gonna happen. "'I Can't Make You Love Me.' Bonnie Raitt."

"Oh, Fiorella."

I glared at him a little as I climbed down. "Was that delightful list for your benefit or mine?"

Frankie grabbed my hand and, when I didn't pull away fast enough, tugged me onto his lap, where he wrapped his arms so tightly around me that I couldn't escape. Sometimes his strength still surprises me. He tickled my cheek with his nose. "Don't hate me just because I'm hateful."

"I never do."

Here's the thing. Frankie's taken a lot of hits in his life. He never stays down for long.

"Excuse me!" The mannequin's evil twin was glaring down at us from her sky-high bootie-heeled heights. Her NM badge told us her name was Victoria. "You cannot do that here!" she snapped.

"Do what?" Frankie returned, matching lockjaw snooty for lockjaw snooty.

She opened and closed her mouth, then hissed, "Canoodle!"

I felt Frankie's hiccup of amusement. "Were we canoodling, snookums?" he asked me. "I rather thought we were about to copulate like bunnies."

I couldn't help it; I laughed out loud. Victoria's mouth thinned into a pale line. The whole thing might have ended with our being escorted out the store's hallowed doors by security. Sadie, as she so often did, momentarily saved us from ourselves.

She stomped out of the dressing room and planted herself in front of us. Ignoring the angry salesgirl completely, she muttered, "I look like a carved pumpkin!"

Frankie took in the skirt, layered shirts, and jacket. "You do not, but I might have been having an overly Michael Kors moment. This will not do for a date. Take it off." He nudged me, then added, "Right here. Every last stitch of it."

As soon as Sadie was back in her own clothing and coat—which got an unwilling frown of respect from Victoria; apparently even Neiman Marcus doesn't carry that line—we moved on. Sadie did better in Frankie's second choice, a lip-printed sweater dress from Betsey Johnson, but wouldn't buy it.

"We're just going to a movie!" she protested. "Besides, Jared's not . . . not . . ." She gestured down at her lippy hips. "He's practical and sensible and quiet."

"Oh, my God!" Frankie slapped both palms to the side of his face, and turned to me. "Sadie has a date with a Prius!"

He had to invoke the sanctity of Truth or Dare before he could even get her into Urban Outfitters. "Sometimes I love you less than other times," she grumbled as he filled her arms with his last choices.

"No, you don't," he said cheerfully, and sent her off to change.

He shepherded me across the store and into the sweater section. He held up a white henley that looked tiny even for me.

"No," I said.

The next one was a little black cardigan with fifties bombshell beading.

"Absolutely not."

He snorted but moved on. A second later, he pounced, grinning, on a narrow turtleneck with blue and white stripes. "Marino . . ."

"No."

"Why?" he demanded, surprised. "It is exactly what every girl in Paris is wearing right now, if she's not wearing the exact same one"—he pointed at my chest—"in black. It is absolutely *made* for you. So again I ask, why?"

"Because . . ." *It is exactly what every girl in Paris is wearing right now, and I don't need reminding that I am not that kind of girl.* "I am broke, and it's—"

"Forty percent off. Come on, Ella, it's a sign."

"Yeah. 'Stop.'" I took the sweater from his hands and folded it neatly into thirds. "Truth or Truth?"

He propped a hip on the edge of the display table. "Shoot."

"Who are you dressing me for? I mean, really? The three nonrelated men playing any part whatsoever in my life right now are, and I will use your terms here, the spawn of Society Hell, dead as the spat, and queer as a football bat."

"Very poetic."

"Bite me."

"Wrong man," Frankie drawled. "That would be the inclination of the hell spawn."

I bared my teeth. "So, who, Frankie? Who is this for?" I waved the sweater. "I just don't get it."

"I know, Grasshopper," he said sadly. "I know."

I blinked at him. "Where—" That's as far as I got. Sadie had come out of the dressing room. She was wearing narrow jeans, a faintly metallic tank, and a guy-styled sweater. She still looked like Sadie, only the magazine version.

"Oh, Sades!" I nearly dislocated my thumbs, I was so enthusiastic in upping them. "You look incredible."

"Hey," she squeaked as Frankie reached down the back of the sweater. "Hey!" He'd ripped the tag off its little plastic string. "I'm not buying—"

"Yes, you are. Or I am. All of it."

"You don't have any money," Sadie reminded him, suddenly looking much more like old Sadie: worried and a little guilty.

"Very little," he agreed. "Now go get your bag and clothes from the dressing room. She'll wear the new ones," he told the guy behind the counter. Then, to Sadie again, "Do you want to fish out the other tags, or should I?"

She disappeared again. The salesclerk smiled at me expectantly. "Will *that* be cash or charge?" he asked.

I looked down at my hands. I was still holding the stripy turtleneck. "Cash, I guess." Beside me, Frankie gave a smug little grunt. "We can live without you, I know," I told him.

"Of course you can. But why would you? I am here for youse, Marino, forevah and evah."

Half an hour and a pair of Frye boots later, Sadie eyed the food court options. "I think I'll do sushi."

Frankie and I had decided to split a meatball hoagie. It

wouldn't be my dad's, but it was safe. There was something about the shopping mall/raw fish combo that just seemed wrong.

"Sadie," I began, but didn't have the heart.

Frankie did. "A hoagie it is." When she protested, he gave her the reptile eye. "Ever hear of salmonella? And I don't mean the dish Ella's uncle named in her honor."

We think that might have been what killed Ricky's *Top Chef* chances last year. Too bad. Disastrous name aside, it had actually been pretty good.

Frankie bought us an extra order of french fries.

"Okay, three things, and one of them has to be in French."

I was back in the weird squashy chair; Alex was flopped on the bed. This time, along with the lemon soda, there were two bags of Doritos on the floor between us. He'd had one waiting. I'd brought one.

"I don't think this is what Mademoiselle Winslow had in mind," I told him.

Truth: Despite all my good intentions to keep Frankie happy and my hopes down, I'd been looking forward to this all week, hoping Alex wouldn't forget. I'd thought up and rethought clever things I could say.

Further Truth: I didn't want to sound like I'd been looking forward to it all week and thinking up what I wanted to say.

Home truth: Yes, I am that pitiful.

"Winslow wants you to learn this"—he waved a few sheets of stapled pages—"and that." He pointed to the book in my lap. *Fifty*

French Conversations. It was one of our textbooks. I'd stopped at the seventeenth: *Mon hamster a mangé trop de fromage. Il a mal au ventre maintenant.* "The rest is the Bainbridge Method."

"You have a method?"

"Patented and proven."

I waved the book. "Does it include greedy, cheese-guzzling hamsters with stomachaches?"

He nodded. "Absolutely. French conversation is nothing without rodents and cheese. Is there something shameful in your past involving either?"

"Not that I can think of off the top of my head."

"Tant pis."

"And that means . . . ?"

"Fuhgeddaboudit," he translated, grinning.

I sighed. "Do people make Russian jokes in your presence?"

"How do you get five Russians to agree on anything?"

"How?" I asked.

"Shoot four of them."

I thought for a sec. "I'm not sure that's funny."

"No," Alex said. "People don't tell many Russian jokes in my presence."

"I should start my three things list, huh?"

"Yeah. That would be good."

I did some speedy translating in my head. *"Je n'ai jamais lu* Huckleberry Finn, Beloved, *ou* Moby-Dick.*"*

"Ella, no one has read *Moby-Dick*. The French was passable, but as far as revelations go, that sucked."

"Ah, but there's a part *deux*. All three of those books were required reading last year in my American lit class. I used SparkNotes."

"You're kidding, right?"

"See?" I daintily brushed Dorito crumbs from my fingertips. "Changes your perception of me, doesn't it?"

"No, I meant, '*That's* a revelation?' You can do better that that."

"Maybe," I agreed, "but it's still early in the game." His room had two dormer windows and a skylight. I must have been facing west, because he was haloed by the late-afternoon sun. It made his hair glow like real bronze and shadowed his features. That made everything easier somehow. "Two: Anna Lombardi and I used to be pretty good friends before we got to Willing and suddenly weren't."

I said it quickly, evenly. Not a plea for sympathy, just an explanation, a truth.

"*Nous avons été amies,*" I added. "There, that's two in French, and using past perfect, no less."

I couldn't see his expression clearly. It felt like a long time before he said anything. "Ella . . ." He paused, then, "What happened? Between you and Anna?"

"Other than the fact that I'm a fashion-impaired poor kid who draws doorknobs? Haven't a clue."

Alex leaned forward. Now I could see his face. He looked annoyed. "Why do you do that? Diminish yourself?"

"I don't—"

"Bullshit."

I could feel my cheeks flaming, feel my shoulders curving inward. "I don't—"

"Right. Don't. Just don't, with me, anyway. I like you better feisty."

I couldn't help it; that made me smile. "Did you really just say 'feisty'?"

"I did. It's a good word."

"It's an *old* word, favored by granddads and pirates."

"Yar," Alex sighed.

"Face it. You're just an old-fashioned guy."

"Whatever. Three . . . ?"

"Three," I said, and changed my mind midthought. "I haven't been able to decide if Willing is the second best thing that ever happened to me, or the second worst."

"What are the firsts?"

"Nope. Uh-uh. It is not for you to ask, Alexander Bainbridge, but to reveal."

He drained his glass and rolled it back and forth between his hands. "I had all these funny admissions planned, but you've screwed up my plans. Hey. Don't go all wounded-wide-eyed on me. It's cute, that Bambi thing you have going, but beside the point. Now I have to rethink."

"You don't—"

"Quiet. One: My name isn't Alexander." He sat up straight and gave his chest a resounding thump. "*Menya zavut* Alexei Pavlovich Dillwyn Bainbridge. Not Alexander. I don't think anyone outside my family knows that."

"Not even Amanda?" It came out before I could stop it.

"Not even Amanda." He reached for the soda. "Two," he muttered as he poured, "I wish more people knew that Amanda and I are not a single unit and fewer people knew that she dumped me temporarily over the summer for a lifeguard in Loveladies named Biff." While I processed that, he finished, "Three. I bombed the PSATs."

"Oh. Well, isn't the point of preliminary tests to help you learn how to do well on the later ones?"

"Tell that to my dad. He has decided that I am now on the fast track toward a future digging ditches."

"Come on. I'm sure he sees that it's just a prep test."

"What he sees," Alex corrected me, "is that the path of Yale, followed by Powel Law and the family firm, has gotten a little slippery."

I had no idea what to say. In my family, whatever we want to do, as long as it involves getting out of bed every morning and satisfying our souls, is considered just splendid. And that coming from multiple generations who've struggled to pay the mortgage. I couldn't imagine being able to give my children everything, and then to demand that they follow the exact same path I did.

"So, twice a week I have my own tutor," he said shortly. "Who, trust me, makes my father look like a marshmallow. And on that note . . ." He picked up the sheaf of French lessons again. "We'll start with the imperfect, used to express actions that are—"

"Incomplete, unfulfilled, or repeated over and over." I slumped back in the weird chair. "*That* I know."

At the end of the very imperfect session, Alex gave me a full ten minutes in the downstairs bathroom before showing up. All I'd figured out was that Edward's faceless girl had had wide feet, and the Bainbridge's decorator had a preference for green that might merit an intervention.

"I could probably give you the stupid thing"—Alex gestured to the picture when he came in—"and my folks would never notice."

I winced inwardly. "I can't advocate theft," I told him, "no matter how noble the intent."

I knew I had to figure out what to do with the photograph and the letters. Beyond the fact that I didn't think I wanted anything to do with them, stealing them had probably been the worst thing I'd ever done. *Something I don't want anyone to know, Alex? I am a disillusioned former hopeless romantic with larcenous tendencies. But I did kill the verbal part of the PSATs.*

The way I saw it, I had three options:

1. I could take the stuff to Maxine. "Hey, look what I found." Confession of theft optional and probably not smart.

2. I could slip them back into the book and pretend they never existed.

3. I could destroy them.

Option two sounded just marvelous.

"So, I'm curious." Alex dragged me from my pleasant contemplation of cowardice and back into the bathroom. He was leaning against the wall, arms crossed, his feet almost touching mine. "What is it you like so much about this guy? I looked up his stuff. It's good, but nothing out of the ordinary."

What a difference a week and a shock to the ideals makes. I felt my defense of Edward sticking a little in my throat. "I like his portraits. He really saw people. It was his great strength, that intensity."

Alex tilted his chin toward the picture. "Not to seem crude, but she could be any girl with a nice ass." When I glared at him, he uncrossed his arms quickly and held up his hands in surrender. "Hey, all I mean is that if I were all about really seeing someone, that's not the angle I would choose."

He was probably right. No matter how I looked at it, he was probably right. "You're probably right," I told him.

He bowed. The small space suddenly got a lot smaller. "Stick with me, Grasshopper. I will never lead you wrong."

⌐⊶⊷⌐

At midnight, I was still at my desk. The drawing was still tacked over Edward's face. I hadn't heard any more of his faint protests recently.

I had my battered copy of *The Collected Works of Edward Willing* open in front of me. Of course, not every piece he ever did is in it, but it's a pretty comprehensive collection. The book itself has been out of print for twenty years. For most of freshman year, I read it in the school library, under Edward's portrait. Amazon and all of my fifteenth-birthday money finally made a copy mine. I've read it so many times that the spine is as yielding as linen.

This time, my search was very specific. Edward used dozens

of models for his paintings: women, men, old, young, friends, students. I was looking for one particular blonde.

I found her first on page 279. *Woman #6, 1906.* It was a watercolor, just a seated figure, anonymous and amorphous. There was another watercolor on page 298: *Summer,* 1907. She had her face buried in an armful of flowers. The same year, she was the central figure, on a bicycle, in a large oil painting called *Boathouse Row.* I found her as a shrouded *Eurydice,* 1908, in a series called *Wissahickon,* 1910–1912, where she sat in profile on a bunch of different rocks, and once more, *Marina, Marseilles,* 1914. In that one, she was seated on the beach, looking toward the marina filled with fishing boats and beyond. It wasn't Edward's best work. Seascapes never were.

He'd painted her over at least eight years. She had traveled with him to France. Only Diana had ever been featured in as many paintings, in multiple locations.

I ripped the sketch from the wall.

"Liar."

Edward looked more ravaged than usual. "That is a terrible word, coming from you."

"Yup."

"And not entirely fair."

"You had an affair with this . . . Woman number 6 . . . Were there five others? Seven, eight, and onward?" When he didn't answer, I waved at the (admittedly small) stack of Edward Willing books on my desk. "She isn't mentioned anywhere. What did you do, keep her tucked away for your private entertainment?"

"Tsk, Ella."

"Oh, no, don't you go all proper and disapproving on me. Was it that she wasn't posh enough for your social circle? Or did you just know it was a bad thing—bad—to follow Diana with . . . her? What's her name, anyway?"

He didn't answer, just stared at me with his pained expression.

"I looked up *dorogaya*. It isn't a name. It's a Russian endearment. There's no mention I can find anywhere that has anything to do with you and anyone Russian. So who was she, a model? Is this just one of those clichés?"

He didn't answer that, either.

"I believed in you," I told him. "I have this stupid project all planned on your muse—how Diana made you the painter you are. How it was all about love."

"Didn't we decide it's all about love or money? Everything."

"Oh, shut up, Edward," I snapped. "Now I don't know what to think of you."

He sighed. "I'm a tad confused here. What is it that bothers you so much? That I might have had a deliberately clandestine relationship with this person who was socially beneath me, or that I didn't spend the last seventeen years of my life alone in desperate mourning for my wife?"

"I . . . I . . ." I discovered that I didn't have a quick answer. I didn't have any answer.

"You need to figure that out, darling girl. You were counting on this passionate, extensively researched, impeccably written paper to be your entrée into NYU."

I had. I was.

"And," the voice went on," you really need to take the photo and letters back to the museum."

"Oh, great. Thank you. Tell me something I don't already know!"

Edward looked at me sadly from his printed frame. "But I can't do that, Ella. That's the one thing I have never been able to do."

And that little tidbit was the icing. Because I'd known from the beginning. Edward couldn't tell me anything I didn't already know. The real Edward Willing was dead. My Edward was a figment of my imagination. And while I have a very good imagination, I can't conjure up the truth. It either is or it isn't.

"You can count on me to always *be* here," said the metal head in the postcard. "Beyond that . . . I'm not going to offer you much."

"Yeah," I said sadly. "I know that, too."

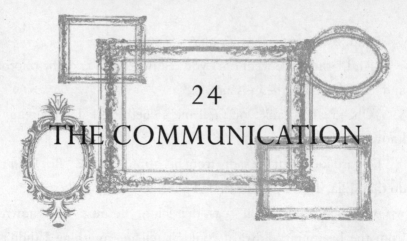

24
THE COMMUNICATION

From: abainbr@thewillingschool.org

To: fmarino@thewillingschool.org

Date: November 17, 9:57 p.m.

Subject: Sorry

Can't do French tomorrow.

—Alex

From: fmarino@thewillingschool.org

To: abainbr@thewillingschool.org

Date: November 18, 7:12 a.m.

Subject: Fine

Okay.

From: abainbr@thewillingschool.org

To: fmarino@thewillingschool.org

Date: November 21, 4:41 p.m.

Subject: Re: Fine

Ella,

Not fine, actually. Well, doing better now, but I spent a seriously hairy two days . . . let's just say "ill." My mother is convinced it was the tuna sandwich I had for dinner Thursday. Personally, I think it was just the bug that's been doing the rounds at school, but I'm not telling her that. Guilt for being an absentee parent had her on the phone with Svichkar's. Now I'm getting a different, three-course Ukrainian meal delivered every night. Chicken Kiev is not what the school kitchen thinks it is.

Anyway, I'm really sorry about Friday. I guess I'll see you after Thanksgiving. We're leaving tomorrow for the week. Going to Martha's Vineyard with another political family. Lots of talking turkey.

—Alex

From: fmarino@thewillingschool.org
To: abainbr@thewillingschool.org
Date: November 21, 8:25 p.m.
Subject: Now I'm Sorry

Alex,

I feel badly.

You probably feel worse.

My grandmother thinks canned tuna is a disaster waiting to happen. She used to stand in the door of the fridge and make protective hand symbols over my mom's leftover tuna casserole. We don't keep Starkist in the house anymore.

Have a great TG.

—Ella

From: abainbr@thewillingschool.org

To: fmarino@thewillingschool.org

Date: November 22, 12:05a.m.

Subject: Here's one for you

Knock knock.

From: fmarino@thewillingschool.org

To: abainbr@thewillingschool.org

Date: November 22, 10:34 a.m.

Subject: Um . . .

Who's there?

From: abainbr@thewillingschool.org

To: fmarino@thewillingschool.org

Date: November 22, 10:56 a.m.

Subject: Re: Um . . .

Tuna.

From: fmarino@thewillingschool.org

To: abainbr@thewillingschool.org

Date: November 22, 10:34 a.m.

Subject: Re: Re: Um . . .

Tuna who?

From: abainbr@thewillingschool.org

To: fmarino@thewillingschool.org

Date: November 22, 9:02 p.m.

Subject: Re: Re: Re: Um . . .

Tuna down ya radio. I'm'a tryin' to sleep here!

From: fmarino@thewillingschool.org

To: abainbr@thewillingschool.org

Date: November 22, 11:32 p.m.

Subject: Sigh.

> Okay. Since we're on the subject . . .
>
> Q. What is the Tsar of Russia's favorite fish?
>
> A. Tsardines, of course.
>
> Q. What does the son of a Ukrainian newscaster and a U.S. congressman eat for Thanksgiving dinner on an island off the coast of Massachusetts?
>
> A.?
>
> —Ella

From: abainbr@thewillingschool.org

To: fmarino@thewillingschool.org

Date: November 23, 9:59 a.m.

Subject: TG

> A. Republicans.
>
> Nah. I'm sure we'll have all the traditional stuff: turkey, stuffing, mashed potatoes. I'm hoping for apple pie. Our hosts have a cook who takes requests, but the island is kinda limited as far as shopping goes. The seven of us will probably spend the morning on a boat, then have a civilized chow-down. I predict Pictionary. I will win.
>
> You?
>
> —Alex

From: fmarino@thewillingschool.org

To: abainbr@thewillingschool.org

Date: November 23, 1:11 p.m.

Subject: Re: TG

Alex,

I will be having my turkey (there will be one, but it will be somewhat lost among the pumpkin fettuccine, sausage-stuffed artichokes, garlic with green beans, and at least four lasagnas, not to mention the sweet potato cannoli and chocolate ricotta pie) with at least forty members of my close family, most of whom will spend the entire meal screaming at each other. Some will actually be fighting, probably over football.

I am hoping to be seated with the adults. It's not a sure thing.

What's Martha's Vineyard like? I hear it's gorgeous. I hear it's favored by presidential types, past and present.

—Ella

From: abainbr@thewillingschool.org
To: fmarino@thewillingschool.org
Date: November 23, 5:28 p.m.
Subject: Can I Have TG with You?

Please??? There's a 6 a.m. flight off the island. I can be back in Philadelphia by noon. I've never had Thanksgiving with more than four or five other people. Only child of two only children. My grandmother usually hosts dinner at the Hunt Club. She doesn't like turkey. Last year we had Scottish salmon. I like salmon, but . . .

The Vineyard is pretty great. The house we're staying in is in Chilmark, which, if you weren't so woefully ignorant of defunct television, is the birthplace of Fox Mulder. I can see the Menemsha fishing fleet out my window. Ever heard of Menemsha Blues? I should bring you a T-shirt. Everyone has Black Dogs; I prefer a good fish on the chest.

(Q. What do you call a fish with no eyes? A. Fsh.)

We went out on a boat this afternoon and actually saw a humpback whale. See pics below. That fuzzy gray lump in the bumpy gray water is a fin. A photographer I am not. Apparently, they're usually gone by now, heading for the Caribbean. It's way too cold to swim, but amazing in the summer. I swear I got bumped by a sea turtle here last July 4, but no one believes me.

Any chance of saving me a cannoli?

—A

From: fmarino@thewillingschool.org
To: abainbr@thewillingschool.org
Date: November 23, 8:43 p.m.
Subject: Some boat

Alex,

I know Fox Mulder. My mom watched *The X-Files*. She says it was because she liked the creepy story lines. I think she liked David Duchovny. She tried *Californication*, but I don't think her heart was in it. I think she was just sticking it to my grandmother, who has decided it's the work of the devil. She says that about most current music, too, but God help anyone who gets between her and *American Idol*.

The fuzzy whale was very nice, if a little hard to identify. The profile of the guy between you and the whale in the third pic was very familiar, if a little fuzzy. I won't ask. No, no. I have to ask.

I won't ask.

My mother loves his wife's suits.

I Googled. There are sharks off the coast of the Vineyard. Great
big white ones. I believe you about the turtle. Did I mention that
there are sharks there? I go to Surf City for a week every summer
with my cousins. I eat too much ice cream. I play miniature golf—
badly. I don't complain about sand in my hot dog buns or sheets.
I even spend enough time on the beach to get sand in more
uncomfortable places. I do not swim. I mean, I could if I wanted to,
but I figure that if we were meant to share the water with sharks, we
would have a few extra rows of teeth, too.

I'll save you some cannoli.
—Ella

From: abainbr@thewillingschool.org
To: fmarino@thewillingschool.org
Date: November 24, 12:44 a.m.
Subject: Shh
.Fiorella,
Yes, Fiorella. I looked it up. It means Flower. Which, when paired
with MArino, means Flower of the Sea. What shark would dare to
touch you?

I won't touch the uncomfrotable sand mention, hard as it is to resist.
I also will not think of you in a bikini (Note to self: Do not think of

Ellla in a bikini under any circumstances. Note from self: Are you f-ing kidding me?).

Okay.

Two pieces of info for you. One: Our host has an excellent wine cellar and my mother is Europaen. Meaning she doesn't begrudge me the occasionsl glass. Or four.

Two: Our hostess says to thank yur mother very much. Most people say nasty things about her suits.
Three: We have a house kinda near Surf City. Maybe I'll be there when your there.

You'd better burn this after reading.
—Alexei

From: fmarino@thewillingschool.org
To: abainbr@thewillingschool.org
Date: November 24, 8:09 p.m.
Subject: Happy Thanksgiving

Alexei,

Consider it burned. Don't worry. I'm not showing your e-mails to anybody. Matter of national security, of course.
Well, I got to sit at the adult table. In between my great-great-aunt Jo, who is ninety-three and deaf, and her daughter, JoJo, who had to repeat everyone's conversations across me. Loudly.
The food was great, even my uncle Ricky's cranberry lasagna. In fact, it would have been a perfectly good TG if the Eagles hadn't been playing the Jets. My cousin Joey (other side of the family)

lives in Hoboken. His sister married a Philly guy. It started out as
a lively across-the-table debate: Jets v. Iggles. It ended up with
Joey flinging himself across the table at his brother-in-law and my
grandmother saying loud prayers to Saint Bridget. At least I think it
was Saint Bridget. Hard to tell. She was speaking Italian.

She caught me trying to freeze a half-dozen cannoli. She yelled
at me. Apparently, the shells get really soggy when they defrost. I
guess you'll have to come have a fresh one when you get back.

—F/E

From: fmarino@thewillingschool.org
To: abainbr@thewillingschool.org
Date: November 26
Subject: Hey. <unsent>

Just thought I would check and make sure you weren't felled by a
rogue turkey bacteria.

From: fmarino@thewillingschool.org
To: abainbr@thewillingschool.org
Date: November 27
Subject: <unsent>

A,

I really hope I didn't

From: fmarino@thewillingschool.org
To: abainbr@thewillingschool.org
Date: November 27
Subject: <unsent>

Alex,

25
THE MESSAGE

1.

"Ahem. I know you hate Mondays, madam, but you picked the absolutely wrong one to play hooky. Or be sick. Yes, I suppose it's vaguely possible that you are actually sick. Anyway, here we are at lunch, Sadie and I, witnessing total social disorder. Your friend Alexander Bainbridge is sitting at the usual table, but facing the room. Amanda Alstead is sitting at Table One. Or, should I say, sitting more or less on a Phillite senior boy, whose name is unimportant, at Table One. A very nice young lady at the next table over—you know, the one who writes about Mr. Darcy—has just informed us that Amanda dumped Alex over the break. On Thanksgiving Day, no less. By e-mail. No telling how much truth is there, but a lot more than a kernel, I would say. We have a large, seven-dollar bag o' movie popcorn here. Thought you'd like to know. Call me."

2.

"Ella?" My dad appeared in my doorway, holding a tray with a napkin draped over the top of it. "How're you doing, hon?"

I covered my phone with a Kleenex. Not that it mattered. Against all the black designs on the quilt, it pretty much blended in. "Okay."

"You still don't look too good." He set the tray down on my desk. "Beautiful, but not too good. I brought you soup."

It was minestrone, and it smelled really, really good. He and my mother hadn't suspected a thing when I'd told them I was sick. ("She barely stepped over the threshold all weekend," Mom lamented. "It's no wonder she's looking like an empty shell.") She left for work, trailing vague threats involving Macy's. Dad had tried to feed me. I was hungry, but figured he might catch on if I ate more than half a piece of toast. My stomach grumbled now. I was definitely feeling like an empty shell. Only part of it had to do with food.

"You wanna tell me about it, sweetheart?"

Dad was holding out a bowl and spoon, and looking at me like he used to when I ran into the restaurant kitchen, crying because I'd crashed my bike into the Grecos' front steps. Again.

"I don't think so," I answered, taking the soup. "It's no big deal."

"And I have a bridge to sell you." He sighed. "How 'bout I ask questions and you can answer the ones you want?"

"Okay." I couldn't say no, not when his face and the smell of warm tomatoes reminded me how I'd never cried for more than a minute once I got into the kitchen and to him.

"Okay." He flipped the desk chair around to face the bed and sat, hands over his knees. There were two long, green stains on the front of his apron, one on each side where he'd rubbed basil residue off his hands. I could smell it, behind the minestrone. "School?"

"No."

"Boy?"

"Yeah, partly."

"Boyfriend?" His heavy eyebrows drew together at that one.

I quickly assured him, "No."

"Ah. But you want him to be."

"Kinda."

"And he—blind, stupid, and probably nutty as a squirrel—doesn't feel the same way."

I smiled a little at the paternal outrage. "No. Maybe. I don't know. That's the problem. I . . . can't trust what I think I know anymore."

Dad didn't say anything for a few seconds, just rocked a little in his seat. Then, "You remember when you used to want me to take you to the museum every single Sunday?"

I smiled again. "You always wanted to look at the Dutch still-life paintings."

"What can I say? I like a good plate of food."

"I hated the ones with the dead rabbits."

"Not my favorites, either, hon. But you really loved that room with all the kooky stuff. The bicycle wheel stuck in a stool, the urinal."

"The Marcel Duchamp room. Wow. I haven't been in there in

ages." I took a sip of the minestrone. It was perfect.

"Yeah, and that really famous painting. You know, the one you used to stand in front of for the longest time."

"Nude Descending a Staircase."

"That's the one. I never saw it, the nude. Or the staircase, either. I saw a bunch of brown shapes in a row. But you . . . You looked and looked, every time we were there, and made me read the title out loud. Then, one day, you grabbed my hand. I dunno, you were maybe six. Like this—'" He placed his own palm flat in the air at waist level. "Tiny, but man, you had a grip on you. 'I see it, Daddy! I see the nude depending on the stairs!" He grinned. "Took you another few months to learn that *nude* didn't mean every person in a painting. You shocked the girdles off some old gals in the portrait rooms. God, you were a fantastic little thing."

I'd almost finished the soup. I still felt pretty hollow, but I was a lot warmer.

"Anyway, here's the point . . ." He reached up and tugged at one earlobe. His fingertips were purple. Pesto and beets on the menu, I guessed. "I had a point . . . Oh, right. You, my fantastic little shrimp, knew what was in front of you. Maybe it wasn't obvious, but you hung in there until it all got clear in your mind and in front of your eyes."

He slapped both knees and stood up. "That was my point. But what do I know about it? I like pictures of peaches that look like peaches." He took the bowl and spoon from me. "Okay?"

"Um . . ."

"I don't mean the soup, hon."

"I know."

"So." He picked up the tray and headed for the door. "You digest."

"You don't mean the soup."

"See? You know what you think you know."

He left chocolate biscotti for my dessert.

I heard the beep of the answering machine in the kitchen. Nonna always turns the volume down ("Like the voices of the dead, that awful box!"). Considering the fact that she is the only one who spends any real time in the house kitchen, messages can wait a long time to be answered.

"Ella," Dad called up to me. "Some boy named Alex left a message. You want I should erase it . . . ?"

My phone thudded to the floor when I got tangled in the quilt trying to get of bed headfirst.

3.

"Ella, um, it's Alex. I hope this is the right number. I had to get it from a really old phone book. I would have gotten your cell number from Sadie Winslow, but . . . well, every time I got near her today, Frankie Hobbes showed his teeth. He's a little scary for such a skinny guy . . . Anyway. You weren't in English today. You weren't anywhere that I could see today. Um . . . call me. I was thinking I could come over . . ."

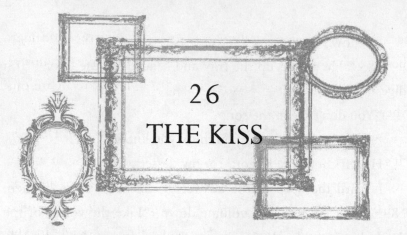

26
THE KISS

My closet door wouldn't close. I pushed. I leaned on it. I eventually realized that my bathrobe sleeve was blocking the latch. When I opened the door to deal with the problem, most of the clothing I had tried and rejected tumbled out onto my feet. I shoveled my jeans, two of Sienna's sweaters, and one of her skirts back in. She would have a fit if she saw, but I reasoned she would have more of a fit if I shoved her things under the bed, with its resident dust wombats and lost charcoal pencils.

Alex was late. I was grateful. I was also incredibly nervous, and I'd gotten mascara in my eye. I blinked a lot as I did a last check. Actually, everything looked pretty much like it usually did, including me. I'd wiped off most of the mascara and all of the lipstick. I was wearing the new blue-and-white turtleneck Frankie had made me buy. I thought I looked very slightly French.

I went into the hall and looked out the front window for the twentieth time and told myself to relax for the fiftieth. It could not be healthy, this breathless, silly, heart-pounding state I'd been in since I'd called him back and left a message and he'd called me back and I'd been convinced he could hear my heartbeat through the phone. All so I could run around my room like a hamster on crack, tripping over discarded jeans and trying to figure out where I'd dropped yesterday's bra.

"Oh, for God's sake," I scolded myself, channeling Frankie. "It's just a French session. It's just a French session with a cute guy. It's just a French session with a cute guy who no longer has a girlfriend, who drunk-e-mailed me about my name, and who makes me feel like I've swallowed a caterpillar." I thought maybe I should sit down.

The green hood of Alex's car nosed into view at 5:09. I flung myself out of my room, down the stairs, and then had to lean against the sofa for a second to compose myself. Then I stood right behind the door, counting a slow ten after he knocked before opening it. Wouldn't want to look too eager, now, would I?

"Hi," he said.

"Hi." What else could I say?

It had turned seriously cold over the break. He was wearing a big black peacoat with Russian symbols on the buttons. I tried to remember if I'd ever known the Russian world for "hi." I didn't think so. He waited patiently for a minute, then asked, "Okay if I come in?"

I flushed and stepped back. We don't have a foyer. Alex walked a few paces into our living room. I imagined what he was seeing: the matchy-matchy three-piece sofa set (a slightly dingy beige on beige, with some flowery throw pillows), the pastel beach scene (seagulls on a broken dune fence) on the wall, Nonna's Madonna statue (brilliantly blue). For a fleeting second, I was embarrassed. Then, suddenly, it didn't matter. It was what it was and wasn't going to change until my mother got another bee in her brain and decided to go Southwestern Chic with rough wood and cow skulls.

"Can I . . . take that?" I asked, pointing to the paper bag in his hand.

Alex looked away from the mantelpiece. The uprights are copies of pillars from the Colosseum in Rome. They're big. "Oh, yeah. It's *pierogis*. From Svichkar's. Probably cold. It seemed . . . Oh, crap. It was a really stupid thing to bring, wasn't it? My mom just has this thing about never arriving empty-handed."

I tugged the bag out of his hands. "It's perfect. *Merci beaucoup,* Monsieur Bainbridge."

"Je t'en prie, Mademoiselle Marino."

Okay, so it's just the semiformal way to say "You're welcome" in French, but anyone who says Italian is the language of romance is probably Italian. I carried the bag into the kitchen and put it on the counter between the freshness-guaranteed Handi-Vac ("put the food in the bag, suck the air out . . .") Mom bought on the Home Shopping Network and Nonna's hand-painted biscotti jar ("What, you think they stay there long enough to go *stale*?") that she carried with her from Calabria. It's decorated with fig leaves and, for some reason, fish. I never look too closely when raiding it; the fish that makes up the handle always seems to be giving me the serious *malocchio*.

I opened the fridge to get the waiting lemon soda. I looked at the paper bag again and grinned. I'd expected Doritos. This was just so much better, even if slightly less appetizing.

"Do you want a *pierogi*?" I called.

"I really don't," Alex called back. Then, "I mean, they're good, and if you want one—"

"Cookie?"

"Excellent."

I got a plate for biscotti. To avoid the fish eye, I flipped the lid over in my hand. There was a little painted scroll on the inside. I'd never really thought about it before. Now I looked closely. And looked again. This time, instead of just a pretty design, I saw an *M*, entwined with an *E*, encircled by a *C*. Michelangelo Costa, I thought. Nonna's Darcy of a great-granddad. And Elisabetta. Then again, it could just have been Nonna's parents: Magda and Euplio.

I put a few biscotti on the plate, balanced a pair of tall plastic tumblers over the neck of the soda bottle, and went back to the living room. Alex was right in front of the mantel now, bent forward, his nose mere inches from a picture of me.

"Oh, God. Don't look at that!"

It was from the year-end recital of my one and only year of ballet class. I was six: twig legs, a huge gap where my two front teeth had recently been, and a bumblebee costume. Nonna had done her best, but there was only so much she could do with yellow and black spandex and a bee butt. Dad had found one of those headbands with springy antennae attached. I'd loved the antennae. The more enthusiastic my *jetés*, the more they bounced. Of course, I'd also *jetéd* my flat-chested little self out of the top of my costume so many times that, during the actual recital itself, I'd barely moved at all, victim to the overwhelming modesty of the six-year-old. Now, looking at the little girl I'd been, I wished someone had told her not to worry so much, that within a year, that smooth, skinny, little bare shoulder would have turned into the bane of her existence. That she was absolutely perfect.

"Nice stripes," Alex said casually, straightening up.

That stung. It shouldn't have—it was just a photo—but it did. I don't know what I'd expected him to say about the picture. It wasn't that. But then, I didn't expect the wide grin that spread across his face when he got a good look at mine, either.

"Those," he announced, pointing to a photo of my mulleted dad leaning against the painted hood of his Mustang, "are nice stripes. That"—he pointed to the me-bee—"is seriously cute."

"You're insane," I muttered, insanely pleased.

"Yeah, well, tell me something I don't know." He took the bottle and plate from me. "I like knowing you have a little vanity in there somewhere." He stood, hands full, looking expectant and completely beautiful.

The reality of the situation hadn't really been all that real before. Now, as I started up the stairs to my bedroom, Alex Bainbridge in tow, it hit me. I was leading a boy, *this* boy, into my very personal space.

Then he started singing.

"'You're so vain, I bet you think this song is about you. You're sooo *vain* . . . !'" He had a pretty good voice. It was a truly excellent AM radio song.

And just like that, I was officially In Deep:

1. *Interested in art.* (Me, charcoal; him, colored ink.)

2. *Not afraid of love.* He'd stuck with Cruella de Vil for a long time.

3. *Or of telling the truth.* "Three things it costs a little to tell."

4. *Hot.* Like, smokin'.

5. *Daring.* Sharks. Ocean. He swims where Here Be Monsters.

5, subsection a. *Daring enough to take a chance on me.*

Oh, that one, always the glitch in *If My Prince Does, in Fact, Come Someday, It Would Be Great If He Could Meet These Five Criteria.* But I had one thing when it came to Alex that I'd never had with Edward. Hope. Well, that and a drunk e-mail.

So up we went. His house had paintings going up the stairs. Mine has . . . yup, school pictures. Sienna, Leo, Ella. Sienna, Leo, Ella. A few different schools, more than a dozen years. Sienna looking beautiful and dissatisfied, even at six. Leo in second grade with the last vestiges of a black eye from a fight he'd picked with three fourth graders. Me with one missing incisor and my hair in two pigtails. Sienna looking beautiful and bored, in the huge hoop earrings that she'd bought with her twelfth-birthday money and that my father kept threatening to smelt. Leo with gelled hair. Me with my hair half over my face and completely covering my neck. Sienna with boobs and pale pink eye shadow. Leo with an earring Dad pretended not to see. Me with my hair half over my face and covering most of my chest.

This time Alex didn't say anything. He did, however, pause

at the life-size framed print that took up most of the landing. "Wow."

That was one way of putting it.

"My mother likes Klimt," I explained. She had this, *The Kiss*, on coasters, a tote bag, and a tea set she'd bought herself for her twentieth wedding anniversary.

It wasn't Klimt the painter she liked, so much as the combination of lots and lots of metallic paint and a red-haired woman in the arms of a dark-haired man. "It's me and your dad," she used to say to our collective distress. Little kids don't want to see their parents canoodling. Older kids *really* don't want to see it. "Hey. You keep rolling your eyes, Sienna Donatella," she would snap, "and they're gonna stick like that. See then if you can find a guy to kiss you!"

Sienna's Tommy is a nice guy. He's okay with the fact that she wants as much metallic gold in their future home as possible.

"Edward Willing called it 'the most beautiful monstrosity in the history of art,'" I told Alex. "He saw it in Vienna the year after it was painted. I've never been able to decide whether he *liked* it."

"Everyone likes *The Kiss*," was Alex's response.

I'm not so sure. But I know my mother would agree completely. She had a half-dozen much smaller versions framed. She puts them in the houses she stages for sale, convinced that no one can resist a little bit of gold and smooching.

Now, standing under our beautiful monstrosity, I couldn't help thinking that if Alex were to kiss me, it would look like that:

me small and blissful and clinging, him so much taller, completely enfolding me.

I averted my red face as I headed down the hall.

My room is a quarter the size of his. It felt even smaller with him in it. "Make yourself at—"

He'd plunked the snack on my desk, deposited his coat on my chair, and was already roaming the room, looking at the walls. "Wow," he said again, staring at a quartet of Victorian door knockers made to look like hands. "Cool. You are seriously good." He stared for a long time at the single study I'd put up from the Willing Romance Languages Room door: the leering devil. "I would put that on my wall," he said.

I hadn't said anything while he browsed, swallowing all the automatic denials of my abilities.

He turned and grinned at me, looking exactly like the little demon. No surprise, since it was essentially his face in miniature. "This is the part where you remove that tack and give me the picture. For keeps."

"Are you serious?" I wasn't sure.

"Yes, Ella. I am serious."

So I removed the tack and handed him the picture. He rolled it up very gently and put it in his coat pocket. Then he wandered over to look out my window. "That's the restaurant, right?"

"Yep."

"Is that your dad?"

I went to stand next to him. He radiated heat. It was distracting. "Um . . . Yeah. And my mom." She was brandishing a piece of paper. Dad had pulled out his pants pockets so they stood out on either side of his apron like mouse ears. "My sister and mom want surf 'n' turf at the wedding. My dad doesn't want to pay for it. It's been a long battle, and we're down to the wire. The wedding's in three weeks."

Mom threw her hands up into the air and stalked away. Dad picked up a really big chef's knife and went to work hacking up an eggplant.

Alex turned his back to the window and leaned against the sill. "Just out of curiosity, do they know I'm here?"

"Yep." My mother did, anyway. Mention of a French tutor had effectively headed off any possibility of shopping.

"I take it they trust you not to do anything inappropriate."

I couldn't tell if he was being serious. I assumed not. "Absolutely. In fact, my mother would probably pay you to do something to make them trust me a little less." I took a look at his face. He looked a little stunned. "Oh, no. I didn't mean—"

Or maybe I did. But Alex was backing away from me, hands raised. "Okay."

"*J'étais stupide.*"

He sat down heavily on the edge of my desk, narrowly missing the biscotti. "I wouldn't say that. But your use of the imperfect is improving."

"Just what I always wanted," I said sadly, "to get better at imperfection."

"Look, Ella . . ." He stared down at his hands, opening and closing his fists. I waited.

I think we might have little bit of a misunderstanding here . . .

You're a nice girl and all, but . . .

I really like you, but I don't really like you . . .

The unmistakable notes of "Don't Stop Believin'," electronic version, suddenly filled my room, followed by the audible and visual treat of my phone vibrating its way across my desk toward Alex's hip. I flung myself on it. In a clearer-headed moment, I would have just turned it off. As it was, I did manage a "Sorry!" to Alex before flipping it open.

"Are you dead?" Frankie demanded from the other end.

"No." I edged away from Alex, who was very politely pretending to be interested in the biscotti.

"Are you even sick?"

"No," I admitted.

"Of course not. Okay, I'm coming over."

"No!" I cringed as Alex jumped a little. I took a breath. "God, no. Don't. It's wedding central here. Sienna will have you tying up birdseed in little purple pouches."

There was a long pause. "You okay, Marino?"

"Yeah," I managed.

"Truth time. Where were you today?"

Could I do it? Could I actually use the word *cramps* with Alex Bainbridge standing three feet away? I could only imagine how the actual truth would sound. *Here, in bed, hiding because I thought I'd made the queen of all fools out of myself e-mailing Alex Bainbridge over the break, and I can't even tell you about it because I promised . . . But it's okay—or maybe not—because he's here now, in my bedroom. Just about to tell me I made the queen of all fools out of myself. Sure. Come on over. The two of you can bond over my idiocy.*

"The archive," I said, stepping away from the desk, like a few feet was going to make a difference. "Look, I gotta go. I'll call you later."

"Promise?"

"Absolutely. Love you."

"Love you, too."

I turned off my phone before putting it in my pocket. "Frankie," I said. Like Alex cared.

"Does *he* know I'm here?"

"Didn't come up."

Alex shrugged. He clearly didn't care. "Not the friendliest guy."

I could have. I could have invoked the swirlies and body slams and cracks about limp wrists and cheap jeans. Maybe I hadn't been there, but I believed every word of Frankie's stories. And knew it had cost him something to relive them. So I didn't. "You just have to get to know him," I said instead.

"Right." Alex nodded. Clearly, he didn't care. "Anyway, I was saying . . . I know you've heard about Amanda and me. I mean, everyone has heard that we broke up."

I waited, standing statue still in the exact middle of my room.

"It's just that the story going around isn't the whole truth. I figured you deserve that." His gaze met mine, but just for a second before sliding away. "Ah, you want to sit down?"

It was getting worse. Not much good has ever been prefaced by variations of "Have a seat." I thought of headmasters' offices and electric chairs. I wondered what I could say to head him off.

Alex studied me for a second. "You look scared. It won't hurt much. I promise."

I am scared of a lot of things, including scary now-ex-girlfriends, sharks, pit bulls, and the odds of being struck by lightning. The possibility that Alex might hurt me, even unintentionally, again was petrifying.

"Okay," I managed.

"Okay. So, here's the thing. Amanda and I have just been split for a few days. Everyone thinks it's temporary . . ."

Maybe if he hadn't paused to take an audible breath, we wouldn't have heard it. But as it was, the creak from the floor outside my half-open door came in loud and clear. Alex shot up like he'd been poked with a sharp stick. I crossed the room in a single breath and jerked open the door.

Nonna, halfway past my room and clearly heading for the stairs, looked like something out of a cartoon. Her shoulders were hunched, she had one foot lifted off the floor, and she was cringing. "Oh, Fiorella. I am sorry!"

In an alternate universe, another Ella was frantically reassuring her shrieking grandmother that nothing had happened, she had not endangered her immortal soul, and it would be a very good thing, please, if Poppa's revolver went back into its dusty case.

In this one, Nonna had a gun forefinger to her own temple. She popped her thumb and rolled her eyes.

Not knowing what else to do, I stepped aside. "Um . . . Nonna, this is Alex Bainbridge. Alex, this is my grandmother . . ."

He was already across the room, hand extended. "*Buongiorno, Signora Marino. Piacere di conosceria.*"

She responded with a delighted cackle and a torrent of Italian. I caught "welcome" and "sausage." Of course, I might have been wrong about both. Alex listened attentively, then gave her a crooked smile. "*Scusi, signora.* I don't speak Italian. Well, much, anyway. I just practiced a couple of phrases for . . . um . . . practice."

"Ah"— Nonna reached up to pinch Alex's cheek, not too hard—"it doesn't matter. You have me at *buongiorno*. Now, come, come."

We went, Nonna leading the way, through the house, across the yard, and into the restaurant kitchen. Mom's car wasn't in the lot. I figured she'd left to sulk over lobsters or shoes. Monday is always a slow night. Leo was cleaning the espresso machine and cursing under his breath. It's the only thing he hates more than waiting tables with Sienna. He didn't even look up when we came in.

At his station, Ricky was up to his elbows in ground sausage meat. He tossed Alex a friendly "Hey, kid," and went back to it.

"This is Alex," I told anyone who cared. "From Willing."

Dad was still holding the big knife. He gave Alex a very long look. Then he set down the knife, wiped his hands on his apron, and extended one. "Ronnie Marino."

Alex almost leaped forward to take it. "Alex Bainbridge."

He gave a tiny wince, and I figured Dad had squeezed.

"Yeah. The congressman's kid. I remember."

I didn't think they'd crossed paths that night. But Dad doesn't forget much that happens in his restaurant.

"We had an amazing dinner," Alex told him. Just as I started to worry that he might launch into just the sort of flattery that doesn't work on my dad, his face got a slightly goofy look and he announced, "I've dreamed about that antipasto plate."

And that was that.

"You hungry?" Dad asked.

"Starving," Alex answered.

"Good." Dad scooped up the knife again. "Ella, find out what the young gentleman would like to eat, and all will be well in the world."

"Sit!" Nonna commanded, pushing Alex from behind. All that was visible of her was a flash of black skirt behind his knees.

"Purple beet ravioli," Uncle Ricky announced to the room, "stuffed with sausage, dried apricots, and Asiago cheese."

"Try," Nonna commanded, one hand in the middle of Alex's chest now to make him sit on one of the stainless stools, the other reaching for a crostini. She makes them every afternoon out of yesterday's *ciabatta* bread, and varies the topping. This one looked suspiciously like anchovy paste, mashed beans, and garlic. Yummy, but not the first thing I would hand a guest.

He took it.

"So, you a ravioli man?" Ricky asked.

"Um, yeah, sure," Alex answered around a mouthful of very

crunchy toast and the hand he'd lifted to prevent crumb spray. "Yours sounds really . . . good."

"Not good, my friend. To die for. A classic in the making. So, you ever watch *Top Chef* . . . ?"

Tina stuck her head through the dining room doors. "Yo, Leo, you got a table! Put your rear in gear." She spied Alex. "Hey. Whaddya know." Her eyes settled on me for a second. "Bag o' chips?" she asked me. I shrugged. "Whatever. Leo!"

He jogged across the floor, shaking coffee grinds off his hands.

"Hey!" Dad snapped. "I just mopped."

Leo grabbed a dish towel and peered past Tina's tower of curls. "It's the Nguyens," he hissed at her. "They've been here every friggin' Monday for ten years, like family. You couldn't just ask them what they want to eat?"

Tina shrugged and examined a scarlet nail. "Not my job, sweetie."

Leo stomped off to get a fresh apron. Tina went back into the dining room. Ten seconds later, we could hear her laughing with the Nguyens, who invariably ordered Caesar salads and *linguine alle vongole*. There was a loud clatter as Dad tipped a bunch of clams into a skillet. It was followed by a clang and a hiss. I spun back toward Nonna.

"*Aiee! San Lorenzo.*" She was hopping in place, one hand cupped in the other. "So stupid."

Dad was already halfway across the kitchen. "Mama, you okay?"

She waved him off with her elbow. "*Sì, sì.* I grab a hot pot.

You go back to your *vongole*. You"—she called to me—"go get me some ice in a towel and honey. *Presto!* Ah, so *stupido* . . ."

I froze. I'd never seen Nonna so much as stub her toe in the kitchen, let alone burn herself. Suddenly, I was remembering the urn and the yelling and the searing, screaming pain . . .

"Fiorella!" Nonna's voice cut through the memory. I had my left hand clamped to my shoulder. She was waving both of her hands at me. "I am fine, *piccola*. Look." One palm might have been a little pink; that was all I could see. I let out my breath in a shaky whoosh. "Ice, now. And the honey."

I darted a glance at Alex. He'd frozen, midchew, and was watching the scene, a little wide-eyed. I gave him a smile that was probably more of a grimace and headed for the storeroom. Even though I was calm, it took me way too long to find the honey. Someone had put it on the highest shelf, behind a gallon jar of olives. I ended up going up the stepladder two separate times.

When I got back to the kitchen, my heart nearly stopped. Dad was leaning across the stainless worktable, over a pile of shrimp, almost right in Alex's face. He was holding a new knife, this one small and very sharp. "You got that, kid, or should I say it again?" he was demanding.

Alex looked more nervous than I'd ever seen him. But only for a second. Then his face hardened, and he slapped both palms flat on the table. "I've got it," he said. He shoved up his sleeves and reached for the knife. Moments later, he was deveining shrimp with a lot of enthusiasm and a little skill.

Dad turned and caught me gaping. He tilted his head in

obvious warning. Raw, icky, slippery: This was the task he'd given the boy I brought into his kitchen, and I was not to interfere.

Poor Alex. He was being tested for a position he didn't even want.

I handed Nonna the ice and set the honey in front of her. She'd already collected a couple of clean dish towels and a butter knife.

"Do you want me to walk you over to the house?" I asked.

"No, no. I put this on my hand, and it will all be fine." She actually slathered honey over her palm, then settled the towel-wrapped ice over it. "Your young man will do the shrimp. You go do the linen. The boys will do the rest." The boys, forty-three and forty-eight respectively, were moving a little faster than usual, but everything was back to calm and cheerful.

Alex looked up from his shrimp. "My mom used to do that, put honey on me when I got little scrapes. She said it prevents infection."

"Did it work?" I asked.

Alex grinned. "Who knows. She usually started with Neosporin."

"Leo!" Dad yelled. "These salads aren't going to serve themselves! Oh, hi, Huong." Mrs. Nguyen was halfway into the kitchen. "Ah! Not a chance. You go sit down, ma'am, and wait for the waiter. Leo!"

Mrs. Nguyen waved and left; Leo came in, scooped up the salads, and followed. Ten seconds later, we could hear them all laughing. Another family came in, another order. Then another, and another, and the night was on. It got busy, especially for a Monday. Tina condescended to serve a few orders—and take the tips that came later. I folded napkins and bused tables and checked in on Alex when I could. Ricky and Dad did what they did. Nonna supervised from a high stool. Alex went from deveining shrimp to cleaning mushrooms.

Poor guy. They were really giving him the dirty work.

He didn't complain, of course. More than that, he was kinda terrific with my family. He was a very good sport when his proud allergy recitation got loud laughter and no sympathy. Apparently, he'd been telling people he was allergic to the kind of nuts that don't have anything to do with food. Apparently, his mother didn't read the English–Italian translation quite carefully enough. Nonna, determined to rectify the situation, gave him the Italian word for everything in the entire kitchen. He repeated them cheerfully. He argued with Ricky over the Phillies' lousy season and agreed with Dad that the Eagles looked good for the Super Bowl.

He ate whatever anyone put in front of him. Including the, yes, *bagna cauda*, whose primary ingredients are anchovies, garlic, and sardines, and some purple ravioli. Dad smacked Leo on the back of the head when he laughed. Leo gave Alex half a loaf of Nonna's *pane* right out of the oven.

Sitting next to him, having my second bowl of soup of the day, and, yes, *bagna cauda* on *pane*, I didn't want the night to end. Simple as that. Because, if one ignored the fact that we were in the middle of a loud kitchen, surrounded by my family, that we were both wearing stained aprons and he smelled like shrimp, it could almost be a date.

At least surrounded and stinky and stuffing his face with warm bread, Alex couldn't dump me. Or whatever a guy does with a girl he isn't dating. Lets her down easy, I guess, if he's a nice guy.

At ten fifteen, the last customers left. Dad, always a step ahead, had seven little chocolate *budinos*—little puddings— baking in the oven. We ate them with the strawberry candy Mrs. Nguyen left for us.

Dad wouldn't let Alex help with the cleanup. Alex tried to refuse the money Dad pushed on him. "Don't you insult me!" Dad snapped. "This is a family business!" Alex missed the smile; he was busy trying to get the folded bills into his pocket. "Now, you go home to your family before they think you've run off to join a circus. You"—pointing to me—"go to bed. You're sick. Remember?"

Of course I'd forgotten. I gave a small cough. He rolled his eyes and waved me off.

I moved a lot more slowly as Alex went out of my day than I had when he came into it. I figured he had some things to say that I didn't want to hear, and I tried to think of any way I could ask him just not to talk, please, without sounding sullen or slightly insane.

I walked him out to his car. Mr. Greco had gone up a ladder and loosened the lightbulb in the streetlamp again. He complains that it shines right into his bedroom. So he disables the light,

PECO sends a crew to fix it, and it all begins again. It's been going on for years. The Grecos are nice people, especially Mrs. Greco. If she's home when the electric guys arrive, she takes them coffee and doughnuts.

Alex unlocked the car and opened the door. "Well, good night," he said cheerfully. "Thanks for dinner."

"Oh. Right." I took a half step back toward the house. "You're welcome."

"Ella."

"Yeah?"

"You've gotta be kidding."

PECO hadn't come yet, so it was pretty dark where we were standing. I don't know how his hand found mine so fast, but one second I was thinking about how much I didn't want to say good night, and the next I was up against his chest, standing on my toes with my feet between his.

"Is this okay?" he asked, his breath chocolaty and warm against my forehead.

"Yeah," I answered, my own breath coming in quick little jumps. "Yeah."

"Good. I have something I have to tell you."

I waited.

"I hate that Klimt painting," he said. "I really hate it."

Then he was folding me into his coat and his face was right above mine, and there was only one kiss that mattered.

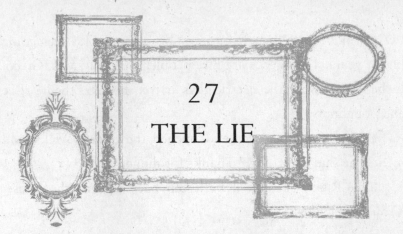

27
THE LIE

I didn't want to play. Frankie was in a mood for some reason, and when Frankie is in a mood, he can be a little mean. Sadie, on the other hand, was glowing slightly, and she hadn't even hit the Chloe's stage yet. She'd had a second date with Jared the night before. It had gone well.

I took a quick look at my phone. No message, but I didn't really expect one. My plans were already made. What I really needed was to see the time: 8:37.

"Why don't you just go already?" Frankie said snarkily. "We don't want to hold you up."

"I have plenty of time." I'd told them that I had to be home, that wedding plans were beginning to go into overdrive. Both statements were true, to a point. It was pretty much all wedding all the time these days. But the real truth there was that I stayed out of the way as much as possible. My shiny purple bridesmaid's dress and shoes fit, I knew the church drill, and I really didn't care what ultimately would be on the menu.

But I did have to go home. Alex was picking me up there.

For two weeks now, we'd been meeting when we could. Which, tragically, had been all of four short times: three at his house, once at mine, for a small amount of French before a lot of kissing. We'd had one furtive little interlude in an empty music room at school, but I'd been too nervous to really get into that one. At home, we were entwined, fingers and lips. At school, we barely spoke. It was still too new, too strange, maybe, to make public. I was still convinced that I was going to wake up, or walk out of a bathroom, or look up from my homework to discover I'd imagined the whole thing.

"Sades," I said, pointing a *pepperoncini* I probably wouldn't eat. "Truth or Dare."

"Truth. I'm eating." She and Frankie were. I wasn't, not really. Alex had said something about food, so I'd been moving my salad around my plate.

"Okay." It had to be a good one, something she would really want to share with her two best friends. It had to be a good one to make up for the fact that I was keeping some big secrets from my two best friends for the past two weeks. "Five years from today. Where, exactly, do you want to be?"

Her eyes lit up. Sadie loves that kind of question. "Ooh. Wow. Let me think. December, getting close to Christmas. I'll be twenty-one . . ."

"Passed out under the tree with a fifth of Jack, half a 7-Eleven rotisserie chicken, and a cat who poops in your shoes." Frankie returned our startled glances with his lizard look. "Oh, wait. That's me. Sorry."

I opted to ignore him. "Five years to the day, Sadie."

She glanced quickly between Frankie and me. "Do we need a time-out here?"

"Nope," I said. "Carry on."

"Okay. Five years. I will be in New York visiting the pair of you because, while NYU is fab, I will be halfway through my final year of classics at Cambridge, trying to decide whether I want to be a psychologist or a pastry chef. You," she said sternly to Frankie, "will be drinking appropriate amounts of champagne with your boyfriend, a six-three blond from Helsinki who happens to design for Tory Burch. Ah! Don't say anything. It's my future. You can choose a different designer when it's your go. I want the Tory freebies." She turned to me. "We will be sipping said champagne in the middle of the Gagosian Gallery, because it is the opening night of your first solo exhibit. At which everything will sell."

She punctuated the sentence by poking the air with a speared black olive.

"I love you," I told her. Then, "But that wasn't really about you."

"Oh, but it was," she disagreed, going back to her salad. "It's exactly where I want to be. Although"—she grinned over a tomato wedge—"I might have the next David Beckham in tow."

"The next David Beckham is a five-foot-tall Welshman named Madog Cadwalader. He has extra teeth and bow legs."

"Really?" Sadie asked.

Frankie snorted. "No. Not really."

"What is up with you tonight?" I demanded before I could stop myself.

He turned, very slowly, to face me. "Not a thing, as it happens. Why don't you tell us what's up with you? Hmm?"

"This isn't about me."

"No?" Frankie tapped his fingers on the table. "Well, something about you is not quite right these days, Marino. And it's not just me who's noticed. Sadie?"

"Oh. Well, I don't know . . . yeah . . . maybe . . ."

"So, what is it?" Frankie demanded. "You're not eating, you've cut more classes in the last month than in the last two years, and you haven't mentioned Edward Willing in three weeks."

"You hate when I talk about—"

"Three weeks, madam. And that's only as long as I've been keeping track. It's weird, and we're worried. Sadie?"

Sadie was twisting pleats into her sweater. It was blue, narrow, and new to her wardrobe. It was obviously also not one of her mother's picks. "Um . . . yeah. Maybe a little."

"See?" Frankie gestured toward Sadie with both hands. "She's completely distraught."

"Frankie." I wanted to reach across the table and touch him, but didn't. I didn't think I could take it if he pulled away. "There is absolutely nothing wrong with me."

"Yeah?"

"Yeah."

He leaned back and crossed his arms over his chest. For a second, he looked exactly like Daniel: cynical, bored, and liable to bite. "Well, that's funny," he drawled. "I think you're lying through your teeth."

My stomach clenched. "Why?"

"Because," he said calmly, "in all the time I've known you, you have never once said those words."

"What words?"

"'There is nothing wrong with me.'"

"Oh, don't—"

"Never. You are a walking litany of imaginary flaws. So." Frankie unfolded himself and rested his elbows on the table. It wobbled. He didn't. He studied me over his tented fingers. "Truth or Dare?"

"It's Sadie's turn to ask."

"She passes," he snapped.

"Hey," I protested.

"Hey." Sadie actually waved a hand between us. "Maybe we can talk about this tomorrow."

"We could," Frankie replied with suspicious agreeability. "Except I want to do it now. So, here's the question, Marino. What—"

"Dare."

"Sorry?" he said.

"Dare. I'll take a dare."

"Really?" he demanded.

"As long as it takes ten minutes or less. I have to go." All I wanted, really, was to leave.

Frankie didn't say anything—or move—for the longest time.

He just stared at me. Then, finally, he blinked, lowered his hands, and shrugged. "Sing."

"Oh, come on—"

"Sing," he repeated. "You know how. Or concede."

That, I thought, would be so easy. It would also break something precious. In all our time together, none of us had ever conceded a dare. "Sadie. Sing with me?"

She nodded, but Frankie shook a finger at her. "You will not. Marino, you're on your own here."

I pretty much stomped my way to the stage. Stavros's son Nic was manning the karaoke machine. His brows shot up when he saw me. "A first."

It wasn't, actually. Frankie had bullied me into doing a duet on Sadie's birthday. We sang—surprise surprise—"Birthday" by the Beatles. It might have bombed, but it turned out that a third-string player for the Flyers was celebrating his birthday that day, too, so we ended up sharing the stage with four drunk hockey players, two female hockey groupies, and a die-hard Ringo fan. The crowd loved it.

"I have to do this," I muttered. "I can do this."

I didn't realize I was shaking slightly until Nic tapped my hand. "You want some advice?"

"Sure."

"Choose one of these." He flipped to a battered page. "And undo a few buttons."

I didn't know if he was serious about the buttons—I suspected he probably was—but he'd given me a page full of crowd-pleasers.

I contemplated "Good Riddance," "Forget You," and "Here's a Quarter, Call Someone Who Cares." Only I didn't know that one, and wasn't really out to stick it to Frankie. Well, maybe just a little.

"I can do this," I said, pointing.

"Kill 'em" was Nic's comment as I hit the stage.

I took one look at Frankie's sulky face before settling my gaze on the back of the room. I could do this, because when I was done, I could go.

The music started. I hit the cue. "'You walked into the party like you were walking onto a yacht . . .'"

I wasn't bad. A little wavery in places, but pretty confident on. "'I bet you think this song is about you, don't you?'" When I was done, a group of girls who reminded me of Cat Vernon and her crowd cheered loudly in back. Sadie was whistling, that two-fingers-in-the-mouth trick that I've always wanted to be able to do. She uses it for taxis and for Chloe's. On the very rare occasions that I am in a cab, Sadie is there, too, so I figure I'll live without that particular skill. It was nice, though, to hear her over the polite applause.

Frankie, I noticed as I flipped the mic up to its normal position, was staring at me through narrowed eyes, clapping so slowly that I could actually measure the silence in between beats.

I felt about three inches tall as I stepped off the stage.

<hr />

". . . and went down like a rock. Bam."

"Oh, man. What did you do?"

"What could I do?" I shrugged. "I hopped up, took a bow, and ran. I was late to meet you."

Alex was gently rubbing my bare knee. I'd rolled up my jeans leg to show him the bruise already blossoming there. "I would have caught you," he said, fingers sliding to the inside of my leg and making my insides feel like jelly.

"Not likely, O Gallant One. The stage is only a foot high."

"I gotta see this place sometime."

"Sure." I knew better, somehow. I wasn't going to take him. I couldn't, for more reasons than I wanted to list. Not that I could even picture him sitting there while people sang bad covers on a plywood stage, the food smells battling with polish and shoe leather.

We were sitting on the big, nice-smelling leather sofa in his den, me with my legs across his, a plate balanced in my lap. We'd stopped at Hikaru on our way from my house to his. I've walked by it enough times when I'd been to Head House Books or Hepburn's, the vintage clothing store across the street. But sushi isn't a big part of my life; Frankie and I inevitably vote Sadie down in favor of the South Street Diner. She always offers to pay. We always tell her that isn't the point. Even if it kind of is.

"What looks good?" Alex asked as we scanned the menu. Then, "Just no blowfish." And, "I'm buying."

I hadn't even heard of most of the options: fluke, conger, porgy. And those I had—mackerel, abalone, octopus—weren't all that appealing raw. "Um. Tempura?" I suggested, thinking you couldn't go too terribly wrong with something dipped and fried.

He shook his head. "This from a girl who likes anchovies?" He shared a sympathetic smile with the very nice waitress, then proceeded to order octopus, mackerel, yellowtail, and several different kinds of tuna. Raw.

"I am not eating that," I told him in the den as he held out his chopsticks, loaded with a slice of octopus that had visible tentacles. I'd been fine with the tuna (I am the Tuna King of the Sea's great-great-granddaughter, after all), but had to draw the line somewhere.

"You have to trust me here. Come on. Be a brave girl. Open up."

Duh. I am not a brave girl. But I opened my mouth and let him feed me. "Mmm."

"See? Excellent stuff."

Actually, it was like eating a pencil eraser. With a vaguely fishy taste. "Delicious," I managed after much chewing.

"All right. Fine. I give up." Alex ate the remainder of the octopus and most of the pickled ginger in quick bites. Then he removed the plate from my thighs. I snagged the last piece of ginger before it was out of my reach. That I liked. "So, what shall we do now?"

Oh, the possibilities. I wiggled my eyebrows at him. He laughed.

"Yeah, absolutely," he agreed. "But first . . . three things . . ."

He was determined. Every time we were together, we traded revelations and did some French. It wasn't usually the first thing, but eventually we got around to it. "You are an enigma wrapped in a mystery," he teased me once. "And you're failing French."

Of all the things I am, I don't think enigmatic is one of them. But I liked that he used the word. So I leaned back against the arm of the sofa and thought. "I don't know what you want to know."

"Well, that's easy. Everything."

"No. You don't. No one wants to know everything about . . ." I found myself at a loss for words. *His girlfriend? His pupil with benefits?* We weren't at the noun stage. I wasn't sure if I would recognize the noun stage if I landed in it. ". . . another person. Mystery is good."

He drummed his fingertips on my thigh. "Maybe. Maybe not. But I'll let it go. How about this: If I were to open the top drawer of your dresser, what would I find?"

"Are we back to discussing my underwear again?"

"Only in graphic detail . . ." He flicked my sore knee, but not where the bruise was. "*I* keep loose change and my oldest comic books in mine. Some people have journals or photographs or awards . . ."

"Okay, okay." I sighed. "Underwear," I said. "Two ancient swimsuits, and a magazine file."

"Of . . . ?"

"Pictures I've pulled out of magazines."

"Yes, thank you. I gathered that. What's in it?"

I squirmed a little and contemplated lying. Travel pix, shoes, hints on getting glue off of Ultrasuede . . . "Mostly pictures of models with short hair," I confessed finally. "It's sort of a goal of mine."

Alex reached up and wrapped a strand around his finger. "I

like your hair," he said quietly, "but I think you'd look great whatever you did with it."

Here's the thing. He looked like he meant it, and like it had been the most natural thing in the world to say. I blinked at him.

"Okay," I said. "You want to know something about me that I don't really want to tell you? How about this. I don't get it. This. I hate that I don't. I wish I were the kind of girl who took guys like you as my sovereign right in life. But I don't."

"Yeah, I've sorta figured that out, too." He let go of my hair and put his hand on my waist, so his thumb was against my skin. I shivered. "Here's my first reveal for the night. One day, not so long ago, I'm just sitting in the dining room, digesting, minding my own business—literally. Trying to decide whether the second hamburger had been such a good idea and whether to break up with my girlfriend of a year and a half. Then I try to stand up, and suddenly there's this really pretty girl doubled over and looking at my book like it was covered with crap—"

"I wasn't."

"Yeah. You were. So there you were, with that amazing face and a yard of hair that smelled like flowers, and all this stuff drawn on your jeans. I really liked that."

"You liked my jeans."

"Among other things. But, jeez, Ella. After that, if you weren't making me feel like I had the IQ of a stone, your friends were looking at me like I'd crawled out from under one. I won't even go into what you obviously think of *my* friends."

"Chase Vere is a reptile."

"Chase Vere has been my friend since we were nine. Hey," he said when I made a face, "the thing about friends is that we pick them for ourselves and don't worry too much about what other people think. Right?"

I got the pointed point, but couldn't help asking, "Do you have any friends who aren't Phillites?"

He scowled at me. "I hate that word. I really hate it."

"Why?" I asked, genuinely confused. I gestured around the room, with its leather furniture and slick electronics. "It fits."

"So do Speedos, but I don't want to wear those, either." He stared at me through narrowed eyes. "Let's try this: You tell me something you actually like about me."

I snuggled into his lap. "I like everything about you."

"Except my friends and socioeconomic status."

I looked up at him. "Are you mad?"

"No, Ella, I'm not mad."

I wasn't entirely sure I believed him. He looked a little grim. I felt a tug of worry. "I like your mouth," I whispered, tracing his lips with my fingertip, coaxing them up at the corner. "Among many, many other things."

The mouth was a good start. I especially liked what he did with it. So much that I didn't realize what his hands were doing until I felt cool air.

"Alex—"

"Come on, Ella. Let me. Please."

I scooted away from him, pushing at his hands. My sweater fell back to my waist. "No. Just . . . no."

"Let me get this straight. I can touch. Here." His palm was warm, even through the cabled cotton. "But I can't look? That's a little messed up, isn't it?"

"Maybe, but that's me."

He sighed. "You're going to have to let me see sometime."

I wasn't quite as sure, but kept that to myself. "Not tonight." *Or tomorrow or tomorrow or tomorrow.*

"Okay." He wrapped both hands around my waist and tugged until I was in his lap again. "But you still have to tell me a third thing. You only did two tonight."

I tried to come up with something light and innocuous. It wasn't easy, with his hands on me and my knee aching again. All I could think of was the fact that, like the piano or French or pulling quarters out of people's ears, lying was easier the more you practiced.

"I'm changing . . ." I said.

"Don't do that," Alex said into my hair. Then he scooped me up and over so I was below him, his knees bracketing mine, his arms curving around my head. "Don't change."

Truth: When he kissed me again, I couldn't have cared less about being a good person. I felt amazing.

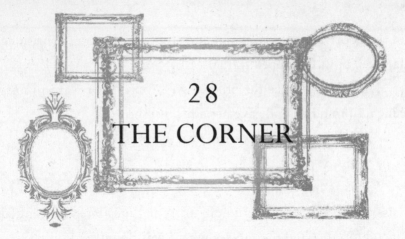

28
THE CORNER

Sadie surprised me at the top of the stairs when I came up from French. "Well?"

"Eighty-seven." I waved the quiz at her.

"Yay!" She actually bounced up and down for a sec. For a French quiz. "Yay, you! Yay, Alex!"

"Yeah, well." I gave all my attention to folding the paper perfectly in half. "It's a start."

"It's a B-plus. C'mon, let's celebrate. I have a real, true Famous Fourth Street cookie in my lunch. I was going to share it with Jared, but how often is it that one's best friend conquers the French?"

"*Merci, mademoiselle*. But you should share with the cute boy. I have to go sort through charcoal in the art studio."

"Need help?"

"Sades, you're wearing white." She actually was. "You look great."

Jared tended to rush in and out of the dining room; he had Willing worlds to conquer every day. But he made sure to stop in the doorway on his way out and give Sadie a huge, flourishing farewell bow. It stopped traffic.

I spun her to face the other way. "You do not want to miss lunch," I told her, and gave her a helpful shove.

"But, Ella, really. It's no big deal. Friends . . ."

I went the other way.

"This is not exactly what I had in mind when I agreed to miss lunch," Alex said grumpily forty minutes later. He shifted uncomfortably and tried to see what I was doing.

I stared him back into submission. "Wait."

The art room is usually empty Thursday afternoons except for me. Ms. Evers leaves early to teach her UArts class and locks up. Of course, I am one of the few entrusted with the Secret Location of the Key.

A few feet away from where I sat perched on a stool, Alex was posed on the ancient chaise we use for figure drawing. It's a relic, probably from the Palladinetti years: chipped mahogany and dusty velvet, what little remaining stuffing pokes out from a century of holes. It was probably luxurious once. Now it's like sitting on a slightly smelly board. But I'd wanted to sketch Alex as I so often saw him, reclining with his head propped on one hand, listening or talking or coaxing me to put down the glass, already, Ella, and come here.

"I don't like this," he complained. He'd been complaining since I'd scooted off the chaise ten minutes earlier, leaving him on it.

"Just a little longer. I know it's not your sofa, but it's not that bad."

He grimaced. "It smells like wet dog. But what I meant was that I don't think I like posing. How do I know you're not going to give me a beer gut or a third eye?"

"I've always thought a third eye would be pretty useful." I pictured the Indian miniature art Cat Vernon had introduced me to and imagined Alex blue, with multiple arms. It was, probably, just what he expected. "And in what universe would there be an even remotely compelling reason for me to give you any sort of gut whatsoever? You're gonna have to trust me, Sushi Boy."

I don't usually draw people. Too many angles. But this was Alex coming through my pencil: the little lifts at the corners of his mouth, the almost invisible bump on his nose where an errant lacrosse ball took a funny bounce ("I was on the sidelines—took me a whole year to convince my mother that I didn't need to wear a helmet twenty-four/seven . . ."), the lean muscles in his bent arm. I was pretty clear on the fact that I wouldn't always have the original, so I was serious about the copy.

"Put down the pencil, already, Ella. Come here."

"Five minutes."

"We only have ten before the end of the period."

"So we'll each get five." But I stopped drawing and rested the sketchbook on my knees. "I'm going to the art museum tomorrow. Do you want to come with me? They have some good Japanese woodblock prints."

I wanted to pay a visit to the Willing collection. It had been a while. Nothing that the Sheridan-Brown had was helpful. I thought I would try the Big House. But what I was really thinking of was the hushed room tucked into the depths of the museum with the real Japanese teahouse. It was one of my favorite places to go in the museum, with its cool stone floor and running water. It felt private, even if it wasn't. I wanted to be there with Alex.

"Wish I could, but I have something I have to do." He sat up and rolled his shoulders.

"So I won't see you tomorrow?"

"Not after school. But we'll do something Saturday, right? Maybe my house?"

"No parents again?"

He shrugged. "Last days of the congressional session for my dad. Mom's doing a piece on holiday shopping. We on?"

"Sure. But no sushi."

"Whatever you want," he said. "Will you please come here now?"

I slipped a piece of protective tissue over my drawing and flipped the book closed. A piece of blue scratch paper slid out, the line I'd copied from Edward's poetry book. "Hey. Translate for me, Monsieur Bainbridge."

I set the sketchbook on my stool and joined him on the chaise. He tugged me onto his lap and read over my head. " '*Qu'ieu sui avinen, leu lo sai.*' 'That I am handsome, I know.' "

"Very funny."

"Very true." He grinned. "The translation. That's what it says. Old-fashionedly."

I thought of Edward's notation on the page, the reminder to read the poem to Diana in bed, and rolled my eyes. *You're so vain. I bet you think this song is about you* . . . "Boys and their egos."

Alex cupped my face in his hands. *"Que tu est belle, tu le sais."*

"Oh, I am not—"

"Shh," he shushed me, and leaned in.

The first bell came way too soon. I reluctantly loosened my grip on his shirt and ran my hands over my hair. He promptly thrust both hands in and messed it up again. "Stop," I scolded, but without much force.

"I have physics," he told me. "We're studying weak interaction."

I sandwiched his open hand between mine. "You know absolutely nothing about that."

"Don't be so quick to accept the obvious," he mock-scolded me. "Weak interaction can actually change the flavor of quarks."

The flavor of quirks, I thought, and vaguely remembered something about being charmed. I'd sat through a term of introductory physics before switching to basic biology. I'd forgotten most of that as soon as I'd been tested on it, too.

"I gotta go." Alex pushed me to my feet and followed. "Last person to get to class always gets the first question, and I didn't do the reading."

"Go," I told him. "I have history. By definition, we get to history late."

"Ha-ha. I'll talk to you later." He kissed me again, then walked out, closing the door quietly behind him.

I slung my bag over my shoulder and picked up my sketchbook. By the time I'd locked the room and rehidden the key in the antique wall sconce, he was long gone. I could hear the patter of feet and voices in another part of the floor, but the hall around me was empty. There isn't much on the corridor except for the art rooms and a girls' bathroom that is usually empty except for the occasional senior Phillite or two using a forbidden phone (apparently the reception was great and the only teacher around was the one least likely to care). I headed for it.

I got there just as the Hannandas and Chase Vere rounded the corner. There was a scattered moment when Anna tried to cover her iPad with a textbook and I tried to decide if I should turn around and run the other way. Then Chase looked up.

"Hey. Freddy," he greeted me affably.

In the second it took the Hannandas to realize who I was, and that I wasn't exactly a threat to the new toy, I made it all of one step backward.

"Freak." Amanda wrinkled her nose in the imaginary stink diss of the unimaginative.

I made a quick choice and started to walk past them. In a world of fight or flight, I was the one with feathers.

She stepped into my path. "I thought I told you to stay away from me, skank." Her repertoire was definitely both limited and predictable, but that realization didn't make her any less scary. "Are you stalking me? There is no reason for you to be in this corridor."

She stared at me expectantly. I hadn't planned on saying

anything, but it seemed required. "I was in the art room," I offered. *With him*, I didn't say.

I don't know if it was that I unconsciously lifted my chin, or if there was something in my voice that her attack mode detected. Whatever the reason, Amanda's eyes narrowed, and her smile turned seriously evil. Before I could even think to protect myself, her arm darted out, fast as a snake, and grabbed my sketchbook. I went after it, but Chase, master defenseman that he is, blocked me with one hand.

Amanda was already flipping roughly through the pages, bending them as she went. It was like she knew what she was looking for. And then she found it.

"Oh. My. God. You are such a freak." She laughed, horsey and startling. "You are worse than a stalker!"

She held up the picture of Alex. I felt the blood flowing into my face, my empty hands tightening into fists.

"I am so going to copy and post this. When Alex sees it—"

"Give it back to her."

It was a toss-up who was more surprised, Amanda or me. We both ended up gaping at Anna. She was holding out the iPad, face completely blank.

In another story, the dauntless heroine would have peppered the mind-controlled Annamaria Lombardi with memories of her past, relentlessly insisting that she was *good* inside. That all she had to do was remember. Then, of course, the glowing red would fade from mind-controlled Annamaria's eyes. She would turn, literally and figuratively, and squash the Evil Amanda before crumpling to the ground, irrevocably weakened by the poison she'd been fed for so long. Her last words would be a plea for forgiveness and, "We always got the strawberry—"

"Ella was always a loser. She can't help it." Anna pushed the iPad toward Amanda, who automatically took it. In that second, Anna pulled my book from Amanda's other hand and passed it back to me. She didn't look at me at all. "Come on. The invite to Harrison's party is on YouTube. He's hidden some stupid password thing in a video, and we need to find it. Adam says he's putting a doorman outside, and it's the last party before break."

Amanda didn't move immediately. But then she flicked her ponytail, did the nostril thing again (I wondered why I'd never noticed exactly how much she resembled a horse), and tilted the iPad in my direction.

"Just in case you doubt it, I could ruin your life so easily." She tapped the screen with a glossy gunmetal nail. "A few lines on Facebook that will follow you *forever*." Then, as if she'd been discussing the weather, she shrugged and turned her back on me. "The signal sucks out here. Let's go in. You," she said to Chase, "can wait."

They filed into the bathroom, Anna and Hannah in their places. The door swung to with a heavy thump. And I came unfrozen. Unfortunately, Chase was a beat ahead. He stepped into my path, forcing me to stop, my back to the wall.

"Man, I thought you two were going to go at it like cats," he announced, grinning. "She does not like you, Freddy. If she knew you were spending time under Bainbridge, she would have ripped you to shreds. You show up at Harrison's with him tomorrow night, and I'm standing back to watch." He tilted his head and studied me through slightly bloodshot eyes. "You *are* doing him, aren't you?"

I didn't answer.

"Well, he's keeping you a dirty little secret. It's that smokin' little bod, right? I mean, what else would it be?"

With that, he reached for me, actually thrust out both hands out like some cartoon monster. I don't know if he would really have grabbed. Maybe not, but it didn't matter. I hit him with the sketchbook, slamming his left elbow hard enough to send him stumbling to his right. I'm small, but I had the advantage of surprise. As I pushed past him, I swung again, this time at his hip. I didn't wait around to see how quickly he regained his balance. I ran, down the few feet of hall and around the corner.

Almost right into Frankie. He was standing in the middle of the hallway, vintage dangerous from the fedora to the black overcoat to the weapon he had gripped in both hands.

"You okay?" he asked, even while he was stepping past me to look where I'd just been. I heard the thud of a weighted door. Chase, I thought, going into the girls' room with the Hannandas.

"Yeah," I said after a shaky second. "Thanks."

Frankie didn't look at me as he returned the fire extinguisher to its clip on the wall.

"I never thought I would see you armed." I was trying for levity. It worked like a lead balloon. Frankie just frowned and reached into an inside coat pocket for one of his ubiquitous handkerchiefs.

He used it to wipe something, dust maybe, from his hands.

"You think I was going to take on three bitchy girls empty-handed? I figured a good blast of this near their Uggs would get them moving the other way fast. Then I thought I could just throw it at Vere's head."

"My hero," I said. I meant it.

He shrugged. "Turns out you didn't need me. But then, you decided that a while ago, right?"

"Of course I need you. You're my best friend."

"Kind of an interesting statement considering the circumstances, wouldn't you say?"

I could have played dumb. But with Frankie, it would only have made matters worse. "How much did you hear?"

"How much would you have rather I hadn't?" he shot back. "I heard it all. No"—he tucked the handkerchief away—"I saw and heard it all, starting with Alex Bainbridge whistling his way down the hall, zipping up his pants as he went."

"He never unzipped them!" I protested, before realizing that Frankie was just being snarky. And that he was very, very angry. "I'm sorry."

"I don't especially care."

"Frankie—"

"Ah!" He gave me the Hand. "I came looking for you to see if you wanted to walk to history, stayed to save your ass, and now I am leaving." He did a slick turn on his heel and started to walk away.

I caught up with him and grabbed his wrist with both hands.

He let me pull him to a stop, but didn't turn around. "I didn't think you'd understand. You *hate* him. Besides, you made me promise—"

He jerked his hand free and snapped, "No way, Ella. No way I'm letting you turn this around and put it on me. You know me. You *know me*. Not telling has done infinitely more damage than just breaking a half-ass promise. Or even a full-ass one. Like promising to call me back, oh, a half-dozen times or so, and just not."

I've seen Frankie angry plenty of times. Even once or twice at me, when I'd been having a good pity party or spilled something on his old cashmere. But I'd never seen him like this.

"I can imagine how it looks . . ." I began.

"How it looks?" He shook his head in disbelief. "Knowing you, you don't have a clue. So let me tell you how it looks. It looks like you chose to lie to me, and to Sadie, to completely abandon friendship and honor for . . . what? The privilege of being available for Alex Bainbridge's booty calls?"

"You don't mean that."

"Don't I? What is it you think you're gonna get from him, Ella? A seat at the Phillite lunch table? A date for the prom? Small children with good teeth and tiny noses?" His mouth twisted. "You might want to rethink those expectations, because from where I'm standing, I don't see him taking you for a walk between classrooms, let alone home to his parents.

"Face it," he said coldly. "Vere was telling the truth. You're a dirty little secret."

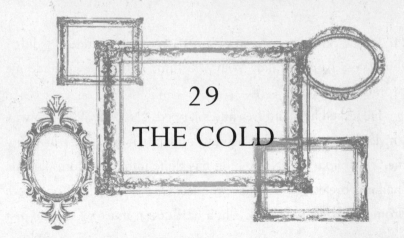

29
THE COLD

I watched Frankie walk away from me, his frame so stiff that I knew if I threw myself at his back, I would bounce off before I could get my arms around him to hold on. In a long line of good exits, that was one of his best.

I cut history. And PE. And algebra. And really cut, no note this time. Willing teachers are famously forgiving in the week before winter or summer break. Exams were done, half the students were either already off on their skiing trip in the Alps or about to depart. But then, it was just as likely my parents would be getting a phone call from the headmaster's office. I was a Willing Girl willing to take the chance.

I went to the museum, a day earlier than planned, and all by myself.

For the last couple of years, I've always started in the same place. It's a little room, more like a little hallway, off one of the Impressionist galleries. That always bothered me. I mean, even in my most Edward-centric moments, I knew he didn't merit a big room of his own. But to tack his work onto the wrong era, not to mention any conceivable style, always chafed.

The upside is that the Willing Room is usually empty. There are eighteen pictures there: seven canvases and eleven pencil sketches. There are two bronzes, too, a pair of portrait busts on pillars. I took a seat between them, on the one bench that fits in the space. The museum guard standing in the archway between this room and the next was shifting on her feet, probably waiting for a break. I knew no one was going to chase me for cutting school, especially not in a museum ("Hey, you! What do you think you're doing, hanging out in a cultural institution! Just wait till your parents hear about this!"), but I still felt a little twitchy.

More than that, I felt sad and pretty scared.

Truth: I had done some real damage to my relationship with Frankie, and I had no idea what I was going to do to fix it.

Hiding in the museum seemed like a perfectly good start.

I had Edward's *Collected Works* closed on my lap. I'd pretty much expended its usefulness. All of the museum's paintings but one were in it: a sunrise-over-water scene that even I, a devotee, thought verged on OTT. *Untitled*, the accompanying placard read, 1901, Gift of an Anonymous Donor, 1942. Someone hadn't wanted the painting on their wall, maybe, and didn't want their name on the museum's.

I'd never paid much attention to where the collection came from before. This time, I did. The paintings were varied, three purchased by the museum, including the one of the bicycle riders on Boathouse Row that had Her in the foreground. Two, portraits of pretty but bland Willings, were gifts from the family. Pretty arrogant, I'd always thought, donating a picture of yourself to major American museum. Another portrait, the pretty, unhappy Mrs. John Girard Hamilton on her pink sofa, was part of a bigger collection that had come to the museum.

And, of course, there was the one anonymous donation.

All eleven sketches had the same origin; they were, with Sad Sofa Lady, from the estate of Vera H. Erasmus, who, if one went by the acquisition dates, had died in 1997. I could have known her, this woman who was such an Edward fan. The bronzes, titled simply *Mother* and *Child*, had been hers, too. My book suggested they were Mary and Murray, Edward's sister and nephew. He'd been kind. I've seen photographs of Mary and Murray Girvan. They weren't that pretty. Of course, Edward hadn't known that some years later they would do some terrible things with his personal papers.

As for the sketches themselves, they were a varied lot and spanned the last fifteen years of his life. Two were of dogs, three of what looked like a garden (I'd always liked the one of the stone bench), and six were of Her. For the first time, I realized it was the same woman in all of them. I'd never thought about it much on previous visits, just assumed they were different models, some clothed, some dressed, some visibly older and softer. Now I could see the similarities in the curve of her neck, the line of her arm and hip and profile.

Not one was of a face. None had names. None had dates. Only the throwaway word *Study*. It read like a command, even though I knew it just referred to the fact that they were quick sketches of what would be part of a larger work. But now, for the first time, I realized that none of the sketched figures were from Edward's paintings. I knew Edward's paintings—the ones that had been catalogued, anyway. These weren't studies for other works. They were like snapshots, little pieces of his life after Diana. Of whatever his life with Her was.

Truth: Edward had painted this woman lovingly.

Truth: He'd never shown her face.

Probability: She was his dirty little secret.

I checked the notes I'd made. There weren't many. A few dates, a few quick descriptions of the sketches, acquisition info. I had no idea how it was going to help. It seemed that Edward had very deliberately not left any clues to Her identity other than the art itself.

"One unpopular connection was enough for him, ya think?" I asked the bronze Mary above me. "If you Phillites are scary now, I can only imagine what you were like a hundred years ago."

No shocker, she didn't respond. The guard, however, gave me the hairy eyeball.

A couple stepped through the archway. They were older than me, early twenties, both blond, both wearing nerdy cool black specs and boots and black canvas clothing that reminded me of Sadie's wardrobe—only infinitely better suited to the wearers. They were holding a map of the museum between them, talking softly in an unfamiliar language. I didn't catch much, just a questioning *"Villink?"* and wondered if they were Russian. I didn't think so. The language sounded more Germanic to me, maybe Dutch. They'd clearly never heard of Edward Willing.

They came in to look. I watched them. Most people go through museums like they do Macy's: eyes sweeping the display, stopping only if something really grabs their attention. These two looked at everything. They both clearly liked the bicycle picture. Yup, Dutch, I decided.

He was a few steps ahead when he got to my favorite painting there. *Diana and the Moon.* It was—surprise surprise— of Diana, framed by a big open window, the moon dominating the sky outside. She was perched on the windowsill, dressed in a gauzy wrap that could have been nightclothes or a nod to her goddess namesake. She looked beautiful, of course, and happy, but if you looked for more than a second, you could see that her smile had a teasing curve to it and one of her hands was actually wrapped around the outside frame. I thought she looked like she might swing her legs over the sill and jump, turning into a moth or owl or breath of wind even before she was completely out of the room. I thought she looked, too, like she was daring the viewer to come along. Or at least to try.

The Dutch guy didn't say anything. He just reached out a hand. His girlfriend stepped in, folding herself into the circle of his outstretched arm. They stood like that, in front of the painting, for a full minute. Then he sneezed.

She reached into her pocket and pulled out a tissue. He took it and, without letting go of her, did a surprisingly graceful one-handed blow. Then he crumpled the tissue and looked around for a trash can. There wasn't one in sight. She held out her free hand;

he passed over the tissue, and she stuck it right back into her pocket. I wanted to be grossed out. Instead, I had the surprising thought that I really really wanted someone who would do that: put my used Kleenex in his pocket. It seemed like a declaration of something pretty big.

Finally, they finished their examination of Diana and moved on. There wasn't much else, just the arrogant Willings and the overblown sunrise. They came over to examine the bronzes.

She saw my book. "Excuse me. You know this artist?"

Intimately just didn't seem as true anymore. "Pretty well," I answered.

"He is famous here?"

"Not very."

"I like him," she said thoughtfully. "He has . . . oh, the word . . . personism?"

"Personality?" I offered.

"Yes!" she said, delighted. "Personality." She reached behind her without looking. Her boyfriend immediately twined his fingers with hers. They left, unfolding the map again as they went, she chattering cheerfully. I think she was telling him he had personality. They might as well have had exhibit information plaques on their backs: "COUPLE." CONTEMPORARY DUTCH. COURTESY OF THE ESTATE OF LOVE, FOR THE VIEWING PLEASURE (OR NOT) OF ANYONE AND EVERYONE.

Truth: When Alex and I got together—his house, my house, empty classrooms at school, there was never anyone else around.

Truth: He was happy to be with me.

Probability: He just didn't want anyone else to know that.

I wondered what he was doing the following night and why he hadn't told me.

Harrison Kinuye of the YouTube video and doorman was part of the Phillite circle. He was on the lacrosse team. He and Alex were buds. I wondered if Alex was going to the party. Taking me out of the equation, it would have almost been a certainty.

I gathered up my things and moved on. The Impressionist galleries seemed to be full of tourist couples: young and hip and clearly from faraway places I might never see. There were only two people in my Duchamp room, a pair of older women in matching marled wool sweaters, standing shoulder to shoulder in front of *Nude Descending a Staircase*.

"Let's go to Paris," one said dreamily.

The other promptly whipped out a Droid and tapped away. "March."

"Perfect."

I could have told them that Duchamp had become an American, a New Yorker, but that would have just been envy talking. I wanted to pick up and run for Paris, too.

I wandered upstairs to the reconstructed tea garden, where I was chased out of any possibility of Zen by a group of schoolkids, each paired with another so they wouldn't get lost. Because that's who's in an art museum midday on a freezing Friday right before Christmas: woolly older women, bored schoolkids, and lovers on holiday. I gave up.

So it wasn't even quite three when I bundled myself into my coat and hit the front steps. Everyone knows the steps. The movie *Rocky* made them famous. There're always a few runners or tourists jogging up, just to say they could.

For a bitterly cold day, the steps seemed crowded. It didn't seem to be by either athletes or tourists, but by people around my age. For the most part, they were coatless, wearing layers of thermal shirts or hoodies, all in heavy knit caps. They were heading up the stairs, milling around the top level in groups of five or six, hunched on the balustrades. I could feel something in the air—not a threat, but a palpable excitement. I quietly moved to the side, where I had a view of both the plaza and the stairs, and waited.

It wasn't long. In the distance, a clock chimed the hour. In front of me, the plaza erupted. Fifty people, mostly male, suddenly had skateboards in their hands. Skateboarding is pretty fiercely forbidden at the museum. I hadn't even noticed the backpacks and duffels and other bags that were now quickly being folded into themselves. With a series of shouts and clatters, the boarders were off.

Some went down the stone ramps that flanked the stairs, going at breakneck speed, jumping between the levels. Unbelievably, a handful tried the steps themselves, flying off each landing to slam into the next. Most did the descent in a combination of boards and running and big leaps. A few fell on the jumps; a few more veered and tumbled, trying to avoid hitting one another and uninvolved stair climbers. A few of the falls looked bad to me. But they were up in a beat, chasing boards or finishing their descent.

I watched one, a girl with dozens of braids flying out from under her helmet, take the last ramp. She looked almost fluid as she lifted off, one hand on her board as she soared. Then she hit the pavement at the bottom with an audible bang, veered sharply to the right, and disappeared from my sight. The back of her hoodie had "Yes!" across it in huge yellow appliquéd letters. A big Yes to . . . whatever. Everything, maybe. Stupid, yeah, probably the whole endeavor had been stupid. Dangerous, absolutely. But as far as bravery and joy went, it was pretty amazing.

By the time security got out onto the plaza, the show was over. I knew there were a couple of boarders in the bushes below, nursing what I hoped weren't bad injuries. No one ratted them out. Who would even think of it?

It was still too early to go home. I ended up at Pat's King of Steaks, a usual happy-place, where I bought myself a Coke and a cheesesteak. My cup had pictures of candy canes all over it. Christmas had arrived in Philadelphia pretty much the day after Halloween. There were still three weeks to go, and the cardboard Santa and reindeer taped to the windows looked ready to call it a year already and take off for Boca. In spite of the cold I took a seat at one of the sidewalk tables. It felt like a slab of ice under my butt. I shivered, but stuck it out.

"Hey, Loco Girl!"

Shout out "Hey, Gorgeous!" or "Einstein," and I don't budge. But this one had me at "Loco." Go figure. I looked across the sidewalk to see Daniel's face, so much like Frankie's, framed in the window of his Jeep. I felt a sad little tug in my chest.

"You are aware it's only forty degrees out there, aren't you?" he asked. I shrugged. "Meeting someone?"

"No," I admitted.

"Then get in. Your hands look like wax. It's seriously creepy."

I looked down at the hand gripping the blindingly cheerful cup. He was right.

He also got out to open the passenger's-side door for me. I was a little charmed, until he pointed at my partially eaten cheesesteak in its wilted paper wrapper. "You are not bringing that thing into my car. It's an abomination."

I eyed the cigarette he'd dropped in the gutter. He did his teeth-baring thing. I tossed my cold meal in the trash, knowing I wouldn't have eaten it anyway. The inside of the Jeep wasn't all that much warmer than out. "Here." Daniel took off his black leather jacket and held it out for me. It was heavy and smelled a little bit like a burned cookie. It went on over my own coat; the sleeves went past my fingertips. "You look like frozen—"

"Don't say it," I muttered as I settled into the battered seat.

"You have no idea what I was going to say," he shot back, grinning. "Something rotten in the state of Marino?"

"And you ask that because . . . ?"

"Really? It's four in the afternoon, and instead of being with Sadie and my brother or at home, eating something colorful, you're sitting outside by yourself here. Not exactly rocket science. Care to share?"

"Do I have to?" There was a comforting hollow in the seat. I snuggled into it, coat and all.

"Nope." There was a pair of thick wool gloves on the dash. Daniel handed them to me, then pulled away from the curb. "I'll take you home. I'm on my way to drop some stuff in Fishtown."

I looked around; the backseat of the Jeep was filled with sealed cardboard boxes. They looked like they'd been loaded in a hurry. There was also some sheet music. And an empty condom wrapper.

Maybe it was because I was wearing his stuff, or maybe it was just that he was there and looked just enough like my best friend. "Tell me about your girlfriend," I said.

The music—this time it sounded surprisingly Irish and traditional—was loud enough that I had to shout a little.

"I don't have a girlfriend."

"Right."

Daniel looked at me just long enough to make me squirm, and only just avoid flattening a granny who was crossing against the light with her shopping cart. "Excuse me?"

I sighed. "Let me guess. She's as tall as you are and looks like she spends her leisure time in a lace bra and angel wings."

"Jesus, Ella, what was in that cup?"

"What? Guys like you always have girlfriends like that."

He reached out and jabbed a button on the dash. It took two tries, but the music stopped. "Sounds good to me, but there's no girlfriend—"

I got it, a little late. Apparently, I'm slow that way. "Ah. I get it now." I slapped my forehead. It was unsatisfactorily silent; his glove was that thick. "Slow. Okay."

"You *look* like an ordinary girl, but in truth—"

I gave him the Hand. It looked silly in his glove. "**Truth:** I am a completely ordinary girl. There are tons of us around. Always have been."

Here's the thing about South Philly. My part of it is small. Daniel was already turning onto my street. There was an electrical crew fixing the light in front of the Grecos'. They were holding doughnuts.

I was halfway out the door before Daniel had even stopped. I slipped off his coat and gloves. "Thanks," I told him.

"Hey." Quick as a snake, he leaned across the passenger seat and thrust out his hand, stopping the door from closing. "Hey! I have something to say here."

"Absolutely. Shoot."

"You're welcome," he said.

"*That's* the something?"

"Nope. That's *a* something. This is *the* something . . ." He pinned me with those almost-black eyes, and I had absolutely no doubt as to why his invisible girl climbed happily into the back of the Jeep with him. "You listening?"

"Sure." A little hypnotized, maybe, but functioning.

"There is not a single ordinary thing about you, Loco Girl." He pulled the door closed with a snap and was gone.

"He's right, you know," Edward was saying almost before

I'd made it into my room. I had crept through the house unnecessarily. No one was home.

"Your assertions have lost a bit of their value these days, Mr. Willing."

"You *know*," he repeated.

I tossed my coat onto the bed. The stark black and white of my quilt was broken by a purple stain now, the result of a peaceful interlude with grape juice turning into a gentle wrestling match. The stain was the size of my palm and shaped like, I thought, an alligator. Alex insisted it was a map of Italy. Later, we'd dripped the rest of the juice onto the thick pages of my drawing pad, finding pictures in the splotches like the Rorschach inkblots used in psychology.

"Well," he'd said in response to my pagoda, anteater, and Viking, "verdict's in. You're nuts."

The pictures were tacked to my wall, unaccustomed spots of color. I'd penciled in our choices. *Viking (E), pineapple (A). Lantern (E), cheese (A). Crown (E), birthday cake (A)* were over my desk, over Edward.

I turned on my computer. It *bing*ed cheerfully at me. I had mail.

From: abainbr@thewillingschool.org

To: fmarino@thewillingschool.org

Date: December 15, 3:50 p.m.

Subject: Should you choose to accept . . .

Tuesday. I'll pick you up at 10:00 a.m. Ask no questions. Tell no one.

—Alex

"Ah, subterfuge" came from over the desk.

"Shut up, Edward," I said.

As much as I disliked the sensation of keeping secrets, I hated being one so very much more.

30
THE PARTY

There was no doorman outside Harrison Kinuye's house, just a Phillite senior leaning into a huge stone urn. He extricated himself as I reached the door. "Hey," he greeted me, sending out plumes of condensed breath and beer fumes. "Thought I was gonna heave."

"Okay," I said. Apparently, that satisfied him, because he opened the front door for me with a clumsy flourish.

I was in. That simple. I'd spent the entire walk over worried that I wasn't going to get past the door. I'd watched Harrison's YouTube video (cleverly posted under the complicated name "Harrison Kinuye's Party") three times to be sure of the password. The whole video consisted of Harrison holding a piece of paper with the address, date, and time of the party. Of course, it read backward, but that wasn't much of a challenge, and I suspected it wasn't deliberate on his part. At the eighteen-second mark, he opened his mouth and let out a massive, echoing belch. Fade to black. I'd been afraid that was the password and that I would have to burp for admittance.

The music was deafening. I couldn't believe I hadn't heard

it from outside. But I figured that's the way it was with these houses. Harrison actually didn't live all that far away from me—maybe seven blocks, but there were only four houses on his, all with gates and front gardens. None of them touched their neighbors'. We can set our clocks by the Channel 6 Eleven O'clock News theme that comes through our walls from the Grecos' every night.

The hall opened into a massive living room. It was full of familiar faces: mostly Phillite juniors and seniors, but I saw a few sophomores, too, and even a handful of Bees. One was wrapped around Chase Vere. I edged away. He looked pretty involved and pretty intent.

I scanned the room. Everyone seemed to be having a grand old time. The boy who'd let me in was now talking intently to a group of my classmates, waving a half-filled bottle of something clear. He offered it to one of the girls. When she lifted it to take a swig, I could see it was Hannah. I shuddered and ducked behind a convenient sophomore. Where Hannah was to be found, Amanda and Anna wouldn't be far away. There was a group dancing to the crazily loud music in one corner. I was pretty sure Amanda was in the middle of it.

I didn't see Alex. True, there was a lot I was probably missing, being short and half hidden, but I was also starting to think that maybe this had been a wild-goose chase and a really stupid idea. He wasn't there. I was feeling incredibly uncomfortable and not very brave anymore.

Wandering the seemingly unending downstairs, I peeked into

a den, a closet, and what looked like a complete gym. Two doors were locked, but I figured whatever was behind them wasn't of much interest to me. He wasn't there.

It was time to go home. No Alex, no one I knew well enough to chat with, and I was still wearing my coat anyway. Unfortunately, I was completely turned around. I found myself in the kitchen. It was twice the size of the one at the restaurant, with much shinier appliances. There were six miles of counter. A few people were sitting on it, but there wasn't a toaster or coffeemaker or jar full of mismatched wooden spoons to hint that any cooking or eating actually took place there. The dinged keg in the middle of the floor looked as out of place as I felt.

Harrison was manning the tap. "Hey, Ella," he greeted me, looking completely unsurprised to see me there. "Beer?"

"Um . . . no," I said, shocked that he knew my name. "Thanks."

He shrugged and handed a plastic cup to a hovering senior girl. "There's other stuff there." He jerked his chin toward the sink. I saw a few lonely Coke cans and one bunch of celery in a bed of ice.

I wasn't really planning on staying. "Thanks," I said again, and headed for yet another door.

This one led to a dining room with a table that could easily seat twenty. Six busy Bees were grouped in one corner, playing Quarters on the shiny surface. Beyond them, I could see the hallway and the graceful sweep of a staircase. As I watched the parade of feet going up and down, a familiar pair of gray suede Adidas came into view. Feeling cold suddenly, I went out to meet them.

Amanda was just hitting the bottom stair. Alex was right behind her.

She saw me first. Her eyes narrowed dangerously. I probably would have taken a step backward, but a group of girls pushed behind me, heading for the Quarters game. I had a choice: hold my ground, or go stumbling forward, probably ending up at Amanda's feet. I held my ground.

"Are you freakin' kidding?" She loomed over me. "Do you not understand the basic laws of nature? You are nothing. You do not exist."

I thought of the girl on the skateboard, who had made her existence known in such a bold and impressive way. Then I thought of Edward's lover, who never got to show her face.

"Is your nasty natural?" I heard myself asking. "Or did you get it implanted?"

It wasn't my line; it was Frankie's. We'd all enjoyed it immensely before, and it slipped out so smoothly now. I wasn't staring at Amanda's chest deliberately. But my bravado only went so far, and she was still one step up.

"You bitch!" she snapped, and, raising one clawed hand, launched herself off the step.

Chase was there before she touched the floor, one arm sliding around her waist. "Come on, princess," he said cheerfully, carrying her off. "Let's dance."

She kicked and hissed a little, but he was bigger and, I thought, drunker. I didn't watch where they went. I didn't care.

Alex came down the last couple of steps. "What are you doing here?"

"Looking for you." It was that honesty thing he brought out in me.

"Why?"

That one was harder, not to answer, but to say aloud. "Can we talk about this somewhere other than right here?"

He shrugged. "Want a beer?"

"No."

"Good. Me, either. Let's go."

"Go where?" I asked. He had his hand on my back and was propelling me down the hall.

"Elsewhere." He pulled his black Russian coat from a pile in the foyer. "Unless you want to stay . . . ?"

"No."

"Good. So . . ."

A minute later we were on the sidewalk. He pulled on a knit cap and buttoned up his coat. I hoped he would reach for my hand, but he didn't. He just shoved his back into his pockets.

"Some party," I said, staving off the inevitable.

"Not really. He does it whenever his parents are out of the country."

From the sound of it, that was often. "Who cleans up?"

"The Kinuyes have a staff of many. They're used to it."

"Typical," I muttered.

Alex shot me a look. "Hey. Don't get pissy at me. I don't throw parties in my house."

He started walking toward South Street. I hurried to catch up. "Where are we going?"

"That depends. Answer the original question. Why did you come looking for me?"

Truth thing aside, there didn't seem to be much point in lying. I'd come looking for him. He was found, and fully aware of it. "I wanted to know if you were there, if that was the thing you were doing that you wouldn't tell me about."

"Why didn't you just ask?"

"Would you have invited me along?" Before he could answer, I blurted, "You wouldn't have. You don't want anyone to know about us. I just . . . needed to see it for myself."

He stopped in his tracks. I could see his breath in the cold air—short, sharp puffs.

"You know, Ella, if you'd said just about anything else— that you missed me and wanted to see me, or even that you were jealous of . . . I don't know what you might be jealous of—it would be a completely different thing. I would be thrilled. But this . . . this is bullshit."

In that moment, I felt something slipping away. It's a pretty distinct, unmistakable feeling. "You didn't exactly look overjoyed to see me, however I came to be there."

He grunted. "Don't do that. Don't try to turn this around. *You* were at the bottom of the stairs, looking at me like I'd peed on you over the banister. I know the look, Ella. It's pretty familiar."

"You were with Amanda."

"I was not with Amanda. I was using a bathroom upstairs.

She was waiting for me when I came out. No"—he shook his head when I opened my mouth—"I am not going to tell you what she said. It's none of your business. But I will tell you that the entire conversation took place in the middle of a hallway and lasted maybe three minutes."

"Did you tell her about us?"

"No."

My heart did a pretty decent cannonball. "So I was right."

He started walking again, fast. I had to run to keep up.

"You really don't want anyone to know," I pressed.

He stopped again. I couldn't look at his face, so I looked down, at our feet. Between us, carved into the sidewalk, were the words *Bainbridge Street*. I was sure it was a sign; I just didn't know of what.

"What I didn't want," he said tightly, "was to rub Amanda's face in the fact that less than a week after we split up, I'd already gotten involved with someone else. You might not like her—I might not blame you—but I used to like her a lot. What sort of asshole would I be if I were to broadcast the fact that I *dumped* her for someone else? Huh?"

"Especially someone like me," I shot back. I read somewhere that women take longer than men to end an argument. That we're almost guaranteed to say something we might regret, just because we're determined to make our point. I was determined to make my point. "Someone beneath the lofty Phillite sphere."

Alex just stared at me for what seemed like a very long time. Then he sighed. "You really don't get it, do you? Me being a snob—which I'm not—isn't the issue. It's the fact that you actually believe I might have something to be snobby about."

"What is that supposed to mean?"

"It means, Fiorella Marino, that only the person who thinks crappily of you is you. That is really sad."

He touched me then, pulled me into a one-armed hug. Just as I started to wrap my arms around his waist, he stepped away. A taxi was stopping at the curb beside us. I hadn't seen him flag it.

Alex opened the door. I climbed in and scooted over, waiting for him to slide in next to me. He didn't. He handed the driver ten dollars and gave him my address. "I'll see you later," he said, and closed me in.

As the taxi pulled away, I realized neither of us had mentioned Tuesday. I had no idea if he was even going to show up. I had no idea if he'd just dumped me on the corner of the street that shared his name.

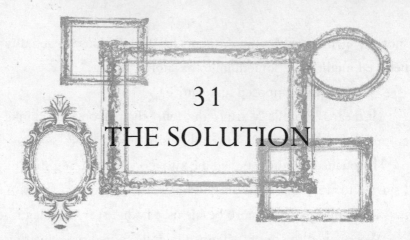

31

THE SOLUTION

From *Who's Who, Ladies of Pennsylvania*, ed. Lee Addison
Elkins. Elkins Press, 1958:

Erasmus, Vera Hamilton (Mrs. Harold N. Erasmus).
Born: Philadelphia, November 6, 1912. Daughter of Mr. John Girard
and Marina (Kulikovsky) Hamilton. Educated at the Agnes Irwin
School and the University of Pennsylvania. Married Harold Norton
Erasmus, March 11, 1935; children: Thomas, Lillian, Edward, Alice.
Affiliations: the Acorn Club, the Cosmopolitan Club, the Daughters
of the American Revolution, the National Society of the Colonial
Dames of America. Trustee of the Willing School, Philadelphia,
and the Barbara Ryan College for Women, Bryn Mawr. Member
of the Board of Directors of numerous organizations, including the
Athenaeum of Philadelphia, the Free Library of Philadelphia, the
Historical Society of Pennsylvania, and the Philadelphia Museum
of Art. Current address: c/o the American Embassy, Moscow.
Permanent address: Selavy, Bryn Mawr.

I turned off my computer and went back to my books.

From *Incomplete: The Life and Art of Edward Willing,* by Ash Anderson. University of Pennsylvania Press, 1983:

<photo courtesy of the Estate of John Jacob Addison>
Attendants at the funeral of Edward Willing, Père Lachaise Cemetery, January 20, 1916. Pictured: Edith Wharton (foreground), Gaston Leroux, Phillip J. Addison, Unidentified Woman (in veil), Pablo Picasso . . .

"Lots of people came," I said, looking up from the book.

"It was January in Paris," Edward replied. "What else did they have to do?"

I studied the picture as best I could. It was grainy, black and white, and the book wasn't expensively printed. "I expected Edith Wharton to be prettier."

"Well, I expected Picasso to have three noses, so you never can tell." He rotated a shoulder, like he was working out a kink. "I have to say, Ella, it's nice to have you voluntarily speaking to me again."

"It's probably temporary."

"As perhaps it should be. Have you learned what you wanted to learn?"

"Maybe." I tapped the photo in the book. "I think this is Marina Hamilton. Is it?"

Edward didn't answer.

"Of course," I sighed. "You won't give me answers. How about this, then? I'll talk. You listen. Nod if anything sounds good."

He gave a small jerk of his chin.

I took a breath and began. "After Diana died, you painted a portrait of a friend's new wife. She was young and unhappy." I looked, but Edward didn't move. "You fell in love." Still nothing.

"I think she was Russian. You called her 'Dorogaya.'" I thought I saw him flinch at that, but it might have just been the old bulb in my desk lamp flickering. "It's what you call the person who has your heart. That's why I think it was love and not just an affair. That and the photo I found of the two of you. I think the bronzes in the museum are of Marina and her daughter, Vera, not your sister and your nephew. I think maybe Vera was yours. I doubt I could ever prove it, but I figure if I dig, I can find pictures of her, maybe even meet her kids. She named one Edward. Coincidence? Maybe. There's an Edward Erasmus living in Radnor. I bet it's him.

"Anyway, I think Marina traveled with you to Europe. She might or might not have left her husband. I'm pretty sure she was with you when you died. I'm also pretty sure she made you happy. In the last photos of you, you look it. I *hope* the fact that you don't name her or talk about her or show her face, for God's sake, was a matter of discretion and not embarrassment. And I really hope you made her happy."

He blinked at that. I was sure I saw him blink. "That's important?" he asked.

"It should be. All of us invisible girls deserve that at least."

"So, do you think Alexei Bainbridge is going to make you happy?"

I shrugged. "Haven't a clue. I might have screwed it up with him. I'll tell you this, though, Frankie makes me happy. So does Sadie. I don't want to canoodle with either of them, but I love them to death."

"Must you use those words in my presence?"

"Sorry. But. **Truth:** You are dead as the spat."

Edward sighed. "You're right. You're absolutely right. So I suppose you'd best go to sleep, darling Ella. It's late. And, as was famously said, 'tomorrow—'"

"—is another day? Thank you, Scarlett O'Hara."

"Actually"—he scowled at me—"I was going to say, 'Tomorrow comes. Tomorrow brings, tomorrow brings love, in the shape of things.'"

"Shakespeare?" I asked.

"Queen," he shot back. "Not nearly as good as 'Bohemian Rhapsody' or 'Fat Bottomed Girls,' but certainly poetic."

"Good night, Edward."

"Good night, lovely girl."

I turned off the light and climbed into bed. "Oh. By the way."

"Yes?"

"I think I figured out why you called Diana all those nicknames. 'Spring,' 'Cab,' 'Post' . . ."

"Yes?"

"They're all things you wait for. I think Diana was making you wait, and it was making you crazy. Am I right?"

"Oh, Ella. You *know* I can't tell you that. I will, however, leave you with one more lovely old chestnut—"

"'All good things are worth waiting for'?"

"I really wish you would let me finish a thought tonight. I was going to say, 'Ain't nothing like the real thing, baby.'"

"Marvin Gaye," I said.

"The one and only."

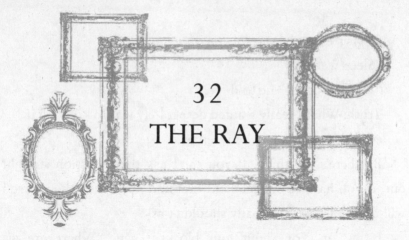

32
THE RAY

Tuesday came.

He showed up.

I was ready, on the off chance that he would, and waiting by the window at nine forty-five. It was a long fifteen minutes. I checked my phone three times. Frankie still wasn't returning my calls. Alex wasn't calling to cancel. Then his car pulled into view, and my heart gave a series of happy little thumps. I didn't make him wait; I was opening the front door before he was all the way out of the car.

He walked around to open the passenger door. "Hi" was all he said.

I climbed in. "Hi."

Neither of us said anything as he turned up Eleventh Street and drove north. I wanted desperately to talk to him, to say something smart and hot and mysterious all at the same time. "Did you go back to the party?" I asked finally. He gave me a sideways look. "Just asking."

"I went home."

Angry? Relieved? Feeling anything at all?

"Sleep well?"

"Like the dead," he told me.

Truth: What I really wanted desperately was to know that everything was okay between us.

But here's the thing. If you can't ask that question straight out, if you have to wriggle and hint and hope the other person will do it for you, you really shouldn't ask.

I shut up. For about four blocks. Then, "Where are we going?"

This got a half smile. One side of his mouth curved. "I was wondering how long it would take you to ask." He looked at his watch. "Three minutes."

"So?"

"So, you're going to have to wait a few more. Here." He did his incomprehensible jiggling thing with the radio dials, and the static came on. "Find something."

I passed a couple of stations that shouted the words "*Goals!,*" "*Spirit!,*" and "*Not in my house!,*" which told me it was religion, sports, or politics. The international station had a couple doing a cover of "Low" in what I thought might be Japanese. I settled on Elvis singing about suspicious minds and hoped it wouldn't make Alex dwell on the scene at Harrison's house.

Suddenly, the sky-blue girders of the bridge to New Jersey were in front of us. Alex headed for it. He reached under his coat, which was balled on the seat between us, and pulled out a Macy's bag. "For you."

It was soft. My heart did its little jumpy thing again. I tipped the bag and pictured cashmere. I pictured him winding it gently around my neck and using the ends to pull me toward him . . .

Jungle-print nylon slithered into my lap.

I lifted it with the tips of my fingers. It was a swimsuit: technically one-piece but composed of very small pieces, a few triangles of various sizes, held together by what looked like jump rings.

"It's a swimsuit," I said, which wasn't really stating the obvious as much as it might have seemed. Frankie's handkerchiefs covered more—and were nicer to look at.

"Yes, it is."

"Let me out."

"Ella—"

"Pull over and let me out!"

"We're in the middle of the Ben Franklin Bridge. What are you going to do, jump?"

I spun in my seat to look at him. He was concentrating on the lane beside us. A tractor trailer the size of Florida was blasting up on the inside, making the car shake and rattle. "Is this payback for that night?" I asked shakily. "Humiliating me in the most effective way possible?"

Lane clear, Alex drifted to the right. He hadn't shaved that morning. He looked a little rough. Beautiful, but rough. And tired. "Look," he said, "I know it's not something you would have chosen in a thousand years, but the options are pretty limited in December. And if I'd told you today's excursion required a bathing suit, would you have come?" When I didn't answer, he grunted. "See?"

We were off the highway now, driving through the empty streets of downtown Camden. I could see Philadelphia just across the river. I wanted to go home.

"You were going to need a suit," he went on. "This looked like it would fit—" I peeked. It was only one size too big. "I won't look at you. I swear. I won't see you in it. No one will see you in it."

He pulled into a parking lot and took a spot. The sign over the entrance read ADVENTURE AQUARIUM. When I looked back at him, he was pulling his shirt up with one hand and the waist of his jeans down with the other. I saw green plaid and a drawstring tie. "I'm wearing one, too."

I couldn't even remotely imagine a scenario that had me coming out feeling anything other than shredded.

"Out." He reached across me and opened the car door. I got a blast of icy air.

"I'm taking you to swim with sharks."

<hr>

"How recently have the sharks been fed?" the guy next to me asked.

Alex and I were in a small room with a dry-erase board, a perky blonde aquarium employee, and three guys from Rutgers who'd won their fraternity Christmas prize. True to Alex's promise, no one had seen me in my minuscule jungle print. Another perky girl had handed me a wet suit and pointed me into a changing room.

So as I listened to the basics of shark tank etiquette, I was fully encased in blue neoprene from ankle to jaw. The frat boys kept sneaking looks at me when they thought I—and Alex—wasn't looking. It made me feel just a little bit better. Alex's promise that I didn't have to get into the water if I really didn't want to helped, too. It had gotten me out of the car and into the aquarium.

"You can do it," he'd coaxed.

"Yes," I'd answered, thinking of the skateboarder a little and "fake it till you make it" more. "I can do it."

"Yesterday." Perky Girl answered the feeding question. "Believe me. They're not hungry."

I wanted to know exactly how she knew that. Did she ask the sharks?

"Okay," she chirped. "Let's get snorkeling."

The five of us followed her to a shallow pool. A few feet away was the shark tank. It looked a lot smaller than it did from the vantage points I'd had on previous visits to the aquarium. And the sharks looked a lot bigger. In fact, they made Jaws look like a pond koi. "That's a nurse shark." Yet another aquarium employee, this time a buoyant guy, pointed out a smaller (yeah, right) one that was lurking near the edge of the tank. "They're cuddlers. They like snuggling up to each other and even us sometimes."

I edged closer to Alex. He grinned and wrapped an arm around my waist. That got me into the practice pool. It was cold.

"Okay," our guide called, "deep breath, then bite down hard on the mouthpiece . . ."

It took me a few minutes and a fair amount of unappealing water down my throat and up my nose. Alex, of course, managed like he'd been snorkeling all his life. Which, I realized, he probably had—in the Pacific, Caribbean, the Mediterranean . . . I still picked it up faster than the frat boys, who seemed to greatly enjoy the "blasting," or blowing hard to shoot any water out of the tube. Eventually, we all passed inspection.

"Ready?" Alex asked as we stood on the edge of the tank.

The cuddler and its buddies were all on the other side. That didn't make me feel much better. I watch Animal Planet. Sharks move fast.

"Tell why I'm doing this again," I whispered.

"Because you want to," Alex whispered back. "Face your fears, Grasshopper, and you will be free. Now, in you go."

"Hey," one of the frat boys asked as I eased myself into the tank, "do the sharks ever eat the fish that are in there with them?" There were dozens of smaller fish flitting through the tank among the sharks.

"Sure," came the response. "But not too often."

The shelf we were on had a low wall to separate it from the main body of the tank, but it also had shark-size cutouts spaced along it. As we waited, just under the surface, one of the sand sharks swam by. I tensed. Beside me, Alex was leaning forward, hands braced against the wall to keep him inside it, but head and shoulders out as far as they could go. He turned back to face me. It's hard to smile with a big tube wedged in your mouth, but he was managing. He was having a blast.

I scooted up a few inches. For countless minutes, we watched the sharks and fish make their swirling patterns through the water of the tank. I started to feel calm, almost, almost convinced that I was really the kind of girl who could swim with sharks. And then a trio swam directly toward us.

They stayed there, swaying a little to keep moving, but never getting more than a few feet away. I thought of the Hannandas. The middle shark did a sharp circle, ending with its snout an arm's length from Alex's face. I grabbed his arm and he thrust it out, a solid if narrow barrier between me and certain death. For the rest of our time in the tank, he let me stay there, pressed against his shoulder blade, his arm curved backward around me. I knew that, even if it was only for this few minutes, he would put himself between me and a ravening Hannanda without a second thought.

Nearby, one of the overexcited frat boys started wildly windmilling his arms. He had overbalanced and now tipped himself right over the wall. In a second, the diver with us had grabbed his ankle and hauled him back. The sharks, instead of being attracted by the flailing, like they are in every single scary underwater movie, took one sideways look and promptly turned tail, heading for the other side of the tank. They stayed there and didn't come back.

The culprit's buddies pounded him when we climbed out of the water. "Smooth move, Ex-Lax," one muttered. "Way to be a buzzkill."

"Hey" was the red-faced retort, "at least I can say I scared off a shark."

They went off to disturb some other sea life on their prize day. I was shivering a little, not entirely from cold, and the horror of a swimsuit had wedged itself firmly in my butt. I was ready to be dressed again. Of course, Alex had more planned.

"Stingrays," I said, almost resigned, as I looked into the shallow pool we were guided to next. "You're putting me in a pond with"—I read the placard—"cownose stingrays."

"Look, no spikes." Alex pointed. Then he shoved a cup of fish bits into my hands. "Come on."

Apparently, this was all familiar to the rays. They had Alex surrounded in a second, flapping their wings on the bottom of the pool and on him, as if to get attention. I could almost hear them calling, "Me, me, me!"

Alex was laughing and lowering bits of fish into the water. They disappeared immediately. Some of the rays did little wiggles, like happy puppies. "Okay," I admitted finally. "They're kinda cute."

"They're incredible," he said, looking like a kid who'd just found said puppy under the Christmas tree, and held out his hand. I took it, fish guts and all, and got in with him.

We went through our ray food pretty quickly. I flinched the first few time and ended up dropping the fish. But then I got used to the gentle nibbling on my fingers. "Kisses," the guide said. He was the same one who'd called the nurse sharks "cuddlers." This time I didn't think he was entirely out of his mind.

Once all the food was gone, Alex and I waded toward the edge of the pool, where we would be able to sit and watch. One large ray kept bumping my ankle. I tried to step out of its way.

It followed, bumping me again. I changed direction; it did, too.

"Sorry, dude," I told it. "I'm all out."

"Oh, he doesn't want food," the guide informed me. "That's Ferdinand."

I looked down at the surprisingly appealing head, with its wide-set eyes and curved snout. "Let me guess. He just likes to float and smell the seaweed."

"Actually, he just likes everyone. He's a lover."

This was my day, surrounded by cuddlers, kissers, and lovers. And Alex. We sat with our feet in the water. The rest of the rays figured out pretty quickly that there was no more food forthcoming, and drifted gracefully around the lagoon. Ferdinand, however, stayed near my feet, flapping and nudging. I reached down and tentatively stroked his back. It felt kind of like a sandy flip-flop: firm and pliable and a little rough. Ferdinand gave what looked like an unmistakably happy wiggle and nudged for more.

"He recognizes a sea goddess when he sees one," Alex said, nudging me with his arm.

"It's a ray," I retorted. "Its brain is the size of a peanut." But I was secretly very, very pleased. I was genuinely sorry to climb out of the pool. The sharks . . . well, the sharks I could do without. But Ferdinand had charmed me.

We talked about all the unimportant stuff on the drive back to the city: the flailing frat boys, the flapping rays, the smell of fish that the mediocre showers hadn't quite gotten off our skin.

The ride going home went so much faster than it had coming.

Alex stopped in front of my house but didn't turn off the car. "Come in?" I asked.

"I don't think—"

"Alex. Please. Just for a few minutes."

He stared out the windshield for a long moment, hands tight around the bumpy steering wheel. Finally, he said, "I really can't stay long. Dad's home, and we're all going out to see my grandmother." We climbed out of the car and headed for the house. "Then it's another family dinner night at another 'Best of Philly' pick: Patsas. Apparently it's the 'place to have something even Zorba couldn't pronounce.'"

My hands were shaking, but I got my key into the lock and the door open. As usual, he gestured me ahead of him. I had other things to say, but I started with "Order the moussaka. Grape leaves, spanakopita, and a salad with lots of feta."

"You sound like an expert on the place."

"Nope. Just a girl who knows restaurants. Trust me. Regulars have their faves; smart diners go for classic. People pleasers order the specials."

"Good advice. So . . . ?"

"So." I stood up a little straighter. "Come upstairs with me."

"Ella, I really can't—"

"It'll just take a couple of minutes, I promise. I have something I want to show you."

I knew the house would be empty. Dad and Nonna would be at the restaurant. Mom was out with Sienna, having a final turn at torturing the flower people and the band and anyone else unlucky enough to be involved in the wedding day itself.

I walked ahead of Alex into my room. I couldn't look at him as I unwrapped my scarf and unbuttoned my coat. I kept my back to him as I pulled my sweater over my head. I left my jeans on, and the pale lace bra that I'd bought a few days after he first kissed me and that I'd never worn. I twisted my hair into a loose knot.

I turned around.

"This is me," I told him. "This is who I am."

Then I closed my eyes. I couldn't look at him while he was looking.

I don't know how long I stood there, hearing the thudding of my heartbeat in my ears and nothing else. A while. Then my floor creaked. I opened my eyes. Alex was a step closer to me, but still a lot closer to the door. "So . . ." I said shakily.

"So."

I took a breath. "Are we okay?"

What I wanted, all I wanted, was for him to take those few more steps and fold me into his coat like he'd done before. I wasn't thinking much beyond that. Maybe because I knew it wasn't going to happen.

"I don't even know what okay would mean," he said. "'Okay.' We've never been okay. We've been kinda scrambling for it. I mean . . . crap . . . Thank you. For showing me. I know it cost you something. But Jesus, Ella, I really don't want to feel like I have to constantly be reassuring you of things you should know for yourself. It's exhausting and takes all the . . . I don't know . . . satisfaction . . . out of saying what I feel."

When he was done, he stood there in the middle of the room, hunched and miserable looking. Neither of us said anything for a long time. Then, "Look, I have to leave. I . . . I'll call you."

"Okay," I said, and let him go.

I heard his footsteps on the stairs and the thud of the door closing behind him. I picked up my sweater with numb fingers. I put it on, backward at first. Then I curled up on my bed and cried.

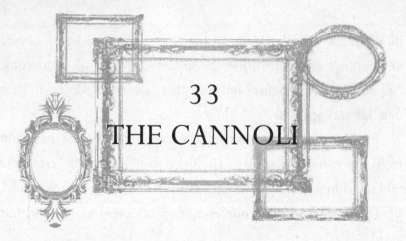

33
THE CANNOLI

It was a toss-up which was worse: that I was sitting in Anthony's Coffee Shop, renowned for its desserts, with a box full of Nonna's cannoli in my bag on the floor, or that the cannoli on the plate in front of me was not Nonna's. She would have scorched me with some choice words, despite the fact that I hadn't touched it. It was part of a peace offering.

Frankie was making me work for my forgiveness. It had taken several days, a thousand phone messages, and a seriously overpriced *Vogue Hommes International* shoved through his mail slot to get him even to speak to me. He was sitting across the table from me now, arms crossed over his chest (to be fair, he did that a lot when wearing that particular cashmere sweater; it covered the repaired moth hole at the point of the V-neck), glowering a little. I nudged the cannoli another millimeter toward him. It was chocolate chip, his fave.

"So I screwed up twice." I was wrapping up my tale of guilt and woe. "Edward I don't mind so much now. We just were too different for it to work out in the end . . ." I chanced a glance at Frankie's sulky face to see if he found that at all humorous. Apparently not. I sighed and went for honesty. "Alex . . . That one has walloped me."

Frankie darted out a finger and scooped a little of the filling from the cannoli. I resisted the urge to fling myself across the table and hug him until he squeaked. "The sharks were good," he acknowledged, and not even too reluctantly. "Insane but good."

"Yeah. And Ferdinand. I'll introduce you sometime."

Frankie wrinkled his perfect nose. "I'll take my stingray as a shagreen wallet, thank you."

I laughed. Not that I appreciated the thought of Ferdinand as an accessory, but I was just so happy to have my Frankie back.

He read my mind and waved a cannoli-tipped finger at me. "Ah. You are not forgiven yet, madam."

I subsided in my chair. "I'm sorry," I told him quietly. "I'm really really sorry. If I could go back and do any of it differently, the very first thing would be to tell you everything as it was happening."

"Hmph." Frankie took a bite of cannoli, delicately wiped his mouth, had a sip of espresso, wiped his mouth. And examined the painted tin ceiling. Then the rows of wooden shelves. Most was bagged coffee; you could smell it from the street. There was a ribbon-and-candy display next to us that was part holiday (red and white and green stripes) and mostly Italy (red and white and green stripes). I waited.

Meeting someplace other than one of our regular hangouts had seemed like a good idea. Sadie was already gone, on her way to London with her father. They were having Christmas at some castle. "I'll freeze," she said as she hugged me fiercely good-bye (she'd listened to my abridged tale of larceny and heartbreak, hugged me fiercely, and told me to return the papers to the Sheridan-Brown), "but at least I'll get to eat real food." The stick-insect girlfriend was gone, and until he found a replacement, Sadie's dad would behave like a normal fifty-year-old with a teenage daughter.

I'd bought her a belt for Christmas. It was black leather cut to look like filigree. She'd put it on then and there. She vowed to wear it in London.

In front of me now, Frankie had turned his attention to the street outside. It was warmer than it had been recently—enough that people were out shopping on foot, bundled but cheerful. There were three shopping days left until Christmas, about twenty-six hours until Sienna's wedding. She was at a spa with Mom, hoping to have that last two pounds steamed and pummeled off. I'd had to take extreme measures to get out of being dragged along. As far as I was concerned, meeting with Frankie was about a zillion times more important, even if it turned out to be just as painful. Nothing had swayed Sienna or Mom until I brandished Nonna's sewing scissors and threatened to cut my own hair. I'd even pulled my magazine file out to show them.

"Don't push it," I'd warned. "I won't be the first bridesmaid with a chop job."

They left without me.

Frankie was looking at me now. I'd barely touched my hair that morning; I hadn't even washed it. Second shower at midnight notwithstanding, I wondered if I still smelled like shark tank from days earlier.

"You know when I said I didn't need you?" I asked. He lifted one brow. "I was so wrong. I can't find words to express quite how wrong I was."

"Try."

"Dramatically wrong," I said. "Terribly."

"Please."

"Okay, terrifically. Horrifically. Catastrophically." I gave him my best meek smile. "Forgivably?"

He rolled his eyes. "I should have bought you a thesaurus for Christmas."

I had his present in my bag (a bow tie that may or may not have once belonged to Dean Martin, courtesy of eBay) and had a vague suspicion that the big lump in his coat pocket was a multicolored scarf I'd drooled over at Urban Outfitters.

"I still think Bainbridge is an ass," he added. "I've been there, y'know. On the edge of where they live, wanting in."

"I know."

"You're better than that."

"I know that, too." Kinda, anyway. I thought Frankie was pretty amazingly brave in about a hundred ways.

He leaned forward then, and pancaked my hands between his. "I am here for youse, Marino. Forevah and evah."

"No matter how stupidly I behave?"

"Don't push it. And don't lie to me again. Now, what are you going to do about the Edward stuff?"

❧

"I didn't want to show it to you until I'd done a little research . . ." I slid the Russian dictionary across the desk to Maxine. The letters and photo were tucked neatly inside the cover, like they'd never been out. I'd gone into the archive to make everything tidy, then come back to the office. "But I'm pretty sure there's an article there I can write."

Maxine did her switchblade-reading-glasses thing and read the three partial letters. Then she scanned my skeleton outline for what would be my honors thesis and, I hoped, an art journal article. She studied the photograph, then looked at my outline again.

"I can't even imagine why anyone would care about something like Edward Willing's sex life, but . . ." She shrugged. "People do. Clever research, Ella. Compelling, even if intrinsically based on a shaky framework of supposition." She got to her feet, all of the papers in hand. "Wait here."

She stalked out of the room. Between her sky-high boot heels and sleek topknot, she only just cleared the doorframe. I'd meant to ask if she'd gotten the Man Ray photograph. I thought it was probably a rhetorical question. I couldn't imagine anyone not giving her exactly what she wanted, as soon as possible.

I waited a little nervously. It was a distinct possibility she knew I wasn't telling the whole truth, but then, somehow, I thought it wouldn't bother her all that much. She seemed like an ends-justifies-the-means kinda person.

It was the first time I'd been in her office without her there, intimidating me into immobility. I took the opportunity to have a glance around. There wasn't much there: one tall wooden bookshelf, the desk, the two uncomfortable guest chairs that faced it.

I dared to leave my seat for a better look at the framed photograph on the bookshelf. I barely recognized Maxine. She was wearing a white shirt and smiling. She was outside, too; it looked like she was standing on a wooden deck in the woods. On one side of her was a tall, gaunt man with crazy eyebrows and brilliantly blue eyes. On the other was a younger man, maybe a couple of years older than me. He had his father's electric eyes and one crazy eyebrow. The other one had stripes shaved through it. Much of his face was covered by spiky blue-and-black hair. He had a ring going through his lower lip. The three had their arms around each other. They all had big goofy grins on their faces.

"Labor Day last year in the Poconos," Maxine said from behind me. "God, the mosquitoes."

"You look like . . . a really good family." I meant it.

"We are. Now . . ."

She fanned a bunch of papers over the desk. I saw the photo and letters, now each encased in its own plastic archival sleeve. The rest were photocopies, and my notes. Maxine separated the outline and a set of copies, one of each letter and the photograph.

On that, she wrote something, then slid the pages to me.

Found by Ella Marino, she'd written, along with the name of the dictionary, the current date (close enough, I thought), and her signature. "Hang on to that," she told me. "I'll put the original, in the department safe for the time being, but in case anyone ever tries to argue provenance . . ."

"Thanks." I had two more things to do, then I was outta there for the next two weeks. I sat up very straight. "Um. Will you mentor me? On the article? I know you probably have way too much to do already, but I think it might really make a difference for me."

"Oh, Ella, I don't do that sort of thing—"

"Okay, I totally understand," I said quickly, and hopped to my feet. The last order of business was on the second chair. I put it on the desk in front of her. "Happy holidays."

She peeked inside the box, then slapped the top back down and glared at me. For a second I wondered if I'd broken some rule of business or cultural propriety. "Homemade?" she demanded.

"My grandmother."

She peeked again, and groaned softly. "I don't know whether I love you or hate you right at this moment." She closed the box firmly. "Of course I'll supervise your article."

"The cannoli weren't meant to be a bribe. I just . . . thought you might like them."

"I'm sure I will," she said crisply, "a great deal. Just as much as I will *not* like the extra twelve hours on the treadmill." Then her face softened. "Thank you. What a treat. What I started to say about mentoring is that I don't normally do it. Apparently, I scare students. But I would be happy to help you however I can."

It was my turn to thank her. I added, "You don't scare me."

"Really?" She stared at me over the sharp frame of her glasses.

"Well, maybe a little," I admitted. "Sometimes."

"Excellent. Now skedaddle. I have a dinner to prepare. My son is bringing home his new girlfriend." For the first time, I saw her look something less than supremely confident. "I don't suppose you know anything about cooking with vegan cheese substitutes?"

We shuddered together. "Google recipes?" I suggested.

"I did."

"And?"

"Maybe we'll take them out to dinner."

"Good plan," I agreed, and skedaddled. I had my own dinner out to contend with. I wondered if I could get away with jeans. Probably not.

The first thing I did when I got home was to tack my labeled copy of the Edward-Marina photograph over my desk. Then I took down the postcard of *Ravaged Man*. "Well, that all worked out nicely," Edward said from my hand.

"Yup." I sat down and propped the postcard upright against my books. "Thanks."

"Whatever for?"

"Being real, I guess. I'm pretty sure this paper about your life will get me into NYU. Which, when you think about it, is a pretty great gift from a guy I've never met who's been dead for a hundred years."

Edward smiled. It was nice to see. "My pleasure, darling girl. I must say, I like this spark of confidence in you."

"About time, huh?"

"Yes, well. Have you forgiven the Bainbridge boy?"

"For . . . ?"

"For hiding you."

"He wasn't. I was hiding me." I gave Edward a look before he could gloat. "Yeah, yeah. You've always been very wise. But this isn't really about my forgiving Alex, is it?"

He had the grace to look a little embarrassed. "I suppose not. So?"

"So. I think you were a good guy, Edward. I think you probably would have told everyone exactly how you felt about Marina if you could have. If she hadn't been married, maybe, or if you'd lived longer. I think maybe all the pictures you did of her were your public declaration. Whaddya think? Can I write that? Is it the truth?"

"Oh, Ella." His face was sad again, just the way he'd cast it in bronze. But it was kinda bittersweet now, not as heartbroken. "I would give my right arm to be able to answer that for you. You know I would."

"You don't have a right arm, Mr. Willing. Left, either." I picked up the card again. "Fuhgeddaboudit," I said to it. "I got this one covered."

I tucked my *Ravaged Man* inside *Collected Works*. It would be there if I wanted it. Who knows. Maybe Edward Willing will come back into fashion someday, and maybe I'll fall for him all over again.

In the meantime, I had another guy to deal with. I sat down in front of my computer. It took me thirty seconds to write the e-mail to Alex. Then it took a couple of hours—some staring, some pacing, an endless rehearsal dinner at Ralph's, and a TiVo'd Christmas special produced by Simon Cowell and Nigel Lythgoe with Nonna and popcorn—for me to hit Send.

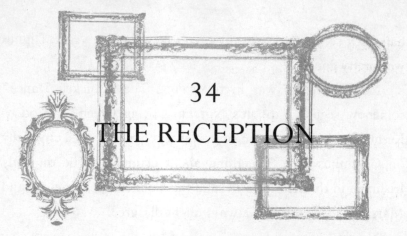

34
THE RECEPTION

The band was playing the "Chicken Dance Song." At least seventy-five assorted Marinos, Palladinettis, and Farneses, not to mention a few Grecos, Nguyens, Giordanos, and Ryans, were on the dance floor, shaking their booties for all they were worth. In the middle of them, gorgeous and glowing in a big white dress, the new Mrs. Thomas Farnese was flapping with abandon. I was sitting this one out. I plan on dying without anyone ever having gotten video of me emulating fowl.

It was only nine o'clock, and I was already exhausted. The first half of the day with Bridezilla hadn't helped, but by two, I think Nonna had slipped her a Xanax (who knows where she got it, although I suspect collusion with Sam Nguyen), and by the time we climbed into the limo at three, Sienna was channeling Grace Kelly in a big way.

The mass was fine, if you like that kinda thing. The photo session was a nightmare, since the flower girl and ring bearer kept kicking each other with their new, hard shoes, and the photographer didn't quite get that, no, I wasn't going to push my hair back so we could see my pretty face, so get over it. Dinner was pretty good.

Now the party was in full swing. The "Chicken Dance" somehow segued into "It's Not Easy Being Green," a nod to Kermit and Mr. Ryan, who sings it every chance he gets, especially on Columbus Day. Something about claiming to be the only Irishman in the vicinity, although the Connellys, Donnellys, and Martinezes (she's from Galway) might disagree.

Nearby, entwined and swaying to the music, were my parents. I catch them like that every so often, dancing together in the restaurant office to whatever's on the radio. Mom had spent the day alternating between beaming and sobbing. Aunt Gina kept whisking her into the bathroom for concealer touch-ups. Dad looked proud and relieved. There's no question that he loves Sienna more than life, but I think a little less of her will be good for his blood pressure.

"So. Leo will be next." Nonna plopped herself down next to me. She was wearing black, as usual, but it had a ruffle at the neck. "Just I hope not this one."

Leo's latest girlfriend is a preschool teacher, which should have the entire family over the moon, right? But it's the sort of preschool where the kids get to wear paint, and the teachers sport incredible ink. I think the *Venus de Milo* on Julie's forearm is pretty fabulous. I like Julie. Nonna is convinced that the ink from tattoos gets way inside and, like the mercury in tinned tuna, causes brain damage. She doesn't know that Leo has a lip print tattooed on his left butt cheek. Now, maybe Leo's not the best argument against ink as brain damager, but heaven help him when someone lets that secret out to Nonna.

She was giving the moderately tattooed band the evil eye at the moment. They were actually Julie's friends; the bassist works with her, teaching small children to make loud noises. So far, I hadn't paid too much attention. They knew their Sinatra and Dino, did a mean Kermit, and had good-naturedly performed their only slightly funky version of the Chicken.

Nonna and I sat in amicable silence for a few minutes. I wished Sadie and Frankie were there, but she, of course, was in London, and Frankie refuses to go to any weddings on principle.

"Make poverty, sickness, and death central issues in the contract," he says, "it's no wonder the divorce rate is fifty percent."

I wouldn't have minded having Alex around, either, but the less I thought about him, the better. He'd said he would call. And even if that was a cliché, a convenient lie, I had two weeks until we were back in school. Maybe I would figure it all out by then.

I actually jumped when the band started the next song. It was fast, fierce, and pretty catchy. It wasn't Sinatra. The lead singer was bouncing behind his mic. Then the guy at the keyboards did a quick spoken section. I paid attention, not because of what he was saying, but because I knew that voice. He had his back to me and was partly hidden by one of the light-studded topiaries that Sienna insisted were absolutely required for any stylish wedding these days. But I knew that voice.

I left Nonna to my cousin Alyssa and more champagne and

crept around to the other side of the floor. It took a while. Lots of people wanted to admire my dress or pinch my cheek. By the time I got a clear view of the guy's face, the song had ended. "Thank you. We'll be back in ten," the lead singer informed the crowd. One of Leo's buddies stepped in to man the DJ-in-a-box. I went after the keyboardist.

I found him outside, smoking behind the limo. "Daniel."

He looked up. "El-la. I was wondering if you'd catch me." He offered me a cigarette. I gave him a shame-on-you look; he grinned.

"*This* is your band?" I asked. Visible piercings aside, no one looked like they went by the name Ax.

"Nope, but I go to school with the lead's sister. Regular guy got food poisoning at a Christmas party last night. I've played with them before."

"Weddings?" It wasn't quite how I'd pictured him performing.

"Usually clubs, but the last one was a bar mitzvah. Musicians have to eat, too," he added, a little sharply.

"Sorry." I wanted to wave the smoke away, but figured that might be adding insult to injury. "I thought you played the guitar."

"Guitar, piano, a little violin, but badly, and I'll have to garrote you with one of the strings if you tell anyone."

That's the thing about Daniel. Obviously—the violin being a case in point—I don't know him very well, but he seems to hold a grudge for even less time than Frankie. "Secret's safe with me."

He shrugged, telling me he didn't really care. Then, "Nice dress."

"Just when I start liking you a little . . ."

He made his vampire-boy face. I could see why it usually worked. "You like me, Ella. Wanna do something when this is over?"

"Tempting," I said. "No, I mean that. But no, thanks. I'm not at my best these days."

"You're good," he said quietly, blowing out a stream of smoke. "You'll be fine."

"Yeah." I shivered. It was bitter outside. "I should go in."

"You should." The cold didn't seem to be bothering him at all, and he wasn't even wearing a jacket over his white dress shirt.

I turned to go. "Oh, I think I figured it out, by the way."

"Figured out what?"

"The question. The one everyone should ask before getting involved with someone. Not 'Will he-slash-she make me happy?' but 'Does it bring out the best in me, being with him?'"

"Him-slash-her," Daniel corrected, clearly amused. Then, "Nope. No way. Wasn't me who posed the question to you, Marino. I would never be so Emo."

"Of course not. But it was one smart boy." I waved. "Hug Frankie for me."

"Will do. Hey. Any requests for the band?"

"'Don't Stop Believin','" I shot back. He rolled his eyes. "I'm curious, in that last song—are the words really 'I cut my chest wide open'?"

"Yup. Followed by, 'They come and watch us bleed. Is it art like I was hoping now?' Avett Brothers. Too gruesome for you?"

"You have no idea," I told him. *How much I get it.*

I missed the cake cutting. I got back in to find everyone with loaded plates and Sienna with frosting in her eyebrows. Never my favorite part of the night, the bride and groom smearing cake on each other's face. I'm with Frankie; it can't be an auspicious start.

I got myself a piece without any purple on it and found a seat at the edge of the crowd. Great-Aunt Jo was dozing in her chair. The band wasn't back yet. Celine Dion came up on the speakers. I cringed and gave my full attention to my cake.

"Would you like to dance?"

I knew I had frosting on my nose.

Alex leaned over and wiped it off with his thumb. "Well?"

I could only nod. I had a full mouth, too. I stood up, swallowed, and accepted the napkin he was holding. "You're here."

"I'm here," he agreed, like it hadn't been a ridiculous thing to say. "I am crashing your sister's wedding. Hope she won't mind."

"She won't mind."

He was wearing a tux. A real tux, complete with bow tie and silk lapels. I stroked one. "I'm guessing this isn't a rental."

He squirmed a little. "No, it's mine. Nice dress."

I looked down at the snug purple monstrosity my sister had chosen. At least it had a mandarin collar and some sleeves. "It's a cheongsam," she'd announced proudly. "It's Eggplant Ho Lee Mess" was Frankie's take. My pear-shaped cousin Vanessa got strapless. Now *she* looked like an eggplant.

"You look beautiful," Alex said, but the corner of his mouth was twitching.

"Well, you look like . . . like . . ." I sighed. "Okay, you look really really good." Then, again, "You're here."

"I'm here."

"Why?"

"I missed you," he said simply.

"It's only been four days."

"A very, very long four days. But your e-mail helped." He reached for my hand. "Now, are we dancing or not?"

We did, and it wasn't as complicated as I'd thought it might be. I stood on my toes, he bent down a little, and we fit together pretty well. The song ended way too soon.

"So," Alex said.

"So."

"We can stay here if you want to . . . or if you have to. But I have another suggestion. Let's go watch the sun rise."

It sounded like a good idea to me. Except . . . "It's ten o'clock. And it's freezing out there."

"Trust me," he said.

"Okay."

I went to tell my father. He was alone at the front table, leaning back in his chair, vest unbuttoned and a spot that I was pretty sure was lobster butter on his tie. There was a glass of amber liquid in front of him. Dad drinks scotch only at weddings and funerals. The rest of the time, he's strictly a one-beer kinda guy. He looked happy and a little glazed.

"Dad, I'm going."

"Yeah? Got your own party?"

"Something like that. I might be really late home, okay? We're thinking of finding someplace to watch the sunrise."

He didn't even blink. "You got your phone?"

"It's here." I waved the little purple bag that was Sienna's bridesmaids' gift. Apparently, Tommy's sister knows someone who's dating someone at Kate Spade.

"Good. Here. You'll need some money." He wiggled until he could reach his wallet. He handed me forty dollars. "Enough?"

"More than. Thanks, Dad."

"Ella." He held on to my hand, pulled me down for a whiskey-scented kiss on my forehead. "You have a good time. Be careful. I won't wait up."

For once, he probably wouldn't.

Alex gave me his jacket as we were walking to the parking lot. It wasn't much warmer inside the car. "Give it a few minutes," he said, fiddling with the vents.

We pulled away from the hotel. "How did you find me?" I asked.

"Easy. I looked in the school directory and called Frankie Hobbes this morning."

"You *what*?"

"He was okay, only called me 'Dickhead' twice."

I winced. "Sorry."

"Not a problem. From his viewpoint I deserve it." He shrugged. "He'll come around. We'll be down to one negative nickname per conversation by summer."

I noticed then that we weren't heading back toward the city, but driving deeper into New Jersey. "Where are we going?"

"East. To where the sun rises."

"Seriously?"

He thumped the dash—not too hard—and I actually felt a little burst of warm air. "You've been to Long Beach Island, right? You told me that in an e-mail."

"Yeah, Surf City."

"We have a house in Barnegat Light. I thought we'd go there. We'll have breakfast somewhere and come back. You okay with that?"

The beach. In late December. At night. "I'm absolutely fine with it."

"So," he said.

"So."

"We okay?"

"I think so," I answered. "I hope we'll be a lot better than that."

"Yeah, me, too."

Here's the thing about the road to the island. A lot of it is one long, straight stretch through the Pine Barrens. Alex didn't have to shift gears nearly as much. Here's the thing about bench seats. There's a seat belt in the middle, too. I spent most of the drive tucked against his side, his arm around my shoulders.

LBI is a totally different place in the winter. There were almost no cars, very few lights in the windows of the houses. I recognized a few places we went to: the little market, the pizza place, the miniature golf-course, all closed for the season. Alex pointed to Scojo's Restaurant. "They open early. We can have breakfast there."

We kept driving. The higher-rent district, I thought. The houses were bigger, with fewer on a block. When it seemed like we were almost out of island, Alex turned down a small street. He drove to the very end and pulled into the drive. He reached in back, grabbed what looked like his schoolbag, and then climbed out of the car.

A single light burned on the porch. I'd expected huge, modern, lots of plate glass and pale exterior walls. Instead, we walked up a stone path toward weathered shingles and a gabled copper roof, oxidized green. It wasn't exactly a small house; I saw a second story and a dormer room, but it was quirky and cool. The floorboards in the entryway groaned when we walked over them.

"I wouldn't have expected this," I told Alex. He'd stopped to turn on the thermostat. I heard the boom and whoosh of a furnace igniting.

"It was built around 1890 by a ship captain. My grandparents bought it when my dad was a kid. Mom hates it. She keeps begging Dad to tear it down and build something new."

He led the way into a big living room. I could smell cedar and leather, and just a hint of damp. "He won't, will he?"

"Never." He turned on a leaded-glass lamp that looked as old as the house. "I don't know about you, but I have to get out of this suit."

I stood, in the middle of the floor in my purple dress and stupid shoes and his coat, and froze.

"Come on." He held out his hand. I waited a long moment. Then I took it. This was Alex. I trusted him.

I counted six doors on the second floor, all open onto dark rooms. Alex pointed to one. "Mine." Then he gave me a little shove toward another. "Mom keeps a bunch of stuff in the closet for guests. Help yourself."

He flicked a switch, illuminating a modern bed with an old patchwork quilt and a few pieces of mismatched but pretty furniture. When I turned back, he was halfway down the hall, whistling. So I headed for the closet.

A "bunch of stuff," it turned out, was T-shirts, shorts, flip-flops, sweatshirts, and even a small stack of cashmere cardigans. I looked at one closely. It didn't have a single moth hole. It was just . . . a spare. No-brainer, I was going to wear it.

"Come back downstairs when you're ready," Alex called a minute later.

I took a peek in the freestanding mirror. The sweats were a size too big, the shirt (a Menemsha bluefish, I'd been happy to read the front) more than that. But the sweater was heaven, and I was comfy.

I found Alex crouched in front of the stone fireplace, playing with sticks and matches. He glanced around and grinned. "Excellent." He had MENEMSHA BLUES written across the back of his sweatshirt. "Now for some fye-ore." He gave a caveman thump on his chest and plied what looked like a miniature blowtorch. "Hey. Harrison's having a New Year's party. You have plans already?"

"Nope," I said, feeling a little thrill at the question. I wondered if Sienna had left anything interesting in her closet.

"Good."

I wandered over to the new-looking glass door. It was all black beyond. Alex reached past me for the handle. "Just for a sec," he said.

We walked to the edge of the creaky deck. He stood with his chest pressed against my back, arms tight around me. It was cold enough to make my nose hurt, and my feet were frozen, but I wanted to stand right where I was for a long time, breathing in the smell of the ocean. "There's the lighthouse." He pointed. I could just see a tall shadow. Then the light on top blinked. "In the daytime, you can see down to the water."

"It's amazing."

"We'll come back. Whenever you want."

I liked the sound of that.

Back inside, his fire was crackling away. "Okay." He actually rubbed his hands together. "Action." In two minutes, he'd pulled cushions and a couple throws from the two sofas and made a sort of nest in front of the fire. Then he grabbed his backpack. "Refreshments."

I half expected to see a bottle of wine or something similar. Instead, he pulled out a thermos. Followed by a bag of marshmallows, a box of graham crackers, and, absolutely, enough Hershey's chocolate bars to feed a small army.

"S'mores!" I said happily.

"And cocoa. Sit." He waited until I was in the middle of the nest, then disappeared through a doorway. I heard a few squeaks and rattles. When he came back, he was carrying a tray, loaded with mugs, napkins, and real, three-pointed skewers.

"You're kidding," I teased when he handed me one. "You actually own s'mores implements?"

"Roast, then laugh."

I didn't laugh in the end. We didn't talk much for a while, either. After the wedding dinner, I only managed three s'mores. Alex had eight. He took his marshmallows seriously, too, turning and examining and turning until they were perfectly, evenly browned. Me, I just waited until they caught fire and assumed they were done.

Finally, stuffed and a little jittery from all the sugar, I collapsed against the pillows. I waited for Alex to join me. Instead, he shoved the leftovers to the side, carefully wiped his hands, and went back to his bag.

"I have something to show you."

He sank down next to me and handed me a sketchbook. I opened it.

And saw the mermaid. She was drawn in colored ink, exquisitely detailed; each scale had a little picture in it: a pyramid, a rocket, a peacock, a lamp. Her torso was patterned red, like a tattoo, like coral. She had a thin strand of seaweed around her neck, with a starfish holding on to the center. Her hair was a tumble of loose black curls. She had my face.

I turned the page. And another and another. There she was fighting a creature that was half human, half octopus. Exploring a cave. Riding a shark. Laughing and petting a stingray that rested on her lap.

"I'm calling her Cora Lia for the moment," Alex told me. "I thought about Corella, but it sounded like cheap dishware."

"She's . . . amazing."

"She's fierce. Fighting the Evil Sea-Dragon King and his minions."

I traced the red tattoo on her chest. "This is beautiful."

Alex reached into my sweater, pulled the loose neck of the T-shirt away from my shoulder. I didn't stop him. "It looks like coral to me."

He touched me, then, the pad of his thumb tracing the outline of the scar. It felt strange, partly because of the difference in the tissue, but more because in the last few years, the only hands that had touched me there were mine.

I set the book aside carefully. "Guess I don't see what you do."

"That's too bad, because I see you perfectly."

I curved myself into him. "Maybe you're exactly what I need."

"Like there's any doubt?" He buried his face in my neck. I didn't stop him. "So."

"So?"

"We'll kill a few hours, watch the sunrise, have pancakes, and you'll drive home."

"*What?*"

I felt him smile against my skin. "I got you swimming with

sharks. Next on the Conquer Your Fears list is driving a stick shift. Right?"

"One thing at a time," I said. Then, "Oh. Do *that* again."

In another story, the intrepid heroine would have gone running out and splashed in the surf, hypothermia be damned. She would have driven the Mustang home, booked a haircut, taken up stand-up comedy, and danced on the observation deck of the Empire State Building.

But this was me, and I was moving at my own pace.

Truth: My story started a hundred years ago. There's time.

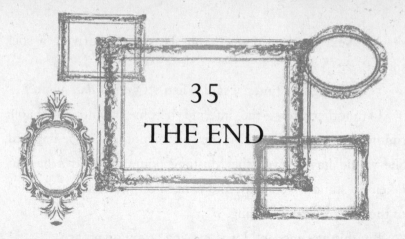

35
THE END

From: fmarino@thewillingschool.org

To: abainbr@thewillingschool.org

Date: December 19, 6:54 p.m.

Subject: Three Things

1. **Truth**: I'm terrified of an embarrassing number of things, including Ferris wheels, rusty nails, being alone, and being with someone.

2. **Truth**: I'm working on that.

3. **Dare**: Take a chance on me, Alex Bainbridge. *Qu'ieu sui precieuse, Ieu Io sai.* *

Turn the page for a preview of

falling in love with english boys

The Cat's Cat-astrophic Cat-aclysmic Cat-atonic Summer Blog

June 22

....

Transatlanticism

Airplane bathrooms are only a step above the ones found in gas stations. Unless you're in first class, which I'm not. I haven't even seen first class on this plane. It's upstairs. Apparently you sit in your own private little pod. Which, when you think about it, must be kinda like sitting in the lavatory here in coach, but with your own movie screen and room service.

Airplane food (*"This evening, ladies and gentlemen, we are offering you a choice of spinach-stuffed chicken in a lemon-tomahto sauce or two-cheese ravioli in a spinach-chicken sauce."*) is disgusting. Unless you're in first class, which I'm not. Or flying Air France, which I'm not. I would much rather be going to Paris than to London. Paris has croissants and Dior and boys who look like Orlando Bloom but say things like *"eet geeves me such ennui"* and *"merde."* London has sandwiches made with cucumber and butter, guys with bad teeth, and the library where my (s)mother will be spending the summer trying to get to know some woman who did absolutely nothing of import and has been dead for two hundred years.

I so wanted to stay with Dad, but apparently the soon-to-be-stepmonster needs his spare bedroom for her "office." Like she can't keep her teetering towers of bridal mags, sample menus, and bad band demos in her own office until the wedding. But then, I've never actually seen her place of work. Perhaps she is not the on-the-rise cleaning-product executive she claims to be. Perhaps she is but a lowly soap-bar wrapper without so much as a cubicle to call her own. Wouldn't surprise me.

So then I'm thinking, I'm sixteen, totally old enough to stay on my own for a few weeks. Mom actually laughed when I suggested it, which wasn't entirely unexpected. Then told me it was a moot point as she was renting the apartment to a visiting professor from Kazakhstan, which kinda was. But I Plan B'd her and suggested staying with Grandma in the burbs. GM would have been happy to have me and offered to drive me to and from the SEPTA train station every day so I could get a job in the city.

Mom's response to that? According to her, since discovering Dr. Phil, GM has become "Freud with a chain saw." Whatever that means. Then she said that GM is also developing a "pernicious mochaccino habit that makes her a caffeinated hazard behind the wheel," and an even worse eBay addiction, which has resulted in a closetful of designer knockoffs made in Chinese sweatshops. (Mom is so obsessed with Third World labor issues.) With all due fondness, Mom sez, she wouldn't leave the dog with her mother for more than an afternoon.

As jolly olde, horsey-houndy England has never had a single case of rabies, there's this bizarre pet passport thing and the dog can't come with us because Mom missed the deadline. He's staying with Mom's teaching assistant. Apparently my passion for reality TV isn't the kind of "rabid" they fear, so here I am jetting over the Atlantic.

For the next ten weeks, while you, my beloved friends, have the CW and texting and weekends at the Shore, I'll have buttered cucumber and the Queen and this blog. Mom swears the apartment . . . excuse me . . . the "flat" has high-speed Internet access. Guess I'll find out when we land at 6 a.m. tomorrow.

Merde.

One pale, tiny glimmer of light has just pierced the gloom. (One other than the "Occupied" light over the lavatory door.) London might actually have Orlando Bloom.

June 23

....

Who Knew

I've learned these English things:

✦ Their "ground floor" is our "first floor." Hence, when they say "third floor," it's actually the fourth. As in: "Charming third-floor flat a stone's throw from Regent's Park. No lift."

✦ They say "lift"; we say "elevator."

✦ They must all be champion shot-putters. I figure I could throw a stone to the park . . . oh, with the aid of a grenade launcher. If you lean all the way out the window—avoiding the copious pigeon *merde*—and think creatively, you can kinda see some green over all the brick chimneys.

✦ When a girl with serious jet lag sleeps until three in the afternoon, the only sandwiches left at the so-called sandwich shop are egg-mayo (egg salad), yoghurt-prawn (shrimp), and chicken-rocket (I have no idea, but it was very yellow and very green).

✦ There is nothing on the "telly" at 3 a.m. except test match cricket (read: will test your viewing endurance with its endlessness) and reruns from the third season of *Friends*.

✦ High-speed Internet access here is an oxymoron.

June 25

Why Does It Always Rain on Me

Day 3 in London. It's raining. Hard. It rained yesterday. And the day before. I'm alone in the flat. Pix below. The distance between my bed and both walls, in case you're curious, is exactly twenty-two inches. The living-room sofa is, yes, truly that orange, the carpet truly that stunning brown. That row of books below the painting of the cows (and that third cow from the left is going to make me crazy—you just *know* it's going to go headfirst into the river) . . . *The Complete Guide to British Fungus, Volumes I–XVII.* Only *III* and *VII* are missing. Apparently the flat belongs to King's College's foremost expert on creeping mold. Who, according to Mom, is spending the summer doing research in the middle of some African desert. What is wrong with that picture, folks (not to mention the cows!)? And where are *III* and *VII*? Being dragged around by some poor camel?

Mom has been at the library since eight this morning. She was there from eight to four yesterday. I've been here, and here, and within three blocks of here. The "newsagent" down the street sells every magazine known to woman—except *InStyle*. And thirty-seven different kinds of chocolate. I counted. Mom tried to get me to go to the BM with her. Really. That's what they call the British Museum. She's working in some dusty back room, just her, some boxes of old papers, and the occasional presence of some old archivist named Mr. Reade. Really. She says I could entertain myself for days in the museum part of the BM, that it's the most famous museum in England. No *merde*. Ha ha.

My mother is full of BM. Ha ha. She loves that crap. Ha ha. Dusty papers, dusty old costumes. Stuff belonging to dead people, most of whom weren't even famous when they were alive. Like I want to spend the day with two-hundred-year-old shopping lists.

I could have done this in Philly, sat in the apartment for three days while it rained. But there it would be raining *and 80* degrees, which, while weird, has a kind of tropical vibe. Here it's 14 degrees Celsius, which means 58.

What I did today:

✦ Slept until 11:00.

✦ Put a sweater on over my pajamas. In June.

✦ Sent fourteen e-mails, including one to Adam the Scum, requesting the return of my DVDs. He has forfeited his right to ever watch *Eternal Sunshine* again. Or even *Borat*, for that matter.

✦ Took digi-pix of the flat (all four rooms; see below).

✦ Read *Elle*, *Vogue*, and something called *Hello!*, which is like *People* on meth.

◆ Ate one bar Aero (chocolate with little airholes), one bar Curly Wurly (chocolate-covered caramel), and one bag Maltesers (chocolate-covered malt balls).

What I would do if I were in Philadelphia:

◆ Wear shorts.

◆ Send three e-mails, because I would probably be seeing the four people who got the other eleven. Including Adam the Scum. But I wouldn't say anything to him, of course.

◆ Take Andouille for a walk, maybe all the way to South Street, because the Java Company allows dogs and Sophie and Jen and Keri would meet me there.

◆ Have some pizza, have some gossip, do some good browsing, because South Street has decent stores and miniature dachshunds will sit quite happily and quietly in your tote bag as long as you give them a regular stream of doggie treats.

◆ Go back to Keri's house because no one is ever there and she has a plasma screen. Watch an episode of *Grey's Anatomy* or *Ugly Betty*. Have a good Abuse Adam the Scum session. Slag him off with the help of my best girls. Probably cry.

Another English thing I've learned:

◆ "Slag" has rahther a lot of meanings.

Are We Having Fun Yet?

Help!

I have experienced boredom of the sort that numbs the soul and reduces the cerebellum to a desiccated and crunchy mass of no substance whatsoever. Kinda like an Aero without the chocolate.

O my friends, why hast thou deserted me? No e-mail since last night. No reports on Hannah's party and whether Adam the Scum was to be seen still in the company of that slag (*see?*) Mandy?

I did finally get e-mail from Dad, apologizing profusely for bailing on dinner the night before we left and promising to make it up to me in a Big Way when he comes to visit. So, what is an appropriate Big Way, do you think? Some Citizens jeans? A new iPod? Nah, I'll take just having him here without the soon-to-be-stepmonster.

Today the temperature has risen to a blistering 16 Celsius. Got math? That's 66 degrees, give or take. I need another sweater. I brought one. Twelve tees (Mom made me leave eight behind—as if she was going to have to carry them), one sweater. God, I miss H&M. Go, O my friends, and tell me what is on display. Even better, take pix. I walked by a clothes store this morning on the long way back from the newsagent (Cadbury Twirl). The sweaters had, like, plaid trim. Really. Help.

Mom says I need to get farther afield, expand my horizons. She also told me to go to Carnaby Street, where the Beatles used to hang out. Can someone please tell me where to go where the Ting Tings or Keane hang out???

✦ ✦ ✦

(later)

I found H&M. Resisted the urge to kiss the floor.

It stopped raining. Mom threatened to disconnect the Internet service, such as it is, if I didn't venture past the newsagent today. Sometimes I really hate my mother.

She pointed me in the direction of Oxford Street and gave me thirty pounds (about fifty-eight dollars). Sometimes I can almost tolerate my mother. Turns out that Oxford Street is pretty cool. H&M, Virgin Records, and Selfridges (kinda like Macy's with attitude). See pix. It's a lot like New York. Wiiiiide street. Most of the cars are cabs—although their cabs look like everything around them should be black and white. Like Cary Grant should be getting out instead of guys with spiky yellow hair and girls with pink cigarettes. Half of the stores sell things with pictures of the Queen or red double-decker buses on them. Most of the others sell Rolexes. Everything is crazy crowded, everyone is carrying designer knockoff handbags, and everyone is making sure to look totally grim. Except the tourists.

H&M here is enormous. Shiny. Overflowing. Mecca, Valhalla, the Emerald City. I wandered. I basked. I worshipped.

I bought myself a boyfriend cardigan with Union Jack buttons. Most cute. See pix. If only finding a boyfriend could be accomplished in a similar fashion. "I'm looking for a medium in some variation of beige or brown. No, this isn't a good fit. Lemme try that one . . ."

Tried on some jeans. I couldn't get them past my knees.

More English things learned:

✦ English clothing sizes are two numbers bigger. Like even a skeleton would need a 4.

◆ English shoe sizes are tiny. My size 9s? Here, I am a 6½.
  Go figure.

Mom and I went out for Indian food tonight in Soho. It's all Indian restaurants, where the Indian waiters sound like Colin Firth, and pubs, where everyone spills out onto the sidewalk and sounds like Adam Sandler. On the way we passed the house Mom's research subject lived in. Lots of the houses in the neighborhood have these round blue plaques on them. *"Frances Hodgson Burnett, Writer, lived here."* (For those of you who have forgotten your childhood, she wrote *The Secret Garden*.) Or *"Martin Van Buren, Eighth U.S. President, lived here."* What our president was doing living in London is a mystery. My fave (see pix): *"Beau Brummell, Leader of Fashion, lived here."* Leader of Fashion. Gotta like that. Mom says he lived at the same time as the woman she's studying, that if he didn't like the way a girl dressed, she could just about give up any hope of being a "success." She says he polished his boots with champagne bubbles. I get the idea she doesn't much care for Beau Brummell. He sounds okay to me. *What Not to Wear*, Regency Edition.

So we walked by the house Mom's Mary Percival lived in. Not so much as a tiny little blue bathroom tile there. Apparently her books didn't make her famous enough for a plaque. Pretty house, though, red brick with lots of windows and a fancy black stair rail that Mom says is definitely original. She touched it and got all emotional. Help.

Tomorrow maybe I'll stroll over to Clarence House. According to a very reliable source (*Hello!*), it's Prince William's official London residence. You never know . . .

Someday My Prince Will Come

No William. Too bad. He's on holiday somewhere, according to my knows-it-all source. (*OK!— Hello!*'s poorer and slightly funny-looking cousin.)

Mom brought home ("home," hah! Home is currently being occupied by the world's foremost expert on 18th century Cossack poetry) a photocopy of Mary's daughter's diary. She thinks I should read it. Apparently Miss Percival and I have a lot in common. So far, I've managed to get through the first ten pages. Her handwriting is almost disgusting, it's so perfect.

Here's what we have in common so far:

✦ A name (she's Katherine with a *K*).

✦ Approximate age (she's 18).

✦ (S)mothers.

✦ Fab dads who are really busy.

Here's where we diverge:

✦ Katherine is a bit of a twit. All she talks about is parties and some boy she calls "Mister" Whatever and who writes poetry.

✦ She never actually went to school. I keep seeing the word "governess." Think *Jane Eyre*. Or *The Nanny Diaries*.

- She has big boobs. There's a b&w photo of a painting of her with the journal. She looks like Rachel Weisz.

- She thinks dancing the waltz is naughty.

- She gets to drink at every party she goes to.

- She never saw a television, car, hair dryer, or flush toilet.

Yawn.

Onward. Thanks, Kelly, for the partay update and the pix. I especially liked the one of Adam being French-kissed by Hannah's pug. Who, as we know, is an inveterate butt licker. Most funny. And yeah, absolutely, I think She Who Shall Not Be Named must be taking diet pills. She's definitely got that pink, crazy, anatrim look going. Josh used to duck whenever she slid her Ford fender into the desk next to him.

I will acknowledge casting stones and glass houses, yada yada. My booty cannot help but expand if I continue with my experiments in English chocolate. They don't call it Bounty (same as U.S., chocolate and coconut, but so much better . . .) for nuthin'. So I took my booty out for a walk. I thought I would find a bookstore, see what Bridget Jones is up to. So, didja know they paint LOOK RIGHT on street corners to keep us dim-witted tourists from stepping into oncoming traffic. They drive on the left side.

Did I look right? Do I look right? Jeans, UPenn tee, my new sweater . . .

I walked past the American embassy today. Bit of a shocker there. It's on this really pretty square, one of those London–Jane Austen–Hugh Grant places with brick buildings all around and grass in the middle. But the embassy is this huge, hideous building with concrete barricades all around it. And there were all these people outside, waving signs and screaming about American troops in Afghanistan.

I'm starting to get the idea that they don't like Americans all that much these days. Lots of postcards of our former pres looking stupid and our current pres looking worried. And I think the guy who owns my chocolate store might have a picture of Saddam Hussein on the wall behind the counter.

Anyway. Keep the e-mails coming. Barring rain, and the BBC seems somewhat confused on the matter, I plan to devote much of tomorrow to Notting Hill. In the event of rain, it's just me and prissy Miss Percival here. Jane Austen she is not. I guess when you think about it, diaries then were the blogs of today. Think of it . . . *June 27. Met the hottest guy yesterday, but his 'tude makes him a total loser. I am so not going to go there. Fitzwilliam Darcy can go dance with himself for all I care.*

Farewell, gentle readers, until next we meet . . .